SAVING THE DARK SIDE

BOOK 2: THE HARBINGERS

JOSEPH PARADIS

Cover design and interior
www.ebooklaunch.com

Edited by Mike Waitz of Sticks and Stones Freelance Editing
www.stickandstonesediting.net

Author Website
www.AenerialsComing.com

From the World of Aeneria

For all Hate mail and love letters:
www.AeneriaIsComing.com/contact/

This book is dedicated to those to braved it first.

Mike Waitz
Timothy Charest
Trevor Hornbeck
Melanie Kasparian
Terri Paradis

And to Brandon Courcy,
who placed the snowflake that started an avalanche.

CHAPTER 1

SAFE AND SOUND

Cole inched closer to the fire, warming himself as he waited for Roth to return from hunting. He marveled at the flames, basking in the heat and enjoying how the glow played off the ferns that walled their hiding spot. The fire was taller than Cole, and he was quite sure it would be large enough to cook whatever Roth brought back. Along with the comfort it provided, the fire ignited within him a genuine sense of pride. Not because of how big it was, but because of how he'd created it; with magic and without help. Recalling his lesson from Deekus, he had convinced the latent heat from the surrounding forest to transfer into the wood. It didn't take much for the first flames to crackle into existence, which was a very good thing because the spell had taxed his Wisdom to its limits.

The fire pulsed warm against his face, massaging his eyes shut. The idea of never waking seemed appealing to him at the moment. He was trapped in a world thoroughly doomed to eternal nightmare. Surely his dreams would be a safer place than Aeneria. As he neared sleep, however, he realized how very wrong he was. Just as he slipped under his conscious self, memories of Costas assaulted him with horrible images of bodies burning by the thousands. The memory triggered his senses, filling his nose with the stench of burnt hair and fat, the taste of boiling Despair, and the roars of Hate.

Cole woke with a jolt. He couldn't sleep, not now. He wasn't ready. He could barely keep his mind from darker thoughts while awake. The memories slunk back to his subself, waiting for his next moment of weakness. It seemed as if the worst parts of his life were painted on the back of his eyelids, fresh and vivid. If he blinked too long they would surely take him. Cole smacked his forehead and pulled his eyes open with his fingers before Joshy could pull him back to the cobblestone alley.

Cole stretched, walking around the fire to calm himself. He was incredibly sore. He took comfort in the aches and stings as they anchored his mind to the waking world. His muscles were strained from their recent exertions and Rage-fueled abuse. Worst of all were the bruises and blisters from their flight from Costas. Roth had carried Cole in his iron arms for the better part of the last few days. Their pace was nauseating, their surroundings nothing but a blur to Cole. They didn't stop or slow, not even to relieve themselves. Cole faded in and out of consciousness from time to time, and when he thought he might starve to death, Roth fed him with a rough sort of Passion. The magic did not fill his belly, but it did sustain him. Now though, he was beyond hunger. His limbs trembled and his stomach felt as if it were eating itself. No magic would fulfill him now. He needed food.

Wobbling, Cole wandered away from the fire in ever increasing circles, searching for anything edible. He took breaks when his fatigue demanded it, finding it more difficult to start back up again with each passing. Eventually he gave up and returned to his fire with a fistful of herbs for seasoning.

He slouched against the trunk of a tree, rubbing his raw feet. He had grown accustomed to being barefoot, but he usually had his munisica to protect his soles. Try as he might, he couldn't summon his black claws and protective shroud. He was simply too tired. With fuzzy recollection, he recalled the moments in which the black armor had enveloped him in full, his munisica the size of rakes. He was indestructible, unstoppable, and insatiable. He was Rage incarnate. Now, though, he couldn't even find the strength to pick himself up off the ground. Even something that crashed ever nearer through the forest couldn't rouse him. Hopefully it wasn't a Domina.

Roth stepped into the flickering glow of the fire. He looked the same as ever, nearly twice Cole's height and with muscles that put comic book heroes to shame. Though he had just carried Cole at a dead sprint for three days there was no sign of exhaustion on his face, merely a quick disappointed sneer as he saw Cole lying on the ground. Drunk with exhaustion, Cole openly admired his Master's physique, wondering how he was able to constantly maintain his munisica and black armor. The shroud covered all of his body except for his torso, neck and face. Even his hair was a weapon, appearing more as a thicket of bouncing ebony knives. No one at The Sill had managed to cover more than their hands and wrists with the shroud. But here was Roth, calm as a spring breeze with his Rage burning as hot as ever. No one had ever come close to Roth's Rage. No one except Cole.

"Get up and get to work," Roth growled with a voice like polished granite. "I did the hunting. You'll do the cooking." He tossed the bodies of two winged-deer onto a bed of leaves next to the fire.

Cole remained slumped against the trunk, his belly rising and falling slowly. He wondered if Roth's eyebrows were armored too, or if they were just naturally that dark.

Roth stomped over to Cole, his bladed feet crunching through rocks and roots. "You know my rule. I don't care how banged up you are. You give me hesitation and I'll give you a broken arm."

Cole mumbled something so feeble that not even Roth could hear it.

"What did you just say?" Roth barked. "Speak up, whelp."

Cole took a deep breath. Then another. "I said, would you like the left one or the right?" He raised his shaking arms, inspecting them. "The left one's broken already I think, but the right one only has a cut. Here," he said, offering a shaky arm. "Go nuts."

For a moment Roth looked as if he would take him up on his offer, but then Cole withdrew and fell into a fit of coughs. Roth bared his teeth in a grin. "It's a good thing you're abiding by my second rule, or else not even Alvani would be able to fix what I'd do to you."

"Give you everything I have, or something like that. Right?" Cole asked when the coughing subsided.

"Every drop of blood and sweat." Roth crouched directly in front of Cole, raising a single claw. "I'd wager you've got a bit more in you." The tip of Roth's claw hummed with white pulses as little snowflakes of Passion chased themselves around his hand. He flicked a flat part of the shining, bladed finger against Cole's forehead.

It hurt. Cole smacked his hand to his brow, rubbing it. "Ow! Haven't I been through enough?" Cole rose to solid feet, shuffling out of Roth's reach. "I already gave everything…" His voice trailed off, as he felt strength and clarity return to his mind and body. He looked up to Roth with a sheepish smile. "Thanks."

"That meat isn't going to cook itself. Get to it." Roth sat himself cross-legged by the fire, cleaning his munisica on the middle of the flames. "You do know how to dress a kill, don't you?"

Cole spent the better part of the next two hours working on the dead animals. They resembled bats, except they were each the size of a motorcycle and had antlers that cupped behind their ears. Their ugly snub-noses looked like squashed mushrooms, though their velvety fur glittered like rubies in the firelight. Cole had a vague idea as to what he was supposed to do. He'd seen his unit work at it before, but no one had ever bothered to give him a part of the job. Frankly he was glad they hadn't needed his help. The task was gruesome and granted him a mouthful of bile with every armful of organs he scooped out. Eventually he had grown so frustrated that his Rage flared to his aid. Cole stowed his dagger as his munisica made quick work of dressing the kills. By the time he finished, his lethargy returned with a vengeance and he lost his appetite entirely. He could feel Roth judging his work.

"That's enough." Roth shooed him away from the mess of skin and viscera. He waved a lazy emerald claw over the fire and the carcasses floated up off the bed of leaves, settling into a slow spin over the fire. "Not good, even for your first time. But I'm hungry and we can't sit here all day."

Cole stretched, arching his stiff back and reaching for the sky. He watched Roth carefully as his Master snipped off a hardwood branch as thick as his leg with two bladed fingers. The same two fingers then flashed green with Wisdom as he gave the branch a little nudge, sending it hovering over the fire where it nestled itself like a puzzle piece. Cole cleared his throat and as loud as his dry throat would allow, he asked, "How are you able to move that with Wisdom or heal me with Passion while still using your Rage? It seems like one or the other to me."

"Practice. Cycles and cycles of it." Roth brought his face so close to the fire that the orange flames tickled his nose. He indulged in a deep sniff before looking at Cole. "Do you remember the bog angel?"

Cole scrunched his nose, recalling the hideous creatures. "How could I forget? That was the first time I used Rage."

"Remember what you did with that Rage?" Roth asked.

"Yeah, I smashed Chiron's machine." Cole stared at the bed of embers for a moment. "Come to think of it, I probably could have done it without Rage, but it definitely made it easier."

"And how did Chiron's machine come to be in your claw?" Roth asked with an impatient huff.

"It was just there when I needed it," Cole offered, but when Roth's expectant glare intensified, he scoured his memories once more. "I remember the barrel floating towards me. It didn't make it all the way though, and it rolled, I mean I rolled it the rest of the way...with Wisdom."

"Too right you did. You used Wisdom while burning with Rage." Roth flashed a toothy grin. "I could have stopped you. Probably should have. Chiron gave me a good mind-lashing after that. He'd spent a week of his free time making it for me."

"A mind-lashing?" Cole's eyes went wide. "Did he attack your mind?" Cole imagined the two ancient ones locking their mental horns and storming at each other.

"No. It was far worse than that." The air boomed with Roth's chuckling. "He lectured me for hours without relent before finishing me off with a lesson on how to make my own gravity well. Chiron was my teacher, way back when."

"Why did you let me break it then?" Cole asked. "It must have been worth more than my life."

Roth jerked his head to the side, half scowling. "Not even close. For the cost of a fancy trinket, our weakest student earned his munisica. I'd do it again, no hesitation. That is why I let you spend half the day gutting and skinning these horned seraphs. You need the experience. You still have much to learn, and I'm a damn sight curious as to what else you might be capable of."

Even though Cole was frustrated and exhausted, he couldn't help but feel a measure of gratitude for all the help he received. His thoughts wandered to Chiron. "Chiron was your teacher? How long ago was that?"

Roth licked his teeth, his black eyes glistening as they took in the sizzling meat. "Just over thirty cycles. He was a lot more practical back then, but that was before he fell himself in love and mastered Passion."

Cole's jaw dropped. "Chiron is a master of Passion?"

"And Wisdom before that. He was one of the Unbound. One of Varka's fellowship. I was too at the very end, though I never fully mastered any of the magics. We are fortunate to have Chiron among our numbers." Roth poked the flank of one of the seraphs, testing it. "The top layer's done. Cut yourself a steak."

A savage craving replaced his initial queasiness as Cole tasted the first bite. The seraph meat was lean, but sweet as though marinated. He swallowed hard, taking another bite.

"What does it take to master a school of magic?" Cole asked, using his dagger to slice off another cooked layer.

Roth tore a hunk off a leg, bolting down a few mouthfuls before responding. "Officially speaking, one would have to enter the trials in Oberon's Temple. There's one for each school. Once you enter, you either survive the trials or never come out. Or at least that's what the stiff-necks of the Celestial Council would have you believe. Bunch of pampered bureaucrats. They'd likely slap you in prison for your actions in Costas."

"What do you mean?" Cole asked.

Roth looked him square in the eye: "You're a master of Rage, Cole. I watched the whole thing from my shackles. That wench struck you a fatal blow, right in the neck. I saw you die. Then I watched the shroud come up over your face and the havoc you unleashed soon after. No one but a master of Rage could have done what you did."

Cole shook his head. "I've been thinking about that. I'm pretty sure that was just a boost from the power I took from your gratia stone on the baileen. It faded pretty quick. I couldn't do that stuff again if I tried. I'm not sure if I would want to." He took a breath, staring into the fire for a moment. "I almost killed them. I wanted to. I wanted to kill you too." Cole turned away from Roth, shame flooding his cheeks.

"You're wrong. Dead wrong." Roth voice boomed into Cole's chest: "I'm no master of Rage, I've studied the school long enough to know what I saw. And as for the power I gave you, that is not how the magic works. It will fuel your body, but it will not call the munisica and shroud for you. Check your bones. You have yet to use any of it."

Cole rubbed his fingers over his forearms. He could almost sense a dull warmth in his bones, dense and distant. "You're right. I can still feel it in there, but it's more solid. I...I don't think I can even use it anymore."

Roth pulled the leg off the sereph with a loud crack. "The time to call it has come and gone. Your body is claiming it now. Over the next month or so you're going to go through some changes. Be mindful of the magic so you don't surprise yourself at the wrong time."

Cole's hands went to his shoulders absentmindedly, feeling the round muscle beneath. Roth was still wrong. If it wasn't Roth's power that helped Cole, then his mastery had something to do with *Him*. Cole gazed into the fire at a glowing log that looked roughly like *His* face. For some reason Cole didn't want to bring up his imaginary friend just yet; however, there was another question that tugged at him. "If I mastered Rage then why were you still so much stronger than me? Shouldn't I have been able to overpower you?"

Roth's laughter shook the air, scaring a sleeping bird into hasty flight. "You wielded a master's power with a child's arm. At times you were stronger than me, but you were merely a fledgling taking your first jump from the nest. You couldn't hold it steady. If I hadn't reeled you in, your Rage would have run wild. You eventually would have lost yourself to it, or at least until Grotton arrived and snared you with Hunger."

Cole shuddered. "Decreath was bad enough. I hope I never see any of the Three again." He recalled too easily what was left of Kreed when Decreath took him, the soulless, vacant smile of broken teeth and the bloody, empty eyes. "Do you think Kreed died?"

"No." Roth returned his attentions to the fire, speaking through a mouthful of meat. "But he isn't alive either. Decreath has him now. He's a Harbinger. Kreed's body and mind now belong to the Lord of Fear."

Cole watched the meat sizzle and pop. His stomach nearly surrendered its contents as some of the meat overcooked to blackened char, reminding him sickeningly of the Devotion Towers. "What will happen to all the chosen? Will they be added to that Colossus? The thing looked like it was made of nothing but dead bodies."

Roth chewed, spitting a bone into the fire. "Once Decreath has fed on their souls he will likely create a *new* Colossus. That one was already bigger than we could handle so there wouldn't be much use in adding to it. And a Colossus isn't made of dead bodies. They're made from chosen, and chosen can't die. Their endless suffering fuels the magic that powers the whole Colossus. It's a nasty bit of dark magic. We're not sure how it works, but we do know that Sorronis is responsible for the idea. It's some cocktail of Despair and Hatred." Roth growled in disgust. "A Colossus has but one weakness, and if you ever find yourself facing one while fully engulfed in Rage, then you might be able to take it down. At its heart is a single priest tugging the strings to the whole thing. Just a fragile, twisted Aenerian made of flesh and bone. Kill him and the whole machine comes apart. You'd better be fully-shrouded though. Many great warriors have been shredded by the nest of bone that protects the priest. Better to just run away until you learn some better control of the Rage."

It was as Cole Feared. The Colossus was a never-ending nightmare from which Lexy could never wake. His heart wept for her. "I think Habbad broke. Something snapped in him. His sister was at the bottom of one of the towers, right in front of us. Kreed made us watch her burn and turn into one of those...things. A chosen. I want to believe that Kreed put a spell to lure Habbad, but I think he went willingly to the Colossus. He wasn't the same. Did you see the look in his eyes?"

Roth grunted. "I saw, and those are my thoughts as well. Ever since I first saw the little shrike I knew he had some taint in him. I'd wager he spent a bit too much time with Kreed. The darkness was pooled so deep in him we were bound to see it sooner or later. The Three revel in the worst parts of a person, and they have ways of drawing your demons out." Roth locked eyes with Cole, raising a bladed eyebrow. "The Habbad you know is dead. Grieve him if you must, then move on. He and Storn won't be the only friends you lose in this war."

They ate in silence. Cole found himself full before long, falling back and rubbing his bulging belly. Roth kept working his way through the first seraph and then half of the second. He may have been a giant among giants but the serephs were no small meal. It didn't make sense to Cole how the man could put so much food away. Where did it all go?

Seeing his confusion, Roth instructed Cole to draw upon his Rage while he ate, explaining how the magic increased his metabolism and converted the food to raw energy. Cole called upon his Rage, fingers stretching with a painful yet satisfying ache. Within minutes his gurgling stomach shrank as his skin tightened over growing muscles, leaving him with renewed vigor and hunger. He ate his stomach full twice more before succumbing to an overwhelming need for sleep. He fought to stay awake, but it was a fight he couldn't win. Roth encouraged him to sleep with a blast of Passion, knocking him so thoroughly unconscious that not even Cole's nightmares could find him.

When Cole's eyes snapped open he found himself freezing, terrified, and coughing on what felt like cold fire. The hollow rushing of liquid told him he was under water. Thrashing and coughing, he righted himself and stood in knee-deep water. Roth was next to him. Steam rose from his unshrouded skin as he waded out, dunking his blond hair in the river.

Cole shivered, hacking up water. He waited for Roth's head to pop back through the surface. "You could have just woke me up you know!" he shouted through chattering teeth.

Roth wrung his hair out, his hands oddly small without their sweeping munisica. "A falling tree wouldn't have roused you. You've slept for nearly half a day. Wash up and get ready for a long run. There's been a development while you were snoring."

Cole didn't much care for the developments at the moment. The river's icy hands ripped at him with every shrill heartbeat. "How am I supposed to wash up in this? This water is freezing my teeth shut!"

"Then warm it up, whelp. I shouldn't have to explain such things to a warrior from The Sill." The water around Roth bubbled, steam rising as he dunked his head back under.

With an effort, Cole shifted his thoughts to Wisdom. He quickly discovered that there was no way for him to heat an area larger than his fist. It required too much of his focus to maintain the spell in moving water, and the surrounding river was much too cold. He instead transferred the heat to his skin. The heat was barely adequate, but his limbs stopped shivering and his teeth no longer clicked.

"Much better," Roth said as he donned his munisica and shroud. "You no longer smell like the wrong side of a bog angel."

Cole sloshed out of the water onto the sandy shore. "I'm just glad that junk's off me. I never thought a fight would be so gross afterwards. There were bits of priest all over me. Next time I'll be… cleaner about it. Some of that stuff I scraped off my armor…I don't even want to know where it came from." Cole disrobed and slapped his cloth armor onto a flat rock.

Roth growled with laughter. "When you dispatch an entire coven of Sorronis's priests like you did, cleanliness is not your top priority. Though if you could come out the other side without a speck of gore on you, then you might be a step closer to a master's control of the magic. Rage as hot as yours burns the mind. The only way to douse those flames is with buckets of your enemy's blood." He paused, inspecting Cole's nearly naked body. Roth crouched and placed a glowing emerald claw over the cloth armor.

Cole yelped and took a step back as steam rose like a geyser from the cloth armor. Seconds later, Roth tossed him his freshly dried laundry. "Thanks, Master Roth." Cole hastily donned the clothes, which were pleasantly warm and dry.

"Believe me it wasn't a favor. We don't have time to wait for you to figure out how to dry your own clothes. Chiron contacted me while you were sleeping. We need to get to Oberon's temple and I don't want you whining about chafing while we run." He looked up at the sky, which looked as if a sun were about to rise. "Shame that coward-baileen fled at Costas. I'm not sharp enough with Passion to contact it at this distance. The beast could have us there in less than a day."

As Cole buckled the final strap an idea came to him. He searched the recesses of his mind for Goran's primal link, which was much easier to find now that he was rested and fed.

Goran perked his head up from the back of the baileen, pointing his crimson eyes in the direction of his bonded friend. He was hungry. He was tired. He missed his Cole. Gentle fingers scratched under his chin. He liked that. The one who smelled like new rain locked eyes with him. A challenge? No, a message. She had a message for his Cole. Words of the two-legs.

"Cole, if you can hear me I need you to re-establish the link between us. I cannot do it alone," said a familiar, garbled voice.

Cole opened his eyes, finding Roth standing expectantly beside him. Cole looked to his master, joy shaking his voice: "Goran's safe! He's safe and on the baileen! Eliza's there too. She wants me to re-establish the link with her."

Roth folded his arms across his armored chest, "Then why are you staring at me like I'm some pretty flower? Get to it."

Cole's cheeks flushed hotter than his clothes. "I'm new at this, so it'll take me a second... I'm not hesitating," he added, ignoring Roth's impatient growl.

He relaxed his mind, taking a moment to enjoy his warm clothes and full belly. Sitting seemed more suitable for this task, so he found the flat rock and rested himself on it. He closed his eyes and plugged his ears, listening and looking within himself. He could feel familiar whispers, but nothing with substance. Cole tuned his empathy, almost like a radio, but the station was one that only he and Eliza knew. Within that link was contained all of the pain and heartache from their losses, both from Deekus and Joshy. Cole watched through watery eyes as a tear splattered to the leathery back of a baileen.

"*Eliza.*"

"*Cole! It lightens my heart to feel your thoughts. Are you and Master Roth safe?*" Strands of worry crept into their link.

"*Yes, we are perfectly fine. I'm not sure where we are, but we're about to head to Oberon Temple. What about the rest of the unit? Is everyone okay?*" he asked, widening their link. He didn't bother hiding his affection for Lileth. Deceit was impossible through the link.

She sent him images of Sitra and Valen, then indulged his concern and lingered over Lileth. They all smiled softly and tired into Eliza's eyes. Goran cowered in his usual spot at the baileen's dorsal fin, but at least his head perked up with some curiosity. "*All things considered, we are well enough.*"

Cole held onto the image of Lileth a bit longer before responding. "*Can you direct the baileen to come pick us up? We could all go to Oberon's Temple together.*"

"*I'm afraid not,*" she said, chords of bitterness humming in the link. "*After the beast abandoned the two of you it made for open water, and has been unresponsive ever since. We've had to resort to some unconventional applications of Wisdom to sustain ourselves.*"

Cole shrank back from the link, turning to Roth. "They're all stuck on the baileen and it won't listen to them.

"Hmm," Roth grumbled. "It makes sense. The baileen Fear the Three more than anyone else. Tell Eliza to stop her coddling and put the promise of death in its heart. The baileen is not some tender sproutling. It needs good, honest threats. It won't respect the careful pampering that she's likely been giving it. Tell her now." He jabbed his chin at Cole.

Cole waded back into the link, relaying Roth's words. For a moment there was silence, but then he felt a sudden, dropping lurch and crippling terror, not from his link with Eliza, but from Goran.

Cole rubbed his face, glad to be on solid ground. He looked back up at Roth: "It worked. The baileen's listening now. Where do you want them to meet us?"

"It's got to be Morthain. I don't know rightly where we are, but I can get us there. It'll be about a day for us on foot." Roth looked up at the fading stars, mumbling something under his breath.

"*Did you get that?*" Cole asked. He attempted to feed Roth's words directly through the link.

"*Yes. I don't know where the town is myself, but the baileen might. I will let you know if we need further guidance. Will you keep the link open? I don't want to lose you again,*" Eliza trilled as desperation leaked through.

"*Of course. I'll try my best. Take care of Goran for me.*" Cole backed away from the link, keeping it within reach. He knew why she wanted the link open. She needed it for the same reason he needed it. They helped each other share the burden of their grief. Even now Joshy called to him.

"*I'll see to Lileth for you too,*" she added, her smirk palpable.

Ignoring the comment, Cole returned to Roth with flushed cheeks. "They're headed for Morthain now."

Chapter 2

Judgment

Cole's munisica tore through rocks and roots as he chased after Roth. The Rage fueled his strides, sustaining him for hours on end. He was disappointed, though not surprised when the shroud didn't quite cover his whole body. His hair remained its usual unkempt mess while only parts of his arms and legs donned the ebony armor. He was certainly faster and stronger than he'd ever been, though every time he caught up to Roth, his Master would shoot off out of sight around some fern or distant hill. It was difficult to gauge how fast he was running, but Cole thought he might be approaching highway speeds. He laughed to himself, imagining Roth outstripping super cars in a drag race. He wished he could summon the Rage he'd wielded back in Costas. Then Roth would be the one trying to keep up with him. Cole fantasized for a moment, then discounted the idea, remembering how he had almost killed his friends.

Cole slowed his pace. Roth cantered to a stop at the base of a ridge, his clawed hand raised in a halting gesture. Stowing his own munisica, Cole took a moment to relax his Rage and catch his breath.

"There are people on the other side of this hill," Roth said, his voice calm and quiet.

"How can you tell?" Cole asked, massaging a cramp in his side.

Roth squinted, changing the angle of his head. "I can hear them."

Cole held his breath for as long as he could, but the only thing he could hear was the thumping of his heart and the chatter of rodents in the canopy above him. Arching his neck, Cole watched a squadron of squirrels chase each other over the weeping leaves of the towering vines. An imminent sunrise teased through the cracks in the leafy canopy, signaling the end of the house of Allias. Cole jumped, feeling something caress his bare foot. Looking down, he saw a faint orb the size of his fist. It flickered between lavender and soot black.

"Roth look! A soul fly!" Cole gasped, reaching down to caress the creature. The soul fly recoiled, sending shards of panic up Cole's arm. It was scared.

"Be silent," Roth hissed. "Follow me as quietly as you can." Without another word Roth crawled up the hill on all four munisica, his mountainous frame making no louder sound than a falling leaf.

Cole stumbled after him, snapping twigs and slipping his bare feet over wet rocks. Roth looked back, clearly annoyed. Cole mouthed his apology, but Roth's eyes flashed emerald with a quick blast of Wisdom. Wincing, Cole expected a kick to the head. Instead he felt an odd fuzzy sensation in his hands and feet, as if they were buried in cotton. Without waiting, Roth continued up the hill. Cole followed. To his pleasant surprise he found that his hands and feet could make no noise whatsoever, not even when he popped a few dried seeds or scraped his foot over loose bark.

As they neared the crest of the hill other soul flies popped over, rolling and darting towards them like a startled herd. There were dozens of them, all the same shade of blue veined with black. The pain and terror were palpable. Cole looked back and watched them bounce down the hill as if chased by Decreath himself.

Cole joined Roth at the top of the hill, following his gaze down towards a small cluster of four houses. The structures seemed too tall and too crooked to stand, as though held together by magic. Judging by the moss that ran up their walls, and the verdant overgrowth that crowded the yards, the structures had been abandoned for quite some time. Roth nudged Cole with his boulder of an elbow, pointing with his chin towards a stone well behind one of the dilapidated houses. Beside the well were two Aenerian women dashing throughout the yard. At first glance they appeared to be chasing each other in a game. After a few seconds their reckless, desperate movements hinted at something more significant.

Cole dared not speak, instead waiting for Roth's sandpaper whisper to break the silence. "What do you think those two women are doing down there?"

Cole leaned close. "I can't tell. Can't hear them from here. Can you hear anything?"

"Of course I can, idiot," Roth snapped. "I can hear their heartbeats from here. You are a warrior of The Sill. Inspect the situation."

"Yes, Master Roth," Cole replied mechanically, realizing that he was now in one of Roth's lessons.

He knew what to do. He slowed his breath and heartbeat, which were both still racing from his contact with the panicked soul fly. In the quiet of his thoughts he found the Wisdom waiting patiently for him. With his fingertips glowing a dim sage, Cole brought them to his ears, then to his eyes. The magic tickled his eardrums and pulled at the lenses in his orbs, adjusting them perfectly. The faint sounds of the surrounding forest rose to a raucous chorus. Cole could hear beetles taking flight and water dripping onto what had to be a mushroom. He opened his eyes, blinking and disoriented. He could only focus on things at great distances, though the images were crystal clear. He turned his frozen eagle's gaze towards the two women. One had black frizzled hair like a charred shrub, and chased the soul fly in zigzagging circles. The other only helped half-heartedly, complaining all the while. Though Wisdom bombarded his ears with a cacophony of sounds, Cole could make out their words as though they stood right next to him.

"What have you discovered?" Roth's whisper was so loud he might as well have been screaming in Cole's ear.

Cole jumped, dropping the magic. He rubbed his ears, working his jaw as he blinked his eyes back into focus. "They've captured a soul fly. I don't know what they're going to do with it but it doesn't sound good. It's so weird. I think... it sounds like..." his voice trailed off, unsure how to put words to it.

"Speak your mind, Cole. What are they going to do with that soul fly?" Roth anchored his eyes into Cole's.

"It...it sounds like they're going to rape it." Cole shuddered. Even in the Aenerian language the word had a sickening shame to it. "But how can they? It's not like it has a body. How can they...how can they violate it like that?"

"Tell me how Storn met his end," Roth ordered.

The corners of Cole's lips curled in disgust as he recalled the memory. "Kreed had the Corpulants subdue him with their flies. They had some kind of venom or something. Then while he was all drugged up Kreed hurt him. He hurt him really bad. Storn screamed and kicked as hard as he could, but between the venom and Kreed's magic it was too much and he…" Cole paused for a moment, swallowing back the lump in his throat. "It looked like Kreed took Storn's soul right out of his face. He took it when Storn was in the height of all his pain and Fear. Then Kreed ate it. I could feel it happening, like it was happening to me too. He violated Storn's soul." Cole finished, hoping that it would be the last time he would have to tell that story.

Roth's eye twitched, but otherwise he didn't show any reaction. "I thought as much. No one deserves an end like that, Storn least of all. If you found yourself in a similar situation but with the power to stop it, would you?"

"Of course I would," Cole hissed. "It's the worst thing I've ever seen. If I could I would rip Kreed's heart out before he ever had the chance."

"Well then, Warrior of The Sill, I have a task for you." Roth inclined his head: "The two Aenerians down behind that house are about to do something very similar to that soul fly. You find yourself with the power to stop it. Go stop it."

Cole's heart dropped down into his stomach. How exactly was he supposed to stop it? What was he supposed to do, run up to the women and try to kill them? All his feeble attempts at magic and failures in his lessons came rushing to the fore of his mind. There was no way he was ready for this.

"Hesitating will cost you more than confronting your Fears." Roth's voice rose alongside a rumble from deep in his chest. "You let your Fear shake you and you'll be another meal like Storn. Oh, and before I forget," Roth's eyes flashed neon green once more as the fuzzy feeling vanished from Cole's hands and feet. "You do this on your own. Go now. That's the last time I'm going to tell you."

Before he knew it Cole was shuffling down the steep hill, trepidation growing like wildfire with every step. Here he was, barefoot in tattered clothes, appearing as a large Underkin or very small Aenerian, and walking straight towards a crime in progress. What would he say to them? Should he say anything at all or just go for it? Before he could give his predicament another thought, one of the women noticed him blunder over a log hidden beneath a pool of dried leaves.

"Ha! Got it!" The woman with black frizzy hair lunged into a dive before wrestling to her knees with the soul fly trapped between her hands. "Milette, be a dear and fetch me that bucket. Milette?" The woman looked up with eyes sunken and dark. "What's got you so spooked, love?"

Milette spoke from the side of her mouth, keeping her eyes on Cole: "We have a visitor."

The woman grasping the soul fly stood to her full height, taking in Cole and gazing down her nose with an imperious expression. "Come forth, little one. Don't fret, you are in safe hands now. This is a dangerous place for an Underkin to be wandering all on his own. Where did you come from, sweet child?" She then dropped her voice and whispered something to Milette. Cole silently augmented his hearing with Wisdom, picking up on the last few words. "...feed us both."

Cole took one timid step after another, unsure what to say or do. He was close now. Close enough to notice some of the patterns on the women's robes, which bore a striking resemblance to the marking of the priests from Costas. He stopped a few paces away, his Fear preventing him from taking another step. The soul fly didn't appear to be doing much better. It flashed indigo and black, wriggling between iron fingers. Cole could almost smell the terror wafting from it as it trembled and squirmed to escape.

Seeing Cole's eyes on her treasure, the woman recoiled, hiding the soul fly behind her back. "Silent as a statue aren't we? No matter, you don't have to talk to us if you don't want to. My name is Traci, and this here is my lovely Milette. Are you hungry? You look like a starved cat in those tattered clothes." Traci's face scrunched into a patronizing sort of pout. "Oh and look at you, you haven't even any shoes. Please Milette, take him inside and dress him. And see if you can't find something to fill his belly." Her voice was soft but the muscles on her forearms were tight and straining with effort. She carefully angled her body so Cole couldn't see the soul fly.

"Come," Milette said, taking two quick strides over to Cole. She was easily a few feet taller than him. Her hands engulfed his shoulders. "Come with me now."

Before Cole could object, Milette firmly guided him towards the nearest rickety house. He was certain there was no food or footwear in there for him. As a matter of fact, he was quite sure he knew exactly what was waiting in there for him. Cole dug his heels into the grass and stopped. Memories of Storn poked through his clouds of Fear.

"What are you doing?" Milette asked, crushing her massive hands into Cole's shoulders. "Answer me, Underkin."

Cole checked the spark inside himself to make sure his Rage was ready. He steadied his breath, projecting his voice so it wouldn't sound as scared as he felt. "What is Traci doing to that soul fly?"

Milette lifted Cole and turned him around so fast that his neck cracked. She kept one hand on his arm, squeezing so tightly that his hand began to fall asleep. "There are no such things as soul flies. Are you referring to Traci's toy?"

"No, the soul fly. The one she's hiding behind her back." Cole winced as her fingers dug deeper into his arm.

Milette's eyes hardened. "That is no soul fly. Milette is practicing a bit of magic that is far beyond your realm of understanding. How do you know what a soul fly is anyhow? Answer me!"

Cole felt blood trickling down his arm from Milette's fingernails. He ignored the pain. It was nothing compared to even the easiest of Roth's lessons, which Cole just remembered he currently was in the middle of. He leaned around so he could see Traci, who was still pretending as if holding her hands awkwardly behind her back was an everyday occurrence.

"I think that soul fly doesn't like what you're doing to it." His voice was soft and shaky. "Why don't you let it go so it can join its friends. The sun will rise soon and they need to go back to Allias before Aeneria moves on."

"My my, aren't we bold." Traci sneered as she brought the frightened soul fly into plain sight. "And clever too. Too clever for an Underkin. Perhaps too clever for your own good."

"He's no Underkin," said Milette, picking Cole up and inspecting his face. "He's too big and he doesn't look right. Come to think of it, he doesn't look like much of anything I've ever seen. Boy, what manner of beast are you?"

Cole ignored Milette, looking over her shoulder at the soul fly. From Traci's fingertips, inky snakes raced over the orb, causing the soul fly to emit a shrill chime as it wriggled desperately. The sound rang in Cole's ears and mind, itching and pinging off horrible memories he didn't remember having. He didn't have much time.

"Let go of that soul fly. This is the last time I'm going to tell you," he added, mimicking Roth's words. They sounded much more intimidating coming from his Master.

Traci threw her head back with derisive laughter. "Such spirit! I look forward to seeing what fuels that fire in your heart. I can't wait to peel you apart and see where you get your fervor. But I'm afraid my curiosity will have to wait." She shook the soul fly at Cole as more of the dark coils wrapped around it. The chiming stopped suddenly. "Milette dear, put our gallant knight to bed would you? Don't kill him of course. That would put me in a sour mood indeed."

"Of course, mistress Traci," Milette said in a menacing tone. She pulled Cole close to her face and shut her eyes and mouth. Her cheeks popped out round as she heaved, looking as though she were about to vomit. Cole turned his head and tried to raise his arms, but Milette had them pinned to his sides. She opened her mouth as a cloud of sickly mauve smoke poured into Cole's face. He held his breath, but it didn't help.

Fear. The noxious cloud was rife with it, stinging Cole's throat and eyes as it worked its way into his mind. His heart quickened, galloping away from him. Chilling fires of terror lapped at his insides, holding him in place, crushing and snuffing him out. Cole fought for a means to escape as the debilitating clouds replaced his conscious thought. But how? He couldn't remember. In order to escape he would surely need to fight. In order to fight he would need his Rage. That was it. His Rage was the counter to the Fear.

Milette's scream tore through the ghostly dawn. She stumbled backwards, falling over herself as she landed in the dirt, blood spurting from what was left of her arms. The acrid smoke cleared, revealing Cole shrouded entirely in the black armor. Within each of his claws was one of Milette's severed hands.

Cole regarded Milette for a single heartbeat. She writhed on the ground, scrabbling in an attempt to stem the crimson that gushed from her. Weak. Pitiful. Defeated. With a single, swift motion, Cole threw her hands over the tree tops on the other side of the village. He didn't bother watching them as they sailed out of sight. He instead brought his fiery gaze upon the one still standing. Hopefully she would put up a fight. He yearned for the challenge. His Rage demanded it. He placed one clawed foot in front of the other, moving as slowly as he could. He wanted to savor every moment. The cowardice painted on her face aroused him.

Traci's mouth popped open in horror as she took a step back. "What...what *are* you?"

Cole's only answer was the sound of his steady footfalls and the clinking of his bladed hair.

Traci's eyes darted back and forth from Milette to Cole. She tucked the soul fly under one arm and readied a spell with the other. She faltered as an idea lit her eyes. "You...you are powerful indeed. I would surely die if I faced you in combat. You are simply too strong, too fast. I'm no worthy opponent for you." She began to talk faster as Cole closed the gap between them: "I can see the desire burning in your eyes, the desire for challenge, to pit yourself against something formidable. I assure you, I won't be able to oblige those desires, at least not in that way. But there is a way, there is something that not even you can stand against." Traci released a quiet sigh as Cole finally stopped two paces in front of her.

"Say it," Cole ordered. He ground his teeth as his claws stretched longer by the second. He needed an outlet.

Traci relaxed, her voice soothing and intoxicating: "Your worthy adversary is of course...yourself. Your power feels good, yes?"

Cole growled, closing his eyes. It was taking all his effort not to drive his munisica through her. "Yes it is. And right now it wants me to kill you."

"Exactly my point." Traci reached down and ran her fingers over his shrouded cheek. "The power demands it. It feels good to satisfy it. You should give it what it wants. You've earned it." Traci shifted her arms, presenting Cole with the soul fly. "Feel that? Isn't it tremendous? Take it. Your power needs it."

Cole stared into the creature held before his eyes. He knew it was important, but couldn't remember why and didn't much care. His Rage was boiling over, churning and changing into something he didn't recognize. He reached out with a clawed hand and took the orb from her. Even through his munisica he could feel the energy pulsing from it. He brought the soul fly to his mouth, eager to add its power to his own.

"Take it, take the fire into yourself," Traci whispered.

Cole opened his mouth and felt a sudden resistance on his head and arm. Two enormous clawed hands had clamped down on him, preventing him from taking his prize. Roth towered beside him, his booming voice lost in the blood that pounded in his ears. Traci scampered away, leaving Milette to die.

Cole still couldn't hear what Roth said, nor did he want to. Right now the big oaf was the only thing standing between Cole and his meal. With his free hand, Cole gripped his Master's wrist and squeezed. Had Roth's arm not been shrouded, his hand would have come free just as Milette's had. Rage building, Cole pulled Roth's arm away from his head. He could feel the muscles strain and surrender to his Rage. Weak. Pitiful. Cole tightened his grip and twisted, indulging himself in the look of confusion on Roth's face. There was a beautiful crack as both munisica released him.

Roth took a step back, his right arm bent at an odd angle. His eyes flashed with white Passion and Cole felt a memory rush to the front of his mind. Storn swam before his eyes, his final scream hanging in Cole's ears. Just as quickly as he came, Storn was gone. Cole shook off the illusion and felt a sense of clarity through the Rage.

"Release the soul fly," Roth said, his voice deep and calm. "Remember Storn."

Cole had completely forgotten the creature he had clutched in his munisica. Appalled, his bladed fingers snapped open as the sad blue orb shot off out of sight. Fresh Rage suddenly replaced his shock. Cole threw his head back and roared, fury shaking him from head to toe. His burning gaze landed on Roth once more.

Roth took a step forward, placing his uninjured hand on Cole's shoulder. "Don't just stand there and curse the skies. Find her and make her pay for it."

Without a word, Cole shot off after Traci. He found her soon enough. The Rage alone had enhanced his senses to a point where he could hear her breathing from inside one of the houses. Deciding that the stairs would take entirely too long, Cole smashed through a second-story window, landing next to a hysterical Traci. She pleaded, begging and groveling at his clawed feet. The Rage demanded that he rip her and the house into a heap of blood and splinters.

"No no no, please. I've done nothing wrong!" She screamed as she tore from the room, hiding in another down the hall. She screamed again when she saw Cole's dark form waiting for her in there. "Monster you are! Beast!" Flicking her hands about her, she assaulted Cole with various flying objects from the room. It was a desperate, primitive use of Wisdom, none of which had any effect on Cole's shrouded form. After breaking a heavy iron armoire over his head, Traci brought her hands together as a ball of heavy orange fire crackled to life within her fingers. The ball pulsed and grew until she could barely hold it.

"Take one more step and I'll burn this whole house down." She cast her eyes at the windows and doors, which proceeded to close and lock themselves. "I'll kill us both. This is no ordinary fire. It's Hatefire. It burns much quicker and hotter than any you've ever seen. There will be no escape, not even for a monster like you."

Cole grimaced and ground his teeth. The Rage was still building, causing his munisica to twitch and grow painfully.

Traci smirked, laughing softly as Cole had appeared to have come to his senses. "That's right little beasty, now let down that pretty black armor and have yourself a seat. Mistress Traci is going to have a look inside your head and see what…" Traci blinked, looking around the empty room. Cole was nowhere to be found. With trembling hands she readjusted her grip on the shaky ball of fire, only to realize that she was no longer holding it. The fire had dropped to the rotten wooden floor, rapidly jumping throughout the room. Traci hopped back, reaching for the door, only her legs wouldn't move. She looked down, seeing the flames walking their way up her legs. Oddly enough, she couldn't feel a thing, though she was burning just as surely as the room was. Amid the scent of charred wood and cloth, she smelled the meat of her lower legs succumbing to the flames. She couldn't see them however, as the smoke was now too thick. She could see something odd sticking out from her breast, something thin and dark glinting in the flames. The thing should not have been there. Traci groped gently for the mysterious object, but lost interest. Her hands fell to her sides as the rushing void replaced the roaring flames in her ears.

Cole planted a foot on Traci's backside and pulled his munisica from her back, kicking her limp body into the center of the blazing room. He could feel the intensity of the Hatefire through the shroud. To his surprise it pained him, but not unbearably so, as if the Hatred lacked conviction. Curious, he stepped into the hottest part of the fire. It hurt, but his Rage burned all the hotter for it. She was right about the speed of the fire, however. With only a minute to work, the fire had fully enveloped this room and, judging by the sounds from above, had already worked its way into the attic. Cole had the strangest urge to stay in the burning house until the entire thing collapsed, which would likely only be another few minutes. He decided against it after feeling himself lightheaded. There was no telling if he could keep the shroud up should he pass out. The smoke was now so dense that Cole couldn't see his hands. Wading through the burning furniture, Cole slashed at the nearest wall. He followed the river of fire out of the resulting hole, landing clumsily in wild grass beside the house. Taking a deep breath, Cole found Roth standing beside him.

"I assume she took her last?" Roth asked, tilting his head curiously. As if in answer, the crooked house collapsed on itself in a gout of flames and smoke. "Yeah, she's meat now." He crossed his arms, both of which were whole and healed.

Without a word, Cole stood to his feet and took a step towards Roth.

Roth dropped his arms and planted a clawed foot behind him. "I'll lock horns with you again if you wish, but you're getting tossed this time."

Cole ignored Roth and stepped around him, towards Milette. She was still lying on the ground, though she was no longer writhing or making any noise at all. The flames from the house began to spread to the tall grass that enveloped her prone form. Cole hooked one of his claws in the back of her jacket and dragged her over to a patch of plain dirt.

Milette moaned, opening her eyes to find Cole standing above her, a shadow of dark fury in the morning light. Gasping, she crawled backwards, crying out in pain as the stumps that were her wrists plunged into the unforgiving earth.

Milette sat up, panting and biting her lip. She raised her head, sighing with resignation. Unlike Traci, she didn't beg or plead. She accepted her fate and greeted Cole with open eyes.

"Do you know what a soul fly is?" Cole asked, his voice hard as steel.

"Yes," Milette replied.

Cole growled, gnashing his claws and teeth together. "Do you know what she was about to do to that soul fly?" His munisica were still growing and hurting, demanding more.

"No." Milette's voice was steady, though a pallor began to spread across her face and neck.

"Are you lying?" Cole bit the inside of his armored mouth as hard as he could, trying to feel something besides the urge to kill. It was taking everything he had to bottle the violence.

Milette hesitated for half a breath, her face softening before responding, "Why would I lie? I will bleed to death in moments, unless you kill me first." The blood pooling at her sides mixed with the dirt, creating a ruddy crimson mud puddle. "Death's kiss carries the breath of truth."

"NO!" Cole roared, dropping his head and hugging himself. He shuddered, the cool breeze tickling his bare skin as the shroud receded. He refused to let the Rage dictate his actions. If he would take another life it would be with sound mind. Traci deserved to die. She would have tortured and broken countless soul flies if he hadn't taken her life. Milette probably deserved death as well, but it seemed wrong to kill her on an assumption. He would stow the magic for now, or at least try to.

He released as much of the Rage as he could, the shroud ebbing and flowing like a black tide. "What were you doing out here then? Look at me!"

Milette hesitantly brought her eyes back up to him, her pale cheeks flushing pink. "Traci saw the soul flies yesterday and suggested that we catch one. She learned some of Grotton's arts from her aunt and said we could gain immense power if we caught one. She wouldn't tell me exactly what the magic involved, but the promise was too sweet to pass up. Where is Traci now?"

"Dead," Cole said, jerking his head towards the bonfire.

Milette nodded to herself as if it only made sense. "Are you going to kill me or not?"

"That depends," Cole said, ignoring the odd glances she cast up and down his figure. "Were you going to kill me?"

"I didn't plan on it, but Traci would have," she said as her eyelids began to sag.

Groaning, Cole bit down on his cheek again, stifling the Rage. "Would you have stopped her?"

"No." Milette's voice was soft now as the remaining color fell from her face, giving her a gaunt, transparent look.

Cole kept his eyes closed, breathing deeply. Should he kill her too? It would be too easy; all he would have to do is stop fighting himself. The Rage would do it for him. Assuming she was telling the truth, Milette would not have killed him directly, but surely under Traci's tutelage she would have grown into a monster herself. Monster. That's what Traci had called him. It was a fitting name for this part of himself. Cole took savage pleasure in his Rage, but this murder would be his choice, not the magic.

With a final, calming exhale, Cole released the Rage entirely. The air was oddly chilled, and he realized why Milette had been giving him odd looks. The fire had completely burned away his cloth armor and he was now fully naked. His momentary embarrassment subsided as

Milette collapsed. Now that he had decided not to kill her, he felt responsible for keeping her alive. He knew there was no way for him to use Passion to heal her, as there was nothing he could use to link any sort of love to her. He instead called Wisdom to his aid.

Cole felt the flames creeping through the grass, finding no trace of the Hatred. The dark magic must have died along with Traci. He flexed his bare hands as an emerald glow spread from his palms, and he felt the potential of the angry little flames. Two thin wires of flame twisted and twirled themselves away from the burning grass. With his wobbly guidance, they snaked through the air and found Milette's clean-cut stumps. Her eyes snapped open, the pain reviving her for a moment. She thrashed and struggled. There was no way he could guide the flames over her flailing arms, so he used his remaining focus to increase the gravity on her stumps. She fell back as her arms slammed flat against the ground. He rushed the flames to her wounds, searing the top inch of flesh. Milette released a weak cry and stopped struggling entirely. Cole swayed drunkenly, releasing his spells and regaining his mental acuity.

"What have you done?" Milette whispered with what little breath she had left. "Must you torture me first?" Her chest rose and fell in a sharp rhythm as tears raced into her ears.

"I'm saving your life," Cole said, swallowing back the guilt. "I might regret it, but I'm letting you live."

Her only response was weak, squeaky panting.

What was he doing? He was no judge. Nor was he an executioner. How had he come to find himself as an arbiter of justice to this alien woman? She was likely much older and wiser than he was. Not one year ago Cole was fumbling through high school and failing basketball tryouts.

Cole found a modicum of confidence amongst his anxious guilt, projecting his voice so that he at least sounded braver than he felt. "Your wounds will remind you of this day, what it cost to take what you had no right to. You may not have known what Traci was going to do, but you had a pretty good idea." Cole crouched down next to her and placed his palm on her forehead. "I'll show you exactly what you were about to take part in."

Cole used his thumbs to open her eyes as he stared into them. He would force his thoughts into her mind, burn them to the walls of her skull so that every time she recalled this moment she would see them. It was a form of Passion that Alvani had only shown him once, and he wasn't sure he could wield it. Guessing his way through the magic, he forced his knowledge of the Devotion, the towers, the soul flies, and finally Storn's death. He knew the magic was working when he felt the implanted memories echoing back to him. Even in her weakened state Cole could tell she was much more adept with Passion than he was. The exchange was only possible because she permitted it. Should she turn her mind on him, he knew he wouldn't stand a chance. After she accepted his knowledge, she poured some of her own back into him, ensuring that Cole knew without a doubt that she had been telling the truth. With a final impression, she gave her solemn guarantee that she would never harm a soul fly for personal gain. Flashes of her soul winked into his mind. The exchange was as revealing as it was intimate. Cole knew she was not a good person, but neither was she inherently evil.

Cole severed the mental link, taking his palm from her forehead and placing it on her chest. "Here. This will help." Rosy light flowed from his fingers into her breast. He knew enough about her now to provide at least some of his Passion. "It won't bring your hands back, but you'll recover in a few hours."

Milette gasped, taking the healing energies into herself as her breath slowed. After Cole took his hand away, a little moan escaped her trembling lips as her face slackened with sleep. Cole stood, kicking dirt over the flames that had crawled too close. What had he just done?

"Well that was right sweet of you, warrior." Roth's voice startled him from behind. Cole wondered how long he had been standing there. "What have you learned?"

Cole shifted in the dirt, trying to angle his legs and hands to preserve some of his modesty. "I...I don't know. I don't know what the hell I just did."

Roth circled around him, stepping through the burning grass, the flames tall enough now to lick his unarmored parts. "Look at the facts. You found two Aenerians setting themselves to commit a crime against nature. Your task was to stop them. You stumbled down the hill, introduced yourself like a fine young gentleman, then after a fair bit of dancing around you finally decided to start on your task."

"I wasn't sure if I should kill them or not!" Cole blurted. "I'm not going to end a life just on someone's word, not even yours. For all I know-"

Roth was suddenly right in front of Cole, spraying him with dirt. "Clap that mouth shut before I close it for you." Cole jumped back a pace, singeing his naked rear on the burning grass. "Now, after you started your task you crippled your first opponent, leaving her alive and possibly able to retaliate. Then you set upon your second opponent and immediately fell prey to Grotton's magic. You know perfectly well that Grotton's Hunger is the perfect counter to Rage, a magic that you rely upon like a child clinging to his favorite blanket. Her lure of Hunger will likely be the weakest attempt you will ever encounter, so you had better put up a damn fight next time. Don't forget yourself. Don't forget Storn." He jabbed the flat of his knuckle into Cole's chest, bruising him.

Cole winced, shameful tears filling his eyes as he bit his lip. He'd never felt so embarrassed, so disgusted in himself, so…dirty. He turned and tried to cover more of his nakedness with his sooty hands.

"If the act wouldn't have ruined the best parts of your soul, I would have let you destroy that soul fly so you could see what it felt like to ruin the life of another. Besides the shame of it, giving in to the lure of Hunger would have bound you to a magical contract with that hag. You would have been hers, forever. There would have been a measure of power no doubt, probably make you too hot for even me to handle. But when the power eventually faded the Hunger would have bloomed from the ashes and clawed at your insides, making that much easier to justify doing it again. You would've started down a path from which there is no return, a slave to Grotton all the while." Roth's voice lowered, sounding slightly less like an avalanche of blame. "Look at me. You know what you did. I won't harp on it, just do better next time. Don't rely too much on Rage and you'll do just fine. Your Passion and Wisdom will be all happy to protect you from the Hunger."

"Thank you, Master Roth," Cole sniffed.

Roth grunted his approval. "So, after you shamed me, I interrupted you." Roth's face changed from one of stony disappointment to fiery humor. "Then you made me more proud than any student ever has. You broke my damn arm!" He growled with laughter, munisica clanking off his shrouded thigh. "A fitting response, eh? I can't remember how many times I threatened to break your arms."

A smile pulled at Cole's mouth. "You rarely threaten us, Master Roth. You've broken my arms *twice* before."

"At least you learned *that* much." Roth steadied his booming laughter and looked towards the remains of the house. "So you nearly pull my arm off, an admirable feat, but it allowed your opponent to escape. She would have too if I hadn't worked some sense into you. You find her, kill her, then make your way back out here to your first opponent. Instead of dispatching her like you should have, you spare her life, even heal her a bit."

"I couldn't do it." Cole looked over at Milette's unconscious form. "I don't want the Rage making those choices for me. It doesn't seem right."

One of Roth's bladed eyebrows curved up. "Then use a bit of Wisdom to get the job done. This is war, boy. We have whole oceans of enemies out there. If we take our time sweet-talking every single one we'll never gain any ground. Anyone using the Three's magic has already identified themselves as an enemy, plain and simple. How many more dead friends do you need before that sinks in?"

Cole nodded, shame mixing with defiance. He understood what Roth was saying, but he definitely didn't agree with it.

Roth sniffed, as though smelling Cole's feelings. "You spent nearly half an hour fighting these two. Time better spent traveling to Morthain. Personally, I would have just sent a rock through each of their heads and been done with it. But this is *your* lesson, not *mine*, and it's not over."

Cole's eyes widened. "It's not?"

"Not by a long shot," Roth said, lip curling in a half smile that did not reach his eyes. "Now, seeing as you decided not to kill her, you've earned yourself a prisoner. And I'd wager she'll be a good shade of pissed off with you once she wakes up and realizes she's never going to wipe her own ass again. So warrior, what are you going to do with your prisoner?"

After finding some child-size garments in one of the nearby houses, Cole clothed himself and extinguished the fire from the house and surrounding grass. Roth had ordered Cole to put out the fire and cover their tracks, stating plainly that this was Cole's mess and he had better figure out how to clean it up. At first Cole tried suffocating the fire by throwing dirt over it, but the fire had spread to such a large area that he didn't have the focus to move that much matter. He found it much easier, however, to persuade the heat to move into the ground where there was plenty of cool earth to soak it up. He silently thanked Deekus for the lesson in Wisdom.

Once Cole had done his best to cover their tracks, he set a spell over Milette's unconscious body, causing her to bob and float a few feet over the ground behind him. Satisfied that she was properly anchored with strands of Wisdom, Cole started off towards the edge of the village. Roth halted him, looking over the remnants of the scene. The house was still smoking and the whole place smelled like a fresh camp fire.

"If we had the time I would make you do this yourself, but for now just watch and learn." Roth knelt down at the border of the blackened earth and placed a naked hand on the ground. Every weed and shrub within ten paces began to writhe like snakes, spreading thousands of little seeds which sprouted instantly, creating a wave of growth that spread over the remains of the house. Within a minute the vegetation had reclaimed the entire area, making it look as though the house was never there in the first place. It smelled like spring rain.

Roth stood, flexing his naked hand back into its usual ebony dragon claw before setting off. Cole followed with Milette in tow, looking back at the green mound and wondering where Traci's body might be. Roth was right; he'd made a mess. They would have to travel at a much slower pace now that Cole had to maintain focus on Milette's body, not to mention he had just cost them nearly an hour. It was all because Cole let his Rage take control, which once again almost cost him everything. He shuddered, thinking about that poor soul fly. Even through his munisica he could feel the creature's Fear. He was all too willing to dominate and feed on the thing, all for a bit more power. His Rage caused more harm than anything else. It didn't feel like he had mastered anything. Every time he called the Rage into himself it felt more like the magic had mastered him. Cole promised himself to never delve so fully into Rage again. He would avoid the magic altogether if he could. There had to be another way.

CHAPTER 3

THE WHITE SANDS

They cut their way through the forest, sticking to small paths and game trails to avoid running into anyone on the main roads. Roth went so far as to weave a spell over their feet that would erase their footprints as they ran. Though Cole was slowed by the mental burden of carrying Milette, Roth gave no leniency and forced them onward at a maddening pace. Cole begrudgingly called upon a measure of his Rage so he could keep up with his Master. Milette floated along behind them, fully asleep and held by Cole's precarious webs of Wisdom. They drove on for a few hours, the sunlight growing steadily brighter all the while. To Cole's immense relief, Roth slowed at the top of a hill, coming to a stop at a rocky outcropping that loomed over a steep cliff.

Cole sagged, throwing his hands on his knees as he ended his own spells and placed Milette on the most comfortable bit of rock he could find. He panted, shuffling over to the edge of the cliff and gazing out at the landscape. Hundreds of feet below them were unforgiving crags and crevices that softened into a sea of white water stretching out to the horizon. He retreated half a step from the ledge. The height induced a queasiness that spread to his limbs, leaving his legs shaking and wobbly. It reminded him of his jump from the baileen, but this seemed worse as the morning light allowed him to acutely identify the many serrated and solid objects below. With a relaxing breath he quelled the dregs of his Rage and turned away from the ledge. The rising star announced itself from the forest canopy behind them, bathing the little waves below them in morning light.

"Behold the White Sands," Roth said. "Morthain's out there somewhere. We'll have to wait for the sun to rise proper before setting out. I need the stars to tell me where it is."

"Sands?" Cole asked, squinting under his hand. "You mean that's not water down there?"

Roth sat himself on a rock. "It's sand alright. After we cross you'll be picking it out your ears for a month."

"Cross it? It looks like I'd sink right to the bottom. I don't think I could fly myself over, especially with a prisoner." Cole glanced back, checking on Milette.

Roth growled, "There are veins of solid ground throughout the sands. We'll walk through just fine once we have the stars to guide us."

Cole squinted down at the sands again, this time making out branches of solid sand that might have been roads. "So we're leaving Allias then. What planet are we coming to next?"

"Dunhaven," Roth grunted.

"Do you know the stars of every local planet?" Cole asked.

"All twenty-one houses. Dead useful. I learned it the hard way, but you ought to pick up a few cyphers of the star maps next time you're at The Sill, if you can afford them that is. They're top-shelf."

"Couldn't you just give me the knowledge?" Cole asked, rubbing his feet. Not using his munisica had taken a toll on his bare soles.

"Ha! And make it easy for you? I thought you knew my policy on handouts. No, it's better for you to earn knowledge on your own, even if it's taken from a cypher like a pie from the markets. Speaking of taking things you haven't earned, how are your bones feeling?" Roth pointed with a long claw at Cole's legs.

Cole rubbed his forearms feeling Roth's magic thrumming deep in the marrow. "They burn a bit, though not in a painful way. Like there's too much energy in there. Itches like crazy sometimes. How long do you think it will last?"

"Until your body absorbs the Rage. What you took from my gratia stone will make you stronger and harder, but it seems to be quickening your little growth spurt, which isn't supposed to happen mind you. I've seen a few humans in my day and I pegged you at near full grown when I first laid eyes on you." He raked his eyes over Cole's legs. "This growth is unusual, no?"

Cole looked down and pulled his pant legs up so he could see his shins. They looked unusually lanky, as did his arms, but he just thought the gangly appearance had to do with his recent weight loss. Everyone said he was getting taller, but hearing Roth say it put a layer of concrete acceptance to it. "When I came here I was seventeen years old - seventeen of *my* years that is, and we stop growing at about eighteen. I've been here for..." He struggled, trying to grasp the concepts through the lens of the time cypher, "it's odd, judging your time against mine. I arrived at the end of the house of Terra, then there was Pastori and Allias. From what I can tell through the cypher each house is about a third of one of my years, so I shouldn't be growing anymore. I guess I do feel a bit taller. That would explain why I've been so clumsy lately." Cole fell silent as homesickness struck him in the chest. He'd been gone for almost a year. He'd missed his birthday, and Nana Beth's. Joshy's birthday should be coming up too. Sullen, he looked back up to Roth's calculating gaze. "Do you have any idea why I'm shooting up like this? Could it be some of your magic, or Oberon's light or something?"

"Our magic is your magic. That much you have earned," Roth said, standing to his full height. His appraising nod filled Cole with a pride that he hadn't felt in a long time. "Oberon's light will have an effect on you, but it won't change your blood and meddle with nature's intent. I have no answers for you. Perhaps when we get to Oberon Temple you can find one of Terra's Council members and pry an answer from them."

"I remember Ka Reine talking about the Council in the Arts District. Those are the Wisdom Walkers that specialized in one local planet. They form your government, right?" Cole asked.

"One Council member from each house. Twenty-one greedy, single-minded, stiff-necks to tell the rest of us how to lace our boots." Roth's face twisted as though he'd just tasted something foul. "Judge for yourself when we get there. I don't much care for the puffed-up bureaucrats." Roth's eyes perked up. "Ah, finally."

Cole followed Roth's gaze to the sky above. The dim morning light swelled to what felt like a high-noon sun, though he couldn't quite see Allias's star over the trees. Then, just as quickly as it flared, the daylight faded into such a deep shade of night that Cole thought his eyes had stopped working. He pressed his fingers to his eyelids, blinded once more by his lime-green flash of Wisdom. Blinking away the pressure, he cast his blind gaze about, looking for the stars. The first thing he noticed was a brilliant amethyst object at about eye level. Oberon smiled at him from across the White Sands, humming through every shade of purple while bathing the pearly waves in hues of feathery lilac and rich plum. Cole found Roth silhouetted in a robe of magenta that glinted off his shrouded armor. His bladed hair dangled over his broad shoulders, tinkling like glass as he took in the stars that began to sprout in the empty canvas above them.

"I thought as much," Roth said to himself. "Grab the prisoner, we're headed straight out from here." He pointed a claw out over the middle of the White Sands: "See the star that flickers red and white?"

Cole nodded. "Yeah, the little guy in between the triangle looking thing."

He looked back at Roth. Even in Oberon's dim glow Cole could see the smirk on his face. "Just follow me...If you can keep up."

Cole made a squeaking noise as Roth took a step into open air and disappeared off the ledge. Cole crouched, wrapping his arms around his body and legs, feeling as if a piece of himself had just plummeted off the cliff. Taking several deep breaths, he took inventory of his magical tool box and tried to think about it as if this were a simple math problem back in school. He had everything he needed, but would he be able to maintain the spells while falling through the air?

Twisting his thoughts, he forced reality to accept his will. There was an immediate lightening of his body. He poured more of his conviction into the idea until he felt almost completely weightless. The effect spread to his clothes as well, rippling his shirt in waves of distorted gravity. He tested the magic with a few little hops. Using only his toes he floated several feet into the air before falling back down as slow as a feather. Pleased, he reinforced the spell with his trust and remaining focus, spreading the field until the small rocks around him began to float upwards. With barely enough focus left to walk, he bobbed towards Milette, who was no longer lying on the ground, but standing. She looked ready to bolt. Cole would have been shocked if he was not already spell-drunk.

She recoiled, taking a timid step back. "I will *not* be going off that cliff."

"Yes. Yes you will," Cole said with slurred speech. Truthfully he had no idea how he was going to force her to do anything. He could barely keep himself from seeing double.

Milette shook her head dismissively, as though she knew he had no power over her. She turned on the spot and lunged for the forest, only to find that her feet were no longer joined with the rocky ledge. She rose and spun as she kicked her feet like a swimming child. "No... no you can't! Stay away from me!"

Waiting for her spinning to expose her back, Cole hooked his fingers around the collar of her jacket and dragged her towards the edge. Her moans filled the air as she thrashed. She clubbed her newly healed stumps over the back of her neck in a fruitless attempt to free herself. Through the river of magic in Cole's mind, a fuzzy memory of Lileth pulling him off the baileen swam forth as he took a bounding leap off the edge. He trusted the magic, like a child trusting the arms of his parents to catch him. Milette however, did not. Even though they were falling more slowly than heavy smoke, she wailed and cried as though they were plummeting to their deaths.

Cole pulled himself close to her, speaking in a calm, reassuring voice: "Don't worry. I have you."

Milette scrambled and crawled over Cole like a squirrel so that he wore her like an oversized backpack. She buried her eyes in his neck as wisps of her hair stuck to Cole's sweaty face. He was quietly thankful that she had no hands as the death-grip of her severed wrists was nearly enough to choke him.

The cliff was not entirely vertical, and before long his bare feet gently pushed off a boulder, propelling them farther along. He couldn't see Roth yet, but he was confident that his Master was waiting not-so-patiently for him at the bottom. He continued bounding down the rocky wall, loosening and tightening his hold on the magic when needed to speed up their progress. The frequency of his jumps increased as the slope of the wall gentled and the rocks gave way to flat sand.

"Nice rucksack you got there," Roth grunted. "Bet you're re-thinking your policy on prisoners now aren't you?"

Cole ended his spell and heaved Milette off his shoulders, landing her heavily into the sand at his feet. "Don't you go running off!" Cole half panted, half shouted at her as she rose into a defensive crouch. "I'll chase you down and take your feet off if you do." Reluctantly, he drew his munisica to emphasize the point.

Milette eyes darted from Cole's claws to the towering cliff, as though judging her chances of escape. After laying eyes on Roth, she slumped back down into the sand with a look of utter dejection.

Roth's laugh shook the air. "Ha! You're my student after all." He gave Cole a rough pat on the shoulder, sinking his feet several inches into the sand. "Nothing like a sincere threat from the bottom of your heart to make a point, eh?" He laughed again, walking past Cole and stopping directly in front of Milette. "Stand up." His tone hardened to granite, giving no hint of leniency. "I said stand up and look at me."

Milette rose to her feet. She was taller than most Aenerians, but she still had to arch her neck back as far as it would go to meet Roth's eyes.

Roth huffed his approval. He snatched a single blade of his obsidian hair and dragged it slowly across her neck. A neat line of crimson blood crawled across her skin.

He took the blade of hair into his mouth, sucking on it. "You taste like a coward."

Milette whimpered.

"I love cowards," Roth said, bringing his face less than an inch from hers. "You know, you ought to be thanking Cole here. I usually enforce a very strict penalty on those who practice the arts of the Three. I would have taken your head, but luckily your captor has the mercy of a saint and only took your hands. You're his prisoner and you work for him now, but seeing as he works for me I guess that makes me your boss. He'll deal with you as he sees fit, but if you so much as vex me in the slightest…" He brought his munisica to her face, black clawed fingers growing and wrapping all the way around her skull, "…I'll be coming for that head, sweetheart. You get all that?"

Milette's voice trembled as she nodded as much as she could without losing an eye. "Y-yes."

Roth's smile deepened. He held her gaze for a moment longer before turning towards the ocean of sand. "Morthain is about half a day's walk towards that red and white star, so it's a good thing we won't be walking," he said, turning his head towards Cole. "Stay behind me and don't wander off or you'll have to teach yourself how to swim in dust. Hail Eliza if you can. They should be there by now." And without another word Roth shot off at a steady gallop, the twinkling red and white star hanging directly above him.

"Get moving." Cole flattened his ebony claw into a single blade and jabbed it at Milette's back.

She gave him a look of deepest loathing, as though imagining him a painful death. "Do you intend on running behind me the whole time? What if I get tired or decide I've had enough?"

Cole bent his munisica and jabbed her in the ribs with a flat part of his claws. "Then I'll take the rest of your arms off. Less weight to carry, right?" He carefully opened the throttle of his Rage, just enough for the shroud to spread up his shoulders and hair. Hopefully his deeds at the village would be enough to persuade her.

Milette's scowl cracked into a defeated sob as she lowered her head and started after Roth. Cole followed close behind, letting her know that he would have no trouble keeping up with her long legs. The sand was loose, sapping his energy and requiring he maintain his hold on the Rage just to keep pace. Milette slowed soon enough, gasping and panting. Cole felt a swell of satisfaction at not being the slowest one in the group, but he began to worry what Roth might think of her waning speed. He couldn't even see his shadow over the sands anymore. Cole was about to loose a spell to make Milette run faster, when he felt an imposing presence enter his mind like an avalanche of fire.

"*Keep your pace.*" Roth's thoughts filled Cole's mind, making his skin tingle with ambient fury. "*I'll run ahead and trigger any ambushes that might be waiting for us. The Morthainians aren't known for their hospitality. Aim for that star."*

Before Cole could respond, Roth left his mind as quickly as he came. Noticing Milette drifting too far to the left, he shouted at her to keep for the red and white star. Her pace continued to slow, allowing Cole to release his hold on the Rage and reach out to Eliza with his Passion. In his mind he found her strings easily enough, but they were slackened and out of tune. He tried tightening the lines, but couldn't manage to hold on to them. He simply wasn't relaxed enough to attune himself to their usual link. Throwing his doubts aside, he grabbed the line and shouted with his thoughts, calling for Eliza. He felt something on the other side, immediate and fuzzy, but he also sensed her groping her way closer, changing her countenance to match his. With ringing clarity, her voice chimed in his head.

Her presence was emboldening. *"I was wondering when I might hear from you again. Is all well with the two of you?"*

"We are well, but there are three of us now. We stumbled upon two Aenerians torturing a soul fly. Roth made me stop them, and they of course attacked me. I killed one and took the other as prisoner." His embarrassment flooded through the link, so he addressed it. *"I should have been strong enough to kill this one too. Now we're slowed down and I have no idea what I'm going to do with her."*

Cole pushed images of the ordeal through the link. He could feel her Rage flare at the idea of someone attacking him, though there was a measure of serene pride as well. *"It certainly would have been easier to kill them both, but ending a person's life for mere convenience is not who you are. Defending yourself is quite different from murder. Killing her would have killed a part of yourself, and would have made it easier to do so again. I am proud to count you as a friend, Cole."*

"Thanks, Eliza. Where are you now? And how are the others?"

Eliza's wry laughter echoed in his mind. *"You mean 'how's Lileth?' I'm sorry, I shouldn't jest. Hiding one's inner thoughts is impossible through the link. We are well and eager to be off this beast. The baileen has grown irritable and doesn't seem to like the piles that Goran keeps leaving on its back. It has agreed to take us to Morthain, but I doubt it will take us any farther. I can see the sands ahead.*

They look quite stunning under Oberon's current mood. I estimate we'll be there in under an hour. What of you, when will you arrive at Morthain?"

Cole brought his attention back to Milette, barking a command to keep her on course. *"I'm guessing within a few hours. Probably longer, seeing as my prisoner isn't capable of any magic to make her run faster. Roth said that Morthainians might attack us, so be careful when you get there."*

"Then the Morthainians would be in for a lesson in humility. Thank you for the warning. I will see you very soon, brother."

Cole's affection for Eliza gushed into the link, bringing a smile to both their faces. *"See you soon."*

He withdrew from the connection, realizing he had fallen several paces off the trail and was knee deep in soft, powdery sand. With a few awkward leaps he righted himself onto the hard packed dirt and caught up to his prisoner. Milette maintained a limping shuffle, clutching a cramp at her side with both her stumps. Her breath sounded as if her throat were made of rust. Roth had told them to maintain their pace, but this was ridiculous. Even back on Earth Cole could have kept up with her, and she was a good three feet taller than he was. Cole pitied her however. As quietly as he could, he slowly poured his Wisdom into her, lessening the gravity on her body so she might think she was running faster on her own. After several hours of painful slogging, they slowed at Roth's standing figure.

Roth turned, his towering form outlined in a soft lavender glow. "We have arrived at Morthain."

Milette collapsed in a puff of sand as Cole trotted up next to Roth, searching from horizon to horizon. The landscape looked just as barren as when they started, except now he couldn't see the cliffs they'd entered from.

Cole frowned. "I thought Morthain would be some kind of city. This doesn't look like anything."

Roth bent low, sifting his claws through the flowing sands off the trail. "This is where Morthain was the last time I was here. Morthain lies just across the barrier on the Light Side, so no one has had contact with their people since before the banishing. Where's the rest of your unit?"

"They should be here any minute." Cole searched the stars and noticed a small shadow growing larger every second. "That could be them now, right above us."

Milette and Roth followed Cole's arm to the gap in the stars, where five figures descended quickly, each tinged with various shades of green. Cole recognized Goran immediately as his friend was easily twice the size of anyone else. After a minute the five glowing shadows alighted on the hardened path.

Cole ran up to Goran and attempted to pry his massive hand from his face. "Goran! Don't worry you big baby, you're on real ground now."

"Coo...cha?" Goran poked his head up, his ruby eyes scanning the area around him before locking on Cole. He jumped to all fours, pounding his hands on the ground with excitement.

Cole lunged and threw his arms around Goran's neck, hugging him tightly. They wrestled back and forth. Cole dug his bladed feet into the hard path to prevent Goran from dropping back into the powder-sand. "Hey watch it there, Bud. Don't fall back into the loose stuff." He opened their familiar link, impressing upon Goran the significance of the water-like powder behind him.

Goran snorted, dropping his head and bumping it gently into Cole's chest.

"It's good to see you too," Cole said through a mouthful of Goran's snow-white mohawk. He gave him a solid head butt before turning towards the others.

Valen, Eliza, Sitra and Lileth each had a lean, worn look about them, as though they hadn't had a decent meal or night's sleep since Costas. Cole wanted to rush over and hug them all, but there was a grim silence in the air that he was hesitant to penetrate. Sensing his feelings, Eliza walked through the circle and picked Cole up in a deep embrace, pouring all her compassion through their link. He let himself cry against the stained cloth armor of her shoulder. Seeing them all together made Storn's absence painfully obvious. Cole's thoughts even spiraled down to darker places, thinking of Lexy and Joshy. Eliza felt all of it and shared the burden of grief. After she set him back down he felt light and refreshed, as if he had just woken from a perfect nap.

Valen cast a sideways glance at the two of them, apparently waiting for them to pay attention. "Master Roth, we have come as ordered. What is our next task?"

The color fell from Cole's face. Task? They were all exhausted and looked like starved dogs. Roth may be perfectly capable of running all the way to Oberon and back, but Cole didn't think he could make it another mile.

Sitra stepped around Valen, cutting him off. "He means 'where's our next meal?' We haven't had a bite since before Costas. Eliza had to trick some birds into flying close enough for us to snare them, but that was days ago."

Roth bent down, scooping the white sand in his claws and looking off into the distance. "Your next task was supposed to be racking up in Morthain for the night, but it seems as if the entire city is gone. We will leave the sands and seek shelter on the other side."

Lileth twirled her fingers, producing her jade-crystalline telescope from thin air. She put the device to her eye and gazed out under Oberon. "I can't even see the tops of the mountains." She placed the telescope between her palms, closing them until it vanished entirely. "Master Roth, I'm not sure we have the resources to cover such a vast distance. We are more than weary."

Roth inclined his head and looked at them all with a look of steely disappointment. "Do none of you have the Rage that I gifted to you before your mission?"

The group shook their collective heads. Valen spoke for them. "Most of us used it while fighting the Domina, or had it pulled from us by Kreed and his priests. Lileth is correct, we are too diminished to run across the sands."

Roth scowled while considering each of them, sizing them up as though thinking about carrying the lot of them to the mountains himself. "Then you'll have to drag your weary asses to the other side." He raised an eyebrow and glared at them all, daring someone to voice a complaint. No one did. "This is war. The hardest part isn't always fighting or watching your friends take their last. Before this is over you'll find yourselves facing an obstacle thrice as daunting as this little walk, and you'll wish you had as much energy as you do right now.

We will head straight for Oberon Temple. Since the entire group has yet to master flight, we will create our own walking path over the loose sands. Ready your spells. We leave in five minutes."

The group tested the soft sand, wading out into it and trying various means of keeping afloat. Cole hadn't the slightest idea as to how he would navigate the sands. The soft powder was insubstantial and grew steadily deeper the farther he strayed from the hard path.

"Stay near me and you'll be just fine," Lileth said to Cole as he fumbled with a spell to put a cushion of air under his feet. "Goran is of course welcome to join, but if you accrue any more prisoners I'm afraid you'll have to carry them yourself." She gave him a quick smile.

"So you heard?" he asked, stepping up onto Lileth's disc of magically hardened sand.

"Eliza told us all about your encounter." She nodded, stepping off to follow the rest of the group, who had all adopted a similar spell to navigate the soft sands. "I would have killed her myself. She is quite the burden."

"Yeah well I'm trying this new thing where I don't kill people just because it's easier." He looked back to Milette, who gave him a look of pure venom.

"I can hear you both you know." She spat, following Goran up onto Lileth's magical platform. "That oaf said this is to be a full day's march! I don't know who you people are or what you're made of, but I can't march across the planet with no food or sleep. If we go another mile you will have to kill me or I'll throw myself into the sands and be done with you all. So *Master*, what will it be? I am in your charge after all."

Cole was at a loss for words. If he had to he could use his Wisdom to float her along as he did before, but he couldn't keep that up forever. He had no answer, but Goran did. The brindle beast turned and snorted in Milette's face before scooping her up and throwing her on his back. Ignoring her protests, he ambled up to Cole and set his eyes for the horizon.

"Disgusting animal! The smell! What is this thing supposed to be anyway, some sort of cat or ape? Or is it some horrible bastard mix breed that you came up with to satisfy your- oh!" Milette lunged forward as Goran snorted and nearly unseated her. Her stubby wrists gripped his neck to little effect as she eyed the far drop off his flank.

Cole silently thanked Goran through their link before turning to Lileth. "You're right. She is a burden for sure."

They trudged on towards Oberon, Cole chatting with Lileth all the while. She was most interested in discussing his recent mastery of Rage, though Cole was reluctant to delve into the subject. He was ashamed of the Rage, ashamed of how it stripped him of all reason and compassion. He glossed over the details of his encounter with Milette and her partner, making it seem as if he just caught them unawares and overpowered them. Cole sensed Milette about to chime in to fill in the gaps of his tale, but Goran silenced her with another bucking grunt. Lileth would probably never speak to him again if she knew he had almost fed on a soul fly. Eventually the wind picked up, and they were too busy trying to keep the sand out of their faces to talk. After an hour of fiddling with his Wisdom, Cole worked a magical net over his face as well as Lileth's and Goran's, blocking the sand and wind while allowing them to breathe and see. He left Milette to shield her face in Goran's fur, which served a dual purpose as an effective muzzle.

"Stop." Roth's voice cracked like thunder over the whining wind. He held a clawed hand back, halting the rest of the unit. "Spread out and wait here."

They all stopped and took up the best defensive positions they could, though they couldn't make much of a formation in such an open area. Munisica glinted in the moonlight as they readied themselves for anything. Valen summoned his ethereal green wings from under his arms and took flight, circling over the rest of them.

Roth jogged ahead of them until his hulking form was barely visible in the dust. He halted, scanning the ground at his feet before diving headfirst and disappearing beneath the surface. A few minutes passed with no sight of him, just the steady moaning of the wind.

The sand in between them exploded in a cloud of dust. Thankfully Milette's scream was so loud nobody could hear Cole's. The wind carried the cloud away, leaving Roth standing in their center. They closed in around their Master. Valen landed roughly beside him, munisica drawn. Cole admired Valen's flexibility with the different magics.

"Something big is headed our way," Roth addressed the group, a look of savage pleasure in his eyes. "Just stay put and still your munisica until I say so. If we're lucky it's a rock wurm. If we're really lucky it'll be a whole herd."

"There is definitely more than one," Eliza said, her face set in grim terror as her eyes darted about the ground at their feet. "They are upon us."

Cole stepped back, swallowing his heart before it could leap out up his throat. His foot met the edge of Lileth's platform, vanishing beneath the surface of the powder. How was he supposed to fight anything in this state? It was all he could do to maintain a few simple spells to shield their faces. He could summon what was left of his Rage, but what good would that do if he fell over into the loose powder? Cole looked around, desperately searching for something more substantial than a thin layer of magically hardened sand. He was exhausted and supremely vulnerable, as if he were an insect bobbing helplessly at the surface of a pond, just waiting for something from the deep to take him.

By unspoken consent the unit converged on Roth. Valen took flight once more, this time joined by Eliza and Sitra. They waited, listening over the wind and peering through the dust for anything at all.

"There!" Milette cried, pointing with one of her stumps. "Something rises!"

A stone's throw away from their tight circle, something dark slid from the surface. A long pole rose up, trailed quickly by a flapping flag and what could only be a crow's nest. A velvety black sail soon followed, then two masts, one on either side of the first. A ship, long and sharp with triangular black sails appeared before them, rising fully from the sands in a splash of white powder. The vessel circled around them, coming closer as yet another rose up behind it, then another. They all stood in windy silence as the muffled rustling of the black sails came ever closer.

"I don't want a word out of any of you, or I'll personally take it out of your hides," Roth said in a harsh tone, keeping his eyes on the largest ship, which had just halted right next to them.

Cole clenched his fists to steady himself, realizing they had transformed into his deadly claws and the shroud had crawled most of the way up his arms. He exhaled slowly and steadily, releasing the Rage. He instead focused on the nearest ship, which was in such a state of disrepair that it must have relied entirely on magic to stay afloat. A clear membrane covered the upper deck, under which stood a dozen hazy figures. Someone ran to the bow of the vessel and pulled a lever. The clear sheet snapped to the stern of the boat, revealing a crew of well-armed and not-so-well-tempered men.

They were all dressed in rust colored leathers that hugged tightly to thick arms and legs. What appeared to be amber colored glass adorned their clothing, giving a striking beauty to the ugly garments. Judging by the variety of glass weaponry on display, these plates were likely some type of armor. Hiding their faces were shiny tinted masks that gleamed out from under taut hoods.

Just as Cole began to wonder if these hooded sailors meant them harm, doors clanged open all down the hull of the ship, revealing an array of triple-barreled tubes pointed directly at their small group. The tubes appeared to be made of the same amber material as the crew's weapons. Cole was no expert on Aenerian weaponry, but he was positive that they had an arsenal of large-caliber guns pointed at them.

A sailor smaller than the rest stepped to the handrail, looking down at them with his blank mask. Judging by the way he carried himself, Cole guessed him to be some sort of leader. "The three in the sky, call them down now." His voice was distorted and metallic.

Roth raised his chin, his voice calm but booming: "I don't think I will. They only just got up there and I don't want to be rude."

"Then their deaths will be on your head," the sailor called down in his strange voice. He motioned towards the bow of the ship as a figure sitting in a turret nodded, cranking wheels and bringing the barrels of yet another gun to the sky.

Cole winced as a resounding explosion hammered his ears. He looked to the sky expecting to see falling bodies. To his relief he found three apparently unharmed sets of emerald wings circling above them. Cole's eyes flashed back to the gunner, who looked utterly disheveled as he pulled another lever to reload. Sand poured out the breech of his weapon, filling his lap. The gunner looked back to the smallest sailor, shrugging his shoulders and shaking his head.

Their leader signaled to another deck gunner, who had already trained his barrels to the sky. With another concussing thud, the second gunner cried out in frustration as he too was buried in sand. An awkward silence fell over the crew on the ship, broken by Roth's ferocious laughter.

"That fancy weaponry must have cost a fortune," Roth cried out. "You ought to invest in a little maintenance."

The smallest figure looked to Roth. Even under the tinted mask his fury was visible. "Let's see how clever you are after we give you another hole to yapp out of. One of the subdeck guns is bound to work." He leaned over the side of the ship, pounding his fist on the hull and shouting to the crew below. "Let them have it!"

Cole felt the guy with the weird voice had a good point. It would only take one of those huge barrels to tear through the lot of them. He ducked, noticing that Roth's munisica had a dull emerald glow to them. Cole held his breath as countless explosions punched him in the chest. He opened his eyes, waiting for the pain, but there was none. The ringing in his ears subsided, giving over to Roth's booming laughter, which was almost as loud as the guns.

"I never much cared for technology," Roth called out. "All those tricky gadgets are too unreliable. Why don't you invite us up so we can have a little talk?"

The leader turned back to his crew, saying something that Cole couldn't make out over the wind. The guns on each ship withdrew, swiftly replaced by spouts that released a clear liquid into the sands. The concoction spread over the rippling powder, making a light crackling sound as the dancing surface froze. The leader of the sailors reached out as a tall glass staff with a bladed tip was placed into his hand. He set a hand on the rail of the ship and hopped over, landing on the now solid surface. His crew fell in behind him, as did the crews from the other ships. They closed in, forming a tight wall of glass blades.

"Not a word," Roth whispered in a voice barely louder than the wind. His shrouded armor and munisica receded until he was bare skinned and blond-haired. He took a single step towards the leader of the sailors. Roth raised his voice so that all could hear: "You Morthainians follow the path of Rage, do you not?"

With a quick wave from the hooded leader, the advancing sailors halted. He walked ahead, brandishing the glass staff and bringing its blade up to Roth's throat. "And what would an outsider know about the path of Rage?" the leader asked, wagging the blade of his staff in front of Roth's face. Cole could make out tiny munisica poking out from his fingerless leather gloves.

Roth ignored the blade, which now slapped him playfully in the cheek. The entire unit, including Goran, backed away. Roth had maimed each of them for far less. Roth's voice was calm however, with only a trace of his usual threatening menace. "I know enough that you must accept my Trial of Honor, which I invoke. Right now."

There was a smattering of laughter amongst the sailors as their weapons clinked together. The leader cocked his masked head, appraising Roth's nearly naked body. "That's a mighty ambitious request, outsider."

"True words, Rage runner," Roth said. "But you are bound to oblige me, unless you've forsaken the old ways while hiding like frightened rats in your holes."

The laughter ceased immediately, replaced by disciplined silence. The leader turned and whipped his staff behind him. The weapon twanged as it stuck into the side of his ship. He tore off his leather, throwing glass plates and leather straps to the ground. Without command, others followed suit.

"NO!" The leader's metallic voice clanged over the wind. "My Rage will suffice. I alone will kill this giant fool."

"But captain..." said another figure, reaching out towards his leader, "We are all honor-bound to face him. Let at least one of us join you." He then added in an undertone not quite soft enough to go unheard by Cole's magically amplified ears, "He is quite large."

The captain removed his mask as a long rope of white hair fell from the hood. He was not a *he* at all, but an aged woman with a face so marked by scars and wrinkles that she almost looked like a giant Underkin. She tossed her mask to the man at her side. "Should I find myself outmatched by a single man and his troupe of crusty bitches then perhaps it's finally my time to fall. Stand down Quicken, and don't you question me again unless you want my job."

"Yes, Captain," Quicken replied with a little bow.

She gave Quicken a curt nod and he fell back in with the rest of the sailors. Without another word she darted for Roth. As she charged, her munisica stretched, twinkling in Oberon's periwinkle light as her hands grew into black swords longer than Cole's legs. The shroud crept up her wrist and ankles, reaching past her elbows and knees as her sweeping braid dimmed to an ebony rope. Just before she would have collided with Roth, she dug in her clawed feet and leapt high above him. Apparently her black snake of hair was also a weapon. Cole barely noticed Roth's head twitching to the side as the lock of bladed hair swished past his cheek.

The captain wasted no time, landing behind Roth and lunging, bringing her sword-hands together as though determined to dive right through him. This time Cole didn't see the movement, only a horrible screeching clang as she stumbled away from Roth, who had apparently parried the blow with a single bladed finger. The captain gave a curt nod, then set at Roth with a series of elegant swipes and jabs which looked more like an exotic dance. Cole struggled to follow the two fighters. The sheer ferocity of the woman's attacks was more than their entire unit could muster during their training matches against him. While it appeared Roth was pushed to his limits, he only had one finger shrouded and didn't return any of her attacks. It was as if he were testing her as one of his students. He merely blocked and danced along as her swords, hair, and clawed feet whistled through the dusty air. His level of control was impossible. Even Valen's jaw hung loose at the spectacle. Cole wondered just how much Roth had held back on the two occasions that the two of them had locked munisica.

The captain changed her fighting style, a risky maneuver that none of their unit had yet to master. All four munisica worked independently of one another; one sword jabbing like a stork, the other cutting wide arches, one clawed foot planted firmly while the other probed for weakness.

Roth leaped back, his mouth half frowning while his eyes fell with disappointment. He gave the captain a look that could have been sadness, or perhaps encouragement. She returned the look with a bewildered snarl that twisted into agony as she fell to one knee. Her mouth opened and closed as if she were drowning. Her munisica and shroud receded as she clutched her chest and throat. The other sailors looked on through their dark-tinted masks, trepidation apparent in their hushed whispers.

Roth approached her crouched form, his eyes blazing with emerald Wisdom. The back of her pale neck glistened with sweat. Roth lowered his munisica to the top of her spine and pricked it with a spark of green light. Her chest emitted two muffled pops as she hacked and coughed, taking in as much air as her lungs would allow.

Roth waited for her breathing to slow before bending down and speaking into her ear. "Give up, or I won't release it next time."

"But how? How in the rusty hell did you ..." Her voice trailed off in a fit of hacking.

Roth stood tall, throwing his chest out and drawing the full measure of his munisica and shroud, bringing him head and shoulders above the tallest man. His voice thundered loud enough for all to hear: "Your Rage is admirable, but you wield it like a crutch. There are others who would twist it against you until there was nothing left of your own soul. This-" Roth rubbed his bladed thumb and first finger together, the claws producing a screeching sound as a fountain of electric green sparks fell to the sand, "-is Wisdom, a magic which you have shunned for countless cycles. You cast it aside as though it were some trifle not worthy of your time, yet the simplest of spells has brought your captain to my feet and disabled your weapons."

The captain shuffled onto her knees as her shroud faded. She spread her naked arms. "May the sands swallow you, outsider. I cannot best you. Take my life." She shut her eyes and exposed her throat.

"Get up," Roth growled.

The captain's eyes popped open as she cocked her head in confusion. "You know the rules. This ends with my head on the ground."

"Keep your head. Consider it my first gift as leader of your tribe." Roth stepped away from her, waving to the others in the sky.

The captain jumped to her feet, shaking her head as she ran after Roth. "You rule no one except me, outsider. I've not the rank to grant you more than that. I may have been defeated, but every Morthainian before you falls under my second, Lieutenant Quicken. Invoke the Trial of Honor again if you feel you can take the crews of all three of our corsairs."

The crew on the ground took a collective step back. Lieutenant Quicken on the other hand walked up to Roth, taking off his mask and revealing a young, handsome face with hard eyes. "We will accept your challenge, though we all know what the outcome will be. We will fight you to the man." Quicken tightened the grip on his staff as Eliza, Valen, and Lileth landed behind Roth. "What is your name, outsider?"

Roth measured them with a heavy stare. "You haven't earned my name, or a death by my hand. None of you have. You misunderstood my challenge. I invoked the Trial of Honor not on you or your crew, but on Morthain."

Quicken's face drooped with the weight of his shock. "The entire city! You are either very foolish or very powerful. Either way you are but one man! What you propose is impossible!"

Roth closed the gap between them and slammed his forehead into Quicken's. "Then *make* it possible."

Quicken staggered back, clasping his head. "But I haven't the authority." He shot a glance at his defeated captain, who looked as if she had just been fed a mouthful of sand. "None of us does."

Roth growled as the final strands of patience appeared to snap. Cole thought he looked as though he were contemplating killing all three crews just to simplify things. The idea wasn't entirely unreasonable as they had just dry-fired about a dozen high-powered weapons at him and his friends. Cole's own munisica started stretching and he could feel the shroud creeping up his arms. Just as he felt the Rage would boil over into action, a voice cut through the dusty wind.

"That authority would be mine." A figure limped towards them from between two ships. He was not wrapped in rusty leathers, but in elegant crimson finery that looked out of place in the bleak desert. His back was hunched and his face lined with the weight of countless cycles, yet his thick arms and broad shoulders suggested that he had not entirely forgotten the strength of his youth. He stepped in between the formations of sailors, who all fell to one knee as he passed. The shroud covered half the man's face and he wore a crown made of the same amber material of the sailors' weapons. In place of his left hand was a massive munisica-hammer larger than Cole's chest.

The man's boots crunched over the sand and he placed a hand on Roth's shoulder. His grin nearly touched his ears as his eyes glistened. "There is no need to invoke the Trial of Honor, Bonebreaker. Both Morthain and this crown remain your trophies from the last time you challenged us."

Excited whispers broke over the crews at the mention of 'Bone-breaker.' Roth ignored them, placing a clawed hand gently upon the old man's shoulder. "King Auger, I wondered how many of your officers I would have to break before you showed your ugly face."

The captain gasped, summoning her bladed hands and hair like a coiled snake. Seeing her imminent attack on Roth, King Auger moved his hammer-hand in front of her, blocking Roth from view. "Release it, Seive. You haven't a clue who this man is. He could raze our city in an afternoon if it pleased him. Nearly did too when I was a lad." He gave captain Seive a look that brought her back to her senses before turning back towards Roth. "So Bonebreaker, what will it be? Our women? Our riches? The city itself?"

"From the great King Auger? How about a hot meal and a warm bed?" He jerked his head towards Cole and the others: "For them too."

"That I can do." King Auger threw an arm around Roth's shoulders, guiding him towards a small vessel between two of the corsairs. He pulled Roth close, speaking in quiet tone: "And don't call me 'King.' Makes this old man feel a damned fool."

Chapter 4

Metamorphosis

Talin could sense the fibers of his dreams running thin. He held onto the dregs, but they ran from him like water in his hands. He couldn't quite remember why, but the idea of waking was repulsive and terrifying. He clutched at his dream, wringing out a few memories of his family at The Sill. Just as a smile pulled at his lips, crippling agony seared across his face, bringing him fully awake.

He was back in the hospital room. He'd named it that originally because he remembered being dragged to the hospital after his capture in Costas. Now, after being in the room for perhaps a week he decided to call it a workshop. He had only ever seen one wall in the room, but he could hear the squeaky doors whenever the Weeping Man entered, and the gritty sound the drawers made when he drew his tools. This room was in the hospital, though Talin was quite certain that no medicine had ever been practiced here. Not after what he'd been through. He tried recalling how many days he'd been strapped to the upright table with nothing but a wall to look at. Even the chronic beacon spells that Chiron had taught him wouldn't work here. The only means of counting time was the progression of decay on his wounds. That, and the visits of the Weeping Man. After each time the Weeping Man worked on him, he brought Talin a mirror to show him what a wonderful job he'd done.

Talin's heart quickened. He'd been awake for nearly a minute now and the Weeping Man would be back soon. He seemed to know when Talin was sleeping, and usually came back as soon as he woke. Another minute passed. He strained against the bonds on his head, trying to look to either side. He would have tried pulling with his arms and legs, but they were long past useful to him and starting to smell sweet with rot. Perhaps the Weeping Man was already in the room? No, he couldn't be. Talin could hear his blubbering sobs from down the hallway before he even entered the room. The man never stopped crying, except for when he brought out his mirror to show Talin the parts he'd cut off, bent, crushed, or otherwise mutilated. The Weeping Man's countenance was as pitiful as it was repugnant. While he looked like a middle-aged man long gone to seed, his expressions and mannerisms were that of a hapless child who simply didn't know better. He had begun to pity the Weeping Man in these revealing moments. His round, too-close eyes begged for Talin's approval whenever he brought out the mirror. It reminded him of when his son would show a craft he made in school.

No. He could not think of those things now. He must put thoughts of his family in the depths of his subself, locked in his treasure chest where only he had the key. It was the same place he kept the knowledge of his unit, The Sill, and every memory he cherished. He was here for a reason. He was here to defy the Three. Sooner or later he would be tortured to the point where his mind would break. He mustn't have his treasures when that happened. If he were to deny them, he could no longer be who he was. He would have to become something else. Talin did allow himself one candle of hope, however; he clung to the possibility that at least one of the other units had been successful. There were at least a half dozen other strike-teams from The Sill. Surely one of them had been successful in disrupting the Devotion. He and his unit were merely casualties in the war, a price they all paid willingly. In this room Talin lived through nightmares that would have broken even the strongest soul. Throughout his time in the workshop Talin remained resolute, never faltering, for the contents of his treasure chest were worth it all. His training had prepared him for much worse than what the Weeping Man had done. He welcomed the pain. Talin would die whole, even if his body wasn't.

There were footsteps coming from the hallway. Talin set upon his rituals. He studied the wall, a key facet of his new identity. He traced his eyes over the faults in the stonework, the peeling paint, and each new stain made by the Weeping Man's labors. The steps grew closer. He checked his arms and legs. Still no sensation. That fact gave him a sense of pride and control, for he had severed the nerves with a quiet spell halfway through his first session with the Weeping Man. The footsteps were at the door now, but something was off. It sounded as if there were more than one person coming down the hall. Several people in fact. One set of the footsteps was quick and shuffling, as though they belonged to a child. The loudest of the group had a hard clacking that echoed into the workshop.

The door screeched open behind Talin's back.

A man coughed, his voice muffled: "My word, the stench in here. He's not dead is he?"

"No, Father Kreed," said a sullen voice that could only belong to the Weeping Man.

Talin's candle of hope flickered and sputtered.

Kreed coughed again, shoes tapping further into the workshop. "Well, get him turned around then so I can have a look at the boy. Why the hell do you have him up against the wall like a damned child in a time-out? Do you not see how odd that is? Even without eyes I can see it."

The weeping man started his usual, shivering whimper, but cut it short as he waddled across the room. Talin's eyes stretched as wide as they would go as he spun on the spot, bringing the rest of the shop into view. He saw a man in a flawless white suit, but he kept turning until he faced the wall again, spinning round and round. The Weeping Man spun him again and again, a childish giggle sneaking in between his feathery sobs.

"What are you doing? Bring him around to face me!" Kreed's voice rose, derisive and impatient. "That will do, that will do. Yes I see the table swivels quite nicely, now back away from the boy and stand over there, you sweaty little freak. A little farther if you would. Thank you. I swear Florien, your cellar-dwellers make a routine out of becoming the queerest people I see all week."

Talin stopped spinning, as did the room a moment later. Standing before him like a dove in a sewer was Kreed. A silken scarf was pulled tight over his eyes, stained with soot and blood over the sockets. On one side of Kreed stood a man dressed in sterile surgeon's attire.

An Underkin wearing dark-blue wrappings and a gaunt visage skulked at his other side.

Kreed's hands flew over a mouth of broken teeth: "What in the world did you do to him?" He scanned over Talin as though he could see through the tainted scarf.

The Weeping Man stopped weeping. He twisted the hem of his ruddy smock, revealing a shiny gut with long black hair clinging to the skin. An involuntary twitch jerked his head to the side as he jibbered to no one.

"Look at him!" Kreed jabbed a finger at Talin's legs, somehow seeing through the white scarf over his eyes. "His fucking legs are hanging on by the sinew! What in the world possessed you to do this?" He paused, holding up his palm to silence the Weeping Man. "No, never mind, I don't care to hear the answer at this point. I'm already upset and if I hear that crying-giggling thing again I'm going to be *very* upset." Kreed stepped closer and picked up a piece of Talin's hands that was still attached. His voice shook with worry: "The decay looks to be a few days along at the very least. Florien, could you...?"

The man in surgeon's clothes shook his head. He spoke in a bored, tired voice: "Sir, the arms and legs look a little over a week along. There's no saving them, not without a donor. The rest can be patched up easily enough, however." He hissed after walking around to inspect Talin's left side, jabbing a question at the Weeping Man. "Would it be foolishly optimistic to ask if you still have the patient's buccal?"

The Weeping Man's eyes darted from Florien to the floor. His lower lip quivered as his eyes rounded with childish confusion and worry. He obviously had no idea what he was being asked.

"His jowl, the cheek!" Florien huffed. "What did you do with it?"

The Weeping Man resumed his fluttery weeping.

Florien sighed. He ran a gloved hand through his hair and gazed at the ceiling, as though searching for patience in the harsh lights and rusty pipes.

A twisting, contradicting mixture of emotions swam through Talin, momentarily dulling the perpetual agony that wracked him. He felt a strange sense of relief and danger with Kreed's appearance.

Why would Kreed care that Talin had been tortured and broken? It was no worse than what Kreed had done to the rest of the unit before he put them up in the Towers. In spite of his feelings of enmity toward the man, he couldn't help but feel his candle of hope burn a little brighter. It sounded as if Kreed wanted to help him. Perhaps he would be healed enough to bring his Wisdom back to his aid. He could escape, or at least end his own life before he could be of any use to them.

"Stop pestering the man, Florien. He's obviously not prepared for an interrogation." Kreed strode over to one of the cabinets and began rummaging through the clunky drawers. He hummed softly, clicking his tongue as he searched for something. "You know, I try to be a good leader, I really do. I listen to my people, no matter how trivial and arbitrary their concerns may be. I can't please everyone of course. Habbad here can attest to my failures firsthand, but for the most part they are taken care of."

The Underkin inclined his head, the lines on his wrinkled face darkening as his eyes widened with apprehension. "Yes, Father Kreed. We are taken care of."

Kreed hummed in affirmation before continuing, "I build them universities, hospitals, stadiums, markets, provide jobs, whatever they desire. It pleases me to please them, it truly does. Even the Underkin were living like little princes before the Devotion. After I passed the labor laws some of them even had jobs in the upper districts. Florien, you regularly patronize a small bakery on the border, do you not?"

"That is correct, Sir," Florien said, holding his hands behind his back as he continued to inventory Talin's wounds.

"How very generous of you. I wish our fellow Aenerians were as open-minded." Kreed pushed the drawer shut but it wouldn't close all the way. He grunted with frustration, throwing a leg back and slamming the drawer with all his weight. "Damn...thing...won't... there we are. I'll have a word with the hospital staff about the clutter down here." He moved on to the next drawer, delving a little more carefully through its contents. "I'll pat myself on the back a bit and admit that we have quite a nice little society here. I saw no need to ruin such harmony, even when the barrier came down with the arrival of the human. Did we go looking for trouble? No. We didn't go marching over to the Dark Side and cast the first stone. Certainly not! It was the Dark Ones who drew first blood, decimating an entire company of Domina who were just trying to retrieve the Human for me. Even then we were content to leave well enough alone and forgive ancient grudges. Ah! Here we are." Kreed reached deep into the drawer and pulled out a short, serrated tool mounted on a wooden dowel.

Talin had seen that tool before. It had been used on him during his second session with the Weeping Man. His breath ran away from him as he desperately studied every detail of the ceiling.

Kreed held the tool up to the light as if checking it for imperfections. With a little nod and grin, he tossed the tool back and forth in between his hands as he approached Talin. "My father was a terrific leader. He knew how to make a point in such a beautifully simple manner that there was no room for misinterpretation. I- oh for heaven's sake." Bouncing off of Kreed's fingers, the tool clanged to the stone floor. "Habbad, be a good lad and grab that for me, thank you son. Eyesight is a bit diminished at the moment." Kreed turned back towards Talin, who found the ceiling less interesting by the second.

Kreed secured the tool in one hand, reaching for Talin's face with the other as he stared through the white scarf. He ran his fingers over Talin's hair, tugging at the straps that cut into his forehead. "My father was a *genius*. He knew how to make his intentions crystal clear to even the plainest of minds." There was a quick snip and Talin's head came free from its bonds. "I do my best to emulate him, which is why I choose my words with utmost care when I give orders. That way when I say, 'secure the prisoner in the hospital,' I should expect to find said prisoner whole and healthy when I go to talk to him. I should not find said prisoner mangled and spoiled with half his face removed." Kreed's blind eyes moved over Talin's wounds, and he shook his head as his face fell in a disappointed frown. "Florien, give the boy something for the pain would you?"

Florien approached Talin, plunging his hand into the front pocket of his gown. "Will you swallow these pills or are you going to spit them back out at me?" It sounded as if he didn't care what the answer was.

Talin remained silent. He'd nearly finished counting how many bolts were in the room, a task made much easier now that his head was free to move around.

"I thought as much." Florien snapped his fingers at the Underkin. "Turn these to powder."

The Underkin pointed a single tiny finger, touching the pills in Florien's white-gloved hand, producing several tiny pops.

"Thank you, Habbad," Florien said. He then brought his cupped hand up to Talin's ruined face and blew the powder into his mouth and open wounds.

Talin coughed, stifling a moan. The powder stung with vivid, brilliant flashes before a dull haze filled his mind. The foggy indifference quickly spread to the rest of his body, giving Talin a deep peace and well-deserved reprieve from the torture.

Florien blew more of the powder here and there, wherever he found open flesh. "The patient is sedated, Sir," Florien said. He drew his gloved fingers to his mouth and neatly cleaned the rest of the powder off with his tongue. He paused, looking self-conscious as he removed the gloves and set to washing his hands in the corner sink.

"Thank you, Florien. Hopefully that takes a bit of the sting off for the boy. Don't you fret my boy, we'll patch you up in no time at all," Kreed said. His tone was polite and bubbly as he walked backwards, bumping into the workbench next to the Weeping Man. Chuckling at his own clumsiness, he ran his palms down the front of his jacket and straightened the lapels on his snowy suit. "You see how that worked? I gave an order, a very simple one, and it was carried out to the letter. A simple order, followed simply by the execution. Order, execution. Order, execution." Kreed then turned his blind gaze and broken grin to the Weeping Man.

"Yes, Father Kreed," said the weeping man, who nodded like an enthusiastic child.

Kreed's arm whipped about, smacking the tool into the Weeping Man's throat. Florien swore, sloshing water over the floor as the Underkin cried out in alarm. Talin stopped his inventory of all the brown items in the room, looking instead at the slow crimson trickle that came from the Weeping Man's neck. Kreed took his hand from the tool and scratched his fingernails lovingly along the Weeping Man's jaw as he withdrew. The Weeping Man drew a shaking, filthy hand to his throat, his look of confusion quickly blooming to panic as he tried to draw a breath, instead producing an odd whistling sound. He wrapped his chubby fingers around the wooden handle and slid the tool from its warm sheath. Air rushed in and out of the hole as the Weeping Man fell to his knees, eyes bulging and mouth gaping like a fish out of water. His fingers scrabbled over the wound as he gave a squelching, liquid scream. His wooden fingernails pulled and clawed at the hole, catching and snapping the thing wider. The Weeping Man bucked on the floor, looking like a panicked child who swam out into the deep end for the first time. He threw a bloody hand up and grabbed Kreed's leg, his face pleading for the mercy that his voice was no longer capable of asking for.

Kreed's head fell back, swaying like an underwater plant as his grin of broken teeth stretched wider. A sound rose from Kreed's chest, whooshing and howling out of his cracked smile. The sound had no business in the world of the living. Fear in its purest form filled every corner of the ruddy workshop, sucking every hint of light and warmth as it swelled. Decreath had ignited.

The Fear stripped Talin of everything he was; his physical pain, his memories, his desires, his very identity. The anticipation of limitless dread filled him, became him. After what felt like an entire lifetime, the cloud lifted and the horror receded. Talin was first aware of the cold, then the pain. It was almost a relief to find himself back in the workshop.

Florien unraveled his finger from his chest. Disoriented, he clutched from pocket to pocket, pulling out a tiny glass ampule. He cracked it open and huffed it as if his life depended on it. His pupils widened until they filled the whites of his eyes. His trembling ceased immediately. He found the Underkin on the floor beside him, cowering and rambling. Florien dropped to a knee and flipped the Underkin by his royal blue wrappings. "Habbad, breathe this in, now."

A few seconds later Habbad was on his feet, wiping tears from his black eyes.

Kreed was no longer standing, but straddling the Weeping Man with his lips tight around the hole that the tool had just vacated. His cheeks shone bright, as if he had a candle in his mouth. He shuddered with a muffled cough as the Weeping Man's chest sank and the light went out. Pulling himself upright, Kreed gasped with perverse delight as he stared up through the ceiling, running a bloody hand through his slick hair. He stood, making a halfhearted effort to wipe the red from the front of his snowy suit.

Clearing his throat, Kreed twisted his head from side to side as he adjusted his tie. "Well Habbad, looks like we'll be stopping by the cleaner's before our next appointment. I wanted to swing by that part of town anyway; my friends at the Alinite courts promised me tickets for tonight's show." Kreed stepped over the Weeping Man's lifeless body, rounding on Talin once more. He drew a silken towel from his jacket and dabbed the corners of his mouth before speaking: "Don't you worry, Warrior of The Sill. You'll be whole once more. Florien is the best there is at this sort of medicine."

From the furthest reaches of Talin's subself, his treasure chest glowed, lending him the strength he needed. When he was first captured he'd resolved to never say a word while he was prisoner. He would be mute until his final breath. Now though seemed a perfect time to break his rule. Florien's anesthetics and his missing cheek made speech difficult, but he ignored the fuzzy pain and pulled the words together. "You will get nothing from me, Father Liar. Take my soul now, I promise it will make a more fitting meal than that pustule of a man." He tilted his head towards the Weeping Man's corpse.

"Oh my!" Kreed's face lit from under the blood-stained scarf as he rapidly clapped his hands together. "The fire still burns! You are quite right warrior, your soul has some *solid* substance to it. I'm ashamed to admit it, but I find myself nearly overwhelmed with envy. It's all I can do to stop myself from taking it from you. But that would be an awful waste of your talents, wouldn't you agree?"

Talin mustered what was left of his Wisdom and Passion, and buried his treasure chest so far beneath himself that he knew he would never find it again. He stared into the sunken depressions where

Kreed's eyes ought to be and attempted speech once more. "Let's get started then."

"Remarkable!" Kreed said, resting his chin on his intertwined fingers as he bounced on his heels. "Such a display of Wisdom and Passion, even in the gallows. Habbad, did you pick up on that? Did you see what he did there? He just partitioned a portion of his mind!"

"Yes, Father Kreed," Habbad said reluctantly.

"Come here then, son," Kreed said, putting a gentle hand on Habbad's shoulder. "I promised you a practical lesson today, and here it is. He's not going to make it easy for you, but I want you to reach in there and find something for me. Find his shame. You know what magic he used to hide it, so use the Dread Father's magic to counter it. Follow Decreath's trail in the halls of his mind, but do it quickly."

Habbad's eyes fell to the grime on the floor, perhaps studying the shapes and contents like Talin currently was. He shook his head, looking as though he had just made up his mind.

"Go on, Habbad," Kreed said, his voice soft and sweet. "I'm so proud of you, son."

Talin sneered inwardly behind his broken face. If there was one thing he was adept at, it was the subtle art of modifying memories. There was no one at The Sill, save for Chiron, that was his equal. He had already prepared a decoy repository of seemingly important memories for such an occasion. He would feign a struggle and reveal some useless snippet from his life, but only after making them work for it. Talin's lip twitched as he stifled the tiniest of grins. There wasn't the slightest possibility that a child, let alone an Underkin child, could navigate his way through Talin's consciousness.

The Underkin's eyes came up, a dark smile playing across his wrinkled face.

Talin broke from his distracting rituals, drawn by morbid curiosity into the Underkin's ominous visage. Talin felt the Underkin's unwholesome, foreign presence worming its way through the back alleys of his mind. He isolated the alien force, tempting it towards his decoy treasure chest, throwing up barriers and creating false doors and trap stairs all the while. The Underkin darted along, falling for every trick thrown at him. Talin could feel the growing ire in the child's mind. He added to it, kindling it like a little fire with tripping thoughts. Through the Underkin's growing fury, Talin was able to sneak a tendril of thought of his own into the child's mind, tearing secrets away for himself and locking them away. Talin's laughter echoed through the halls of his mind, letting the child know he didn't stand a chance. If need be, he could easily manage another dozen Underkin before he would have to resort to direct mental combat. Talin emphasized his superiority by stabbing the knowledge through the layers of rising emotions.

After a quarter hour, the Underkin's endurance started to wane. Talin could take the child's mind now and have his way with it. However, he brought the chase to a halt so as not to discourage him entirely. Feigning his own exhaustion, Talin allowed himself to be cornered. He left his decoy chest only partially revealed, yet easy enough for a Hungry mind to spot. The Underkin's awareness took in the glinting corner of the chest and without hesitation, dove right for it. Just before the chest opened, suspicion leaked from the Underkin and he paused, looking instead into Talin's focused thoughts. The Underkin's mind went quiet, almost dissipating entirely.

Talin's heart stopped, stumbling for just one beat as a freezing hand of terror pinched at his insides. No, it was impossible. Not even Talin knew where it was. He felt himself free-falling. His treasure chest, the real one, cracked open and one gleaming jewel came rushing out.

Habbad took a long breath, his eyes flashing wide with Talin's ambient Fear. "I have it. I have it all. It's his family, he's bonded to a woman and child. A wife and daughter."

Talin cried out, his Rage tearing through the Fear and pain. If his hands and feet still worked they would have exploded into munisica. It was impossible, but the Underkin took it from him. His most precious memories. The little insect had them all now. He had been laid bare by mere livestock. A simple Underkin.

"That was beautiful, Habbad," Kreed said, rubbing Habbad's shoulders. "It was just as we thought. Florien, go on upstairs and prep the operating room. Habbad, run off to the waiting room if you want. I'm afraid I'm going to be awhile with the boy."

Florien set off at once, disappearing through the squeaky double doors without a backwards glance.

"No, Father Kreed," Habbad said, giving Kreed a stern look and standing as tall as he could. "I will stay with you."

"Thank you very much, son. It's embarrassing, but the surgery rather scares me. Your presence will be comforting." Kreed patted Habbad on the shoulder and then moved behind Talin's table. "Our warrior here will have a practical lesson in the operating room as well. The lesson will be a bit serious, but I believe you're mature enough to witness it. The process is important for your education. We are going to make our warrior into something that has not been seen on Aeneria for an age."

There was a loud clack and the table fell flat, bringing Kreed's upside-down face into Talin's view. Talin roared and thrashed with what was left of his body as he felt the table rumble over the uneven floor. "Curse you, traitor!" Talin spat through his torn mouth. "Rip me to pieces, you'll find nothing! I've nothing left to give."

Kreed raised his voice over the rattling of the table as he pushed Talin through the double doors: "As you are you have nothing left to offer. You'll need to change. After your lessons you'll be quite useful, however. You won't recognize yourself. By the time I'm through with you, the person waiting for you in the operating room won't recognize you either."

Talin's breath caught, halting a steady stream of curses as the cold hand of Fear tickled his heart once more.

Kreed smiled. "And there's the delicious Fear. You know who's up there waiting for you, don't you? Do you know why the Fear torments you so?"

Kreed waited, nodding at Talin's silence. "Of course you don't. Your teachers don't cover that school of magic. You are soaked with Fear, which at this very moment is spreading through your veins and coating your mind. The Fear affects you because you have something, something of a weakness. It's not your fault, it's inherent. We all have it to some degree."

Kreed slowed the table to a silent halt, bringing his mouth to Talin's ear. His voice was a husky whisper. "You have hope. You hope that there is still value to your life. You hope that the person waiting in the operating room is not who you think it is. You hope that there will eventually be an end to it all. Your hope is your bane."

Kreed gently slapped Talin on the good side of his face before leaning into the table and resuming their stroll.

"Don't worry yourself overmuch, my boy. There is a way to cure you of your hope. The person that your hope weeps for is indeed in the operating room, but she's not alone. Florien is there, and so are a few of the hospital guards. You and your wife are each going to give me an eye. I can make do without mine, but it makes things rather awkward at dinner parties, so yours will do. It's the least you can do for me after attempting to sabotage my Devotion."

For the first time since his capture, Talin began to sob, becoming his own Weeping Man. He truly had nothing left to give.

"Oh hush now," Kreed said in a patronizing tone. "You haven't even heard the best part. The surgery hasn't a bit to do with your training. You see, in order to truly break a man down, you must first destroy everything he cherishes, utterly and completely. That is crucial and can't be glossed over. The guards upstairs are not there for anyone's protection as the two of you are hardly any threat. While you still have both of your eyes, you're going to watch as the guards fuck her. They don't get out much, so they likely won't last long, but that's why I had four of them brought down. After they finish we'll start the surgery." Kreed shuddered, suddenly stricken. "I really am terrified of going under the knife, but Florien is the best there is and he just did one of these a few weeks ago. It will be nice to have Habbad there with us."

Kreed rambled on, but Talin couldn't hear him. His Fear choked him as an elevator took them up a level. He wished he were back in the workshop with the Weeping Man. He wished he had never taken the assignment at The Sill. He wished he were dead. He wished his wife were dead. Talin raised his head as high as he could as the foot of the table reached another set of double doors. The doors glided open, blinding him as he entered the operating room.

CHAPTER 5

BENEATH THE CLOUDS

After Cole and Lileth used their combined Wisdom to lift a struggling Goran into King Auger's ship, the two jumped in and joined the rest of their unit. Cole had to lull Goran with his Passion before the mirak would calm down and stop pulling planks from the upper deck. Goran hated not having all four feet on the ground. Sitra helped, nearly putting him asleep by gently raking her munisica through the white tuft of hair on his scalp.

"Forgetting someone?" Lileth asked, inclining her head overboard where someone hollered for Cole.

"Shoot, yeah. I'm not used to having a prisoner," Cole said, running to the side of the ship. "Stay still, or I'll drop you!"

As tired as he was, he could barely wield the necessary Wisdom to lift Milette. Lileth or Eliza could have lifted her in an instant, but Milette was Cole's burden to bear. He hoped when they got to Morthain they could figure out something to do with her. Burden indeed.

After Cole set her down, Milette wandered about the main deck, remarking at the shabbiness and disrepair. Seeing Cole following her like a shadow, Milette turned around and snapped, "Don't worry *Master*, I'm not about to run off. I can't exactly swim away, can I?" She offered her stumps to Cole, pushing them under his nose.

Cole slapped her wrists away. They still smelled horribly like burnt food. "Just don't cause any trouble."

Roth hopped up after King Auger, who had been hoisted up with a small platform on pulleys. A few sailors went to the front of the ship, and used long pikes with glass tips to break apart the hardened sand as other members of the crew cut the sails into favorable winds. Within a minute they were back out on open powder, gliding as smoothly as if they were on a cloud. Oberon watched over them, painting the sails with lavender and magentas while Dunhaven's starscape swarmed above.

King Auger hobbled over to a barrel at the main mast and took a seat. He gave each of them a measuring look before speaking to Roth. "So the Bonebreaker returns to his Kingdom at last. Funny timing I'd say. Funny timing indeed. Up until two months ago the barrier used to run right through these sands. There were rumors that the soul flies had returned as well. Wouldn't have believed it if I didn't see the rivers with my own eyes. We may have been on the Light Side of the barrier, but we never saw hide nor hair of The Three. Now with the barrier down and the soul flies returned, so it seems has the war. Our architects had to break into the old libraries to figure out how to bring Morthain below the sands and out of the Domina's reach." The King raised a wizened eyebrow at Cole. "And someone's been Traveling again. What's this one, Terra? He's certainly not of this world."

The others shifted uncomfortably. Valen opened his mouth to respond but a halting glare from Roth froze him solid. "I'm surprised your eyes still work through all those wrinkles and whiskers. He's from Terra. Human. I won't tell you more than that unless you want me to lie to you, but then I'd be thrown in prison for lying to the King, wouldn't I? And then of course I'd have to go through the trouble of killing your guards and breaking your prison. Then who knows, my lust for blood might not be satisfied until I earned myself a new nickname. Bonebreaker's been getting old. Perhaps Worldshaker, or Chaosweaver...or maybe Kingslayer." Roth scratched his chin with a bladed finger.

One of King Auger's guards tightened the grip on his glass sword, unsure if Roth was joking or not. Cole plopped himself on the deck and leaned up against Goran with Lileth and Eliza, who stroked his brindle fur and jowls. Goran's eyes were rolling with pleasure, and a thick rope of drool bounced from his sweeping canines.

King Auger hefted his hammer-munisica. It was almost too fast for Cole to see. The King's hammer jabbed into Roth's stomach with a solid thump. Roth staggered back, a toothy grin on his face.

The King chuckled. "How about Backbiter, or Fairydancer?" King Auger looked down his broad nose at Cole once more. His mouth opened, a question forming on his lips before he swallowed it back. "I know better than to meddle with you fickle Sill folk. Still, the question burns a hole in this old man's tongue." He gave his head a little shake and addressed Roth: "Maybe when all this is over you and I will once again lock hammer and claw, but for now I'd settle for you getting me caught up on the goings on of the world. Oberon Temple sent envoys our way, no doubt searching for us, but we ducked them as we always have. You scoundrels at The Sill always had at least a scrap of common sense. Come Rothael, join me in my cabin and tell me a tale."

"Of course, King Auger. But in exchange you must feed and water my warriors here. The whelps are ready to drop. They could do with some of the King's hospitality." Roth ran his tongue across his teeth. "And I could use something a little stronger to wash the sand from my throat."

The King waved his bony hand dismissively and nodded to one of his guards, sending him below deck. "You don't have to ask, you know these men are yours. And stop calling me 'King, it makes no damned sense. No sense at all."

"I just like seeing you dole out orders. You've been giving some tall ones it seems; Morthain was *above* the sands last time I was here," Roth said, following King Auger through a glass-paned door. He threw out a hand, stopping Valen and Sitra. "You all wait up here."

Valen stopped and silently acknowledged his Master, throwing a hand over Sitra's mouth before she could talk back. Roth thankfully ignored her hisses and huffing, slamming the door behind him.

"I'm starving!" Sitra snapped at Valen. "The last thing I ate was half a scrawny bird on the back of that lazy baileen. If they don't bring food up in the next five minutes I'm going to eat one of the King's guards." Her long braid whipped over her shoulder as she spun away from Valen, clenching the handrail with her munisica.

"Calm yourself, Sitra," Valen said, his voice steady and soothing. "This is no worse than anything you've been through in training. Think it another trial if you must. Besides, drawing your munisica and devoting energy to your Rage will only increase your body's demand for food. You know this. Master Roth-"

"Enough with the lessons!" Sitra spat, rounding on Valen. "There's no training that can prepare you for what we just did. Where in our training did we ever have to starve ourselves for a week? When did we learn how to get drugged and dragged through the street by Underkin while they groped and shit all over us? In whose lessons did we watch a friend have his soul pulled out of his face? Save your preaching, Valen. Your Wisdom didn't save us from Decreath. It was Rage!" She roared, jabbing a claw at Cole. The guards looked to one another, taking positions around Sitra. "Rage saved us from burning on the towers. Rage saved us from being meals for The Three! Rage gets you results, so that's what I'll use. And what the fuck are you staring at?" she added, shooting a dangerous glare at a guard who had tried to shimmy his way in between her and the door to the lower decks.

The guard froze. He seemed to remember his duties and spoke with an authoritative tone. "You'll step away from the door, Miss. You've been ordered by King...Rothael to stay above deck." Addressing Roth as 'King' gave the man a small fit. He sidestepped, filling the entire frame of the door with his broad shoulders. "I don't care if you're daughter to the King himself, you won't get through this door. Find somewhere else to throw your tantrum."

Sitra may not have been considering going below deck, but she certainly looked it now. With teeth and munisica bared, she stalked closer to the guard, who slammed his tower shield down before him.

"Sitra, do calm yourself. There's no need for it. Food's on the way." Eliza sighed, now slumping droopy-eyed against Goran's belly.

Goran perked up, sniffing and opening one ruby eye as he lifted his head an inch from the deck. Cole thought about using his Rage to stop Sitra, but wasn't sure if he could contain himself. She would just have to make an ass out of herself. Unless someone else stepped in.

Sitra wrapped her claws delicately around the thick glass shield. "You want to see a tantrum?" She growled as she planted one of her clawed feet against the shield's center, still gripping the sides with her hands. Her muscles flexed and rippled. The shield groaned, but held fast. Whatever material the glass was made from must have been incredibly strong, as Cole had seen Sitra bend metal beams with that kind of force. Eyes blind with Rage, Sitra released her grip and punched the shield with a ball of jade light held in between her claws. The glass exploded.

Cole threw an arm over his eyes, but he didn't need to. Lileth was on her feet, hands twirling in front of her as if she were playing an invisible harp. Shards of broken glass hung in midair, tumbling silently.

"Let go of me Lil!" Sitra bellowed.

Both Sitra and the guard were floating in midair and covered in a fuzzy emerald light. Sitra lashed out with her munisica while the guard swung with his glass sword, but neither of them could find any ground for leverage.

"The spell is not strong," Lileth said, tossing the shattered fragments of shield over the edge with a flick of her wrist. "Break yourself free when you have the Wisdom to do so. And you, sheathe your sword before you hurt yourself," she added, addressing the flailing guard.

Without hesitation, the guard slammed his sword back into the scabbard, though his small munisica were still bared and ready. Lileth released her spell on him and he landed in a clanking heap. A moment later, Sitra alighted on the deck without her munisica and shroud. She wrapped her arms around Lileth, crying softly. Lileth embraced her, though her face was emotionless.

The door crashed open as two young sailors stumbled through, arms loaded with canvas bags and wooden boxes.

"Just a bit longer if you've got the patience," piped one of the boys. "Should take us less than an hour to prep the meal."

"We do *not* have the patience," Valen said. "Drop the food on the deck. Thank you."

The boys looked at each other, unsure if they should do as Valen said. After an awkward moment of hesitation, the bags and boxes were lifted from their arms as their contents began to spread themselves across the deck, hovering at chest height.

"Thank you boys." Eliza wrapped her arms around their shoulders as a dreamy expression washed over their faces. Her voice was like honey. "Would it be too much trouble to ask for a bit more? We are somewhat famished from our journey. It would mean the world to me," she added, giving them a little squeeze.

"Whuh…yeah. Sure thing!" stuttered one of the boys.

"We'll be right back, Miss! There's so much more, just wait here," gushed the other as the pair dashed away.

Eliza's eyebrow went up along with the corner of her mouth. "What are you all waiting for? I thought you were hungry."

They attacked the floating food with indiscriminate zeal, flash cooking whatever happened to be in front of them with quick blasts of Wisdom. Cole took an experimental nibble on a white rock, which turned out to be cheese. He melted the brick up and drizzled it over a loaf of bread. Goran was in his own personal heaven. He didn't even bother to stand up to eat. The giant mirak scooted around on his back, knocking food from the air into his mouth. In between bites they all took turns tossing raw vegetables through his overlarge canines. Goran usually avoided vegetables as if they were the vilest of poisons, but didn't seem to mind at the moment. Before long the boys returned with their arms full, this time taking requests for their next trip below deck.

Lileth gave Cole a gentle elbow to the shoulder. "Don't forget your charge."

"My what?" Cole asked, looking around to see Milette poking her head around a bundle of netting. "Oh right. Hey Milette, there's plenty more food coming. Get over here and eat something. Or don't," he added, unsure of how nice he should be to his prisoner.

Milette shot out like a stray cat and used her stumps to grab a few hunks of cold bread before slinking back into the shadows. She struggled to feed herself without the use of her hands. It was indecent, watching a dignified woman driven by desperation as she ate from the floor like a dog. Cole felt a stab of guilt as the food in his mouth turned to dry wood. Her crime against the soul fly certainly deserved punishment, but Cole loathed being the one responsible for her fumbling attempt to feed herself with her scabbed, blunt wrists. It was all because he let the Rage take him.

Lileth gave his arm a gentle squeeze, warming him. "Remember the reasons for your choice. Her suffering is the cost of upholding your morals. If there were another Milette tomorrow, would you spare her life and take her prisoner as well?"

"I'd take a dozen Milettes before I let myself become an executioner. You can kill the next one if you want." Cole sprung to his feet and brought a few servings of meat and fruits over to Milette, cooking them along the way. Milette's eyes flashed at his unexpected appearance. She withdrew, coiling like a snake ready to strike. Without a word Cole tied the food with Wisdom so that it would hover around her head, making it easier for her to eat. Without thanking him she attacked the air with ravenous bites, not bothering to wipe the fruit's juices that ran down her chin. Cole returned to Lileth. She grinned softly and wouldn't look at him.

Sometime during their fifth serving, the shieldless guard interrupted their feasting. "If you'll all stay to the center of the deck, we must draw the sheet caps."

"Are we going under the sand now?" Cole asked with his mouth full.

"Move away from the sides now, unless you want to be picking sand from places you didn't know you had," the guard barked. Even as he spoke, others ran alongside the handrails and up the masts, securing a rippling crystal veil over their heads.

Cole nudged Goran to the center of the deck, grabbing the last few pieces of meat along the way. The vessel sank lower and lower, giving Cole a sense of restrained anxiety as the surface of the powdery sands rose above the deck. Darkness poured up over them, as if they were inside a goblet filling with oil. Cole steadied himself by staring at Oberon's fading glow before it too was swallowed by the sands.

Cole bumped against unknown arms, growing steadily more unbalanced in the pitch black. He used his Wisdom to stretch his eyes to allow more light, but there simply was none. A few uncomfortable seconds later, tiny candles blazed to life throughout the main deck, casting them all in warm light. Cole severed the spell on his eyes and waited for the blind spots in his vision to fade away.

"Flames on a wooden ship?" Valen said, touching one of the flickering candles with his bare fingers. "Such a crude design. Surely a bit of Wisdom would be preferential. Do you Morthainians use Rage exclusively?" he asked a passing member of the crew, who scowled at his criticism of their ship.

"We've no use for the coddling or useless pondering of your other magics," said the sailor as he coiled a rope around his arm. "Nor do we care for the stink that the Three tempt us with. Leave us well enough alone with our fire and tools. Rage is the only magic we need." He threw the rope over his shoulder and stamped off to the upper deck.

Sitra punched Valen in the shoulder. "See? I told you. Rage gets results."

Unsure of how long this portion of their journey would be, Cole found a comfy spot up against Goran and stretched out. Lileth sat down next to him and fell asleep almost immediately. As tired as Cole was, he kept himself awake so he could stare openly at her. She was the most beautiful creature he had ever seen. The candle light danced across the handsome curves of her face, stunning him. Her lips were full and parted slightly, tempting Cole to find out what they might taste like. Travel worn as she was, her raven hair was still tied back with only a few neat strands running down her jaw. He wished she would let her hair down again, like the day she brought him to the Arts District. If only he could touch her face and see if it was as smooth as it looked. For the first time he allowed himself to fully believe what the others said about him growing taller. If he continued at this rate maybe he would be as tall as she was. Then perhaps she'd see him in a different light. A romantic light. He turned his focus to his bones, where Roth's gift still burned in his marrow. He could almost see his arms and legs growing longer as he watched.

Cole suddenly found himself not tired at all. His heart was hammering and he felt a longing warmth spread its way down his lower abdomen. Goran's concern pressed through their bond as he angled an ear towards Cole. Cole patted his barrel ribs, reassuring him as he withdrew himself from their bond. This was a time for privacy. He made quite sure his link with Eliza didn't betray any of his embarrassing thoughts and desires. Lileth turned in her sleep, inching closer to Cole. The strand of hair along her jaw swung forward and rested itself over her lips. Holding his breath, Cole reached a hand out, moving the thread of hair behind her ear. The ship lurched, jostling Lileth awake.

Cole withdrew his hand, but not before she saw him pull away. She turned her back to him, leaving Cole to stew in his shame.

Cole spent the sleepless journey going over a list of reasons as to why he and Lileth could never be together. After an hour's brooding, the darkness around the veil lifted into a hazy amber glow. The others roused themselves and darted to the handrails, peering through the hazy sheet cap.

"So that's what they mean by a city beneath the sands," Eliza said in a dreamy voice as she nuzzled her head against Valen's shoulder. Valen stiffened, but did not withdraw.

Cole hopped up and pressed his nose to the veil. Above them he could make out the vague clouds of sand, but hundreds of feet below looked like a sea of fuzzy torches.

"Step away from the sheet cap!" called one of the sailors.

There was a loud crack from the bow of the ship and the veil snapped over their heads, disappearing in a slot towards the aft.

Cole jumped up so that his chest rested on the handrail, taking in the city under the sands. Morthain lay nestled in a dense pocket at the bottom of a crater. The structures were made of a dark wood with stained-glass embellishments and golden torches that danced like flags. Surrounding the city towered harsh, cragged walls of rock that stretched up into the sand clouds where swaths of garnet lightning flashed without a sound.

"Oberon's ass," Sitra hissed, face slack with shock. "That's the biggest city I've ever seen."

"Wait till you see Oberon's City. You could hide a dozen Morthains inside the temple," Valen replied.

Lileth joined them. She inspected the ship and the city below with a skeptical eye. "I find it hard to believe that the city uses no magic other than Rage. There's magic all around, old and powerful. It's incredible. I can sense it, but I cannot classify it. The sands themselves are swimming with energies, and this ship cannot navigate the clouds by Rage and clever fingers alone. There is magic here."

Cole wondered about the magic himself. The velvety black sails of their ship were drawn and rolled onto the masts, but the ship still moved. Peering down below the ship he saw that they were on some sort of sandy river carved into the jagged walls of Morthain's border. The river spiraled all the way down to a small harbor. Miles away on the other side of Morthain Cole could make out another river winding up the wall. Ships flowed upwards, as if on a sandy escalator. Old magic indeed.

The unit stood in silence for a moment, their eyes wandering out over Morthain's endless details. Even Milette snuck out of her hiding spot to take a look. To the protests of the sailors, Goran climbed halfway up the mast to get a better look at his surroundings.

"Who does that beast belong to?" asked a grumpy sailor.

Cole approached the man, who gave him a patronizing smirk as though Cole were a mere child.

"Goran belongs to no one," Cole said, standing as tall as he could. "But he is my friend."

"Really then? All right, call the thing down." The sailor cracked the top off of a barrel and pulled out a heavy chain. "It's got to be on a leash within the city walls."

Eliza's eyes went wide as she approached the man, palms open in a gesture of peace. "Goran is not some feral beast. He is incredibly bright and a member of our unit. If you chain him you may as well chain the rest of us."

"Oh stop it Liza, don't spoil the fun. I want to see what Goran makes of them," Sitra cut in with a toothy grin. She perched herself atop another barrel as though claiming the best seat for a show.

The man's eyes narrowed as he dropped the chain at their feet. "I don't care if the animal is the mascot of the Celestial Council. We have laws here in Morthain. Within our walls you fall in line or fall out."

Seeing that no one else was about to start a fight, Sitra kicked off the barrel and drew close to the sailor, hands twitching. "Then perhaps we will have to change the laws. It sounds like your leader is a false-king anyway. Why don't we see what King Rothael has to say about you chaining up a member of his unit like a pet dog?"

Eyeing the chains, Milette sank back into her hiding spot under a pile of netting.

Cole stepped in between Sitra and the guard. "No, it's fine. I don't think Goran will have a problem with it. He won't care if he's got chains on him as long as he's with us. He'll probably break them anyway."

The guard chuckled. "Not likely. The chains are made from Morthainian glass. Just get the thing down here so we can throw them on. I take it you'll be the one holding the other end?"

"Sure," Cole replied, taking a length of the cool brown chain. It was incredibly heavy and covered in sticky grease. Cole drew his Rage to protect his hands and grant him the strength needed to bear the weight.

"Then you'll be responsible for the creature. Animals are not permitted within the city, unless they're food of course."

"Whatever," Cole acknowledged. The guard's attitude was starting to get to him. "Don't worry, I'll keep him out of trouble. We're not here for long anyway."

With Cole's nudging, Goran swooped down from the top mast and allowed the chains to be wrapped and locked around his hands, feet, and neck. The process was easier than Cole had expected. Goran chewed and licked at the oil that coated the links. Cole could tell just by looking that the length was much too short and would interfere with Goran's stride, but now seemed like a poor time to bring it up. Better to wait for when they were not riding a sand river down a rock wall.

After what felt like an hour their ship reached the bottom of the flowing ramp, dumping them out into a harbor. The ship bobbed and swayed into the loose powder as they steered off to the right following a pillar of rough stone.

"What is that thing!" Milette cried from her hiding place. Cole looked over to see a scabbed wrist poking out from the netting toward the bow of the ship.

The ship was moving slowly and steadily towards the largest set of jaws Cole had ever seen. The jaws belonged to an ancient rusty skull adorned with torches, creating an archway large enough for two ships to pass through. Each tooth was bigger than Roth and hooked like a sickle. The lower mandible was buried below the flowing sand while the upper hooked up and finished with a large pointed horn.

"That would be a rock wurm," answered Roth's gravelly voice. Milette squeaked with his sudden appearance.

King Auger followed him out of the doorway. He rose his hammer-hand to the colossal skull. "Pass through the ancient maw of Kumahl and be welcomed to the City of Morthain. You are the first outsiders in many cycles to lay eyes upon it."

Cole arched his neck, trying to imagine what a creature that size would look like. Judging by the height of the skull, the wurm could have wrapped itself around the entire city. The rusty horn looked just as capable of cutting through mountains as it would sand.

They passed through the jaws, arriving a few minutes later at the Morthain docks. Workers operated heavy glass machinery, loading and unloading other ships. Eyes peeked out from alleys and windows, eager to see the outsiders on the King's ship. They followed King Auger and his guards off the gangway and onto the pier. A loud crack and flash of sparks brought raised weapons and angry eyes to Goran, who had snapped the bonds from his wrists and ankles and was carrying the broken pieces in his mouth.

Cole smiled awkwardly, holding up the chain that was still connected to Goran's neck. "Hey, at least he's still on a leash."

King Auger's laughter broke the silence. "That he is! We'll have to keep him away from the finery."

The King led them off the pier where they were greeted by the strangest bus Cole had ever seen. Wheels as tall as Roth carried an armored hull nearly as large as the King's ship. It had the Spartan design of a military transport vehicle, though elegant silver emblems and embellishments were tacked on haphazardly, as though an afterthought. A glass engine stuck out the back, shaking and rocking as it growled to life. Smoke poured out the open tail pipes as the driver hopped out, opening the doors for them.

Cole leaned closer to Lileth, hoping some conversation would help to bury the awkward incident on the ship. "We have similar vehicles back on my planet. It's crazy how even in different worlds we have some of the same technology." As he said it, another pang of homesickness struck him. He stifled the thoughts before his emotions could show on his face.

"It's not as crazy as you think," Lileth said without looking at him. "Wisdom Walkers from ages past would share knowledge with sentient life on the local planets. I would not be surprised if other planets adopted similar constructs for transportation."

"Why doesn't The Sill have any vehicles like this?" Cole asked.

"Because they're costly and unnecessary when you have Wisdom," King Auger said, banging his hammer against the side of the bus. "I've been campaigning every cycle to get our citizens to take up another school of magic. We've got a few queer folk that can use the most basic of Wisdom and Passion, but they're shunned like lepers for breaking tradition. Every time someone comes up with a useful spell, the engineers make a show of embarrassing the poor sod and come up with some new machine that makes the spell useless. We've got plenty of gratia stones that we scooped up before the war, but they're nearly useless. No one knows how to fill them properly. Instead we burn wurm oil and gases to power clunkers like this thing here." King Auger smacked his hammer against the bus once more, leaving a fist-sized dent.

"Morthainians were a stubborn folk last time I was here," Roth said. "You couldn't find a tribe more fierce than the people of the White Sands. Now, though, I'm not sure they have the fire, judging by the performance of your welcome party. The Morthainians I remember had no use for weaponry. Their own flesh and munisica were enough to get the job done. I saw some of your guards even carry shields, as if they were afraid of getting hit."

King Auger nodded. "Life under the sands doesn't suit us. Pieces of our culture dwindle a little more every cycle. We've lost sight of the old ways and rusted into a city of sneak-thieves and cutthroats. I pour resources into things like infrastructure and education, but each cycle the city gets a little worse, as if it likes being dirty. The city's fractured into gangs now, each with their own unwritten laws and agendas. I can hardly recruit anyone into the guard nowadays. None of them feel safe when they go back to their homes at night. Afraid they might be greeted with cold glass when they open the door. That reminds me, you're all safe in my company, but don't go wandering off on your own."

"My unit can take care of themselves," Roth said.

King Auger shook his head. "It's not them I'm worried about. I have enough murders without my citizens trying to mug warriors of The Sill. Sorry, *your* citizens I should say." He finished with an accusatory glare at Roth.

The bus was both roomy and comfortable on the inside, with a row of plush seats around the exterior and a nice big open spot for Goran in the middle. The ride to King Auger's brought them through a residential district run by a gang that called themselves the 'Rusty Doves.' Everywhere Cole looked there were unfriendly faces and hungry eyes. They passed by brawls involving seven or more people, shady characters lurking in alleys, and prone figures that may have been sleeping or dead. After half an hour Cole realized they weren't running through a bad part of the city because there didn't seem to be any good parts. Each building looked as if it were about to collapse, though a few had some shoddy glass work patching up the holes. Here and there were pedestals with large, dim gratia stones set in a way that anyone walking by could make an offering, though it seemed people would rather make a crude drawing or smash the stones instead. For a town that prided itself on Rage, Cole thought it funny that so few people wore their munisica. The ones that did had unimpressive claws and nearly no shroud.

The city and its people had an odd familiarity to Cole, not in the way everything looked but in the overall demeanor and tone. It had the same ghetto-trashiness of the tree streets back home. Cole leaned his head into Goran's arm and shook the thoughts out of his head. He hadn't thought about his past life in a while, and he could feel the sadness bubbling up more and more lately. Now however was not the time to think about home. If he had a room to himself at King Auger's, Cole would allow himself some time to break down and cry if he needed to.

The bus screeched to a halt outside a plain building only slightly less run-down than the rest. If it wasn't for the high walls and the guards at the gate, the building wouldn't have stood out at all.

"Not much of a palace," Roth said, ribbing the King with his elbow. "I would have come sooner if I'd known you were living in such squalor."

"That means a lot from folk who live in trees," King Auger said, hopping down from the bus. "It's not right for someone in my position to spend resources on decorating my house or living beyond necessity, when my blasted city is rotting from the inside out. I'd sell the behemoth we rode in on if I didn't need it for safety. There's some places in Morthain that not even I am free to walk through. I'd consider culling a few of the gangs myself if some other litter of rag-tags wouldn't rise up from the blood and shit."

Cole jumped out of the bus, calling after a sleeping Goran, who had chewed off the rest of the chains and left the slobbery pieces scattered on the floor. The driver was none too pleased, especially when he saw the fur and claw marks on the sides of the seats. Cole offered to try and fix the broken parts with his Wisdom, but Valen pushed him along. A broken bus was preferable to making a King wait for you.

Cole set off at a trot to catch up with the others. He stopped suddenly, eyes wide and searching for Milette. He silently berated himself for not keeping better track of her. His worry was for nothing however, as Milette came running out of the bus as fast as she could to catch up. Her face was awash with desperation that did not relax until she was at his side. Perhaps it wouldn't be so hard to keep an eye on her. She shot him a nasty glare, full of accusation and resentment, though she clung to his side like a magnet. He had to think of what to do with her, and soon.

The group followed the Kings through a pair of thick glass gates which took three hulking guards to open. Auger's yard was just as barren as the house itself. Only a few guard shacks and a stone pavilion decorated the grounds. Hard dirt crunched beneath their feet as they walked.

Roth's voice echoed like thunder off the high walls. "These gangs need dealing with, Auger. You ought to stop ruling with your left hand and start using that hammer. When one of these groups steps a toe out of line, you smash the toe. If they're brazen enough to walk over the line, you crush the whole foot. Sooner or later you're going to have to meet them in combat."

"You were always the practical man, Rothael," King Auger sighed, greeting the guard at the main door. "But you're no bureaucrat. I won't govern Morthain with Fear. There's rules here. Old grudges fester until they become laws. I'm no more than a placeholder to some of them because they're waiting for you to return. Then there are others that blame you for the sinking of the city and our decline."

"It seems as though Morthain could do with a change," Roth remarked. "Not a change in leadership - you're not getting off that easy." Roth reached out to a passing guard and took his pike. The guard resisted but the pike came loose as if he had given it freely. Roth waited, daring the guard to make a move, but after a moment of inaction Roth thrust the pike back into his chest, sending the guard sprawling. He turned back to King Auger as though nothing had happened. "It's been too long since someone's tested your mettle. Morthain sat out the last war. This one's going to be much worse. I suggest you pick a side."

"You know full well that would be a death-warrant for us," the King huffed, shaking his head. "They know nothing of battle outside of stabbing each other while their backs are turned."

"Then maybe death is what Morthain deserves," Roth said.

King Auger rubbed his hand over his brow. "Perhaps you are right, Bonebreaker. Everyone has their time, no more, no less. Our time may have already passed and we're holding on to nothing. Even you nutters at The Sill won't be around forever. Perhaps The Three will have their time next."

"We haven't had our time yet," Roth said with pride as he looked at his unit. Cole noticed they all stood a little taller and carried their chins a little higher. "Our time might be over long before this war comes to a head, but we will have it. We'll set fire to the sky before we meet our end."

"I don't doubt it." King Auger took a flask from an inner pocket of his jacket and drained the last few sips before crushing the metal against his hammer hand. "Bah! Enough of these weighty words. The true King has returned. Our battle-fires may have dimmed, but our spirit burns all the brighter. Let us break open a few casks and light the great ovens. There are a few among our numbers that are old enough to know why you are Bonebreaker, and they would be sore to miss a chance to repay your favors."

Roth grinned like a wolf. "Let's not disappoint them then."

Cole felt as if he could drop dead asleep at any moment. Whatever party or feast that the King talked about was the last thing he wanted. He turned to the rest of his unit, who each looked worse than he felt. Sitra was slumped up against a stone pillar and Eliza was already sleeping up on Goran's back. Valen and Lileth were only vaguely paying attention, swaying as though they were on a rocking boat.

Milette elbowed Cole in the shoulder, her dark eyes sunken and wild as she hissed, "You'd better say something! I'm in your care, so take care of me! If you don't I'll put myself into a death-sleep right now and you can carry me until I wake!"

"Okay, just don't touch me with those things. You smell like a bog angel." Cole gagged, eyeing Milette's festering stumps. He would have Eliza take a look at them later. Cole cleared his throat as loudly as he could, interrupting the hammer-handed King. "I uh...I think I speak for the unit, but we're dead tired...Master Roth," he added, unsure if he should address him as 'King.' "Can we find a bed, or at least a spot on the floor to crash?"

A guard led them to an empty portion of the house, which turned out to be unused barracks. They passed by bathrooms and showers, but none of the unit were interested in anything outside of a soft bed. The bunks were double-stacked and lined the walls of the sleeping quarters. There was no bed large enough for Goran, but the mirak didn't seem all that tired. He had slept nearly the whole way from the sands and probably slept the whole time on the back of the baileen. They each fell in whatever bed they came to first. Cole trailed behind, and it wasn't by accident that he ended up in a bed next to Lileth. To Cole's annoyance, Milette wound up in the top bunk of his own bed even though there were countless others available. Without the aid of her hands, she stumbled and clambered her way up to the top bunk, shaking the entire frame. Cole waited in quiet fury for her to stop fidgeting, only to have her trade the wriggling for obnoxious snoring.

Cole rolled in his bed, tricking his mind into thinking the snoring was just a sound from home, like a passing fire truck. Before long he was twitching lightly with sleep as his dreams began to commandeer his conscious thoughts. He cracked his eyes open so he could see Lileth one more time. A pale light fell over her face, catching and twinkling in her long eyelashes. Her closed eyes looked like flowers just about to bloom. Her arm hung out from the bed as if reaching for him. Cole threw a lazy arm out, but it was too short. His first dreams were of his fingers wrapped around hers.

Cole had many strange dreams that night, most of which were not potent enough to remember. As the night wore on, his desires pulled at him like a lodestone, drawing him somewhere even his subself didn't want to go. The more he resisted the harder it became. He knew he could wake himself, so he tried; however, he was thoroughly stuck. Before he knew it he was falling, sinking far beneath himself, beneath the world. He was alone in the river, floating upwards and onwards into aethers unknown. His body was no more, but he didn't need it here. Cole had become a soul fly.

Even with the inexorable current of the river he tried pulling himself back to Aeneria. When that didn't work he tried throwing himself sideways out into infinity, only to discover that he was not alone. *He* was there, as *He* always was, guiding Cole with a firm, paternal hand.

His presence and intention bored into Cole: "*You cast many shadows, Cole Carter, for in your heart and in your mind you are many.*"

Cole pressed his own will inwards, forcing *Him* to elaborate. *He* retaliated with profound compassion, filling Cole with such warmth and comfort that the urge to fight melted from him like frost in the morning sun. Compassion paved the way for understanding and together they swam onward to their destination. Cole knew where he had to go.

A lifetime seemed to pass within the blink of an eye as Cole found himself in the place he was dreading. *He* faded back, watching quietly from the deepest corners of Cole's mind. This was no place for *Him*.

Cole placed a bare foot on the front steps of his little apartment on Blossom Street. The house was barely visible in the orange haze of the street lights, as though someone had painted it with shadow.

Cole took another step, careful not to scratch off any more paint from the stairs. As his hand closed around the dented handle of the door, a feeling of impending doom rushed up to greet him, seemingly from the house itself. He wished he could turn back now, but this was the only way. He pulled the door open, yanking through its familiar sticky spot. The darkness from within reached out to embrace him. Holding his breath, Cole entered his house.

The kitchen and living room were vacant, though there was enough trash and clutter piled up that it looked as though several homeless people had taken up residence. Cole could barely see through the shadows that permeated the air in thick clouds. He flicked on a few lights but they lacked the potency to pierce whatever hung in the room. The air was dank with something sick and unsavory, as if the house were haunted by a vile spirit. Cole felt part of himself stolen with each foggy breath, lost forever to the evil in the house. With grim recognition Cole identified the hallmarks of stale Fear and ripe Despair choking the air. From somewhere deeper in he sensed a burning Hatred.

He took one timid step after the other, checking the hallway and downstairs bathroom. The baleful silence smothered his footsteps and swallowed his drumming heart. He could detect no sound or sign of life, but he certainly was not alone.

"COLE!"

The tearing scream came from upstairs. Tremors rushed through his legs as terror yanked the breath out of him. Steeling himself, Cole squeezed a hand on the broken railing and set up the stairs. The cry had come from up there, but that was where the darkness and foulness was most palpable. He was now breathing so hard he felt he might faint, yet no sound came from his quivering lips. He took one step after another, forcing himself to keep moving, keep breathing. There was no way back now. He felt feeble and helpless, as if his most vulnerable parts had just been peeled back and exposed to an unknown horror. He reached the top step, wondering where to search next. A dreadful, familiar groan came from his mother's room.

The door was open, though the room was bathed in an ominous murk that his eyes couldn't pierce. The groan echoed from the open door once more. Hands groping through empty air, Cole staggered blindly down the hall towards his mother's room. His fingers found the doorway. He dug his nails into the soft wood and pulled himself in.

He was in the room now, too blind to take another step, too afraid to make a noise. Cole realized he forgot to breathe, but suddenly found himself lacking the urge. He was naked. Fully bare to the darkness now.

A moan sounded through the darkness directly in front of him now.

Cole thought the Fear would kill him. He wished it would. But as the moan faded, it was replaced by a rustling of blankets.

A ghostly light trickled over his mother's bed, revealing a lump rolling back and forth. A wiry mop of blond hair poked out next to the pillows.

"Mom?" Cole breathed.

There was nothing but crushing silence. The lump didn't even seem to be breathing.

"Mom?" Cole squeaked again.

The lump stirred, rolling over as the blankets peeled back and Tara's face appeared.

"Colton," she whispered.

Cole lunged forward, throwing his arms around her. Tara recoiled, wailing as if he'd struck her.

"I'm sorry," Cole cried, withdrawing and patting the side of the bed. "I'm so sorry."

Tara fell silent, her lips pulling into a cynical smile that Cole had never seen. She rolled her head away from him and gazed through the ceiling. "I knew you'd come back."

Cole sobbed, wiping the tears as fast as he could so he could see her. "I'm here, Mom. I'm right here for you."

"Is this a dream?" Tara asked in a hollow voice.

"I don't know," Cole said between sobs.

Tara mumbled something Cole couldn't quite make out. She rambled like a mad woman, as though she didn't know who or where she was. Cole looked away, ashamed to see her in such a state. His eyes fell upon the nightstand, where the ghostly light illuminated several bottles of prescription pills. None of them was for her.

A small fire blazed within Cole, bringing clarity through his Despair. "Mom, where's Nana Beth? You shouldn't be alone like this.

I'll go get her. Now." He knew he hadn't much time. He would sprint through the darkness to find Nana Beth and make her come help. Nana Beth would know what to do.

Tara's head fell to the side, her lifeless eyes meeting Cole's for the first time. Her voice was clear and cold: "Nana Beth is dead, Colton. She died after you left me, after you let Joshy die. I hate you, Colton. Go away. Go away and never come back."

CHAPTER 6

WARBREAK

"Valen, Lil, he's back!" Sitra cried. "He's back!"

The others came running back into the sleeping room, eyes wide with alarm. Eliza and Goran had never left, though they had fallen into a catatonic state sometime after Cole disappeared. Cole was back in his bed, mouth open in a silent scream as tears poured down his cheeks.

"What's wrong with him? Where did he come from?" Valen asked.

"He was a soul fly!" Sitra explained, her words rushing out of her mouth faster than she could speak them. "He came right up through the floor and lit up the whole room with this miserable blue light and then his body plopped right into the bed. There's something broken in him, and it's pouring out into Eliza and Goran."

Valen seized Cole, squinting and calculating. Lileth reached out to stop him, but his hands flew to Cole's head, placing his middle fingers on his brow. "What's wrong, Cole? Speak to me, brother."

Valen recoiled as the color drained from his face. There was a sudden movement from the center of the room, startling them all. Goran let out a long, high keen as he stirred, trudging across the room and pushing them aside with his bulk. With a massive shovel of a hand, he scooped Cole out of the bed and closed his teeth around the back of his shirt, carrying him to the center of the room. He set Cole down with astonishing care and grace.

"Why?" Sitra demanded. "Goran why'd you move him over there?" She shot across the room, knocking a bunk over with her shoulder. "I can't take it anymore. Roth is going to cancel his party and come down here right now."

"Wait, Sitra," Lileth breathed, taking a timid step.

Sitra whirled around, her long braid snapping like a whip. "What for?"

Lileth inclined her head towards Cole. "There's a gratia stone embedded in the floor where Cole's lying. I believe he's filling it."

"Take his clothes off," Eliza murmured from her bed as she rose to a shaky elbow. The pallor on her face was even fainter than Valen's. "The stone is drawing it out of him. Take his clothes off so his skin can transfer the Passion."

With a flick of his hand and a flash of green light, Valen ripped the clothes from Cole's back, sending them across the room where they splattered in a sweaty heap. Lileth draped a sheet over Cole, preserving his modesty. Goran nudged him with his nose, making sure his whole body was on the stone.

From under the sheet, a soft lavender hue silhouetted Cole from underneath. The light shone brighter until it filled the entire room, blinding them all. Suddenly, a low hum sounded from far beneath the King's house, as if some ancient beast had just woken. The gratia stone dimmed to a tolerable volume as lights within the room flicked on and the sounds of distant machinery roared to life. Cole stirred, taking deep gasping breaths as he pulled the sheet off his face.

"You're safe Cole, you're back," Lileth said, falling to her knees and wrapping her arms around him. She ran her hands over his side, healing the blisters from the stone.

"I'm sorry," Cole sobbed. "I'm so sorry."

Lileth rubbed his back. "You've nothing to be sorry for, Cole."

"You don't know that," Valen said, ignoring the glares from the others. "Cole, where did you go? What did you do?"

Cole buried his eyes in his elbow, rubbing the tears away. After a moment he regained enough composure to answer. "I went to my house, on Earth."

"You Traveled?" Valen asked, "To Terra? It's not possible, we're not in Terra's house. Not even the ancient Wisdom Walkers Traveled out-of-turn."

"He speaks the truth, Valen," Eliza said, approaching Cole and crouching next to him. "I could feel it through the Passion link. He was certainly not in this reality, and his soul resonated with the familiarity of home." She dropped her eyes, shuddering. "It also wailed with the Fear and Despair that could only come from the loss of a loved one. He was at his home. Someone close to him has died."

Valen shook his head in disbelief.

Lileth stroked Cole's wet hair away from his eyes. "Do you want us to fetch Master Roth? He is old and may have some experience with Traveling."

Cole drew the sheet tight as he looked around, trying to figure out how he got on the floor and why he was naked. "No. I don't think Roth could help me with this one. Where's- oh, hey there Bud." Goran reached over and placed the back of his leathery fingers against Cole's leg.

Rapid footsteps clopped down the hallway, growing louder by the second. Milette, who had somehow acquired a glass dagger clamped between her teeth, jumped from her bed and ran to the other side of the room. A guard entered, breathing heavy with his hands resting on his knees.

He took a moment to catch his breath. "You all okay? Somehow all the old machines fired up and things are going haywire. Some-thing's back-feeding power and generators are blowing up all over the place."

Valen turned towards the guard, blocking Cole from view. "We are fine, thank you. We have inadvertently fed the gratia stone in the floor here, which must be what is causing your machinery to malfunction."

The guard scratched his chin. "A *what* stone?"

Valen motioned towards the glowing stone. "The old power system, it uses magic to fuel things throughout the house. You ought to tell your superiors so they can mitigate the damage."

The guard looked as if he only understood half of what Valen said. "Well, as long as you're all okay."

Growing impatient, Valen shifted his tone. "We are fine, thank you very much. Now leave us, we need privacy."

Getting the hint, the guard nodded and set off down the hall at a much slower pace this time. Valen waited for the footsteps to fade before turning around. "Cole, are you going to recover? Is there anything we can do? Name it and we'll make it so."

"I'm still really tired, but I can't sleep," he said, pulling himself away from Lileth and standing up. "I'm soaked. A shower might be the best thing for me."

"I think your showering would be the best thing for all of us right now," Sitra said with a grin, fanning her nose.

Lileth rose to her feet. "I know I could do with a bath. Let us go see if Cole's contribution woke up the facilities."

Refusing offers to carry him, Cole wrapped the sheets around himself and trudged off towards the baths. He looked in every shadow and for *Him*. Who was this guy and what right did he have to bring him to such terrible nightmares? Cole identified the experience as a nightmare, but in his heart he knew it was much worse. He had indeed Traveled, and what had occurred was real. His mother was alone, and no longer a mother. She had lost everything, even Nana Beth. And she Hated him.

Cole felt every aspect of dark magic within the rickety Blossom Street apartment. Thick, viscous clouds of it hung over him, still clinging to his skin. He felt tainted by it, which was the real reason he wanted a shower. At the moment he couldn't call even the simplest of spells to his aid. The dark magic blocked everything from his munisica to his connection to Goran. Worst of all was the guilt, which somehow fueled the maelstrom of negative energy within him. Why would *He* bring him there?

Cole rounded the corner into the wash room, discovering deep basins cut into the limestone floor. Cole expected the laser-showers he was accustomed to at The Sill, which did the job very effectively but left him cold, raw, and unsatisfied. Following a hunch, he drew the sheet tighter and turned a few spigots on the edge of one of the basins. To his relief, the valves made sense and within a few minutes he had himself a full bathtub covered by a blanket of pinkish bubbles. Cole speared his foot through the foam, but the water was far too hot. He tried using Wisdom to transfer some of the heat, but he couldn't focus. It was all he could do to not break down crying. He needed that water. After ten painful minutes, the water had relinquished some of its bite and Cole sloshed in, sheet and all. He submerged himself completely, screaming as loudly as he could, each sob bringing him closer to the bottom as gouts of air roared past his ears. He remained under long after his lungs demanded he surface. There didn't seem to be a good enough reason for him to get out. Eventually his body rebelled against his emotions and he pushed up from the bottom.

He emerged, sucking both air and bubbles into his mouth. After clearing his throat and eyes he discovered Lileth in the basin next to him. Her eyes were shut and the back of her head rested against the edge of the basin.

"I was just wondering if you had grown gills and forsaken the land altogether. You were under for quite some time." She smiled, though her eyes were still closed. Her hair was slick and droplets clung to her black petal lashes.

"I was washing up," Cole sputtered. "Is there no ladies' room here?"

Lileth opened one eye. "You mean a separate bath for women only? Why would there be such a thing?"

Cole swam to the edge of his basin, holding on with the tips of his fingers. "I...I guess I don't know. Just another thing for me to get used to."

"Would it please you if I left?" she asked. She sounded like she really meant it.

"It would please me if you stayed," Cole said, ready to plunge his head back under.

Lileth's smile deepened as she nestled her head back once more. "Good. The water-baths are lovely. They are not as thorough as the showers at The Sill, but these are immensely gratifying. I could stay in here forever I think."

Cole felt a tiny shard of Rage poke through the clouds in his mind. "I'm not about to kill myself, so you don't need to keep checking on me every five minutes. I know you all felt it back there. That Despair. It didn't come from me, you know. I must have brought it back with me. It came from..." He trailed off, turning his head away so she couldn't see his tears. The dregs of his mother's suicidal thoughts still clung to his heart.

"I am here because you are my friend, Cole. I care about you." Her tone was harsh but genuine. "You saved me once, do you remember? In the meadow? I am not here to pry, but I am here if you need me. Besides, it's not every day one gets to soak in such a comfy bath."

Cole sank a little. "Thank you, Lileth. I'm sorry for snapping ..." He paused a moment, waiting for her to respond. She did not. "Is it okay if we don't talk about it?"

"Of course," she said in a soft voice.

Cole rose from the bubbles, searching for her eyes. Her eyes were still closed, though her hand extended across the tile floor towards him. Without thinking, Cole threw his arm out of the tub, grasping her fingers and squeezing them, conveying all his gratitude and more. She gripped him in return, swirling her thumb over the back of his hand. Cole cherished the moment. He had been linked with certain magics of Passion to Goran and Eliza, but this was different. They were connected with a simple touch, yet it felt so much closer. She began to hum a familiar tune, her voice rich and warm, contradicting Cole's ideas on who Lileth really was. As far as he knew, her cold practicality gave no hints that she was capable of things as frivolous as song. The more he thought on just how little he knew about her, the more he yearned to know. After a few minutes his shoulder began to ache where the edge of the basin dug into his armpit. He did not release her hand, however. He would suffer the discomfort as long as she kept holding him. A moment later he felt invisible hands lift his naked body from below, supporting him into a comfortable position with a nudge of Wisdom. He glanced at her again. Her sleepy head had shifted onto her shoulder, towards him. As Cole drifted into a warm slumber, his mind echoed with the haunting beauty of a whale's song.

Cole woke feeling foggy and sluggish, but the crippling lethargy had lifted from his body and mind. All the bubbles had gone and Lileth's hand was still gripping his, but she appeared fast asleep. Reluctantly, Cole withdrew. Lileth's eyes fluttered awake. The invisible hands holding him up vanished as Cole fished the bottom of the basin with his toes for the bed sheet.

Lileth twirled away from Cole before exploding from the basin with a single, mighty leap. She was entirely naked. Cole averted his eyes and pretended to be busy finding the bed sheet. There was a light hissing in the air followed by a billowing hot fog, which turned out to be the water Lileth evaporated from her skin. After an awkward moment of listening to Lileth dress herself, Cole hoisted himself from the basin and found a stack of clothes folded neatly on a stool. He had been naked in front of his entire unit on several occasions, but he was always sick or unconscious. He ignored his reservations and used his Wisdom to convince the water on his skin to evaporate as Lileth had. Within a few seconds he was concealed by a hot cloud of water and toed his way over to the stool. There was a card sitting atop the pile with words scrawled across in acid green ink.

FOR THE NEW BLOOD

A sad smile pulled across Cole's face. 'New Blood' was the name Storn had given him. He let a couple more tears fall freely before grasping the first piece off the stool and dangling it in front of his eyes. The material was a deep merlot, but as he looked closer he could see something sparkling within the fibers. It was Morthainian glass. He plunged his legs into the tight trousers and snapped the long-sleeved shirt over his head. He ignored the socks and boots, seeing as he had destroyed more than his fair share whenever his munisica decided to detonate from his feet. The clothes were stretchy in all the right places and carried extra layers where his vital organs lay. It was clearly some sort of armor, but it felt so light and breathable that it could have passed for silky nightwear. Cole turned around to find Lileth in a similar, form-fitting armor. She too had forsaken the socks and boots.

There was a slight commotion from down the hall, which turned out to be the rest of the unit, with Milette in tow. They entered the baths caught up in their own conversations. Cole noticed an odd softness to Valen's countenance as he guided Milette with a gentle hand. He helped lower her into the basin, whispering something in her ear and eliciting a girlish giggle from her. Cole suddenly knew what he was going to do with his prisoner.

"There's food out there," Sitra said before cannonballing into the basin closest to Cole, splashing him with fresh water and bubbles. "We ate all the good stuff, but there's some bread and fruit left. Better hurry before Goran finishes it off."

Cole flung the soapy water from him, casting another quiet spell to dry himself off. "Thanks. Care to join me for…what is it, dinner or breakfast now?" he asked Lileth.

She answered with a smile that warmed him in a way that not even a hot bath could.

Goran was fast asleep. The mirak lay on his back with his fat belly rising and falling in low, rumbling snores. Half eaten food lay strewn about him like an epic battle scene. Cole perused the cart of leftover food and managed to build himself a hearty, two-handed sandwich. Lileth took a bowl of untouched fruits from the cart and brought it back to her bed. Cole sat down next to her and tried not to make a mess.

"Where are you from?" Cole asked, swallowing hard. "You didn't grow up at The Sill did you?"

Lileth sucked all the juices out of a plump ruby fruit before looking at him. "I spent my childhood with my parents in a village just outside Oberon City. I have only been at The Sill for two cycles."

His eyes went wide. "Two cycles is a long time… at least to me it is. In Earth-years that's most of my life. I hope you get to visit your parents often enough." Cole paused, trying to find an ambiguous way to ask her age. "Is two cycles a long time for you?"

Lileth's eyes fell to the floor. "It is no small span. I see my parents often enough for their liking. The village I grew up in has a very practical view on reproduction and family bonds. Members of my village descended from Wisdom Walkers and, much like Morthain, scoff at all other magics and lifestyles. It is customary in my village to send your children away at an early age to seek knowledge and Wisdom, eventually returning to contribute to the betterment of the society. My parents jumped at the opportunity to have me trained by Chiron, who trained with Varka himself. They told me in no uncertain terms that I was conceived for the sole purpose of being trained by him. If not for Master Chiron, I would never have been born."

A silence fell between them. Cole shifted closer, wanting to comfort her. "When's the last time you were home?"

Her voice hardened. "The day I left."

Cole put his sandwich in his lap. "I'm sorry to bring it up, I just wanted to learn more about you. You must miss them."

She resumed her usual stoic tone of indifference: "You cannot miss that which you do not remember. When I had the ability, I gave my memories of them to a Wisdom Stone in the necropolis. I..."

Lileth jerked her head around. A few seconds later, familiar footfalls came clopping down the hallway. The footsteps grew louder until the same guard stood before them, huffing with his hands on his knees. Goran's growling head poked up from over his shoulder, his hackles raised and a crimson eye set in a murderous glare.

"King Auger-" The guard shook his head, panting, "King Roth...ah blast it. Your presence is requested in the throne hall. All of you."

Goran's fury spilled over into Cole's mind. He clenched his fists to keep his munisica from erupting. "We were supposed to have at least a night to recover. Is this an emergency?"

Lileth placed a hand over Cole's, soothing him as she addressed the guard, "We will be up within the hour."

The guard twisted his hands together as he made a pained expression. "King Rothael said you'll get your asses up there within the minute, or you'll have no asses to worry about."

"Then we will be up as soon as possible," Lileth said, nodding to the guard, who turned on his heels and trotted off.

Cole stood and kicked his bunk, immediately regretting doing so with bare feet. "I'm sick of always being on the run! It's go-go-go, every day! We've earned some time off."

Lileth reached down and healed Cole's foot with a droplet of rosy light. "We've been here for over two days. You were gone for some time while you Traveled. I don't know if Traveling is the same as sleeping, but if you are tired I suggest you ask Eliza to guide you through a Passion-dream. It's a clever form of hypnosis that can grant you the benefits of a full night's sleep from a few minutes of day-dreaming."

"Two days!" Cole gasped, rubbing his foot. "I hope this isn't like when I disappeared from Earth. I would be gone for days or weeks at a time, over and over for months on end. Maybe this time was just because I was so tired from running around half the planet. I'll talk to Eliza about the hypno-meditation thing."

Eliza's thoughts bloomed in his mind: *"Just tell me when, brother."*

"How long have you been eavesdropping?" Cole demanded.

"I do not actively listen, but when you speak my name I can't help but tune in. It's almost like picking your whispered name out of a noisy crowd. You can sever the connection if you'd like," she offered, her smile palpable through the link.

"Not now, but privacy would be nice sometimes," Cole said, trying to mask his imagination, which had just wandered towards a fantasy that included himself and Lileth alone in the baths. *"Stop laughing at me! Did you hear what the guard said when he came in a minute ago?"*

"With my own ears. Don't worry, we are clothing and hurrying our 'asses' as we speak. See you soon."

Cole looked up at Lileth, hoping she hadn't noticed his sudden lapse in attention. She stirred, as if suddenly rousing from her own day dream. "I thought you wanted to return to Terra. Have you changed your mind about going home?"

"I'm not sure I have much of a home to go back to," he said, swallowing back an ache in his chest.

Lileth swooped down and gave Cole a quick, soft kiss on the cheek. "You have a home here."

Cole suddenly felt as if he was the tallest man on Aeneria.

They wolfed down as much food as they could before heading back upstairs at a steady trot. Cole had no problem keeping up with the rest, but he didn't like how Valen chose to carry Milette in his arms. She was a prisoner after all. Throughout the stone house the gas torches had been extinguished, replaced by the gratia-fed lights that had filled the whole estate with an ambient white glow. Frustrated engineers ran about, dousing fires and tinkering with old machines that had sparked and smoked to life. Guided by urgent instructions from passing guards, the unit found the throne hall where both Kings and several important-looking people were gathered around.

Cole noticed the white-haired captain from the greeting party skulking behind King Auger with her arms crossed.

"Took you long enough," Roth barked without looking at them. "They're all here, go ahead and get started, Auger."

King Auger beckoned them all closer to a wide table he leaned over. "Right then, gather round and take a good look at the overlays here. It's been a lifetime since these things were running so forgive my fumbling."

They all pulled in close, trying to get a good view. Cole hopped up onto Goran's back so he could see over everyone's shoulders. The table was six-sided with little drawers running up its length. King Auger opened one drawer near the top and a ribbon of woven azure light flowed out of a hidden slot, rippling and twisting into a miniature landscape.

King Auger pointed with his hammer: "The old machines powered up a few hours ago, including this map overlay. When the battle-alarms went off we thought it was some sort of glitch in the hardware. It wasn't until our senior engineer took a look that we discovered the alarms to be genuine." He motioned towards a man holding an armful of books and clipboards.

The man dropped one of his books and bent over to pick it up, only to drop the rest in a heap. He ignored the pile and shuffled closer to the table. "That's right! The alarm systems may be old but they work just fine; however, it's taking us a good while to deduce their finer machinations." He pulled a miniscule notebook from a leather pocket on his belt, squinting his eyes and flipping through the tiny pages. "Battle overlays…battle overlays, yes! Sorry Kings, the old runes have me completely flummoxed." He bent down and ran his fingers over the drawers, opening one near the bottom.

The model-landscape shifted to a depiction of the White Sands, including a tiny Morthain buried beneath its center. In stark contrast to the azure map were five red blobs blinking at the edge of the display. Looking closely, Cole saw the blobs crawling steadily towards Morthain.

The engineer replaced his notebook back into his belt. "As you may have guessed, those red things on the edge there are what's setting off our alarms. We don't know what they are, but we've been tracking their trajectory for the last hour and they are certainly headed for Morthain. And, they are certainly humongous. Ships perhaps. Their pace has been erratic, but we estimate their arrival within the hour."

"That will do, Thanis," King Auger said, slamming the drawers shut. The overlays whipped back into their slots. King Auger addressed Roth with a sober look. "Seeing as your lot have an appointment with the Council, I assume you'll be taking your leave before our guests arrive?"

"It pains me to miss a chance to draw munisica with you, but yes, we will be leaving. In your fastest ship," Roth added.

An annoyed huff drew all eyes to Captain Seive. Her mouth looked like a dam holding back a flood. She surveyed the unit with a look of contempt before returning her sneer to Roth. "After nigh on thirty cycles you come here unannounced with your band of tramps from the other side of the planet. You insult our guards at every turn and make a mockery of our navy, and now you have the audacity to demand our fastest ship? What gives you the right? Old ways be damned, I won't grovel and bandy favors for some forget-me-not King who wasn't there for us when we needed him the most."

Without warning King Auger's hammer flashed through the air, pinning Captain Seive face first against the table. "You dare challenge King Roth after he evoked the trial? He had the good graces to spare your life and you spit at him now? You've no idea what this man's done for Morthain, for your ancestors!"

The King's hammer-hand lifted just enough to allow Captain Seive to speak. "I don't care what he's done for my dead uncles. Let them return from the aethers and lick his munisica. I won't. I'm concerned with today's Morthain, not yesterday's half-remembered glories. Forgotten Kings and old traditions hold no sway over the wars of now. I set myself against this false-king with every bone and breath."

"You lack-honored, toothless snake!" The King pressed his hammer deeper into Captain Seive's back. She made no effort to resist. "You know nothing of war. I'd smother you now if I didn't need you. Consider yourself relieved of rank. Report to the sergeants out at the proving grounds." He removed his hammer, producing a muffled crunching from the captain's chest.

Seive pushed herself off the pedestal, clutching her ribs and taking tiny breaths through thin lips. Her brittle gait suggested nearly all of her ribs had been broken by the King's hammer. She walked stiffly towards the door, careful not to touch anyone on the way out. Everyone moved aside and a few of the dignitaries muttered their disapproval.

"Wait," Roth's voice thundered across the hall. Seive paused at the door without turning around. Roth's munisica clacked against the polished tile as he walked over to her, pausing just behind her back. "Look at me."

Seive hesitated, but then hobbled around on the spot, still clutching her chest. The color had vanished from her aged face, turning nearly as pale as her long snowy hair.

He bent down so his eyes were boring straight into hers. "Do you know why they call me Bonebreaker?"

"No." Her voice was as thin and dry as a dead leaf.

Roth brought a dragon clawed hand to her chest, gently moving her hands away with a single bladed finger. For a moment Cole thought he was going to check to make sure all of her ribs had indeed snapped, but the wicked claw shrank and receded back into a naked hand. Roth pressed his palm against her chest, pearly light shining from in between his fingers. There were several loud pops as Seive drew a pained, full breath, followed by her sigh of relief. The color returned to her face as her chest resumed its normal cadence. She looked as if she wanted to thank him, but Cole was sure she was keeping her mouth shut out of spite.

"In my youth, Morthain was a wild, raw land with no one to guide her. So I took it upon myself to invoke the Blood Trial upon the entire city with hopes that I could hammer the separate factions into something useful. Not a single one would bend, so they had to be broken. The Blood Trial brought every citizen to me in single combat, and I defeated them all. The old ways demanded I kill everyone, even the children. Instead, I flouted tradition and took payment in my own way: One broken bone from every single person. Something that takes time to heal and would hurt enough to make them think about it every day. Morthain had to be broken into a thousand pieces and thrown into a furnace before it became something real. You are too young for me to have known you, but I remember the names of your fathers and battle-matrons and they were among the hardest to break. So, tell me, will you bend or will you be broken?"

Seive's eye twitched, but her face betrayed no other emotion. "I will bend myself in half for Morthain, but I won't bend for you."

"Good." Roth's lips pulled back into a wolfish smile as his munisica returned. With the flat of one of his bladed fingers, he struck her upper arm, producing a crack like a gunshot. Seive's eyes went wide.

Roth turned and strode back to the group at the table, "Auger, promote her to War Captain. I want her in charge of all your defenses."

King Auger's jaw dropped. "But that's preposterous! We are not at war, the rank wouldn't make sense."

"She's going to disobey you again," Roth explained. "She's one of your best. It won't take her long to move up the ranks and be a thorn in your ass again. Unless you want to kill her you'll have to promote her. That way her disobedience will be taken for good advice instead of outright defiance. And as for the war," Roth tapped the ends of his claws on the pedestal, "I'd wager these visitors are not your neighbors bringing you a pie. War is upon you, King."

"Damn you Rothael, you're right," King Auger admitted, looking older than ever as he ran a hand over his eyes. "War Captain, muster our navy and every member of the guard. I want your plan on how we are to receive our visitors in half an hour. Rothael, there's a bus waiting outside to take you all to the docks. Ask the port-master for our fastest ship and best crew, though I'm afraid our entire fleet is in a poorly state."

Eliza chimed in, "I believe that can be remedied in no time at all, King Auger."

Auger raised a bladed eyebrow. "Really? And what is your remedy, dear one?"

Eliza walked over to a gratia stone embedded in the wall behind Auger's throne. The surface was dusty and dim, but after rubbing her hand on it, the stone popped with vibrant pink light. Hidden machines buried in the walls of the throne hall vibrated to life, summoning a team of engineers, who set to removing panels and inspecting wires.

"Your gratia stones, where did you get them from?" Eliza asked, drawing the King's attention back to her.

An engineer emerged from a cloud of smoke coughing and waving her arms. "Our records show they were purchased in bulk from a dealer in Oberon City. They worked for some time, but when Morthain sank beneath the sands they dimmed every cycle until they stopped working altogether. We can only put a minimal charge to them, no matter how much Rage is applied."

Eliza rubbed the stone again, which grew so bright that a high ringing filled the air. "That is because they are Passion stones. Every single one I've seen is a Passion stone. I bet the ones on the ships are as well."

Every engineer in the hall broke into a chorus of irritated moans and muttering, kicking circuit boards and banging tools off panels.

"It's settled then!" King Auger slammed his hammer on the table, nearly splitting it in two. His face lit with a hard happiness that made even the shrouded half look cycles younger. "You'll have our sharpest crew and fastest ship, which ought to be a fair shade faster with a contribution from the young lass. Mind you, it wouldn't hurt relations with the local gangs if you showed the other crews how to charge their ships. They might have a few oddballs skilled with Passion. This revelation will go a long way to reforging Morthain to its former glory. Perhaps it'll even open a few eyes to the other magics. Now, begone! All of you!"

The group scattered. Morthain's dignitaries left through the main entrance with the lead engineer. The unit gathered around Roth. Before he lost his chance, Cole ran to the side exit, catching Seive before she could leave.

"Wait! Seive, uh, I mean War Captain, I have a favor to ask," Cole said, blocking the door with his arm.

The newly promoted War Captain halted before him. The hand of her uninjured arm was balled into a fist. "You have thirty seconds. Speak."

Cole ignored her long, pointy munisica growing longer by the second. He called over his shoulder, "Hey Milette! Get over here!"

Milette wrapped her half-arms tightly around Valen. "No!"

Cole felt his own munisica aching and itching as they shot out, making him a few inches taller. "It's going to be real hard for you to walk over here with no *feet!* Move your ass, NOW!"

Milette scowled and jogged over, halting in front of him and averting her eyes. She made it clear she wasn't going to say a word.

Still blocking the door, Cole turned back to Seive: "The guard is low on recruits right?"

"*Desperately* low," Seive replied. "Your thirty seconds are up by the way," She added, glancing down at Cole's munisica.

"Well, here's your newest recruit. Meet Milette, my prisoner of war," Cole said with more confidence than he felt.

Seive measured Milette, her eyes falling on her stumped wrists. "You're joking."

"You are out of your little mind!" Milette's voice became a shrieking wind. "I've no attachment to this wretched city, and absolutely no aspirations to go fight someone else's war. You go too far, *Master*. I won't have my life dictated by a child who clearly has no idea what he's doing. Kill me now if you must, but dignity has a price."

Cole sighed, looking to Seive. "Will you take her?"

"That's not my call." Seive walked around Milette, appraising her as if she were livestock at an auction. "Very lean. Horrible attitude. I can tell by the way she walks that she's hopelessly inflexible, though perhaps not impossible. The lack of hands is an obvious problem, but there are workarounds." She did one more loop before placing her munisica lightly on Cole's outstretched arm. "I could put a word in with the senior sergeants at the proving grounds, but that's all I can do. Now, get out of the way. I have much to do."

Cole took his arm from the doorway, knowing this was the best deal he was going to get. Seive gripped her broken arm and sped off at a dead sprint, her bladed feet tearing up chunks of tile as she went. Cole glanced up at Milette, who looked as if she were readying a spell to fling at him. "Before you start spitting at me, just hear me out. You're right, I'm way younger than you and I've no clue what I'm doing most of the time. You know I'm not going to kill you, but I'm stuck. I can't bring you with me and I won't release you back to where you can hurt more soul flies."

Milette cocked her head with a derisive chuckle. "I refuse to join this gang of sand-sailors, or whatever they call themselves. So, what does the wizened Master wish to do with me?" It sounded more like a challenge than a question.

"I'm not doing *anything* with you," Cole replied with a sneer of his own. "Consider yourself released. You're no longer a prisoner. Go on." He motioned towards the main door.

Milette's jaw worked open and closed a few times, the lashes of her eyes flapping like a bird caught in a storm. "I…but what does that mean for me? I can't go out *there.*" She jabbed her stump towards the door. "I'll die a starving beggar! I'll be mugged every hour! I have nothing, not even the means to defend myself! Even if I could somehow climb out of this pit I'd never make it across the sands. You crippled me human, you owe me more than that!"

"Then I suggest you make nice with the sergeants at the proving grounds," Cole replied, keeping the tortured soul fly in the fore of his thoughts before she could rouse his sympathies. "Or go make nice with the assassins and thieves out on the streets. Either way, I'm done with you." Cole stepped away, leaving Milette babbling with fury.

As he turned away from her, he felt something chilled land on the back of his neck, scrabbling and searching. Goran's primal bellow echoed throughout the hall as he thundered to Cole's side, but Cole's Rage was already there. In the blink of an eye, the shroud enveloped the entirety of his skin and hair, protecting him from whatever Milette had just cast at him. Cole's vision flashed red as his heart hammered in his armored ears like a steel drum. He turned slowly to face Milette. The sheer force of his glare seemed to send her sprawling back against the wall. Cole reached up with savage claws and snatched a smoky, translucent snake from his neck. Without taking his eyes from Milette, he squeezed the phantom creature, which bit and thrashed harmlessly against his shrouded arm. The snake went limp, and with a quick jerk Cole whipped it against the wall where it splattered, covering Milette in chunks of viscous grey smoke.

There was a clinking of glass armor as two guards rushed over, drawing swords to Milette's chest. One of them spoke to Cole from the corner of his mouth. "Say the word and she'll breathe her last."

The guard repeated himself, but Cole couldn't hear it. The Rage was building, growing louder and encompassing his every thought and desire. He wanted to throw Milette through the wall she cowered against. He wanted to plunge his fists through the guards, just because they were there. He wondered how long it would take him to level the entire house, and then see what else he could destroy. The Rage demanded it. A small voice reminded him that he hadn't the mastery to control himself if the Rage swelled any hotter. But he wanted it to consume him. The power was seductive. With supreme effort, he released it. He felt the pressure ebb from his skull as the Rage fizzled, leaving him trembling and unsatisfied.

"Take her away from me," he said, voice shaking as he turned away from her. "Anywhere, just go. Her life is her own now."

"You got it," the guard said, handing his weapon off to his partner and pulling a curved glass dagger from his belt. "Up you get, lass. You save your wicked magic for when you get outside, unless you know a spell to fix whatever my blade will do to your insides. Up now, there you go."

Cole ignored Milette's struggling screams as the guards dragged her out of the hall. He returned to his unit under looks of shock and caution.

"You were right," Cole sighed, addressing Roth. "I should have killed her. I'm pretty sure I just earned myself a mortal enemy." Cole felt Valen's eyes on him and hoped it wasn't *two* mortal enemies.

"It's good to have a few blades out there thirsting for your blood." Roth looked down at Cole, pride burning in his eyes. "Keeps you from getting complacent. Now, all of you draw your munisica and follow me. We've a ship to catch."

"Don't you mean we have a *bus* to catch?" Sitra asked, flexing her claws.

"We're not taking that tank," Roth growled.

They followed Roth out of King Auger's house. The bus driver shoved his pipe back into his jacket and rushed to the front.

The blocky engine roared to life, great gouts of black smoke billowing up to the sandy sky. In single file the unit leaped over the bus, shooting through the dark cloud of exhaust gases. As Cole landed on the nearest rooftop, he heard a resounding crunch and an outraged cry from below. Through his familial link, he tried to impress upon Goran that buses were not okay to jump on, but concepts of property damage were of no concern to a mirak.

Keeping to the rooftops, Roth led them to the base of the ascending ramp that would take them up to the undulating sandy clouds. Afraid to lose himself in the magic, Cole throttled his Rage back to the bare minimum, though he then had some difficulty keeping up with the group. When he felt too far behind he instead called upon Wisdom to pull him along in great, floating leaps. To Cole's relief, Goran stayed with him the whole time, barking and snorting with excitement. It had been a while since the mirak had had a chance to stretch his legs. After what felt like only a few minutes they arrived at the ascending port. The dock workers had yet to receive word of their arrival or demands for a ship and crew. Fortunately the dock captain was old enough to know who Roth was, and guided them over towards a sleek, mahogany vessel with no visible blemishes.

While the captain scrambled his crew together and readied the ship, Roth had the unit walk amongst each of the war ships and charge their gratia stones. As Eliza had predicted they were all Passion stones. Once charged, the ships perked up out of the sand, jumping and bucking like horses. After prepping their fleet, the captain called the unit to their vessel, which was called the Firedancer.

The Firedancer shoved off and they made for the sandy ramp ahead of the other war ships. The ascending ramp was painfully slow, but with the Firedancer's gratia stone fully charged, the crew was able to persuade it to climb a little faster. Cole took one last look at Morthain before the sheet caps were pulled over the upper deck. King Auger's house shone like a gleaming beacon lit by brilliant street lights instead of orange tongues of torches. Guilt clawed at Cole's heart. He couldn't help but feel as if he had sentenced Milette to a harsh and drawn-out death.

Blackness enveloped the top deck as the Firedancer pierced the surging clouds above the city. Instead of gas candles, tiny lightning marbles sprouted to life all along the deck, making it look as if the woodwork had been covered in blankets of shimmering eyes.

"Can't this heaping pile go any faster?" Roth called up to the captain.

"I'm afraid that's all she's got," the captain hollered back from the front wheel. "It's slow going through the sands. Once we get up top we'll set her to a good clip, don't you worry."

A rumbling came from Roth's chest. "Valen, go charge the gratia stone."

"The stone is full already, Master Roth," Valen replied. "It will crack if any more Passion is applied. The ship seems to be running at maximum efficiency."

The side rail creaked under Roth's grip. "Something is close. Eliza, can you detect anything?"

Eliza closed her eyes and turned her head about as though trying to identify the source of a sound. "Nothing. Not a soul, other than the crews behind our ship."

"Maybe it's just their machines acting up," Sitra pointed out. "They're ancient anyway. If Eliza can't sense anything then there's nothing out there."

The ship gave a great shudder, dropping sharply and sending everyone flailing through the air. Cole's munisica sprang forth out of instinct. He felt one of his bladed feet tear a hole through the sheet cap. He landed roughly on the deck, though unharmed. Sand poured through the tear in the sheet cap, carrying with it a lurid moan that he hoped was just the wind.

"Hold on to something!" the captain bellowed from the upper deck.

A second later the ship pitched backwards, groaning as it climbed nearly straight up. Red lightning flashed in the sandy clouds, silhouetting a gargantuan hand in the murk. It was easily half the size of the Firedancer. Another moan shook the chains on the upper deck.

"Colossus!" Roth boomed.

Crimson lightning flashed again, revealing a mountainous form searching and groping through the sands. The ship lurched faster, speeding up and away from the Colossus. Cole grabbed a loose rope and pulled himself upright, though the ship's ascent was so steep he was looking straight at the floor. Sand continued to pour through the hole in the sheet cap, swirling in a rasping dervish. A moment later the Firedancer breached the surface of the powdery ocean. Oberon greeted them with a warm bouquet of colors.

"Stand clear of the sheet cap!" cried one of the crew.

The membrane rippled and flew to the rear deck as the Firedancer shot forward with another burst of speed. Cole ran to the side, peering over the railing, half expecting a monstrous hand to come out to grab them.

"Point this thing towards Oberon and give it everything you've got!" Roth shouted to the captain.

"You heard him boys and girls!" the captain relayed to his crew. "Get me a strong body on each mast and pull those sails free. Our pretty dancer shan't be scuffing her hull on the sands tonight! Raise her up now!"

Like trained squirrels, the crew bounded up the netting and released the sails. Other sailors worked pulleys, cranked on ratchets, or barked warnings to stay out of the way. A moment later the activity subsided and the Firedancer picked up yet another burst of speed, this time rising up out of the sand entirely.

"Hard port! Hard port!" the captain hollered across the deck.

Following everyone's lead, Cole gripped the handrail and the Firedancer banked sharply to the left. Over the side of the ship a humongous arm breached, swiping down and clipping pieces from the stern. The Firedancer wheeled away from Oberon, only to veer again to dodge another crushing hand. Everywhere the Firedancer turned, another arm erupted from the sands. They were surrounded.

"There's nothing for it!" the captain called down to Roth. "I hope your lot has another plan. We can't keep this up for long."

"Lead them to the shallows. As close to the hard-pack as you can," Roth roared. The ship leaned once more, away from the groping hands.

"They are closing on us," Lileth said with stoic calm. "We should take to the air."

Cole turned, following her eyes. Rising out of the sands behind them were four massive heads, followed by four sets of shoulders and swaying arms. They were so large that they barely appeared to be moving, but they grew larger with every stride. Their legs broke the surface next, sending great walls of sand cascading in front as they lumbered on. As they neared, Cole could see the thousands of charred bodies that comprised their towering figures. He hoped to whatever gods might be listening that Lexy was not among them.

"We're over the hard pack now!" the captain shouted.

"Dismount," Roth barked, leaping off the ship.

The others followed without a word. Cole paused, checking with Goran, making sure his friend was okay. Goran's eyes were ablaze with deadly intent, his brindle fur standing up and running along his back. He was ready. Cole grasped the handrail and threw his legs over, realizing too late that enough Fear had crept up through his bones to stifle his Wisdom. His stomach leaped up to his throat as air whipped past his ears. A heartbeat before colliding with the hard sand, Cole managed to wrestle his feeble Wisdom into submission and slow his descent with magic. He crashed into the hardened dirt, rolling and thrashing to a halt. Dizzy, he put a hand on his knee and stood. He was hurt, but there was no time to assess his injuries. The giants were nearly on them. Goran landed next to him in an explosion of dirt. Holding his ribs, Cole jogged over to the others. Roth was already giving instructions.

"Those of you who fly, get up there and try to take their eyes," he ordered, keeping his stony glare on their quickly approaching enemies. "Goran, Cole, and I will do the groundwork. Cole, do you remember what I told you about the Colossus?"

"There's a priest at its heart. You have to kill him to take it down," Cole said, thinking this was not the time for a pop quiz.

"And you'd better be fully shrouded before diving in." Roth looked to all of them. "Their hearts are protected by a nest of hardened bone that will bite through flesh and armor, which means Cole's the only one who can do it."

"I don't know if I can," Cole stammered. "I hurt myself jumping off the ship and I don't know if I'll be able to control the magic. What if the Rage takes over and I hurt one of you? I can't stop myself once it gets going."

"We'll worry about that after," Roth said. "Right now you're our best shot, so do whatever it is to get yourself good and angry. The rest of you stay out of Cole's way and don't get too close to the-"

"Goran!" Cole cried as his brindle-furred friend darted for the Colossus.

CHAPTER 7

MADNESS DRIPPING

Talin opened his eye, waking to find his wife sleeping next to him. The sight of her was one of his most cherished things in the world. Now however, he wished he could cut out his remaining eye so he'd never have to look at her again. If only he could remove his ears as well so he wouldn't have to hear her whimper. If he were able, he would kill Pineah now, saving her from the torture before she woke. Kreed decided Talin was to be healed enough to use his full complement of magic, but his mind was tainted and tethered, limited to the doorless prison cell that he shared with Pineah. Kreed's dark magic prevented him from harming anyone within its confines, including himself.

Talin slid over to Pineah, longing to stroke her face, but held back for fear of waking her. She had earned some uninterrupted sleep. Instead, he hugged himself and caressed her arms, which had replaced his own. He kissed her fingers, rubbing them over his cheek, her cheek. He looked down at her, sleeping soundly in her cot in momentary solace. He ignored her missing arms and legs, as well as the gap where her cheek had been, focusing instead on her beautiful, whole parts. The surgeon, Florien, had done a neat job at transplanting the pieces, but there was no anesthetic or antibiotics. He seemed to keep those for himself. Talin had watched the surgeries from his own table. Immobile and helpless, he'd begged Pineah to allow him to divulge every secret he knew of The Sill, anything to put an end to the torture. Pineah's will was as iron however, and she'd refused to let him give anything to the enemy.

She was always stronger than he, though she had not been through what he had. She had not suffered as he had. Her surgeries were quick. Florien never did more than what was necessary, never caused her more harm than he needed to. Talin knew she scorned him, disappointment evident in her eyes when he begged to reveal their secrets. She had not been worked on by the Weeping Man. She didn't have to feel Decreath's presence inside her. She had it easy. Talin shook himself, grasping his head. Why did he despise her? Why did he resent her for not having been tortured as badly as he? He was breaking, losing himself. He was going mad.

Talin loved her more than he loved himself. He had loved her from their first lessons together at The Sill. She took his love, as mediocre and inept as it was and loved him right back. She made him more than he deserved to be. Now, Talin was forced to watch his temple desecrated over and over. He was helpless under Kreed's spells, sedated with Fear as Florien took parts from her and fixed them to him. At first he hated her limbs. It was an abomination, a perverse violation of his family and body. He would rather have his rotting stumps than her limbs knitted to him. They were too small and frail, but sooner or later he knew they would be all he had to remember her by. He Hated how her limbs started working as well as his own.

After the surgeries, his munisica, her munisica, exploded with useless Rage as the guards came back again and again. The animals threw themselves at her, not bothering to take turns. They seemed to adore Talin's screams, thrusting all the harder. Talin eventually learned to scream without making a sound. With each passing moment he felt parts of himself die many times over. Parts of him that he would never get back. Fortunately, Kreed was so pleased with his new eyes that he allowed Talin to use his Passion to heal Pineah. Talin was weakest with healing magics, but he was able to take her pain away, pulling it into himself instead. Compared to what he'd been through, her agony was only mildly irritating, easily tolerated. He tried using Wisdom to take her memories of what the guards had done to her, but Kreed's taint prevented him from manipulating her mind.

Talin watched her silently, kissing his fingers, her fingers. Tears somehow fell from his empty eye socket. The music of her breathing was suddenly interrupted by a loud pop. Talin wheeled around, dreading the return of the guards. His heart sank. It was not the guards, but Kreed. The Underkin was at his side.

Before Kreed could speak, Talin dropped to the floor, crawling on his knees to Kreed's feet. "Father Kreed! Please end this! Kill her, I'll do it myself. I'll give you anything! I know the secrets of your enemies, their strategies, their battle plans. I can tell you what they know about you, and what they don't! I can help you win this war! All of it is yours, just let me kill her and I'll reveal everything." Talin's begging broke down into incoherent sobbing.

Kreed bent down, placing an arm around Talin's shoulders. His white suit was as pristine as ever. "Hush now Talin, you mustn't get too hasty. It's unbecoming for a warrior such as yourself. You haven't even asked sweet Pineah for permission to take such liberties with her life. Don't you think she ought to have a say?"

Talin looked up, seeing his and Pineah's eyes looking back through Kreed's face. "Please Father Kreed, let me do it. Let me do it while she still sleeps."

"Perhaps, in time," Kreed said, reaching down with a tender grip and picking up Talin's new hand as though plucking a flower from a garden. "The transplants are taking quite well. Florien has truly outdone himself. What do you think, Habbad?"

The Underkin's sunken eyes fell lazily upon Talin. "Very good, Father Kreed."

"Very good indeed!" Kreed gushed. "But how does it feel? Do you have full sensation in your new hands and feet? What about your cheek?"

Talin pulled his sleeves back, eager to show Kreed, eager to please him. "They work perfectly, Father Kreed. I can even call forth the munisica. They are yours, I am yours, let me use them for you."

"In time, my boy. Though when your training is complete I doubt you'll have need for such crude tools." Kreed squinted and gave Talin a wry smile. "I admit I didn't expect you to make such strides in your training, not at just a few weeks in. Habbad here took a couple cycles to come around, yet here you are, a model student. A prodigy even! A month ago you wouldn't have dreamed of harming sweet Pineah. But look at you now, crawling on hands and knees and begging me to let you slit her throat!" Kreed giggled, clapping his fingertips together. "Not even I could bring myself to put a hair out of place on her pretty head. You are changing before my very eyes, or *your* eyes I should say." Talin averted his gaze. He could no longer bear the weight of Pineah's eye from behind Kreed's lashes.

Kreed seemed to notice his faltering. He clucked his tongue. "Your progress is steady, but you're held back by something, something that's no fault of your own of course. You're not entirely cured of that nasty little virus of yours. It still clings to your heart, weakening and diluting the best parts of you."

Talin gripped Kreed's leg. "What is it, Father Kreed, please tell me!"

Kreed paused, seemingly taken aback by Talin's genuine devotion. His eyes softened as he bit down on his lip, rubbing Talin's back.

"Why, it's your hope of course." Kreed looked down at him with his stolen eyes, one green and one brown. "Your hope is still holding you back. It's preventing you from becoming something greater. Something, *divine*. I can still see it in your eye, when you look at her." Kreed nodded towards Pineah's sleeping form. "You still have hope for her. You have given up hope for yourself, and for that I cannot tell you how proud I am. I *want* you to kill her too, I yearn for it more than words can describe, but you must do it for the right reasons." Kreed's fingers flew to his mouth, and he suddenly looked as if he were about to cry.

"What is it?" Talin begged, holding on to Kreed's pocket as if his life depended upon it. "What is the reason? Let me do it, let me kill her."

Kreed's voice shook. "I'm sorry, my boy. I can't tell you. It's an important part of the training. You must work out that little puzzle for yourself." Kreed ran his fingers lovingly through Talin's hair. "Once you do, you will transcend beyond your suffering."

Talin's face hit the floor, weighed down by an avalanche of sorrow. He had not the energy to tinker with mental puzzles. For that he would need sleep, and how could he sleep when the woman he loved the most was laid bare and broken before him? Kreed was his only salvation. His only way out. The only candle in this endless cavern of Despair.

Kreed sat on the floor with Talin, lifting his head and embracing him like a child. He stroked Talin's face, pushing the tears away. "Embrace the Despair, my son. I know it hurts, but you must pull it into yourself. Let it become you. Take it all, and when you can't take any more, I will unmake you."

Talin writhed on the floor, spitting and wailing like a child as he attempted to rip Pineah's limbs from his body. Kreed's magic halted his fingers, her fingers, before they could do any real damage. Talin had nothing, not even freedom with his own body. Everything had been taken from him.

Talin lay on his back, heaving. Eventually his gasping sobs were stilled by a dull indifference. Voice steady and quiet, he spoke: "I give up. I give in. Father Kreed, take me now. I am yours."

Kreed said not a word, shaking his head slowly back and forth, his eyes clearly stating that Talin's mere devotion wouldn't be enough. He needed more from Talin. He needed to take it all.

Talin sank deeper, pulled by the shadow's edge into the Despair. A moan of tedium slipped from his lips. The sound scared him, cracking his mind further until he found himself in a fit of feathery giggles. This had to be a test. If not, there was no longer any purpose to his life. But he hadn't the energy for a test. Not now, not after all he'd been through. He was so very tired. With every breath he felt more of his sanity dripping out through the ragged cracks in his skull. His patience and vitality trickled out soon afterwards. He was losing parts of himself. Talin could feel his magic in the darkness. It was different, however, as though twisted and distorted through a new lens. He used the grotesque magic to wring his very soul, eking out every facet of his pained existence. The process was excruciating, but after a few heaves, he expelled his pride, his comfort, his dignity. With another good push he vomited out his ability to love. He almost lost his sense of who he was. These parts did not go gently, as they were never meant to be separated from the soul. Out they went, screaming and bleeding, dragged by the fresh shadows of his mind. The pain rose to an unacceptable volume, then rose again. The agony ascended until it was no longer a sensation, but a state of being. The tides waxed and roiled, building to a crescendo of colors and smells that assaulted his every nerve and memory.

Somewhere in the madness, a shard of clarity made itself known, or perhaps he merely imagined it. It was the only coherent thought he was capable of, so he clung to it as a child clinging to a parent after waking from a nightmare.

Pineah.

She had done this to him. She hadn't allowed him to stop it, even though it would have been all too easy. He could have feigned his betrayal, lied about his knowledge of The Sill, but not even that was good enough for her. Pineah was a liability; she got herself stuck here, allowed herself to be used against ordering her to stay home. Even now she slumbered peacefully while he suffered. She was no comfort in this room, nor had she been a comfort in life before his capture. She had done nothing for him in the arms of the enemy, no word of solace, no promise of escape. She hadn't even given him a shred of gratitude for his sacrifices. Her mock-lovery did nothing to help see him through his ordeals. She had done nothing other than present herself as a trophy for the enemy. The only memory of her that would live on would be her cold limbs that had been foisted onto him. The wretched whore hadn't even cried out when the guards came for her after the second time. She had indulged in their beasting.

Talin drunkenly brought himself to his feet, her feet. He wobbled, searching for her in the haze of his Despair. He worried he couldn't find her, though part of him wished he never would. The cell was small however, and it didn't take long for him to find her woven auburn hair, her inviting curves. The sight of her was startling, not because of what he must do, but because she was wide awake and staring back at him. Her sunken, missing eye no longer pained him, but her other eye did. She looked at him with such supreme accusation that he felt himself laid naked before her, all his shame and weakness open to her freezing judgment.

"Talin, my love, what have you become?" Pineah whimpered with her whore's mouth.

Talin's heart fell, though the sensation had lost all meaning to him, for his heart simply wasn't there. He no longer had those parts of him that cared about Pineah's squabbling. Her judgment. In fact, he didn't care much about anything. In the quiet of his indifference, something began to fill the voids. It was sweltering, oppressive, and hellishly strong. He could hold onto it, trust it, use it.

His Hatred birthed itself, one facet at a time. Where he felt weak, the Hatred filled him with power. Where he felt shame, the Hatred lit infernos of pride. Where he felt lost, the Hatred forged his will into white-hot conviction. Talin had burned himself to a barren field of scabs and sinew, rising from the ashes as the phoenix of suffering.

Pineah opened her mouth, but stopped herself, instead focusing her eyes elsewhere. A peaceful acceptance softened her features, as though her mind was apart from the nightmare before her.

Talin's munisica, her munisica, creaked and stretched, elongating and twitching with anticipation. His first step was timid, but the intent was clear. The fact that Kreed's magic hadn't stopped him was not lost on him. His next step was confident and stolid. He stood over Pineah, claws trembling at his sides. She was the final piece of the puzzle. After she slid into place, she would fall away and he would be rid of his most crippling weakness; Hope.

Kreed backed away, careful not to make a sound. "Come, Habbad. We're being rude."

Habbad's eyes were glued to the scene before him. Kreed noticed something dark and beautiful gleaming in his little eyes. With a gentle nudging, Kreed led him out of the prison cell.

"But what if he actually does it?" Habbad asked after they popped through the wall. His wrinkled face soured with disappointment.

Kreed smiled. His young protégé had been making him smile more and more of late. "He just might. He is making tremendous strides in his training. With any luck he'll be a different person when next we meet." Kreed waved a hand, dismissing the guards who were lined up outside the cell. "Not today, boys." The guards wilted, looking like starving men who had been denied dinner right at the table.

"But what if we miss it? Or what if he doesn't do it?" Habbad asked, jogging to keep up. "It's important, is it not? I feel I need to see it. For my own training."

Kreed hummed with pride. Such a sweet boy. Kreed slowed his pace and mussed Habbad's hair. "Young Talin is going through the most trying time of his life. The poor man is contemplating killing the person he loves most in this world. It's very personal. We've no right intruding on such an intimate moment. If he goes through with it then we'll find out tomorrow. If not, then his training continues. Think him an artist, a painter if you will. This is his first time. He's painting a one-of-a-kind masterpiece, and he knows it. You can't hover over his shoulder, rushing him and chucking your own ideas at him, not as he bares his very soul to the canvas. You can inspire him, but you cannot do it for him. It must be done with his own hands or not at all. And don't you worry yourself over your own training, Master Habbad. Trust in me. You are right where you should be. You do trust me, don't you?"

Habbad looked as if he wasn't finished making his case. He set his eyes down the dank hallway, resuming his look of stony indifference. "Of course, Father Kreed. I trust you with my life."

"Good boy," Kreed said, steering the two of them up a steep set of stairs. He was winded before he got to the top. "Habbad," he breathed, "Why is it you want to see Talin kill his wife? That is a very nasty thing to want to see."

Habbad floated to the top of the stairs, green light emanating from his palms and feet. "I...I am not quite sure. I suppose I want to see him do it because I know how he feels. If I could, I would have killed my parents...and Lexy. I would have done anything to stop them from hurting. It killed me inside, to witness their pain and not have the strength to end it. I want to see him do what I could not."

Kreed finally caught his breath. He planted a warm hand on Habbad's shoulder. "Do you resent me for what I did to your family?"

Habbad's stoic mask darkened a shade. "I do not resent you, Father Kreed. You only killed the weakest parts of me. I'm stronger for your lessons."

Kreed raised an eyebrow, chuckling though a grin. "And you deserved it, didn't you. You little scoundrel."

The tiniest smile cracked Habbad's grumpy face. "I know I did. I'm sorry for disappointing you so. Will you ever forgive me?"

"I forgive you, my son, but I will never forget. Ever." Kreed bored his stolen eyes into Habbad's. "Ah, Corpulants take me. I never could stay angry with you, Habbad. I've always had a soft spot for you." He gave Habbad's shoulder a squeeze and continued walking.

Kreed saw Habbad's mind working through his lined brow. He decided to give the boy a moment to ponder as they worked their way out of the dingy prison. The hall eventually opened up into a dimly lit atrium, which looked as if its walls and broken statues had survived an age and several fires without a proper cleaning. It was a hideous sight, unfit for use. The building ought to be condemned. Kreed had to stop his mind from drafting the decrees before he got too far. He couldn't shut the place down; where else would he put his prisoners? It was an awful shame that none of the Underkin could be spared. He was desperate for a labor force. A few of those little blighters could have the whole room shining within the hour. In the morning he would send his emissaries to Amoskeag and Faron to broker a trade for more Underkin, if they had any left that was.

They popped through the main door, stepping out into the balmy air and crooked streets of Costas's Infinity District.

"You do seem to take favor with me," Habbad said, eyeing Kreed's misshapen bone-creature, Baedine. She waited obediently for them at the nearest light post. "I must be special. I'm the only Underkin left in Costas. Perhaps even the world. Why is it that you kept me around? The magic that you've taught me is practical and powerful, but you must have priests who are better spell casters than me." Habbad swerved to the opposite side of Kreed when they neared Baedine.

Kreed sucked on his lip. The boy was too smart for his own good. He let the question hang for a moment. "Come Baedine, that's a good girl," Kreed cooed to the nightmarish creature. He tried to whistle, but air rushed through his broken teeth.

Baedine's head bobbed as she whined and skittered over to Kreed, licking his hand. The creature's hobbled framework of bones and open flesh was only half covered with skin. She had taken to eating her own pelt when her next meal didn't come soon enough. She was absolutely repulsive and smelled like a bad wound, but she was the only thing left of his sister. Kreed knew that Habbad abhorred her, though the boy would never say it aloud. The repulsion was not entirely unfounded. Habbad's Hatred for Baedine was matched equally by her desire to tear at him with those broken rib bones that were her teeth.

After walking a few blocks, Kreed finally found words delicate enough to answer Habbad's question. "You are special indeed, Habbad, and I would know. I've been inside more minds than the stars in our skies. However, you have a certain quality inside of you that is very hard to find. This quality is not exclusive to you, but in your case it's an untapped ocean the likes of which I've never seen. It's potent, yet entirely virgin and pure. The fact that you have yet to discover it on your own is no small miracle, given the trials that you've survived. And before you ask, the answer is no. I won't reveal what this quality is, or the purpose of your training. Just as our friend Talin is a painter, you are a sculptor. I'll cut out my own heart before I meddle with your life's work. I will give you one little hint, however. I intend you to be my equal before we are through."

Habbad gazed up at Kreed, utter disbelief etched on his face. "But, how is that possible? You've countless cycles of knowledge and experience. I couldn't hope to equal you in any field of magic, or anything else come to think of it."

Kreed decided to let this question stand unanswered. Both his students were progressing rapidly. Too much too soon and everything would be spoiled. He swooped down and plucked Habbad up, plopping him on his shoulder. "Ah Habbad, I do grow weary of this heavy talk. What do you say we take a turn through the Valley District on our way home? You're overdue for a change of wardrobe. I'd like to see how debonair you'd look in a proper suit. You are my first protégé after all."

CHAPTER 8

DESERT TITANS

"Goran stop! They'll kill you!" Cole's voice broke over the moaning desert wind. He tried forcing Goran's attention through their bond, but Goran's blood-lust was absolute. Cole had never seen the mirak move so fast.

"He'll set the pace then," Roth said, his eyes darkening with a foreboding gloom as if he knew they were charging death. "What are you all hesitating for? Move your hides before I rip them off!"

Even under the shadow of four of the most titanic enemies they had ever encountered, the unit Feared their ancient Master above all else. Emerald wings cut through the wind and munisica burst from their sheaths as the unit sprung to action, leaving Cole and Roth on the ground.

"Don't let them grab you!" Roth roared into the sky. He dropped his gaze, giving Cole a serious look. "Human, you better be ready for the fight of your life. Get that Rage going."

Cole did not hesitate. While the Colossi were certainly the biggest threats, they were not the immediate one. Even in battle Cole knew Roth wouldn't tolerate hesitation. He plodded over the crusty dirt, clutching his broken ribs as Roth kept pace slightly behind him. If only Eliza or Lileth could have healed him before they took off. The rising pain made it exponentially more difficult to focus on any sort of magic. He wasn't ready for the fight of his life. He wasn't even ready to fight off a stiff breeze at this point. At the moment he felt like a very ordinary human limping towards four impossible nightmares. He called for his Rage, demanding it, but the magic wouldn't flow. His hands were bare and his naked feet hurt on the rough crust.

Goran met the smallest Colossus; the mirak was only half the height of its shin. He flew like a brindle missile, scaling the giant's leg, running up its side and around its torso. Goran didn't waste a movement. He constantly tore parts from the Colossus, littering the ground with a steady rain of blackened limbs. The titan struck with its massive fists, but the mirak was too quick, darting and swinging all over its body. The damage was relatively minor, but if Goran had enough time it looked like he would peel the whole thing apart like a rotten onion.

Seeing that Goran was handling himself, the others flew past the first Colossus and assaulted the other three. Cole couldn't tell which set of green wings belonged to whom, but he guessed Sitra to be the one spending entirely too much time perched on the face of one Colossus. She simply wasn't as fast or as perceptive as Goran. Time and time again she narrowly missed being snatched by fingers larger than the whole of her body.

Cole was very close now, but he felt no closer to being any more than a frail liability. Slowed by his injuries and unaided by magic, it was all he could do to keep up his sprint. He could hear Roth's footsteps thundering beside him and feel the disappointment in his glare.

Cole neared Goran's Colossus, Fear taking his heart and thrashing it against his cracked ribs like a dog shaking a rat. He was at its feet now, jumping over the charred limbs of the chosen that Goran had ripped off. They writhed with jerky motions, looking as though they were trying to reassemble themselves. Cole knew this was the time to act, but he hadn't the slightest idea what to do without his magic. Fear froze him in place. He winced, dreading punishment from Roth, but his Master lunged over him, diving headfirst into the belly of the Colossus.

"Roth don't!" Cole screamed, his voice weak with horror. Roth must have been going for the priest, but he wasn't entirely shrouded. He would be torn apart by the hardened bone-nest in the giant's belly.

Cole berated himself, his Rage finally flickering into a little candle that melted his Fear. His friends were risking their lives, missing death by an inch here, a fraction of a second there. But here he was, cowering in his enemy's shadow and indulging in a few cracked bones and bruises. Now was the time to act, he could finally feel it.

A massive hand twisted through the wind, trying to reach Goran. The other sped like a charging elephant towards Roth, who was too busy tearing at the titan's belly to notice. The fist rushed closer and Cole readied himself to jump. He knew his Rage wouldn't carry him that high yet. The magic simply hadn't boiled up enough. He looked to one of the titan's legs instead, imagining how he would scale it.

Like a diving falcon Goran appeared from nowhere, crashing into the arm that was only feet from Roth. Goran tore into the giant's wrist with terrifying violence, his roar so loud that Cole had to clap his hands over his ears. Cole was suddenly glad to be on the ground. Goran was so lost in his own Rage that Cole wasn't entirely confident his friend was capable of distinguishing between friend and foe.

With a horrible wet sound, the hand of the Colossus ripped free from its arm, landing in a heap in front of Cole. The grisly sight froze him with morbid curiosity as a sickening concept struck him in the gut. Countless chosen, all Underkin, made up the body of the Colossus. The more he looked the more he saw. Making up the palm of the hand were dozens of raw torsos, while its fingers were twisted braids of burnt arms, ending in claws made from thousands of fingers sharpened to the bone. Cole could see crispy ribs jerking in and out, drawing ragged breaths through whatever hole they were breathing from. The huge fingers groped at the open air, yearning for anything to come within their grasp. Worst of all was the stench. The burnt flesh reeked of unwholesome rot and excrement; the breath of a thousand corpses.

A second later there was a muffled scream that Cole recognized from Costas. It was the fatal scream of one greeting death. It came from somewhere around the belly of the Colossus, followed by a sudden quiet. The hand in front of Cole disintegrated into a loose pile of unmoving body parts. Other segments fell around Cole, legs at first, then a torrent of limbs and whole corpses. Throwing an arm above him, Cole chanced a glance at Roth, but he was no longer visible in the steady hail of meat. The entire Colossus was coming undone. Cole's munisica rushed out, digging into the dirt as he kicked his way to safety. He felt a flutter of relief as Goran came trotting around the collapsing mountain, his ruby eyes scanning for threats among the building rubble. When the final pieces fell Cole ran to the base of the pile, heaving bodies out of the way. Roth was still nowhere to be found.

Frustration rising with his panic, Cole tried using Wisdom to move some of the bodies, but he could only manage to levitate one at a time.

"Dammit Roth! Where the hell are you?" Cole bellowed, committing more of himself to his Rage. His munisica stretched and his obsidian shroud crawled farther up his arms. As the strength surged, so did his need for action. The tiny bodies of the Underkin flew behind him as he dug into the pile. Somewhere in the back of Cole's mind he could hear Lexy's unbridled laughter and see her dancing in the starlight. He did not want to find her. His only consolation was that her body would likely be immolated beyond all recognition.

The pile gave a sudden lurch as Cole heard a familiar growl from its center. Holding his breath, Cole turned his head and listened again. Eyes snapping wide, he leapt backward as a portion of the mountain exploded, creating a hail of limp Underkin. Roth crawled out of the crevice with the head of an Aenerian woman in his clawed hand. Cole hoped the sheen of crimson on his skin was only a trick of the moonlight, but as Roth approached, the severity of his wounds became apparent. Where his shroud had not protected him, deep gouges and wide swaths of skin were rent like torn paper. An alarming amount of blood poured freely from the injuries, soaking the dusty ground at his feet.

"Here," Roth grunted as he threw the severed head at Cole's feet. "Next time you better do more than stand there and piss yourself."

Cole peered around Roth, taking in the dark hillock of Underkin behind him. At the core of the pile was the nest of black bones, woven in an unforgiving pattern of spikes and blades.

"Master Roth," Cole said, his voice shaking with worry as he watched the pool at Roth's feet grow. "Let me heal you. You're losing a lot of blood."

Roth held Cole in a glare. Whether his voice was quiet with deadly Rage or fatal injuries Cole couldn't tell. "I don't remember begging for your sympathies. I only ask that you do your job. Now go. There are three more to take care of. Go before Goran makes it to the next one."

Cole glanced around. Goran had already set off. He swallowed his shame and shot after the mirak. Roth was one of the most powerful Aenerians on the planet, but even he couldn't survive injuries like that for very long. Perhaps he knew he was too far gone and sent Cole away so he wouldn't watch him die. It would be his fault if Roth bled out. He should have done what he was told, but his Fear had held him back. He was still afraid to loose the entirety of his Rage. It felt like letting a rabid dog off the leash with children around. While fully shrouded he'd almost killed his friends back in Costas, and had nearly violated a soul fly. Even when Milette had attacked him back at King Auger's he'd had to extinguish his Rage immediately so it wouldn't consume him. He was afraid of his Rage, but what scared him most wasn't the thought of hurting his friends. He was scared of how much he liked it.

Shuddering at the thought, Cole ground his teeth and dug in with his munisica, accelerating far beyond his normal speed. He let the Rage boil. Closing the gap to the next Colossus, he saw Goran already at its feet. Cole veered off to the left, away from Goran towards a larger Colossus that the unit had yet to engage. If he were to lose control then he'd rather do it away from others. Goran would have to handle himself. Before his Rage could block it, he opened his heart and thoughts to Eliza, letting his Passion flow.

His Rage surged through the Passion link. *"Friend of my heart, I'm headed for the largest Colossus. Do you see me?"*

Eliza shifted her mood to a tone that soothed Cole. *"I see you. I'm right above, brother of my soul."*

"No!" Cole pleaded. *"You have to stay away. Keep the others away as well. I'm going to let the Rage take me. All of me."*

Her compassion washed over him like dancing autumn leaves. *"I understand. I will do as you ask, but is it the only way?"*

Cole strummed the link with his guilt. *"It is...I'm sorry."*

"Do not feel sorry for me," Eliza replied with a melody of hardened steel. *"You will have to live with whatever happens. I will be there when you emerge from the other side."*

"Thank you. Roth is hurt bad. Real bad." Cole impressed his urgency into every syllable.

A shadow fell over Eliza's heart. *"I felt him tearing himself apart to get to the priest. I will do what I can for the Bonebreaker. Now, go do what you can for that abomination. Goodbye, Cole."*

Cole felt her leave his mind entirely, severing the link. The abrupt silence was unnerving. He had always had some ambient thought or trickling emotion coming from either her or Goran. Now all he could hear was his steady breath and the rapid crunching of his munisica stabbing into the hard-pack. The shroud had nearly reached his abdomen, his Rage roiling into an inferno that fueled his every movement and desire. He was running faster than he had ever run in his life, yet he accelerated even more as his Rage broke free of its chains. Cole was dimly aware of his Morthainian armor coming apart at the seams, tearing and breaking in between his thighs and the gaps of his armpits. The force and friction were too great. His body was now beyond the limits of the physical. He was Rage.

Free of its prison, the red magic rushed up out of Cole, greeting the world with fire and fury. Cole looked at the scene before him in a new light. A savage lens revealed to him the bountiful opportunities for physical destruction, the utter dominance of his environment. He had real enemies, real outlets, and the biggest of the lot was right in front of him.

The mental calculation took but a flicker of thought. Cole slowed himself and planted his munisica, shooting straight for the titan's head. Dusty wind whistled through his bladed hair as he stretched his arms in front of him. The target couldn't come soon enough. The lumbering Colossus was entirely unaware of Cole as he tore through the air like a shrouded spear. A few of the titan's eyes seemed to register his approach, but the vast majority lolled about, weak and useless. Cole let out a snarling grin. This was going to be too easy. He broke into the titan's head, barely halfway through when he knew he was moving too fast. Cole spread his arms, slowing himself with the mass around him. He emerged from the other side amongst a rotten mist. It seemed to take a lifetime for him to reach the ground, his Rage igniting every part of his soul as he descended, revealing the next target to him.

As Cole landed, he twisted in the dirt and shot towards the Colossus once more, this time aiming for a leg. He dove through the limb, this time slowed by a core of woven bone that was the giant's femur. The bone slowed him, but Cole smashed his way through, eager for more. The giant's leg exploded around him, releasing him back into the desert. Cole landed, this time darting away from the Colossus so he could see his work. He allowed himself a moment to indulge in the weakness of his enemy. The Colossus teetered like a hacked tree, not yet aware of its severed leg as its hands flew towards the remains of its head. The titan's girth met the ground with a shuddering report, staggering the two smaller Colossus.

Cole's Rage grew, and so did his desire. The violence was simple and beautiful, but he only just had a taste. He wanted more, needed more. He set his blackened eyes for the chest of his crippled enemy, where his Rage-sharpened ears could hear the muffled cries and panicked heart of a weak spirit.

"I CAN HEAR YOU IN THERE!" Cole roared at the torso. "GET OUT HERE AND LET ME TASTE YOUR WEAKNESS!"

The Colossus sat halfway up on its elbow, its eyeless head twisting and searching as a fist the size of a small house smashed blindly at the ground.

Cole dodged casually to the side as the Colossus struck at him. He was close enough now he could hear the words from the priest inside.

"It's him! The human, he is on me now! Help me you dithering idiots!"

Cole's curiosity drew his eyes to the other giants. The titans ceased their fighting and began sprinting towards Cole.

"I know I mustn't kill him, but he's about to kill me! The rumors are true, we should not have come alone."

"WHAT RUMORS?" Cole bellowed, "WHAT ARE YOU TALKING ABOUT? ANSWER ME!" He chopped his munisica across the layer of Underkin, scooping off broken hunks.

The priest's only response was a frightened squeal that itched at Cole's munisica. Cole wanted nothing more than to extinguish that sound. Anything capable of such a pathetic noise deserved to be killed. Cole's momentary curiosity was suddenly smothered by a need for the priest's head. He cleaved off layer after layer, working himself into a frenzy as the Colossus struggled. Blinded by his growing Rage, Cole didn't notice the giant hand sweep down and grab him, but then again he didn't have to. The hand came apart as easily as the chest, as though the Colossus had just stuck its arm into a running blender. With a satisfying crunch, Cole found the walls of the bone nest.

The Colossus stopped moving, limbs crashing like dead weights against the ground. Cole slashed away the final pieces of the chosen before sinking his claws deep into the bone nest. He gave a good yank, but the armor was thick and held fast. Cole's savage grin deepened. It was about time he found something that didn't simply fall apart under his munisica. He stabbed his feet into the side of the nest, granting him the necessary leverage. Growling, he let the Rage grow, giving more and more of himself until he no longer remembered who he was, only what he needed to do. Inside the walls of the nest his munisica grew like bladed roots, cutting through the bone as if it were rotten wood. Cole heaved, ripping off a large portion and sending it skipping over the hardened dirt.

The priest coughed, choking on the desert dust. His naked body was covered in soggy sheets of pale skin, as though he'd spent his entire life in a well underground. Ropes of white tendon ran from the walls of his cage, suspending him in the center away from the sharpened spikes. A thick bundle of nerves dangled over him, connecting to the base of his skull. There was a bloody ring around his mouth where pinkish strips still clung to a broken tube of flesh that Cole had just torn off.

The priest spat something unintelligible as he thrashed without effect in his morbid machine. As Cole reached his bladed hand into the bone nest, the priest cut his arms free with sizzling purple light from his fingertips. Gritting his teeth, the priest flung his hands towards Cole and showered him in a hail of violet needles. The spell burned holes through what was left of his Morthainian armor before shattering against the shroud. Cole's bladed hand continued its descent. Taking his time, Cole sank his munisica into the priest's chest, careful to avoid his vital organs. Savoring his cries of pain, Cole pulled the priest free, snapping the tendons and nerves that held him in place and dragging him into the open air. The priest screamed as if he were being torn in half as the bundle of nerves snapped from his skull. Cole leapt from the disintegrating Colossus, throwing the priest out onto the ground. The priest rolled to a stop, soggy skin caking with dirt as he clutched his pierced chest. Cole waited, granting the priest a few precious seconds to catch his leaking breath. As Cole had hoped, the priest cast his hands out, flinging another spell at him. Dark, bloody flecks exploded from the priest's palms, covering Cole from head to toe. Cole recognized the rank fragrance of Despair, but the wicked magic evaporated from him like evening dew before a bonfire.

"Sorronis, take me," the priest murmured, placing his palms against the sides of his head. There was a flash of violet light and the priest fell lifeless to the dirt.

Cole stomped the ground, furious that he could no longer make his enemy suffer for his weakness. He needed to kill. To dominate. The Rage demanded it. He turned his burning gaze to the two remaining Colossi that still lumbered towards him. The priests within would not get a chance for such cowardice. He would kill them more quickly.

They were smaller than the one he'd just defeated, but perhaps together they would prove a worthy outlet for his Rage. They drew near enough to shake the ground. Cole readied himself, but then huge chunks of their torsos suddenly broke apart, followed by the distant sounds of cannon fire. Cole wheeled around, his sharpened eyes catching the flapping of velvety sails and twinkling of yet more glass missiles tearing through the air. The Colossi were hit again, this time in the legs. They tripped over themselves and fell with an explosion of dust. Cole growled, his munisica aching for action. Who would dare strike at his enemies before he had a chance to tear at them? He set his blackened eyes for the ships. The Colossi could wait.

Cole shot off across the desert, a blurred shadow of need and violence. He was barely halfway to the ships when he found himself floating in midair, his munisica kicking out at nothing. Thrashing and roaring into the night, he felt his momentum slow as he was raised into the sky. Cole's Rage flared, incensed by the futility of the situation. A woman with rippling emerald wings hovered into his view. If only she were a little closer. His munisica thirsted for her flesh. She said something, though her words went unheard. Cole didn't want her words, he wanted her dead. There was a tug at his insides as some invisible force brought him to her. Before he knew it her arms and legs were wrapped around him, her body pressed tight against his. Cole's munisica twitched, eager to bury themselves in her back. He flexed, feeling her grip yield and slip. He took his time, savoring her weakness.

Something then happened that gave him pause. Her mouth was on his armored lips, kissing him. Even through his shroud he could feel how soft she was. Her touch was as soothing as it was disarming. Before he knew it, Cole's Rage was doused.

As if he were waking from a daydream, the bloody lens of Rage lifted from his eyes. Lileth was in his arms.

"Welcome back," she said, pulling her lips from his.

"Lileth," Cole mumbled, "I'm so sorry. I almost killed..."

She hugged him. "But you didn't. The Morthainian navy is making short work of the remaining Colossi. Look." She twisted them around so Cole could see the titans falling to the naval artillery.

"I wasn't talking about the stupid ships," Cole said, swallowing back hot shame. "I almost killed *you*...I wanted to. I didn't even know who you were."

"But you didn't," she repeated, her voice melting the last bits of Rage from his core. "At least I found a way to defuse you. You were terrifying. You felled the largest Colossus in under half a minute. I shudder to think how long it would take you to disassemble the entire Morthainian navy."

"Don't worry, I'm not going to lose it again." Cole went rigid in her arms. "I couldn't stop myself. It felt too good. I won't let it take me again."

"I hope you do." Lileth gazed down at him with a sly grin. "Your Rage is a part of you, and no part can be ignored forever. Acquaint yourself with it. I will be there to douse your fire should it burn too hot."

"But that's dangerous," Cole mumbled, not knowing what else to say. He thought every day about kissing Lileth, but not like this. It would have been all too easy to maim her with his claws. If not for his Rage wanting to give her a chance to attack him, he would have pulled her in half. There would have been no one there to stop him or hold him accountable, not until his Rage finally subsided. If it ever did.

"Do not dwell on it." She gave him a swift peck on the cheek, stunning him. "You should rejoice, this is our first victory as a unit thanks to you. Even Roth wasn't a match for all four of them."

Cole's heart sank. "Where is Roth? He was hurt real bad after he took down the first one."

"Eliza is tending to him," she said, lowering them back to the ground.

Cole shut his eyes. He tried to reconnect with Eliza, but the link was severed. He could feel Goran's familiar presence, however. The mirak's bloodlust had relaxed enough for Cole to worm his way through, though he approached his friend's mind with caution. Goran acknowledged him, giving Cole's consciousness a solid bump. Cole impressed the danger of the artillery, telling Goran to stay away from the Colossi. Goran responded with another bump.

Cole's bare feet clapped to the dirt as Lileth released him. He turned to the Colossi. They were both on their backs but still moving. "We should go finish off the priests. I think the Colossi can remake themselves. Goran took an entire hand off of one and it kept moving around. I saw other parts crawling around and knitting themselves back together. Once the priest died the whole thing went still though."

"Shall I carry you or are you up for a little jog?" she asked, eyeing Cole's bare feet and hesitance. "Do not fret, I will levitate you should your Rage consume you."

Cole reluctantly drew his munisica, halting his Rage before the shroud could inch past his wrists and ankles. Their eyes met and Cole set off with a nod. Lileth pulled ahead, encouraging Cole to use more of his Rage, but he refused.

"Goran, get off that thing!" Cole hollered before turning to Lileth. "I told him to stay away! Those guns will tear right through him."

Goran was perched on the chest of one Colossus, snapping pieces from the bone nest with his sweeping canines. Valen and Sitra stood nearby.

"The Morthainian ships have ceased fire. I believe they are on their way over," Valen called, trotting over with Sitra.

"I wondered when we'd see your mean side again." Sitra grinned, clinking her munisica against Cole's. "You'll have to show me how you do that."

"I don't think so," Cole said, embarrassment flushing his cheeks. "I Hate it. It makes me forget who I am. I almost killed Lileth again. That much Rage isn't good for anyone. Roth doesn't even shroud himself fully."

"That's because he can't. The old man's on his way over now." Sitra's eyes sharpened with worry. "I thought Liza patched him up."

Cole twisted around, seeing Roth in a gimping run with Eliza at his side. "That first Colossus nearly killed him. I'm surprised to see him standing at all."

Roth skidded to a halt while Eliza hovered closer to him, glancing sideways at his wounds. Thin, membranous sheets of new skin draped over his wounds. The patched skin looked as though it would break loose at the slightest prodding.

Roth ignored their looks of concern. "Are the priests dead yet?"

As if in answer, a vicious barking came from Goran. The unit turned as the mirak wrenched a final piece of bone free. A piercing scream rang from the bone nest, only to be cut short as Goran plunged his head into its depths. The body of the Colossus disintegrated into hundreds of charred Underkin. Goran's white mohawk was covered in blood, looking like a brush dipped in crimson paint. The mirak wasted no time jumping off and galloping for the final Colossus.

Valen sprang into the air, his jade wings cutting through the dust and wind like swords. He alighted on the torso of the Colossus before Goran reached it. Valen raised his hands into the air, his munisica and wings receding entirely as his whole body became enveloped in an emerald glow. Tiny sparks of Wisdom swirled in between his outstretched arms, coalescing into a crystalline spear longer than he was tall. He snapped his arms down, and the spear shot into the Colossus. The titan fell apart as Valen's wings dissolved. He landed rough and ran back to the unit, swaying drunkenly from the exertion of his Wisdom.

"That last one sure put up a fight," Sitra said with a chuckle as she kicked at a blackened limb that rolled too close. "Are the chosen dead for good now that the priests are gone?"

Roth's bladed hair whipped across his shoulders as he scanned the desert. "That's not the last one. There's another one out there somewhere. The battle overlays showed five Colossi. If we don't kill that last priest then the slimeball will cannibalize the others. The Colossi we just fought were toddlers compared to what they can grow into."

"So they're still not dead?" Cole asked. "Can't we do anything for them?"

"The chosen cannot die," Roth grunted. "It's best to crush them into dust so that their bodies can no longer be used. We can break them; however, their ruined spirits will linger on, haunting and poisoning our world. Alvani was working on a way to free them before you all set off for Costas. Too bad she didn't finish it. I'd wager the Underkin from the Costas's Devotion were used against us tonight." He sniffed the air, lips curling. "You can smell the Hatred coming off them. These things are just waiting to get scooped up by one of Sorronis's priests. Auger better dispose of them soon."

The unit mulled around, assessing their injuries and taking turns healing Roth's. Roth flat out refused their help at first, but Eliza persisted, convincing him that it would be good training. Try as they might, however, they were unable to heal him completely. When Cole took his turn, his Passion revealed to him just how badly Roth had been hurt. How the Bonebreaker had managed to survive was a mystery.

A few minutes later the Firedancer pulled up beside them, hovering several feet over the hardened dirt. A dozen other ships circled not far off, each deck gun scanning the desert. With Cole's encouragement Goran leaped up onto the Firedancer while the rest of the unit followed suit. Still disgusted by his Rage, Cole used Wisdom to carry himself up to the top deck.

"Never in all my cycles have I seen such nightmares," the Fire-dancer's captain spat into the wind. He sprinted down the stairs to greet them. "Boil my bones if you didn't make short work of them though. Watched the whole thing through our scopes. Which one of you took the big one down by your damned self?"

"That would be our Rage Master, the little guy right here," Sitra said, and clapped her clawed hand over Cole's shoulders, buckling his knees. "He doesn't look like much, but he's got himself an awful temper."

The captain's jaw swung open. "The human! You're kidding me!"

"Enough!" Roth barked, startling them. "Get us out of here, now. Point this log at Oberon and give it everything you have. Can you communicate with Morthain from here?"

The captain snapped to attention. "Yes, King Roth. Since your lot powered up the gratia stones all sorts of equipment has fired up. The boys just got the relay resonators working not ten minutes ago."

"Send word to King Auger that there's another Colossus out there. And these chosen need to be dealt with before Sorronis's minions come for them," Roth ordered, motioning towards the blackened hills behind him.

"As you say, King Roth." The captain turned and disappeared through a door to the lower deck.

The Firedancer picked up speed, banking towards Oberon and bringing them back over the powdery ocean. Roth and Valen remained vigilant, each warrior climbing a mast to a separate crow's nest for a better view. Cole took a seat up against Goran's flank, listening to the steady thrum of his wild heart. Lileth joined him, her shoulder leaning against his as she gave him a warm grin. Cole's chest swarmed with butterflies and he felt as though he were a foot taller. Something was off, however. As he glanced down at his body, a confusing, disorienting sensation came over him. He did not just *feel* taller, he *was* taller. His eyes were now level with Lileth's chest and his ruined armor was far too small.

"See something interesting?" she asked, grinning.

Cole stuttered, tearing his eyes away from her chest. "S-sorry, I just...I think I just went through another growth spurt. I'm taller than I was when we were in King Auger's house."

"You are taller than you were twenty minutes ago." She looked him up and down. "It seems as if your Rage is encouraging your growth."

Cole shifted uncomfortably as she looked him over. His armor was tattered with dozens of holes, some of which were very revealing. "Roth says the Rage isn't the reason I'm growing, though it definitely feels like it's helping me along. It's got to be something though, some kind of magic. I must have grown a foot taller since I left Earth. Humans can't grow that fast. Do you think Chiron might have an idea?" Cole asked, leaning back and gazing up at Oberon's twisting colors.

Lileth remained unusually silent.

"Yeah he probably doesn't know either. I wonder if Kreed knows. He mentioned that there was something special about me in Costas. I heard one of the priests talking about me from inside the Colossus. I wish I'd had the sense to keep him alive and question him. Maybe take myself another prisoner, eh?" Cole laughed, poking Lileth with his elbow.

She still didn't say a word.

"What's with the silent treatment? You okay?" he asked.

Lileth squinted out into the sands. Her look of confusion bloomed into open horror as her eyes snapped wide.

"Colossus!" Roth bellowed from above.

The stench of burnt meat stung Cole's nostrils as his stomach churned. Cole jumped to his feet, running over to the side of the deck. A dark mountain rose steadily from the powder. The fifth Colossus had finally arrived.

"At least it's smaller than the others," Sitra called out over the wind. "Come on, let's go give it hell before their navy takes all the fun."

Roth landed on the deck, splintering the wood. He approached the balustrade, shaking his head with a look of grim defeat. "I was wrong. That's an Alpha Colossus."

"That's not the whole Colossus. That's only its head." Eliza whimpered. She looked as if she were about to vomit.

Cole rose to his feet, rubbing Wisdom into his eyes to sharpen his vision. From several miles away, what he took to be an entire Colossus was soon joined by two broad shoulders and arms. It was impossible. The figure rising out of the sands was larger than any single object

Cole had ever seen. This Colossus was not only bigger than the others, but faster and more agile. The others were clumsy children compared to this behemoth. The Colossus felt the edge of the hard packed dirt with its hands, then hoisted itself up with alarming grace. A thunderous report of artillery fire broke out from the navy, though Cole couldn't make out any damage to the Colossus. It was simply too large.

The titan's head snapped towards a ship that had fired from at least a mile away. With impossible speed it covered the distance in several bounding strides. It paused over the ship and cocked its head, as if surprised by its own quickness.

With sickening Fear bubbling up his spine, Cole realized none of them were safe. If the giant could close such a gap in just a few steps, then it would be all too easy for it to pick apart the entire navy. Their only hope was that it wouldn't notice the Firedancer in the chaos. From in between the titan's legs, flashes of light were followed by a few deep booms as the deck guns unleashed a volley, though the Colossus didn't seem to notice. The ships then shot off in zigzagging patterns. Unfazed, the Colossus gave a lazy kick to the nearest vessel, sending it careening into a roll and cracking it in half. The titan picked up the biggest piece and brought it to its mouth, shaking the contents down its gullet.

Valen alighted on the deck beside Roth. His voice was weak, as if Fear had sapped him of the strength to talk. "How...how can we hope to combat such a nightmare? Escape seems the only viable option."

"We can't just leave them!" Cole said, standing as tall as he could. "That thing will eat their navy and probably all of Morthain by the end of the day." Unbidden thoughts of Milette came to him. It would be his fault if the Colossus killed her.

"A foe of that scale is beyond any of us," Valen said, laying his steely eyes on Cole. "Escape is our only means of survival."

"It's not beyond *me*," Cole said, hands balling into fists as tears flooded his eyes. "I can do it, but I have to let the Rage take all of me. The other Colossus was easy. This one's bigger so it'll take me longer, but I can do it. I'm sure."

Valen squinted. "And what will be left of you? Even if you should kill that abomination then we would have your unrestrained Rage to deal with. You yourself may very well be the ruin of Morthain if you carry on unchecked." Valen placed a hand on Cole's shoulder. "I do not say this out of disdain for you, brother; however, I cannot pretend that I didn't see the instability of your Rage." Valen's eyes flicked to Lileth. "I am not eager to lose another member of this unit."

Cole nodded, feeling both helpless and crestfallen. Valen was right. He had come far too close to killing Lileth on more than one occasion.

"But we can't just run away. We just can't. A whole city is at stake here." Cole looked back at the Alpha Colossus, which had finished eating another ship and had started working on the remains of one of its smaller brethren. "I'm going back. I'll figure something out. None of you need to come."

"You won't be alone," Eliza said, a grin playing across her face. "Someone needs to carry you over at the very least. You may have a knack for Rage, but the Colossus will tire of waiting for you to figure out how to fly over." She caressed the side of Cole's face and at once he felt her familiar song blooming in his mind. He grasped the link, strengthening it with his own Passion.

"*Perhaps I can keep you from wandering too far down the path of Rage,*" Eliza said with her mouth and mind, brushing roughly up against his Rage. Cole felt his munisica come forth.

"And perhaps I can pull you back if you do." Lileth gripped Cole's bladed hands with her own claws.

"Well that settles it then," Sitra said. She pounded her feet against the deck and hollered at the crew, "Hey, someone turn this heap around! We've got another baddie to tackle!"

Valen shook his head, looking suddenly tired. "I tell you, it's a fool's errand. Master Roth, won't you inject some reason into this madness?"

"I will go. None of you will follow me," Roth said in a quiet rumble. His eyes were locked on the Alpha Colossus. He was as calm and docile as Cole had ever seen him. His tone was soft yet unyielding, like an avalanche of fresh snow. "Go to Oberon City. Find Chiron and

Alvani at the temple. That's an order. On my blood and honor you will follow it."

"But-but what are you talking about?" Sitra stammered. "You're not going anywhere without us. Are you?"

"She's right, Master Roth," Eliza pleaded. "You can't go alone. You shouldn't go at all with those wounds. Master Alvani needs to look at you."

Roth didn't answer. He flexed his shoulders forward as massive emerald wings exploded from his back, sweeping over the entire deck like bladed fans.

"NO!" Sitra screamed, angry tears shaking from her eyes. "You can't, I won't let you! You're hurt! That thing will kill you for sure! We only just lost Storn and now you're going to throw your life away chasing some glorious death or something? You're abandoning us is what you're doing! You're an idiot, a big dumb coward! Don't you dare leave us!"

Roth's eyes turned to Sitra, his granite features melting into fatherly adoration. "I don't remember asking for your tears, Warrior of the Sill." He raised Sitra's trembling chin with a bladed finger. "I have one more order for you. Should I perish in this war, you are to return to Morthain and invoke the Trial of Honor upon the whole damned city. Don't let my people fade into comfort and shadow. They need your strength, Sitra."

Sitra turned her head and winced more tears from her eyes. "Master...no..."

Roth spread his crystalline wings, grinning his toothy grin as he turned to face his colossal enemy.

The rest of the unit summoned wings of their own, crouching and readying themselves for flight. Cole desperately tried to summon wings, feathers, anything to help him make the flight. However, all he could manage was to levitate himself with a wobbly spell, his feet dangling a few feet over the deck. Lileth's arms wrapped around him and pulled him close.

Something then smashed its way into Cole's mind, disarming him with overwhelming ferocity. He was no longer in Lileth's embrace, or even on the Firedancer. It felt as if a hurricane made of mountains had crashed upon him, battering and burying him under their inconceivable mass. The force buried him so far beneath himself that he forgot who he was supposed to be. Recognizing the onslaught as one of Roth's mental assaults, Cole stopped resisting and allowed himself to be carried away. He grasped at the first memory his mind came across, which was of him giving Joshy a ride on the back of his bike. He poured himself into the memory, feeling the wind in his hair as Joshy belly-laughed into his ear. Outside of his memory bubble the storm subsided. He grudgingly popped the memory and returned to the deck of the Firedancer.

Cole was on his back, lying flat on Lileth's stomach. Rubbing his head, he looked around and saw his unit wearing pained faces that matched his own.

"He's gone!" Sitra cried, clawing at the air.

"But he's not too far." Lileth rose swiftly to her feet, picking up Cole along the way. "We can still catch him."

Cole felt her arms tighten around him as Lileth prepared to take flight. She jerked twice, then dropped him on the deck, moaning.

"He's smothered our memories," Valen said, exhaling sharply through pursed lips. "I can't recall any spells for flight, or levitation, or...aghh!" He gripped his hair and fell to his knees. "Or gravity."

"The cocky bastard!" Sitra growled. The handrail split and cracked under her munisica. "He's already injured and now he's going to battle that monster while maintaining spells against us. Probably thought the Colossus would be too easy if we all ganged up on it. He's going to kill himself. I Hate hi-"

There was a blur of movement and Eliza was suddenly upon Sitra, her hand clasped over her mouth. "Not Hate. Not that. Do not allow Sorronis into your heart so easily."

Sitra's eyes blazed as her munisica wrapped slowly around Eliza's bare wrist, pulling it away from her mouth. Her lips parted, baring her teeth as her breath came in deep heaves. Eliza's free hand floated up and cupped Sitra's cheek, pouring a fresh torrent of rosy Passion into her. Sitra broke into heavy sobs as she sheathed her munisica and hugged Eliza.

Cole felt the weight of every sorrow fall upon him like lead blankets. He couldn't lose another person he cared about. Joshy, Deekus, Storn, Lexy, Nana Beth, and probably his mother. It was too much. Each loss crippled and cracked parts off his soul that he could never fit back into place. Only in their absence were the parts fully realized and appreciated. Roth had been an iron mountain, challenging and protecting him every step of the way. He made Cole more than he ever thought he could be. Without Roth what hope did they have?

Cole felt a furry nudge at his hand and a primal mind brush against his own. Goran grunted, nudging him again. Cole's eyes met with the mirak's ruby orbs. Goran was not ready to give up.

Cole rose to his feet and scrambled up the nearest cargo net. He willed his Wisdom to grant his eyes the distance that Roth's magic would not allow. He saw his Master's emerald wings slicing through the air. He was not quite at the Alpha Colossus yet. A wild idea suddenly came to Cole.

"Let's commandeer the ship!" he cried down to the others. "To hell with Morthain! We don't owe them a damned thing. Let's threaten the crew and make them take us back. Just get me over there and give me some space. I've lost everything and I don't really care what happens to me or that dirty city."

"Finally someone with fire in their bones!" Sitra growled, throwing her shoulders back. Her long braid sailed behind her in the wind. "I'll do the honors of persuading the crew."

Valen interjected, "Cole might not care what happens to him, but some of us do." He threw his arms out to halt Sitra, glaring up at Cole. "Humans are more selfish than I thought if you truly believe you've lost everything."

"I'm not being selfish," Cole spat. "I just-"

"You just thought you knew better than Master Roth!" Valen shouted. "He is one of the oldest Aenerians, one of the Unbound! You think you know better than he? Shame on you Cole, shame on all humans if your arrogance is representative of your whole race." He turned his gaze on each of them in turn, burning into them. "If the unit decides to shame our Master then I will not hesitate to join you, but by my death and honor I will be done with you."

A cold, guilty wind seemed to blow across the deck. Even Goran moaned, his fur no longer standing on end as he slumped to the deck at Valen's side.

"I'm sorry, Valen," Cole murmured, hopping back to the deck.

"Do not be sorry, be productive," Valen replied, turning his gaze towards the bow of the ship, Oberon's rainbow hues glinting in his eyes. "As Roth once said, being sorry never helped anyone."

CHAPTER 9

TRANSIENT SOLACE

Deep in the armored belly of the Lead Orchid, War Captain Seive labored over the duties of her new position. Her arm was still broken, but she left it untreated and ignored her body's cries for relief. It would not do for the crew to see even a glimmer of weakness in their newly promoted War Captain. She had already lost two ships and judging by the battle overlays, they would be lucky if any vessel made it out intact. The Alpha Colossus was impossibly fast and moved with a lazy grace, as if it picked them apart at its leisure. Fortunately it was distracted somewhat by consuming the remains of the other four titans.

War Captain Seive was able to direct the fleets more efficiently with the recently mended communications equipment in the war room. It was a testament to the necessity of the old engineers, who until now had been all but obsolete. The engineers bustled around, perusing dusty manuals, calibrating the old machines, and putting out spot fires from old wiring. The machines were mysterious and elegant, yet the controls were simple enough for even the dullest sailor to understand.

"Tell the fleets to stay still!" Seive barked, poring over the battle overlays of her command ship. "The Colossus is attracted to movement, so have the ships alternate their maneuvers. With a scrap of luck we may confuse it. Has anyone managed to land a blow to its face?"

"Negative, War Captain," Lieutenant Harver replied, fidgeting his weather-worn hands over the dials and knobs of the communication overlay. "None of the deck guns can traverse that high. They would have to retreat half a mile to make the angle, but the damned thing moves too fast at that distance. We just lost the Rusty Comet by the way."

"Tell them to stop moving around so much!" Seive shouted, slamming her fist. She watched in helpless fury as the overlay showed a miniature azure model of the Alpha Colossus dumping the Rusty Comet into its mouth. "Roth's crew charged all their gratia stones and now they think they're untouchable."

The battle overlay displayed dozens of ships swarming around the Colossus. The titan tossed another to the heavens before the rest stopped moving entirely, finally heeding Seive's orders. The Colossus halted, darting its head about as though having trouble deciding which to pursue next. One brave vessel shot out, doing a flourishing loop before speeding away. The Colossus jogged casually towards it, but then another ship caught its attention, then another. It was working.

"Lead it into the deep sands, away from Morthain," Seive ordered. "The sands will slow it, and its head might sink low enough for us to fire at it. Concentrate fire on its knee for now. The deck guns are only doing surface damage, but maybe we can cripple the bastard if we hammer down on one spot."

"As you say," Lieutenant Harver replied before relaying her instructions to the fleet.

Seive's brow scrunched up, sweat beading off her nose as she scanned the battle overlay. How in Oberon's bloody light can something so big move so fast? She growled, munisica stretching as two more ships were taken out of the fight, this time by their own clumsiness as they collided with each other. The overlays didn't show the glass missiles from the deck guns, but there were tiny pieces falling from the left knee of the Colossus. Seive let out a savage bark as the Colossus developed the slightest limp, allowing the ships to take advantage of its break in balance. As they approached the shores of the deep sands, the fleets drew their sheet caps and dove in and out of the white powder, staying just out of reach.

Seive's uninjured arm shot out and grabbed her chief engineer by the hood of his robes. "Is the main gun ready yet?"

The engineer coughed as the collar of his robes choked him. His scowl cracked into a look of terror when he realized who had stopped him. "N-not sure ma'am, I m-mean War Captain."

"Well?" She growled.

"Well? Uh… I don't know what you, I mean what we…there are so many factors," he sputtered.

"What's the status?" she snapped. "How much longer? That hammer is our only chance of doing any real damage."

"Oh, of course, p-please f-forgive my ignorance." He stammered as though he were afraid his next word would sentence him to a swift death. "Well, you see it is ready whenever you want it to be. H-however it will be more ready the longer you wait."

"What the hell does that mean?" she asked. "And stop your sniveling, you're the most valuable sod on this ship. No one's about to bite your head off."

The engineer took a calming breath before resuming. "Thank you, I am just a little frightened by all this. I've never been in so much as a street squabble, never mind hostilities of this scale. What I meant to say was that the main gun of the Lead Orchid is not like the others. It is not mechanical, but magnetic. It seems that our glass munitions have a significant magnetic field about them and the Orchid's main gun leverages that field as a propellant. However, the capacitors need adequate time to charge, a charge which comes from the gratia stone. I've diverted nearly all ancillary power to the gun's capacitors, but it's still only at half charge."

Seive considered smacking him in the head just to simplify things. She took her own calming breath. "And to someone who hasn't spent their entire life buried in books and tinkering with machines, what the hell does all that mean?"

The corner of the engineer's mouth twitched. "We can fire now at half strength, or if you wait an hour we can fire at full power. There's only one projectile, however, so do try to make it count." He cast a sideways glance at the tiny Colossus on the battle overlay.

Seive's eyes followed the engineer's. They both watched as the Alpha Colossus shattered another vessel with a playful swat.

"Get back to work then." She nodded to the engineer, who set off at a run. She walked around the battle overlay and rapped the Lead Orchid's captain on the shoulder. "I need a word."

The captain grunted and followed, ignoring the questions from his helmsman. "What is it, War Captain? I ain't got much time for idle talk."

"You will be anything but idle after you hear my words." She stilled her munisica, preventing them from bursting forth. "Should we divert all power to the task, how high and how fast could you fly the Lead Orchid?"

The captain scratched the stubble on his neck. "If I were ripe crazy, I'd wager we could get it up pretty damn high. The speed's no matter, but the higher we go the more draw we take from the gratia stone. How high though, I ain't got the fuzziest. Nothin' of the sort's been done before. It's best to keep our ships nearer the ground. There's no tellin' if we'd have enough juice to make it back down slower than a fallin' anvil. Now, why would you be askin' somethin' so harebrained for?"

Seive threw an arm around the captain and dropped her voice so the crew couldn't hear. "That Colossus is big. Too big, plain and simple. There's no way under Oberon's light that we're going to win this one. Not by conventional means anyhow. The main gun is going to give that rotten bastard a little kiss, then if it's still standing, were going to fly the Lead Orchid up and give it another. Should we survive the impact, every sailor able to swing a mallet is going to board the giant and see what more we can hack off. It's not the perfect plan, but unless you have anything better that's what we're going to do." Her eyes darted to the battle overlay. "We've lost another three ships since we've been *chatting idly*, so speak up if you have any ideas. If not, then get ready to take to the skies."

A savage grin had been growing on the captain's face as Seive spoke. She knew that grin, and she knew his answer before he even said it. "Well then, call me ripe crazy. That's the most beautiful thing these ears have heard in an age."

"Can it be done?" Seive hissed.

The captain's voice dropped to a grating whisper: "Beats the pants off me, but we hafta try then, don't we? The helms-crew is a little green, but I'll grab the wheel myself if it comes to it. You've got balls of munisica, War Captain, and you've got me word. The Orchid will fly."

"Good." She gave him a curt nod, masking her relief.

The ship's captain slapped a rough hand on her broken arm, giving her an excited shake before returning to the helmsmen. Seive held her breath, waiting for the pain to ebb away. She could feel hot fire stabbing along with her heartbeat as blood pooled under the skin of her broken arm.

"War Captain!" Lieutenant Harver shouted across the battle overlay. "There's something... odd. The fleets are reporting something flying towards the Colossus. Something green and fast."

Seive was already on the overlay. "Why isn't it showing up on the map? This thing is real-time isn't it?"

"I...don't know," Harver replied, listening closely to his earpiece. "It's already on the Colossus. It's...it's a man. He's tearing at it, doing a good job by the sounds of it."

Seive watched as sizeable chunks fell from the miniature Colossus. It was still surface damage, but it was more than their fleet was doing. Her arm throbbed again. She had a sneaking suspicion as to who the invisible man was.

"Should we initiate ceasefire?" Harver asked.

"No. Keep it up." She smirked. "Have them switch to offensive maneuvers and keep hammering that knee. It looks like our invisible friend is holding the beast's attention."

Lieutenant Harver relayed her commands. On the battle overlay the remaining ships popped out of the deep sands and pressed on with their deck guns.

"Captain!" Seive barked.

"I'm all ears, War Captain," he shouted in return.

"Bring us around to the Colossus and ready the main gun." Without waiting for his reply, she bolted across the war room towards the door to the upper deck.

"You heard her, lads! Crank this old bitch hard starboard and give her hell!" he barked, sending the helmsmen into a flurry of activity. He addressed the targeting officer, a young woman barely of age. "Where's she at then?"

"Just under a two third's charge, sir," she replied without looking at him. Her nimble fingers danced over the controls as though playing an instrument.

"Well that's better than nothin' I suppose," the captain sighed, clapping the targeting officer on the back. "Certainly gonna give the rotten bastard a nice kiss on the cheek. Fire when ready."

Sure that the crew was on track, Seive ran out to the top deck, her munisica clacking over the glass planks. She needed to see the Colossus with her own eyes. The overlays had to be off. The thing couldn't be that big.

"Clear the sheet cap!" she hollered to the deck crew.

The ancient latches clanked open with clouds of rust as the sheet cap raced over the deck, letting in the abrasive winds. Seive tucked her face into her scarf and ran for the bow, ignoring the protests of the crew. She leapt up the final staircase, dropping her scarf as her mouth hung wide open.

The Alpha Colossus was not big. *Big* was wildly insufficient. There were few words for things of this scale. Even the mountains at the far reaches of the White Sands were not useful for comparison. The thing was impossible, inconceivable. Her ships, the smallest of which held eighty men, looked like rats darting about at its feet. It was no wonder they had been so timid in their maneuvers. To draw the attention of such an enemy meant sure death. The Alpha Colossus was bigger than big, huger than huge. It was colossal, nigh on god-like. A tiny mote of Despair took root in Seive's heart.

As the Lead Orchid raced closer she could make out the glinting and slashing of Roth's wings. The Bonebreaker was untouchable. He seemed to know how the Colossus would react before it made a move. He was deadly yet elegant, dancing about and removing huge swaths of blackened flesh with every twirl and dive. To Seive, his tactics were confusing, however, as though he were merely drawing the giant's attention to the sands. In between attacks Roth spent an unusual amount of effort luring the titan into striking the ground. After darting in for a strike he would land in the hard sands, appearing to take a break. Each time the Colossus followed him down with a lightning-quick fist or foot, and each time Roth shot out of the way with not a blink to spare. Roth was nimble, but there was something amiss with his gait, as though he nursed an injury. Each passing moment he appeared just a little clumsier, and his escapes were becoming more and more narrow. With each miss, the Colossus struck the ground, sending a mountainous geyser of powder up into the air.

The Lead Orchid was now close enough that Seive could feel the concussions reverberating through the hull, though they were still a little over a mile away. Seeing Roth take such risks rekindled the Rage in the War Captain. Her Despair wilted and crisped before its flame. She yearned for battle. Beneath her bladed feet she could feel the main gun stirring, a low hum rising to a high whine. Seive hoped that Roth wouldn't catch the impact. She didn't like him, but friendly-fire was no way for a warrior to die.

The gun's whine rose higher and higher, sending itching vibrations up Seive's legs. She let go of the balustrade and sheathed her munisica, plunging her thumbs into her ears not a moment too soon. An explosion slammed into her chest, taking the breath from her as a massive cloud of flame erupted from the bow of the Lead Orchid. She withdrew her thumbs as a screaming, tearing sound filled the skies. Squinting, Seive beheld the glass projectile cutting through the dusty air like a spear thrown by a god. The missile found its home within a heartbeat.

A river of bodies erupted from the torso as the Colossus stumbled and fell over its injured knee. The ship shook and nearly rattled apart as the titan's bulk struck the sands. A glimmer of emerald wings and a tiny dark figure emerged from the clouds, rising higher with belabored flapping. Roth had survived.

The Lead Orchid was near the cloud now. Seive could make out Roth's stony face as he sailed towards them.

"King Rothael!" Seive called out. "Get your ass over here and take a breather!"

Roth folded his wings and dove for the Orchid, half-falling, half-gliding just above the billowing cloud of white dust. He was hurt.

Seive watched in silent horror as a dark mountain of a hand shot out of the rising fog, closing around Roth with a sickening crunch. Roth's wings stuck out from in between its fingers, flickering and fading.

"Stars no…" Seive groaned.

The Colossus rose from the dust, a gaping crevice exposing the grotesque piping and framework of the chosen. Its fist swung up to its crooked maw, giving Roth a final squeeze before releasing him to the hungry hole.

Seive knew better than to waste time with shock or grief. Roth was an egotistical, forgotten King after all. It was only fitting that his arrogance tie him to a foe that was so clearly beyond mortal means. The Lead Orchid banked hard and veered away from the Colossus. The rest of the fleets retreated as well, racing away as if death were nipping at their tails.

"Cowards!" Seive spat, digging her munisica into the deck and stomping off to the lower decks. Retreat was not an option, not when they were the only thing that stood between the Alpha Colossus and Morthain. She would slit the throats of every captain herself, if they survived that was.

Her uninjured hand was about to close on the handle of the door to the lower decks when out spilled the ship's captain, breathless and pale.

"Explain!" Seive's icy voice cut into him as she raised her sword-munisica to the captain's chin.

"There's somethin' on the way," he gasped. "Somethin big. Bigger'n *that* even!" He jabbed a finger at the Colossus. "Wouldn't have believed it if I didn't see the overlays with me own eyes."

"What the hell are you talking about?" Seive asked, scanning the desert. "Nothing's bigger than that. We would see it coming at the very least. Turn us around now, or forfeit your life."

The captain's face slackened as his eyes cast out over her shoulder. His mouth fell open as his gaze climbed higher and higher. Seive lowered her munisica and wheeled around, steeling herself.

A serpentine creature rose from the sands, its flank shining with bioluminescent orbs that ran along its length. The monster's girth was as thick as the leg of the Colossus and there seemed to be no end to its length as it rose up from the world. The creature was clearly a rock wurm, though a specimen of such a scale was unprecedented. Seive suddenly realized why Roth had baited the Colossus into striking the ground; he was calling for it.

The rock wurm opened its bifurcated jaws as it speared into the neck of the Colossus, throwing the titan to the ground once more. Coil after coil wrapped around as the wurm attacked with primordial ferocity born from the depths of Aeneria itself. The Colossus twisted and buckled as the wurm dragged it down. A moment later the two monsters fell down the crater the rock wurm had come from. An eerie silence fell over the desert as the two behemoths disappeared far below the world.

• • • •

"Can you see anything?" Cole asked Lileth, leaning over the balustrade and squinting hard. He used Wisdom to sharpen his eyes as much as he could, but the dust billowing over the sands obscured his view.

"Nothing at all." Lileth threw her crystalline telescope out into the sands. "I worry we shall never see him again. He is the strongest man I know, but how can a mere man stand up to something the size of a mountain?" She shut her glassy eyes as a single tear rolled down her dusty cheek.

Cole swirled his hand on her back. "Don't count Roth out just yet. He probably used to fight those things ten at a time back in his day. And I'm pretty sure he could level a mountain if he caught it hesitating."

A sad smile tugged at a corner of her mouth. "I am sure you are right, Cole."

Cole twitched as something popped into his mind. An image of a cauldron with contents thick and delicious pressed through Cole's thoughts. The scent of cooked meat and spices wafted up from the lower decks.

"Food's ready." Cole nudged Lileth's arm. "Goran's going to suck it all down if we don't get down there soon."

Lileth waved her hand. "Lead the way."

Cole and Lileth passed through the doors to the lower decks of the Firedancer. Cole noticed claw marks and patches of brindle fur caught on the stairs and walls. Goran was entirely too large for the narrow ship's passages. Shoving past bustling members of the crew, they followed the savory aroma to an open patio that ran along the stern. The rest of the unit was already gathered. A small sheet cap rippled against the tearing winds, though Oberon's rainbow hues bled through and coated them all in warm light.

"Goran, that's disgusting!" Cole punched the mirak in the ribs.

Goran took his head out of the cauldron, frothy chunks of soup clinging to his jowls. He gave Cole an eager grunt before diving back in.

"I'm afraid there's nothing for it." Eliza giggled, picking up a bowl from a nearby serving table. "We'll just have to eat around him."

"It'll take more than a giant cat-monkey to stop me." Sitra snatched a bowl in each hand and heaved her shoulder into Goran. "Make some room furball!" Goran seemed not to notice, but he did come up for air, granting them a moment to take their share.

Grabbing his own bowl, Cole glanced down into the cauldron. He had no idea what was in the soup, but by smell alone he knew that a bit of Goran-drool wouldn't dilute the hearty flavor. When he finally scooped some out he tipped the bowl right back and drank it in. It tasted even better than he imagined.

Valen walked to the very front of the patio and flipped open a latch, sending the small sheet cap rolling back into the stern. He then waved an emerald hand through the air, replacing the sheet cap with a clear spell before the sand rushed in. "We certainly have the swiftest vessel in the fleet. The mountains are already in view."

Cole put his soup down for a moment and squinted. He could only see Oberon perched just above the horizon like a beach ball. He stretched his eyes with a quick spell as his vision zoomed and sharpened, revealing jagged teeth poking up out of the sands.

Lileth sat herself down in a chair alongside the hull. "Has anyone ever been to Oberon City?"

No one answered, other than their intermittent slurping and gulping.

"Deekus grew up in the capital," Eliza replied, sliding her bowl across the table. "From what he told me the city is predominantly Wisdom followers. He said the people there are as stiff as frozen pines and hold no tolerance for those guided by emotions. They take their Wisdom very seriously, and most claim to have descended from the Wisdom Walkers of old. Though that is unlikely as the Wisdom Walkers live at the temple and rarely procreate."

"Why'd he leave then?" Sitra asked through a mouthful of soup. "Deekus was pretty damned good with Wisdom. Remember that time he beat Chiron in a memory scan?"

"I do, but I also remember he had some of Chiron's memory cyphers hidden in his robes. He was a trickster at heart, which is why the city bored him and his family ostracized him. Also, his aptitude with Passion made life among the Wisdom followers troublesome, so he left for The Sill."

Sitra clicked her tongue disapprovingly as she scooped another helping from the cauldron. "The place must be duller than dirt if they keep only to logic and reason. Imagine a whole city full of people like Whind? You could set yourself on fire and they wouldn't look twice at you. Probably just tell you you're doing it wrong and show you how to burn more *efficiently*." She spat out the last word. Cole hid his smile behind his bowl. Sitra had performed terribly whenever Whind had taken over for Chiron's lessons.

"Oberon city is not unlike where I am from," Lileth added. "Wisdom followers are brilliant of course, and when they gather in numbers they can change any society into a utopia. However, I find their utopia sterile and tasteless, completely lacking color or creativity. When logic and reason are your only guiding stars, contention is scarce; however, so is the flavor of life."

"Is that why you left?" Sitra inclined her chin. "Didn't want to be another gear in the machine?"

Lileth's eyes glanced to Cole. Had she not told them about her parents? Unsure if he should speak on the matter, he remained silent.

"I came to The Sill to be more than I once was. I have succeeded," Lileth said, her tone making it clear that she was finished with the subject.

"What of *your* home, Cole?" Valen asked, "You don't speak much about Terra, but I would hear it. Tell of your world, your family."

Cole's heart seemed to forget that it was supposed to be beating. He didn't talk about his home for good reason. He kept his eyes down in his bowl as he swirled the soup around. "I...don't want to talk about my family. As far as I'm concerned, you're all my family now." He waited for quippy retort, but none came and he continued. "Terra is like Aeneria in a lot of ways. I mean, we have forests and deserts and mountains and stuff, though your trees are way bigger and our sands don't flow like water. We definitely don't have any magic, though our technology makes up for it. We have machines that fly, and allow us to talk from any distance, there are even some machines that think for us."

"I think you will find that Oberon City has a lot in common with your Terra," Eliza said, running her fingers through her short hair. "Deekus said they had machines that did everything for them. He said they relied upon them too much, that it made them lazy and their magic weaker."

"Yeah that sounds a lot like humans." Cole chuckled. "Me included. We're always trying to do more with less. We want all the riches in the world but we're not about to go work for it. I grew up kind of poor. We didn't have much compared to other people, but man did I want those things. I should have worked harder." Cole stared off, drifting into a sweet day-dream about driving his own car to school.

"You mean material things?" Valen asked. "Fine machines and jewelries? Slaves?"

"Not so much slaves." Cole tried not to laugh at the genuine look of interest that Valen gave him. "That was outlawed long before I was born. But yeah, we like material things. Nice clothes and...cars." Cole paused, surprised that the word 'cars' had translated through the language cypher. "If you have expensive things, it shows you have ..." Cole paused again, surprised this time that there was no Aenerian word for 'money.' "...it shows that you have a lot of currency. What is your currency on Aeneria? People at the Sill seem to barter with gratia stones and their energies."

Lileth raised her hand. A torrent of electric green sparks erupted from her palm, rising up the roof of the patio and tinkling over them like floating Christmas lights. Where each landed, a miniscule crystal flower bloomed. Goran sneezed as a flower sprouted from his nose.

Lileth turned to Cole, her hand now a pair of ebony dragon's claws. "When you have magic, you have the means to sustain yourself independent from the support of others. We have no need for currency, at least not in the way that you think of it." She brought her munisica to a tear in Cole's leather armor. Glittery strands of jade shot from the tips of her claws as she worked them with controlled alacrity, swiftly repairing the hole. "Certain things have value to us. Helping a friend, for example."

Cole had only just noticed how tattered his armor was. Battling the Colossus had ruined a good portion of it, exposing his skin beneath. At least he wasn't as pale and chubby as the first time he met the unit.

"I have to disagree," Valen said, joining Lileth in mending Cole's armor. "Or at least I agree that The Sill uses no traditional form of currency. Those of us adept with Wisdom have the means to shape the world to support ourselves, though other villages that are predominantly Passion or Rage followers must have currency. Look at Morthain and their gratia stones. No doubt some deviant swindled them into outfitting their entire city with Passion stones, knowing full well they could never charge them properly. Now Morthain is a city full of tricksters cutting each other's throats over material things." Cole felt a comforting warmth as the armor on his back side stitched back together. Valen reached over and gave him a pat on the shoulder. "Has Terra adapted better to a currency-based system?"

Cole twisted, checking the flexibility of his newly repaired armor. Satisfied, he turned to Valen. "I want to say yes, but I can't say we're much better. People spend half their time trying to build up enough currency just to live. It's too expensive to build a home, so we work more than a third of our time to make small payments for it. Then whoever we pay uses those payments to build more homes. Education is treated similarly. Our society pretty much makes it a requirement to get educated, even though you'll end up owing more than you can pay off. Most people are in debt one way or another."

"That sounds exhausting," Eliza said with a scowl. "If only you could Travel at will. You could do some good for your world, just like the Wisdom Walkers of old."

"Yeah…" Cole trailed off, shoving back memories of his last venture to Earth. "It might cause too much trouble though. Humans are really good at making a big deal out of little things. If you introduced magic to them, then all the world would come together and figure out a way to make a profit from it. Besides, I couldn't do much more than light a candle with Wisdom. I wouldn't be much help to anyone."

"Last I checked you were an absolute nightmare on the battlefield," Sitra said, wagging a bladed finger at him. "That's gotta be worth something. Is there no one over there that could use a good beating?"

Cole allowed himself a brief fantasy of flying around Earth as some sort of superhero, kicking down doors and fighting terrorists with Rage. "Oh there is for sure, but I wouldn't want to be the one to do it. Honestly I don't like my Rage. I'm not myself when it takes over. Every time I almost end up hurting someone I care about."

"Control will come from experience," Valen said. "Fear of your Rage would be most counterproductive. Embrace it. Learn from it. But do not lose sight of our other magics."

"I would rather be better with Wisdom than anything else," Cole said. "Chiron seems like he could change the world on a whim. Why do you think they want us to go to Oberon City anyway?"

Valen bit back his reply and averted his eyes. There was an uncomfortable silence among the others as well. Cole felt Eliza pressing on him, a mental tap on the shoulder.

"If no one tells you then I will." Her reluctance mingled with a tone of compassion. *"The elders didn't want you to know, but I think you've earned it. You are more important to this war than they let on."*

Cole scanned Eliza's face, though she revealed nothing. Whatever this secret was, he wanted to hear it. It might have to do with how he came to Aeneria in the first place. He returned his gaze on Valen, making it clear he was looking for a response.

"You said we're all family here, brother," he jabbed. "Secrets among family don't end well where I come from."

Valen winced. "The knowledge is not ours to give. Not even to you. We never would have heard it in the first place had Storn not been eavesdropping on the elders. I don't know for sure, but it is safe to assume we have been called to Oberon City because of you."

"But why?" Cole asked, getting angry now. "Do they want to punish me for bringing down the barrier? How the hell can they hold that against me?"

"I'm sorry, Cole, but I cannot tell you." Valen held on to Cole's burning glare.

"Then I will," Lileth said, rising to her feet.

Valen shook his head. "I won't stop you. I only ask that you trust our elders. They have reasons for withholding the knowledge from us."

"And I have good reason to give the knowledge to him," Lileth replied. "He has been ripped from his home and thrust into ours with little choice and even less explanation. The least we can do is fill him in before we cast him into the wolves' den."

Cole swallowed hard. "You make it seem like we're off to my execution." He gave her a weak smile, hoping she would return it. She did not.

"Storn isn't the only one with sharp ears. I have also listened when I should not have." Even under Oberon's changing light Cole could see Lileth blushing. "Cole, you are the key. To all of it. You took down the barrier. You are the reason the soul flies have returned. You remain the only one who is capable of Traveling, and you are the key for others to do the same. The Three need you like a virus needs a host. They need you to bring more cattle to replenish their herds, and through you they can funnel every soul fly into their waiting mouths. This is one reason the Council has summoned you. They seek to use you as well, though their motives will be wrapped in gold and lace."

"I don't want to be used by anyone!" Cole blurted. His Rage flared as his munisica cut into the patio decking. "Chiron said I could come and go as I please, choose my own destiny and all that. But now it sounds like you're all bringing me to the gallows! You're my unit, my family! I chose you guys, unless you're all using me too and there's some other grand plan that you're not telling me."

"That's a bit of a reach, don't you think? I for one cannot deceive you, just as you can hide nothing from me." Eliza injected golden strands of integrity and honesty into their link.

"I know, I'm just...frustrated. I don't like having other people decide what's best for me." Cole's mind became a murky storm, but Eliza's golden link had no problem piercing the clouds.

Lileth's face fell, stung by his accusation. She spoke with a stern, yet not unkind voice, "I will say this to you just one time and never again henceforth; I will never lie to you. Judge me by my actions, you will find no trickery in me."

"Nor from me," Eliza sang, smiling from her chair as she held her bowl in her lap.

"I will never tell a secret that is not my own, but I too will never lie to you," Valen added.

A long black claw suddenly appeared under Cole's neck, picking his chin up and bringing his eyes to Sitra.

"And if you're even *hinting* at calling *me* a liar, I'll...oh how does Roth put it? Take it out of your hide?" She struck Cole with a blunt kiss on the cheek. He could feel the bruise forming even as she pulled away and slumped into a chair. "Don't worry about the Council, you're not facing them alone. We'll be with you during the trial; I'll say what a brave little hero you've been."

"Trial?" Cole rubbed his cheek. "What trial?"

"What are *you* talking about?" Lileth asked Sitra, an eyebrow curving sharply.

"Oh come on, you're not the only one sticking their ears where they don't belong." Sitra waved her munisica. "While you were all sleeping and lounging in Morthain, I went to go see what Roth was up to."

"You mean you went to go find what Roth was drinking." Eliza gave her a sly grin.

Sitra rolled her eyes. "I'm perfectly entitled to a bit of fun. That includes a drink from time to time. After finding the liquor casks I went to go find Roth, but he wasn't there. He wasn't at Auger's little party at all. I did some exploring and found him up on the roof. He was talking to Alvani with the same sort of mental link you and Cole have, except he was talking out loud. Oh, and you're totally right Liza, those two are definitely bonded."

"Of course they are." Eliza nodded.

"Imagine having a heart-to-heart with Roth? I hope she doesn't hesitate!" Sitra covered her mouth as a fit of giggles hissed through her munisica. "Anyway, I heard Roth blabbing on about Cole's trial. He's in some sort of trouble with the Celestial Council. They're talking about putting him to work. They want to study him or something." She inclined her head towards Cole. "One thing's for sure though; you can't tell anyone you've mastered Rage. Roth didn't explain why, but it sounded like you'd be turned into a weapon."

"The Council seems less friendly the more I hear about them," Cole said. "What if I refuse to go to Oberon City?"

"You certainly could, and no one would stop you," Lileth said. "But the Council is as resourceful as it is cunning. Not to mention they are among the most powerful Wisdom users on the planet. They won't have to find you, not directly anyway. Should they want you badly enough, they will shape events around you so that you will stand before them eventually."

"Do not worry yourself overmuch," Valen interjected. "You will have us there with you, and as powerful as the Council is, they are but moths before eagles compared to Chiron and Alvani. You'll find no safer place on Aeneria than in their company, unless Roth was with them as well of course." Valen's eyes drifted to the aft of the Firedancer, back where the Bonebreaker was hopefully winning his fight against the Alpha Colossus.

"The elders can't be *that* powerful," Sitra remarked, flicking her clawed fingers against the hull. "The Council is a bunch of Wisdom Walkers, each one a Master of the school. There's one for each of the local planets right?"

"Twenty-one in all," Lileth replied. "They are a force worthy of pause, of that there is no doubt. However, Chiron fought during the last war while the Council hid in the temple. He was one of the Unbound, trained by Varka himself. Alvani has worked under Chiron ever since."

"The Unbound?" Cole asked. "The old storyteller lady talked about them at the theater. They were the only ones who stood a chance against The Three right?"

"That old storyteller lady's name is Ka Reine, and you would do yourself a service to address her properly," Valen scolded him. "She is most revered throughout the Dark Side. Her age is greater than any other, as is her gift for memory. But you are correct, the Unbound were the only ones who had any sort of effect on The Three. The Council, being Masters of Wisdom, were perfect prey for those adept with Fear. Even if they all gathered as one, a single minion of Decreath could devastate their numbers. Decreath himself would lay waste to the lot of them, the city included. Alvani is a master of Passion and expert of Wisdom, and Chiron is master of both. They will have no trouble protecting you from the Council."

"I think I get it," Cole said, glancing at Lileth. The memory of her kiss played before his mind's eye. "Even though I was fully engulfed in Rage you were able to lift me into the air no sweat. My Rage was useless with the simplest of Wisdom spells. The council's Wisdom would be similarly crippled by strong Passion."

Lileth locked eyes with him, smirking with a look of playful guile that was meant for him alone. "That is also why Kreed, or I should say Decreath in Kreed's body, fled Costas. Decreath is not only a master of Fear, he *is* Fear. But as powerful as his putrid magic is, he would have been no match for your Rage."

Cole felt a surge of pride, though his guilt quickly stifled it. His Rage was perfect against Decreath and his Fear, but it only made him more vulnerable to Grotton and his Hunger. Not even a week ago Hunger was used on him, and he fell right for it. If not for Roth he would have fed on that soul fly just as Kreed had fed on Storn.

"And to think," Cole murmured. "As powerful as our Masters are, not even they can stand up to The Three. In Costas Roth was easy prey for Decreath and now trying to fight Sorronis's Colossus."

No one spoke. They had all seen the shape Roth was in before he flew at the Alpha Colossus. A somber mood fell over the patio. Losing Roth was hard to accept; it didn't even make sense in Cole's mind. It was as if a mountain he had seen every day had suddenly vanished.

Sitra sprang to her feet. "And on that cheery note, I'm going to bed." Without another word she left through the deck door.

"I am tired as well," Eliza sighed, rising to her feet and following Sitra.

Eliza's bell rang in Cole's mind: "*I have more to tell you. Come find me in the crow's nest if you want to talk.*" She gave him a warm, comforting mental hug before reducing their link to a single strand. It was a gesture of etiquette; the thin link would allow them to find each other in the dark while allowing for privacy in their thoughts.

Cole sat in silence for a moment, pondering over what he could have done to save Roth. He hoped Lileth was likewise engaged and that Valen would be the next to leave.

"The ship is slowing." Valen strode across the patio, taking another bowl of soup before stepping to the door. "The gratia stone may need another charge. I should go talk with the captain."

The door slammed shut as Valen disappeared through it, leaving Cole alone with Lileth and a very sleepy Goran. The mirak had eaten himself into a stupor. He swayed on the spot as his ruby eyes rolled with drowsiness.

Lileth strode to the edge of the patio, placing her elbows on the railing and gazing out into the White Sands. "You know, I've seen almost all that Aeneria has to offer, and in moments like this it still takes my breath away. I always thought the sands a harsh and unforgiving land. But now, looking out from the comfort of a Morthainian ship, I find it captivating."

"Aeneria is like nothing I've ever seen," Cole said, leaning awkwardly against the railing, which was just a bit too high for him. He felt close to her. Drawn to her. It was as if in that moment Lileth understood him better than anyone else. "Just about everywhere I look I find something beautiful." He didn't realize he was gawking at Lileth until her eyes locked onto his, startling him.

"There is much to appreciate here." She unfolded her arms, laying a hand on the railing, close to Cole's.

"There certainly is." Cole swallowed back the butterflies that tried climbing out from his chest. His heart and mind were a flutter of activity, swirling with elation and longing. He had felt these things before, but not like this. It was as if his recently developed Passion had amplified his yearning to an unbearable level. He didn't know if he should throw himself at her or run away before his desire made the choice for him. He felt hot. His skin was wet. Things stirred in him in places he wished she would help him explore.

"Are you well, Cole? You look flushed." Her brow mushed with concern as her lips pouted, looking full and inviting. If only he could reach them. She traced a finger alongside his face. "I could inspect you. I'm not as adept with the medicinal facets of Passion as Eliza, but I will do what I can." There was a hint of bitterness in the way she moved her lips when she said Eliza's name. Was it jealousy?

"No, no, I'm good." Cole wiped his forehead with a tablecloth. "Just a little warm out here, you know?"

She placed her hand back on the railing. Was it even closer than before? Cole leaned towards her until his arm touched hers. He could feel her taut skin on his.

"I'm here if you need me, Cole," she said, her voice rich and sweet to his ears. "Your life has not been an easy one, yet you keep moving where others would have given up. You are special."

Cole felt her eyes on him, looking down and raking over his face. For some reason he couldn't bring himself to meet her gaze. His heart thumped so loudly he worried she would hear it. His eyes remained glued to the White Sands, studying the craggy teeth of the distant mountains.

"I don't..." His voice tapered off. He was about to say that he didn't feel special at all, but in truth he had never felt more important, more a part of something than he did right now. "Thank you, Lileth. You have been...very important to me since I came to The Sill. Before that even. I still remember the dream in the meadow. Or at least it was a dream to me."

"I remember the meadow as well." Her eyes smiled, but her lips quivered with sorrow. "I don't know how to thank you for that. I am embarrassed to admit what I went to that meadow to do. I've told no one." Her eyes darted about, stricken with panic and pain. "I would not be here if the aethers had not brought you to me."

Cole's hand fell over her white knuckles. The tips of her fingers had hardened into little munisica. "I don't know what brought me to you, but I'm glad I found you. Don't forget, I wouldn't be here either if you hadn't saved me in the lagoon." Cole gripped her hand and her claws receded. "Lileth, why was it that you were able to heal me when Alvani wasn't? She is a master of Passion. If she couldn't fix me then why could you?"

A heavy silence filled the air between them. Her hand stiffened under his little fingers. A splinter of Fear snuck in between the hammer blows of his Passion-fueled heart.

She brought her gaze to Cole, making his legs wobble. "I was able to heal you for the same reason you were able to save me from my doom in the meadow. There is something in you. The same thing is in me as well. It is potent, yet invisible. It is profound, yet it transcends both worlds and time. Do you know of what I speak?"

Cole's thumping heart clanged like a machine gun. He knew what she meant, but there was no way he could put words to it. He had to try, however. She was staring at him, her eyes yearning for a response.

"I know what you mean," he breathed. "I...don't know how to describe it. But I feel as if I knew you all along, and you knew me. Like we were old friends before we even met."

"That is as fine a point as I could describe." She smiled, placing her other hand over his. It was so warm and comforting. Cole only wished he was taller. He was sick of being smaller than everyone. Especially Lileth.

From the other side of the patio Goran's barking snarls shattered their moment.

"What's wrong with him?" Lileth asked, her eyes wide.

Cole dug into Goran's link. He felt teeth gnashing and claws tearing into enemies unknown, somewhere high on a mountain.

"He's dreaming." Cole smiled as Goran's misty visions switched to fantasies of triumph and feasting. "I forgot he was out here."

Lileth sighed with relief. "I didn't know animals could dream. Then again, Goran is unlike any other animal I have ever seen. Just as like you are unlike any other person I have ever met."

"Alvani mentioned how Goran and I were growing together." Cole watched the rapid rise and fall of Goran's ribs as steamy air rushed from his snout. "He dreams all the time now. He's grown a lot too. When I first met him he was no taller than my shin, and I was way smaller than I am now. He was my first friend on Aeneria, the first person I could trust. He taught me how to survive in the woods, showed me how to adapt. Then Domina attacked us and he just went off like a bomb. Practically exploded! The next time I saw him he was the giant furball that we have now."

Lileth gave Goran a look of adoration, before returning her eyes to Cole. Oberon's light trickled through the loose strands of her black hair, revealing a sheen of blue. "He had no choice but to grow, just as you had no choice. We have all grown since you joined us. I've been with the unit for quite some time, and with The Sill even longer. Though I knew you were something else, you were just an Underkin to the rest of them. You were as weak and inept as we all expected, but only at first. Soon you grew faster than any of us had. It pushed us, drove us harder. We took our lessons more seriously. You elevated us."

To this, Cole had no response. His unit had always been on a higher level than he could comprehend. They were practically superheroes from movies. The fact that Lileth looked up to him, even as he had to crane his neck to meet her eyes, was paradoxical to the extreme.

Lileth's head snapped out towards the sands. Oberon's fickle hues painted a violent rainbow on her sharp features. Cole followed her gaze to the sky, where he beheld swirling droves of soul flies far above them. The orbs danced in unseen tunnels, racing and twirling their way down. Cole recognized the rivers, for he had led them in his dreams. The veins twisted and joined, forming a funnel of color and lights that coalesced into a single torrent of lights. Though the spinning tower was miles away, Cole still felt their warmth on his cheeks.

The sight was too beautiful for words. Cole's head fell against Lileth's shoulder just as her head fell against his. They watched in serenity as the bleak sands turned into a roiling ocean of life and fire.

CHAPTER 10

SIN BLOSSOM

He had found peace within the heart of the enemy. Talin was no longer Talin, but something else entirely. He was no longer in his cell, but deep within what was left of his consciousness. A barren wasteland of echoed Despair and smoldered Hatred was all that remained of his mind. Somewhere in the furthest reaches of his worthlessness was a pit, deep and decayed. The pit became Talin's new home, for in his waking hours he could feel the phantoms of his memories calling to him, begging that he dive back in. The phantoms demanded payment for what he had done.

The pit was where Talin lay now, at the very bottom. The phantoms swirled about him, closing and calling to him. A ghostly figure of a much younger Pineah swam forth, taking him back to the beautiful shallows of The Sill's lagoon. Images flashed before his mind's eyes with increasing lucidity. He was running down the beach in search of a more intimate location for the two of them. The azure moonlight painted the curves of Pineah's body. Pearly sand scratched in between his toes as they waded out in the warm water. Her legs wrapped around his waist as their fingers wove together. Her unbridled laughter filled him as they spun about. Her lips were a conduit of raw Passion.

The phantom howled as the memory curdled in Talin's mouth like soured milk. Sinking its claws deep, the phantom latched onto Talin's soul and with indulgent slowness, tore its payment from him. Talin curled into a ball, his scream rising with the phantom's wails. The wraith drifted away, taking with it the final piece of his sense of comfort.

Talin heaved his lungs empty, shaking and sweating. He didn't have time to catch his breath before the next phantom was on him, dragging him flailing and screaming to another treasured memory. His first month at The Sill was trying to the extreme. Talin was lost, depressed, and tired. Most of all he felt a sense of severe isolation, a profound loneliness that smothered him like a heavy blanket. Sneaking out on the night of a sunrise, he broke into a pub down in the markets and made off with a bottle of iced moonwine. Retreating to an isolated pine, he climbed to the very top, where he planned on watching the birth of the new sky. At the uppermost platform he was surprised to discover his Pineah. They spent the entire sunrise chasing the bottom of the bottle while captivated by the new constellations. For the first time in far too long, Talin felt at home.

The phantom's howl echoed throughout the pit as it dug into the raw flesh of his inner-self, ripping and jerking its payment from him. Talin couldn't catch his breath, let alone brace himself for the mutilation of his soul. The phantom wept as it faded back into the shadows of the pit, taking with it Talin's capacity for joy.

Pineah's phantoms came and went. With each passing Talin lost another part of himself; desire, curiosity, pride, empathy, conviction, self-preservation. He had nothing left of his core self, yet still the phantoms came, ripping and raking over raw wounds, greedy claws searching and scraping. Talin willingly thrust it all upon them, for he had no use for these parts of himself outside the pit. There was no point to any of it.

The cries of the phantoms died away as they slipped back into the crags of his mind. He knew they would come calling again, but for now they were sated. Talin lay at the very bottom of the pit, bathing in the nothingness. He had crawled in and out of the pit more times than he could recall, each time emerging with less of himself. Soon he knew there would be nothing left to give. He would emerge an empty husk. Perhaps he already was.

Talin rose to his feet, wincing. It was time to crawl out again. Eyes sunken and heavy, he reached from foothold to handhold as he prepared himself for the harsh, ripping winds of his wasteland.

Opening his eye, Talin found himself back in his body. Back in the doorless cell. As bleak as it had been, his prison had lost what little color and light it had. Even the sour decay of Pineah's body had failed to rouse his disgust. He had no urge or desire to speak of. He only vaguely registered Kreed's white suit in the corner of the room.

Kreed leaned forward in his chair. His eyes lit with vicious intrigue as he looked Talin over. "Aethers take me, that was marvelous. Truly spectacular. How does it feel?"

Talin did not move.

Kreed giggled, clapping his hands together as if they were on fire. "Oh I think we're nearly there! Scraping the bottom of the barrel indeed! It's a shame young Habbad was tied up with an appointment. He practically begged me to see you do it."

A wet snapping sound came from the corner of the cell. Kreed's lip curled in revulsion as he glanced over at Pineah's corpse. "Ugh, disgusting. I hope you don't mind if Baedine indulges. She hasn't fed in some time and has taken to nipping at her own hide again. Fucking repulsive I know, but she wasn't my idea. Decreath pulled her from my sister and now I'm stuck with the beast. But that's all blood under the bridge now. I assumed you were quite finished with your darling Pineah anyhow. I do hope Baedine's actions are not a touch indelicate?"

Talin was still as stone as he slumped in the chair he was only now aware of sitting in. His hands, Pineah's hands, fell from his lap and hung by his sides.

"Not a damn thing?" Kreed's voice was ablaze with accusation. "You just murdered your wife and now my dog is eating her corpse. Does that not upset you? Don't you have anything to say? What kind of monster can live such horror without so much as a twinge of guilt? For heaven's sake man, at least look at what you've done."

Kreed's scowl twisted with annoyance as he jumped to his feet. Baedine paused in her feeding, looking up at her Master with wet, lidless eyes. Kreed stormed across the cell and grasped the cuff of Talin's shirt, dragging him over to Pineah. Baedine folded her wings and skittered off.

"Behold her!" Kreed spat, shoving Talin's face into the decaying folds. "Look at her, look at what you've wrought you piece of shit!"

Talin hung limply, choking on Pineah's remains.

Kreed planted his feet and threw Talin across the cell, where he crashed into a cot. Gasping, Kreed ran his fingers through his hair and circled the room.

"You truly are ready." Tears welled as Kreed's lip quivered. "I hope you are, because I certainly am not."

Kreed straightened his lapels and sighed through pursed lips before stepping to the wall. He took his little finger to his mouth and pulled it across his broken teeth. He removed the finger, which now wore a jagged gash that bled freely. He smeared the blood on the wall with careful strokes as if he were working a canvas. The blood bubbled and crawled of its own accord, spreading into a disk the size of a large serving platter. The disk changed from a ruddy crimson to a dark plum as Kreed waved his hands over it.

A sticky gurgling came from the puddle before it became smooth as a mirror, its reflection showing Habbad in the woods. He had a squealing mirak cornered against a hulking fern. The little creature jumped and clawed its way away up the bark, only to slide back down as though pulled by invisible weights. Indigo lightning shot from Habbad's fingers, striking the mirak with a sizzling crack each time it attempted to escape.

"Really?" Kreed said into the mirror. "A mirak?"

Habbad jumped. The mirak seized the momentary distraction and shot off into nearby underbrush. Habbad's wrinkled face darkened into a frown as he cast a hand out to the mirak. A high screeching rang from the mirror as Habbad's spell dragged the creature back to him.

"You said I could choose any one I wanted," Habbad said, turning his face towards the mirror.

Kreed pinched the bridge of his nose with his thumb and first finger. "Yes, I certainly recall saying that, but why wouldn't you go for something a bit more formidable? You know for a fact that your first Domina will have the greatest effect on you."

Habbad's eyes fell to the ground. He raised his hand and hooked his fingers into claws. The mirak floated into sight, its limbs and tail stretched straight out as it screeched in mortal terror. Habbad returned his gaze to Kreed, his tone becoming defensive. "I am well aware of the nuances of Domina possession. I chose the mirak for good reason. They are the most ferocious fighters I've ever seen and regularly take down prey many times their size. And I do recall a certain mirak giving you some trouble not too long ago."

"That it did. And if I were not so pressed for time I would have lit a plague-fire on the entire forest and rid the land of the parasitic blighters. What you do with your soul is your choice my son, though I wouldn't be doing my duty as your father if I didn't question your motives." Kreed peeled the mirror from the wall and aimed it at Talin. "Now, for our other little project. You will notice he *seems* ready to make the leap, but I want you to come verify."

"He does look ready, but I'm busy." Habbad's voice echoed across the cell. "You can do it better than I can anyway."

"Come now, Habbad." Kreed spun the mirror back around. His tone was patronizing, but thick notes of menace stabbed through. "You were the one who first broke into his mind. You were a bit more forceful than necessity called for, as you very well know. His mental scars belong to you and you alone. Should I enter him, my foreign presence would set him back a great deal. It's bad practice, sloppy work. You'll come down here and finish the job, now."

"But..." Habbad's head turned towards the mirak. "I've been working on this for hours. If I leave now I'll lose everything. I'm very close to breaking its will. Give me just another hour."

The mirror shook in Kreed's hand, the shards of his broken teeth bared as darkness filled the room. His voice became a venomous wind: "I'll *give* you an eon of terror and melt you to your nightmares if you don't come to me now. It is not lost on me that you seek the mirak's submission for personal reasons. I can see your envy, even through the mirror. You wish to be bonded to a mirak because the human is bonded to one with Passion. TELL ME I AM WRONG!"

Habbad's face slackened with dread. "You are not wrong, Father Kreed."

Kreed sneered. He ran his tongue over his jagged teeth, his voice hissing with restrained fury. "Of course I'm not wrong. I know you, Habbad. I know everything you're made of. Never forget, I am the one tugging your strings. Your Fear, your hope and shame, all of it is mine. Don't give me reason to use them against you, lest you desire another audience with sweet Lexy."

"No, Father Kreed. My apologies, Father Kreed." Habbad's voice trembled as he dropped his head.

"Well then, that's settled." Kreed shook his head as though shooing a fly. He resumed his usual exuberance. "You, young man, have a job to do. Take your little prize with you if you want, but I expect you within a half hour. Don't dawdle, our warrior grows more lucid by the minute. And fetch Florien on your way, won't you?"

"Right away, Father Kreed." Habbad nodded, dashing out of the mirror's frame, his mirak floating behind him.

Kreed laughed, tossing the mirror aside as it shattered into purple smoke. "Kids these days. I swear I wasn't such a ripe little bastard when I was his age. My father would have boiled my marrow if I were half as flippant as that one." He raised an eyebrow to Talin, checking to see if he was listening.

Talin was now swaying in small circles, tiny moans slipping out of his cracked lips. He gazed straight out into nothing as Baedine returned to eating her meal.

"Finally coming 'round?" Kreed asked, his voice feathery and soothing as he removed his snow-white jacket and hung it off a nail in the wall. "Very good. You need to be in tip-top shape for this next part. I'm ashamed to admit it, but I've never done this before. We're not blazing any *new* trails so to speak, but for me this is uncharted." Kreed rolled his sleeves and sucked on his lip, inspecting Talin's lifeless form. "Come now Talin, let's get you cleaned up at least. I may even remember a trick or two with Passion to spruce you up a bit. If not I'm sure Florien can do something."

Kreed hoisted Talin to his feet, carrying him over to a deep wash basin in the corner of the room. He cracked open a valve and cold water rushed out, filling the hollow. Kreed began humming a sweet lullaby as he stripped the soiled clothes from Talin with tender hands. He lowered Talin into the basin. The broken warrior moaned like a child at the sting of the chilly water.

"Oh dear, that must be terribly cold," Kreed apologized before waving a casual hand over the tub. "There, how's that?"

Steam rose from the water as Talin released an involuntary sigh of pleasure.

Kreed took a sponge and chunk of soap from a shelf embedded in the wall, and sat himself in a stool behind Talin. He massaged the sponge into a thick lather and set to washing Talin from head to toe, cooing his lullaby all the while.

Talin began weeping, rejoicing in the momentary solace from the phantoms. For now at least, all he had to do was relax and enjoy the simple pleasures of the hot water and soothing aromas. He didn't need to be anyone, or do anything. For now, he could unclench his screaming mind and indulge in his empty soul.

"Bit of an oddity, me washing you up. Don't you think?" Kreed asked, wringing out a sponge. "A month ago I would have a whole team of Underkin clean you up. I daresay the little critters would do a better job than I could." Kreed sighed, working the sponge into a fluffy lather once more. "But we no longer have such luxuries. I knew it was ambitious of me to use our entire stock on the Devotion, and now here I am doing their work and lamenting their absence. I could of course order one of the priests or aristocrats to wash you up. But then I'd never hear the end of the complaining, the rumors, oh you wouldn't believe the *attitude.* You would think I was asking them to shovel shit with a spoon! Then of course I'd have to kill whoever found out about you. You're top secret, you know. Highly classified. No one else knows about you besides Habbad, Florien, and The Three. Even the guards that worked on Pineah were disposed of. Does any of this at least tickle your curiosity?"

Kreed's mouth curved into a frown as he raised an expectant eyebrow. Talin heard every word, but he couldn't care any less. His curiosity had been taken from him at the bottom of the pit.

Kreed let out a long, low whistle. He lowered his lips until they were touching Talin's ear. "My my, you're quite the empty shell aren't you. You're nearly there, my son. Just one more test to be sure there's nothing left. I promise it will be over soon."

"I have nothing. I am nothing," Talin responded with a hoarse, robotic voice.

It was true. Talin hadn't a thing left to offer. He vaguely recalled a treasure chest of memories, but he couldn't remember its contents. The chest had long rotted in places forgotten. He couldn't recall a life before this moment.

"What do you mean by that?" Kreed asked, clasping both hands on Talin's shoulders.

"I no longer have the memories," Talin croaked. "I feel I was supposed to be guarding secrets from you, but they're gone. Everything is gone, even my loyalty. I would give it all to you now if I knew what it was. I no longer care for the fate of this world. I have nothing more for you. I am nothing."

"Oh come now," Kreed scoffed. "Don't be such a pessimist, brave warrior. You most certainly are not *nothing*. You have potential to be as great as I. Potential that will be tapped very soon, unless I am woefully mistaken."

"You are mistaken," Talin said, his voice rising to a slightly louder whisper. "I have nothing more. You broke me. You've ruined all of me. I am barren."

Kreed's voice dropped into a seductive, leathery tone. Talin could hear his manic grin through his words. "My dear warrior, I'm not after your information."

Confused, Talin forced his weakened body to turn and look Kreed in the eyes. One blue and one brown gleamed back at him. "What do you mean?"

Kreed lowered his gaze. "I'm so sorry Talin. It seems you've been laboring under some empty bravado. I'm not at all interested in your adventures from The Sill. Not now at least. Please, don't be offended by this. I value your past, I really do. One day I would love to sit with you and hear all about it, though nothing will be of any use to me in a strategic sense."

Kreed stared into Talin. Feathery giggles escaped between his broken teeth as he saw the sickening realization click on Talin's face. Vague memories of Talin's past life bubbled up through the ashes of his wasteland.

"You see, Decreath lives inside me now. I am his Harbinger, therefore I live inside the hearts of every Aenerian that has ever been graced by Fear. Even now, there is a little girl in a tree at Kulkicka who has climbed too high and is terrified to come down. In Galdebron, a husband dreads coming home early because he knows he'll discover his wife courting another man. I am everywhere now. There are few secrets I am not privy to. Thousands of skipped heartbeats and jumping horrors bombard me day and night. The knowledge was overwhelming at first, a bit too much to process. But Decreath has been patient. He helps me manage it all."

Teetering at the edge of the pit, Talin heard the phantoms calling his name. Another wave of Despair crashed over him, bringing with it fuzzy memories of the last few weeks. Had it all been for nothing? What was the point of such a desolation of his mind and soul? Why in Oberon's bloody light did he have to kill Pineah?

Before the spark of curiosity could fade entirely, Talin opened his cracked lips. "Why?"

"You sell yourself short yet again. We've only just begun to see what you can do with Despair, and let's not forget her brother, Hatred. Yes, the Hatred. I see it in you, plain as moonlight. The Hatred fuels you now, feeding and nursing you like a mother to her babe. As I told you before, you must take the Despair into you, let it become you. When you can't take any more I will unmake you. Then, hopefully the Hatred will still be there to save you." Kreed shivered, digging his fingernails into Talin's arms." It's going to be beautiful, my boy. A part of me is very envious of you. Not for what you've done, but for what you are about to become."

Talin focused on breathing, doing his best to ignore the siren calls from the pit. A taunting sickness welled up inside him. "What will I become?"

"You'll see soon enough!" Kreed slapped Talin on the shoulder. "It's not my place to ruin the surprise. Now, up you get. Let's dry you off and put some proper clothes on you."

Talin fell back, tipping down into the pit. The phantoms were ready and wailing from the shadows. They lunged and lashed at him, tearing him from one memory to the next. It had never been so bad before. They attacked him in pairs, with a third reaching in between gaps in the maelstrom. It was as if they knew he was about to be taken from them and wanted one last kiss goodbye. At first Talin didn't bother fighting. He was familiar with the pain and had no use for the pieces they continued to steal from him. But long after they took their fill the phantoms didn't relent. Their howling tenacity redoubled, scraping and ripping at things never meant to be touched, things they had no right to. Talin was unravelling.

A blinding beam of light shot down the hole, falling on Talin as the phantoms screamed in pain, fleeing back to the shadows. An angel garbed in white floated down into the pit, bending low and picking up what remained of Talin's torment.

Talin's eye opened, bringing Kreed's tear-streaked face into view. Kreed pressed his hand into Talin's chest and a warm, comforting sensation replaced the brittle decay infecting his body. Talin returned to his body as dank air rushed into his lungs.

"There there, warrior." Kreed stroked the side of Talin's face. "I thought I lost you there for a moment. You are very hard on yourself, you know that? I promise it will all be over soon."

With Kreed's assistance, Talin rose to his feet. He had been dressed in a smoky grey suit and matching shoes. His soul was raw and his head seemed to be trying to rip itself in half. He was steady now, steady enough to feel the familiar sensation of magic working in him, healing him. The magic stirred memories in his mind, distant and thin. He knew the magic was called Passion, but more than that he could not recall.

Two soft *pops* announced the arrival of Habbad and the doctor, Florien. Habbad now sported a crimson suit of a cut that matched Kreed's, and now Talin's. Florien was dressed in sleek eveningwear and snapping on a pair of gloves. They both kept their eyes on Talin, measuring him as if he were some dangerous animal who had just escaped his cage. Habbad hissed and kicked at Baedine, sending her scuttling to the far side of the cell.

"Quick as a flash, thank you Habbad." Kreed gave a small bow to the Underkin, and then a nod to Florien. "And you as well, doctor. I hope my sudden appointment didn't put you in a bind?"

Talin recognized these people. He remembered them from the workshop. He also knew that he Hated them, but he could not recall what for. The doctor stepped closer, his eyes leaking bloody tears. Talin certainly didn't remember him having such a pronounced twitch.

"No. No not at all." Florien's words were crammed into one rushed breath. "I was in the next district anyway, recreation. Nothing more important than what you're paying me for."

"Florien," Kreed said, tone rising with halfhearted warning. "You've been at the clubs again, haven't you?"

Florien's eyes followed something unseen to an empty corner of the cell. He winced, jerking his head away. "You know I frequent the clubs. I frequent a whole host of establishments in the city. I assure you I am a master of the body, especially my own. I am fit for duty." Even as he said it, his hand plunged into his pocket, pulling out a small pouch and shaking a few pills out. He popped the pills into his mouth and swallowed them dry.

"Oh don't be so defensive, Florien," Kreed huffed. "I'm not judging, and I'm surely not questioning your abilities. But I do worry about you sometimes. Why, only just last month you had to be pulled out of the fire. I worry some of your *recreations* might cause you to harm yourself. It's my job to worry, being in charge of Costas and all."

A steadying calm replaced Florien's jittery look of unease as his pupils shrank to pin pricks, leaving nothing but the blood-stained whites and irises. He took a deep breath before addressing Kreed.

"As I said, master of the body." Florien strode over to Talin, assessing him as if he were a piece of art at auction. From his jacket he pulled a silver cup, which he began swirling over Talin's forehead and neck. He put the cup to the light, shaking it. "The boy is in perfect health, physically speaking. What do you need me for then, and why didn't you tell me you were adept with Passion? You know I'm useless with magic. You could have saved me hours of work and prevented unneeded suffering for the boy."

"Because using Passion disgusts me, and you are paid handsomely to do a job. A job to be done without the assistance of Decreath's Harbinger," Kreed added with a real warning now rising into his tone.

"What is it that I am supposed to do then?" Florien demanded, crossing his arms.

"Always with the attitude," Kreed said under his breath, closing his eyes as though trying to remember where he put his patience. He slapped Talin on the arm. "You see. This is what I'm talking about! No one's willing to go an inch beyond what's required. Not even the highest paid surgeon in the city."

Kreed shook his head as he sauntered behind Florien. He dangled his arms around Florien's neck in a loose hug. "Your job today is to keep *him*-," Kreed jerked Florien's head to face Talin, "-alive. Keep the boy alive while *he*-," he then snapped his face to Habbad. "-does his job. Can you do that, or is that asking too much?" Kreed asked in a dangerous, honeyed tone, nuzzling his chin onto Florien's shoulder.

Florien shrugged Kreed away, his face souring with embarrassment. "That depends on what's being done to the boy this time."

"Unfortunately, I can't tell you exactly what's going to happen," Kreed said. He walked back to Talin and gave him a gentle shake. "What he's about to go through, well, I've never seen it in my lifetime. That's why I have you here. He needs the best should the worst happen."

Florien gave a lazy nod. "I'll need supplies. And tools."

Kreed nodded at a marble chest behind Florien.

Florien sifted through the chest's drawers and doors, filling his pockets with needle packs, ampules, and salves. "This will do. Unless you pull the boy's head off, there's enough here to keep his heart beating at the very least."

"Outstanding!" Kreed gushed, leaping across the room and pulling Habbad out into Talin's view. Kreed bent low, speaking in hushed whispers into Habbad's ear.

Talin couldn't hear what was being said and he didn't much care. The prison cell no longer held his interest. His Hatred demanded he strike out at everyone in the room, but Kreed's magical shackles held him fast. Instead, Talin retreated within himself to the barren wasteland of his mind.

He was utterly alone in the empty, lifeless fields. Hatred blazed from horizon to horizon, choking and burning the skies with black clouds lined with red lightning. Bitter winds and a bleak landscape drained all thoughts and desires. Despair bubbled from the pit below as it always did, though the phantoms no longer called his name.

A gout of bloody flame erupted in front of Talin, leaving a small figure in its wake.

"I have something for you," Habbad said. "Are you ready to accept it?"

"In the prison cell I am forbidden from harming you." Talin opened his arms like a crow's wings. "This is my realm. You will find no such protection here."

Habbad took a step forward. Fiery lightning roared above them as Talin prepared to bring the entire sky down upon the Underkin. Hatred seething in his bones, Talin raised Pineah's arms, summoning a swirling tornado of malice from the sky; Hatefire. He would cast the entire column down on the both of them.

Habbad smirked up at the Hatefire, then a figure stepped out from behind the Underkin. She was impossibly small in her periwinkle dress and mess of curly hair. Her trembling lips and round eyes were disarmingly familiar.

"Daddy?" the girl whimpered.

Talin's heart leaped back into his chest, flooding him with life and love.

"Penelope..." Talin quailed, falling to his knees. The Hatefire shrank back into the clouds. "My sweet flower..."

She winced as a gust of salty wind tore at her face. A bolt of lightning made her squeal and jump. "Daddy I don't like this place!" She ran to Talin, crashing into him and grasping her hands behind his waist. "Please Daddy, take me home! I don't like it here! I want mommy!"

"Penelope..." Talin breathed. Hugging her close as Habbad took another step towards them.

Habbad cocked his head, an evil grin contorting his wrinkled face. "It's time for you to return. Awake and face your shame, warrior!"

Talin gasped, returning fully to his prison cell. Florien was at his side, fiddling with needles in his arm. Habbad was in front of him, grinning. Kreed was standing just behind the Underkin. Penelope was cradled in his arms.

Munisica erupted from Talin as he screamed in horror. He set his foot back and prepared to charge, but Kreed's magic rang in his mind like a jarring bell, holding him fast.

"KREE-" Talin's voice went silent, though he continued to scream at the top of his lungs. He felt the familiar taint of Kreed's magic stealing his voice.

"She has been brought here for you, Talin," Kreed said, holding out Penelope's body in offering. She was still, though she appeared to be sleeping. "She's the final piece of the puzzle. The way out of the maze."

Kreed pulled her back to his chest and hugged Penelope tightly. Her sleeping arms wrapped around his neck, pulling him in search of comfort. Kreed lowered his head and placed his lips to her cheek, kissing her softly. When he pulled away, the flesh on her smoldered and smoked. She was chosen.

"You and Pineah have suffered," Habbad said, his voice slick and oily. "Your sufferings will now be passed down to your child. Everything that has been done to the both of you shall be done to her. You will be the one to do it."

"*Penelope...*" Talin whispered.

Kreed slinked forward, holding Penelope to Talin. "Here you are, warrior. Hold her one last time before it starts."

Talin pulled his daughter into his chest. His world fractured around him, his mind splitting in two realities. Out of his remaining eye, he beheld the prison cell and his sleeping Penelope. Out of the empty socket, he beheld the wasteland, the sky igniting with Hatred and the pit writhing with Despair. Through Pineah's arms he could feel Penelope quiver, a lamb ready for slaughter in both worlds of pain.

Talin hugged her, crushed her into him as he fell to the ground. Penelope's little body began to smoke and char as she curled tightly against his chest. From her smoldering skin a dense cloud of noxious gases churned about the room. Talin choked, his hacking so violent that he could no longer draw breath. Clutching his daughter, Talin threw his head back as a noise rose from within his chest, a noise that had no business in the world of the living. It was the sounds of Despair and Hatred in their purest forms.

The gas filled the whole of the room, melting paint and boiling the floor tiles. Florien ran from the room, snatching Habbad along the way. Kreed remained, Decreath's taint pouring out of his broken teeth as he stood with his arms spread wide.

An otherworldly cry blared from Kreed's mouth: "Arise, Sorronis the Hated, Sorronis the Despaired!"

CHAPTER 11

FIRE DANCER

"There is no shame in it, Cole. No shame at all," Eliza said, leaning out over the edge of the crow's nest. "At the very least, you're more self-aware. Most people are never ready to face parts of themselves they're afraid of. They bury it, leaving it to fester and accumulate. Acknowledgement and awareness will give you strength."

"You don't get it," Cole said as he turned away. "I could have betrayed any of you without a second thought. I came so close to killing Lileth. It still gives me nightmares, though you probably already knew that. Have you ever dreamed about killing your friends?"

"I can't say I have," Eliza replied. She closed her eyes as a warm breeze whipped her spiked hair to one side.

"The thing that sickens me the most is that I wanted to kill her. I wanted to pull her apart for no other reason than she might have put up a good fight. Given the chance, I would have killed anyone." The words tasted foul in Cole's mouth.

"Then it's nothing personal," Eliza said. "There is no part of you that really wants to kill Lileth, or any of us. No one has ever had a nightmare dreading their desires. You'll sort it out eventually. And don't be so hard on yourself, you've only just begun using our magic."

"You may be right, but that doesn't make it any easier." Cole forced a weak smile.

"Of course not." She shook her head as if dodging a fly. "Rage like yours hasn't been seen since before the banishing. You may very well never be able to control it, but as long as you have someone adept with Passion nearby then you *can* be defused. That is why we're a unit and not solitary vigilantes." She placed the palm of her hand to his chest.

A gentle rosy glow pulsed between her fingers, filling Cole with wholesome sensations of companionship and love.

"Why don't we go find something to do?" he said, unable to hide his smile. "I can't rest anymore and I've just about had it with this ship-food. There's got to be something fun to do around here."

Eliza's eyebrow disappeared in her hair. "You mean something other than sneaking off into the shadows with Lileth?"

Cole checked over the edge of the crow's nest before dropping his voice to a low whisper. "I thought you weren't listening! We talked about privacy and boundaries, remember? I don't go snooping around your thoughts at all hours of the night."

"Nor do I snoop around yours," she said through a fox's smile. "The others have been gossiping about you."

Cole was determined to find out exactly what they were saying, but Eliza disarmed him with another blast of Passion. It was a low trick in Cole's opinion, but he followed her down to the main deck without complaint.

Cole had been spending quite a bit of time with Eliza, though their interactions were usually through their link. He'd never had an older sibling and Eliza fit the role perfectly. She had been one of the first in the unit to befriend him, ignoring the prejudices that were common at The Sill. Whenever memories of Joshy swam up from nowhere, Eliza was always there to share the burden and ease his suffering. He had done the same for her when memories of Deekus pained her. They kept each other afloat in the darkest of times.

The Firedancer had been cruising over the sands for a week now, Oberon growing larger and brighter while it climbed up from the horizon. The soul flies came and went, dancing and flowing about the ship. The captain complained whenever they boarded. He shooed them off with a length of pole, shouting about vulnerabilities as the Firedancer was lit up like a beacon with each visit. The crew made no such complaints, however. The soul flies danced on and around the crew, leaving them awestruck and dreamy-eyed. Often the soul flies would leave them gifts before departing to the sands or up into the aethers.

One pair of soul flies chased each other about the ship, producing endless trails of rope that wound throughout every nook and cranny of the upper deck. The crew initially cursed the soul flies for leaving such a mess. However, after closer inspection they cried out in joy, praising their visitors as they discovered one rope to be woven from strands of sapphire, and the other from woven platinum. Afraid to ruin the work of art, the crew made painstaking efforts and took an entire day unravelling the gifts.

Following Eliza down the pegs of the main mast, Cole leapt from halfway down, using Wisdom to slow his fall at the last second.

"Beat you," he said, standing tall.

Eliza took her time climbing down the rest of the way, joining Cole on the main deck with a neat hop. "Had I known we were racing, I think I would have let you win anyway. It's good for you to win at some things now and again, little human."

"You better watch yourself, Aenerian." Cole stood next to her, using his hand to measure the top of his head to her shoulder. "I'm almost up to your chin now. I've only been here a few months. I might turn out bigger than you before long."

"You of all people should know that size is no indication of one's abilities. Your friend Habbad was unusually gifted with Wisdom, and you yourself made a mockery of the Colossus." She waggled her shining pink finger in front of her grin. "And don't think I won't charm you if you get too brash with me."

Cole's smile faded as he thought about Habbad. He wondered how his friend was holding up under Kreed's shadow. Habbad's grim smile and vacant eyes still haunted him.

Shaking the dreary thoughts, Cole looked about the ship. "Why don't we change things up a bit?"

"What do you mean?" she asked.

"Since I came to Aeneria, almost every day has been filled with training or running or fighting. It's non-stop stress, you know? We never take time to just have a bit of fun. There's got to be something we can do." He kicked at a barrel, sending a soul fly rushing out blaring a sun-yellow hue. The soul fly bumped into a cross-beam above them, producing a ringing peal as it showered them with hot sparks.

The cascade of sparks gave Cole an idea. He turned to Eliza, a wild grin spreading on his face. "Eliza, what do you say we play a little joke on someone?"

"A what?" she asked, taking interest in his mischievous expression.

He searched the deck, making sure no one was around. "Have you seen Valen? I feel like he could use a good joke."

"I'm not sure I follow," she replied. "Is it the same as what the jesters do in the arts district? They tell jokes, though they are rather boorish for my taste."

"Not anything like that," Cole said, remembering how the jesters spouted off cruel but true jokes about outsiders and other races. "I'm thinking more of a harmless prank. You know, to have fun at someone else's...misfortune."

Eliza stiffened, gawking at him with a look of shock. "Well that sounds awful. At least the jesters don't assault others directly."

"It's not as bad as it sounds," Cole said, picking up a loose nut perched atop a bundle of rope. He hefted the iron in between his hands. "Come with me, and try to be quiet."

Valen had just come up from below deck, his hands dirty and his face sagging with exhaustion from a long day tinkering on the Firedancer. He walked to the bow and summoned a crystalline telescope just like Lileth's. As he scanned the horizon, Cole led Eliza to a tall stack of wooden traps.

Cole crouched low and peered at Valen between the gaps in the traps. "*He won't be able to see us from here.*"

"*And why would we need to hide from him?*" Eliza asked, giving him a suspicious look.

"*You'll see.*"

Cole held out the iron nut in the flat of his hand. With a green spark from his finger, the nut shot into the air, weaving through the netting of the front mast and coming to a halt above Valen. Cole's eye twitched with effort as the nut dropped into a guided dive, bouncing off Valen's shoulder with a sharp *thwack.*

Valen's telescope came apart, the emerald pieces clinking over the deck before flickering and fading. Confused, he looked around the bow, his eyes falling upon the rogue nut. He plucked it off the deck and looked above him to the front mast, his lips thin and eyes wide.

Cole bit down on his knuckles, shaking with stifled giggles. *"I'll bet you anything he goes up and checks every bolt on the front mast."*

Eliza's budding amusement began trickling through. *"I think you are making a gross underestimation of Valen's attention to detail."*

As Cole suspected, Valen jumped to the base of the front mast, checking the joinery by the decking. Eliza pulled Cole tight to her. With a quick wiggle of her fingers she folded a spell around them, rendering the two invisible. Valen passed right over them in his search. Conjuring a small crystalline wrench, he tightened every nut and bolt on his way up the front mast. Once at the top, he sprouted wings and leapt to the main mast, setting to work at once with his tool.

"You weren't kidding. This'll take him half an hour at least!" Cole whispered with his thoughts, as though Valen might somehow hear them.

Eliza shook with silent giggles. *"That's if he finds the culprit."*

After only a few minutes of laughing at Valen's fervent bustling, Cole swore under his breath. Valen cried out victorious as he set his tool to the cross beam of the main mast, fitting the missing nut back to its home. Apparently unsatisfied, he continued down the main mast and checked every nut on the rear mast as well.

Eliza recalled her invisible curtain. "Well, at least the ship is in better shape. Is that part of the prank?"

"Definitely not," Cole scowled. His bare feet slapped over the deck as he trotted closer to Valen, who was now checking the riggings of some cargo straps up on the rearmost deck.

Eliza glided along next to him silent as a shadow. "I'm afraid I don't understand the meaning of your prank. What end are you seeking here?"

Cole pressed his finger to his lips, silencing her. He flexed his hand as his thumb and forefinger stretched into blackened claws. He darted to the door to the lower decks and used his talons to loosen one of the nuts on an ornate lantern. Cole retracted his claws. Clamping the nut between his teeth, he jumped up and grabbed the bannisters of the rear deck. Pulling his head just above the floor, he spied Valen hunched over and fiddling with a latch that secured a large stack of barrels.

Holding on with only one hand, Cole snatched the nut from his teeth and flung it as hard as he could, hitting Valen square in the back of his head.

Cole landed as softly as a falling leaf. *"Walk away...walk away and act as if nothing happened."*

"This is utterly absurd." Eliza shook her head, striding off towards the bow of the ship.

Cole sat himself on a bench next to the rear mast and feigned interest in a school of soul flies that kept pace next to the ship. Valen's footsteps pounded close.

"Cole!" Valen barked. "Go find the captain...please. His rotten ship is falling apart."

Cole painted his face with a look of quiet shock, a tactic he'd mastered in middle school. "What do you mean the ship's falling apart? Is this thing not safe?" His eyes darted about, as if the decking might catch fire any moment.

"This is what I mean!" Valen whipped his arm about, showing Cole the little lump of iron. "I don't know what shoddy engineers built this boat, but it's clearly not meant for sustained sprints like this. Please Cole, get the captain now! It's raining nuts out here!"

Cole's ears twitched. With supreme effort, he kept his face blank as he nodded. "I'll go find him."

"Thank you, Cole." Valen's emerald wings flashed to life once more. "I'll go see what in Oberon's bloody light is falling apart this time."

Cole's belly shook with laughter as he cast his face in stony determination. He approached the rear door, and heard wind flapping and filling Valen's wings as he took flight. Cole was about to grab the handle when the door flung open.

"What's Valen spouting off about? Are we under attack?" Sitra asked, teeth baring as her eyes followed Valen up the rear mast.

"You could say that," Eliza's silky voice sounded from nowhere. Appearing from thin air, she grinned like a fox as she held out a handful of iron nuts. "We are assaulting Valen with a hail of hardware. Would you care to join?"

"What are you talking about, Liza?" Sitra said, plucking one of the nuts from her outstretched hand.

Eliza turned her grin to Cole. *"Why don't you explain it to her?"*

Cole took a nut and hefted it in his palm. *"Gladly."*

It didn't take much explaining for Sitra to get the idea, though Cole didn't like the savage grin that lit her face. They waited for Valen to finish checking all three masts, crafting new ways to trick him all the while.

"When he gets down to the last one, I'm going to light his pants on fire," Sitra whispered.

Cole winced. "Sitra! That's not how pranks work. You're not supposed to hurt anyone."

"Then what's the point?" she asked, her lips curving in a half-frown. "It's not very exciting if there's no danger. All you two have managed to do is to make him climb up and down a pole. *I'm* gonna make him *dance*." Grinning, she rubbed her hands together as fiery stars sparked out from her fingertips. "Yeah, I'm gonna light his pants on fire."

Cole shook his head, suddenly remembering why he'd retired from his pranking career. The last thing they needed was a magical duel between his friends. He made for the door to the lower decks, but a sudden flapping of wind stopped him mid-stride.

"Cole!" Valen said, hovering above. "Where is the captain? You haven't been dawdling have you? This is important."

A nervous tingling had filled Cole's chest as he looked from Valen to Sitra, who strode casually away from them, her face hidden from view. Eliza meandered off to the side, suddenly very interested in Oberon. Cole's mind raced as he inventoried his scant spells to put out a fire.

"I was just discussing the issue with the others. I'll go get the captain now..." Cole's voice trailed off as Valen's wings vanished and he dropped to the deck.

"Don't bother," Valen said, storming past him. "It's obvious you don't realize the danger we're in. If one of those cross beams comes loose..." He stopped at the door, turning around slowly. "What is that in your hand, Cole?"

Cole shifted his hand slightly to hide the nut from view. "I...I don't have anything."

In the blink of an eye, Valen shot across the space between them and snatched Cole's wrist, wrenching it upwards. The nut fell from his hand, bouncing and rolling its way across the deck, then it slipped between two bannisters as it fell overboard. Eyes locked on Cole, Valen released his wrist as his hand glowed a dull jade. The nut came sailing up from the sands and smacked into his palm.

Cole swallowed. "Another one fell while you were up there."

"I find that unlikely. What are you up to, human? If there's something you're not-oh!" Valen yelped as a gout of flame erupted from a nearby gas pipe.

The flame snaked its way around Cole, dousing Valen's legs in dripping fire. Valen jumped up and down, slapping the flames while he cried out for help.

"Fire on deck!" a voice hollered from a crow's nest. "Fire on deck!"

His words were echoed from the crew as a few sailors came running with large rifles with red tanks fixed to the stocks. Water shot out of the barrels, spraying in narrow cones over Valen's legs. The flames did not die, however; they flared and grew, as if angered by the water.

Arms flailing, Valen yanked and pulled at his pants, but the smoldering cloth fell apart in his hands. "Someone, please!" he pleaded.

The fire showed no sign of relenting as the water guns sputtered and died. The crew dropped their extinguishers and bustled around Valen, stomping at any flames that dripped onto the polished wooden deck.

Cole ran through every memory and trick he used to put out fires. Water of course was of no use. He could transfer the heat into another object, but everything around them was flammable. Unsure, he took a small step towards Valen, who now hopped from foot to foot, slapping his legs and screaming in pain.

The door behind Valen burst open, revealing Lileth, her eyes wide with apprehension. She scanned the deck as spells shimmered to life in her hands. A powerful burst of air charged across the deck, knocking Cole to his backside. He scrambled to his feet, his ears ringing. Both Valen and the broken pipe ceased burning.

Silence fell over the deck, broken only by Valen's panting and his sizzling trousers.

"What happened?" Lileth asked, directing her question towards Cole and Eliza.

Cole's mouth opened and closed, but no words came out. He looked to Eliza, but she remained silent as well, wearing a look of polite amusement.

Boisterous laughter exploded from above them. Sitra hung from the netting of the rear mast, holding her belly as she sniggered. She took a deep breath as if to speak, only to laugh even harder. The *Firedancer's* crew took a step back, putting space between them and the lunatic above.

"Sitra?" Lileth called up. "What's so funny? Your war-brother is hurt."

"Never mind, me!" Valen spat, covering his nakedness. "This rusty bucket is falling apart! It's been raining nuts and now the ship is spitting fire!"

Sitra's howling rose as she fell from the netting, crashing through a crate below the rear mast in an explosion of splinters. Cackling madly, she rose from the wreckage, gasping for air and limping.

"Did you see him dance?" she squealed when she finally found her breath. "Valen the wise, dancing with fire! Aboard a ship called the *Firedancer!*"

Valen picked up a few scraps of his pants and tried to cover himself. "Sitra, did you have something to do with this?"

Sitra held her stomach, massaging it with her fist. "Oh don't be such a worry-worm. You weren't in any real danger, you only thought you were. And now we know how good of a dancer you are!" A fit of giggles took her breath from her once more. "Ow, ow, ow, my stomach's cramping!"

Valen face darkened. "What do you mean I was in no danger? You lit me on fire, Sitra! What in Oberon's light would possess you to light me on fire? On a wooden ship!"

Sitra took a steadying breath, wiping tears from her eyes. "Look at your skin. Look at the wood. Do you see any damage?"

Dripping wet, Valen's eyes darted about his legs as he assessed himself. While his pants were nothing but a charred pile on the deck, there was no visible injury to his skin or the wood. Confused, he looked back to Sitra. "What was the point of it then?"

"To laugh at your misfortune of course!" she said in a sing-song voice, dancing over to Valen and putting her arms around his shoulders. "Loosen up, brother, my fire only ate your pants. Not every day needs to be about rules and tasks. Cole was right, we owe it to ourselves to have some fun now and again." She bent down and picked up an unburnt scrap of his pants and clapped it to Valen's backside.

Valen's face flushed through several shades of red as he fumbled between hiding his front and batting away Sitra's hand.

Sitra pulled her hand away, revealing tendrils of green light streaming from her palm. The patch of Morthainian armor began to stretch and flow over Valen's naked skin. "Give me a hand Liza, I was never good with the seamstress stuff."

"Of course." Eliza smiled, adding her magic to Sitra's. "Be sure to leave him extra room around the knees and groin, we never know when our fire-dancer might lose himself to another bout of frolicking."

"You took part in this sneakery as well?" Valen asked, a look of utter betrayal on his face.

Eliza held her fist above Valen's head and sprinkled him with a handful of iron nuts. "It's a more likely story than a *rain of nuts*." She chuckled, slapping him softly on the cheek. "Don't be so serious, Valen. It was only a game."

"*A game* you say?" Valen said, adjusting the belt of his newly mended trousers. "And I assume our little Cole was in on the plot as well, weren't you?"

Cole rubbed his jaw. "I may have found a nut lying around. I just brought it to your attention, didn't I? And you went and checked all the masts twice! The ship's in better shape than it's ever been. What's wrong with that?"

A hint of a smile twitched at Valen's jaw. "So I see. I think I understand your game now. We will have another match soon enough, though next time you may find *yourself* the fool." He nodded to Lileth. "Please don't tell me you were involved."

Lileth crossed her arms, a wry half-grin pulling across her cheek. "Would you believe me if I said I wasn't?"

Valen squinted at her. "Probably not."

"In that case, count me in on all games henceforth," Lileth said in an offhanded tone. "A bit of friendly competition will keep our minds sharp, which ought to come in useful as we're headed to a city full of Wisdom-followers. Cole may even be forced to solve a problem without Rage for once." She winked at Cole, walking over to the burst pipe, which now bled oil all over the deck. "Though I think we ought to leave the Firedancer out of it. The ship that is, not you, Valen."

Valen's stony glare cracked like brittle glass as laughter finally took him. The rest of the unit joined in, releasing weeks of bottled-up tension. Cole had never heard Valen laugh before. Throughout the collective mirth, Cole thought he felt Eliza in the back of his mind, nudging Valen's elation with Passion.

A gunshot brought their attention to a crewman standing up on the stern deck. He leaned against a rifle longer than he was tall. The sailor spat at his feet before addressing the unit. "Your lot has done nuthin' but stir the sands since yer arrivals. Good men is dyin' back there, yer Roth included. And here ya are, jokin and bayin like a bunch o giddy prats! We're only bringin' ya's cross the sands as a favor to our King, the true King mind. We won't bring ya's no farther, and we won't hold with any more of yer games. Disrespectin' the Firedancer, bah! Not while there's still marrow in my bones."

A dozen crewmen appeared while the man spoke, appearing from nowhere as though they had popped right up from the planks. They all grumbled and growled their agreement as they hefted clubs and Morthainian weapons.

Cole assessed the man holding the rifle. He was not the captain, but judging by the way the others fell in around him he was well-listened to. He had a hard, dangerous stare that implied he was accustomed to getting his way.

In a flash almost too fast for Cole to see, Sitra appeared on the stern deck directly in front of the crew. Before they could finish flinching, she snatched the rifle from the man's hands.

Sitra admired the rifle, taking aim at the stars and flipping it in the air. "You know, if you boys wanted a part in our game you only had to ask. And don't you fret, we'll put your Firedancer back together before we leave. And maybe I'll give you your toy back if you ask real nice," she said, slinging the rifle over her back.

The man puffed his chest and stood to his full height, which was a half-head shorter than Sitra. "Darlin, you just made yerself an enemy o' the crew. Keep the gun. Yer gonna need it."

"Hmm," Sitra huffed, turning her back to the man and walking down the stairs, patting the stock of her new rifle.

Tension twisted the air as Sitra mended the broken crate with Wisdom. Lines of emerald light shot from her palms, pulling the broken pieces back together. Eliza collected the loose nuts in her cupped hands, bringing them to her lips and whispering something. The nuts glowed a dull jade before shooting off like bees back to their nests. Valen went below deck to speak to the captain as Lileth siphoned up the oil and fixed the burst pipe with a quick spell. Cole tried to help with the clean-up, but his grasp of Wisdom was useless outside of the most basic tasks. He hoped that the crew's threat didn't extend beyond Sitra. Lileth was right; he only had his Rage to get him out of trouble. He had no desire to wield his munisica against these men. As if in answer to his doubts, a wild growl bumped against his mind.

Cole hardened his thoughts and returned the mirak's mental bump. *"Yeah, yeah. I've always got you too, Goran. They'd think twice about messing with me when you're around."*

From somewhere below deck, Cole felt Goran shove an entire pie into his mouth before rolling over and falling back asleep, his treat dripping from his jowls.

• • • •

The next few days aboard the Firedancer were wrought with sticky surprises and complex traps that taxed Cole's Wisdom to the limits. There was no reprieve from the assault, as every inch of the Firedancer seemed to have some unseen trick ready to spring at him. Cole drank from a water jug offered to him by Valen, and for several hours afterwards his mind had reversed its definition of left and right. He would try to use his right hand to grab hold of a railing, only to have his left reach out into thin air as he went barreling down a flight of stairs. Eventually he became accustomed to the vertigo, only to have the effects wear off as his usual faculties then became his handicap.

On an evening when the soul flies were particularly active, he secured a spot for Lileth and himself to watch the show. Lileth offered Cole one of her conjured telescopes. He gazed through it but knew at once something was wrong. Cole looked to Lileth and fell, quite literally, into her eyes, smashing his forehead against hers. He had lost all sense of depth perception, making the crow's nest more like an angel's nest as high as the heavens. He cowered in the nest long after she left, though she promised that the effects would relent once he reached the bottom of the mast. It took him nearly an hour to muster the courage to make the descent, and another hour to actually make it to the main deck.

Not all of the jokes were mentally debilitating, however. Cole never found out who the culprit was, but he woke every morning to find himself completely naked. At first he thought someone had stolen his clothes, but as it turned out, they had merely been made invisible. Tired of waiting around for his clothes to reappear every day, he started hiding them under Goran before bed. The fight with the Colossus had revealed the full measure of Goran's savagery, and no one dared give him reason to display it again.

While the rest of the unit enjoyed unravelling each other's spells, Cole's ineptitude with Wisdom left him helpless to the hazing. Often Eliza would take pity on him and relieve him of the magical fetters. While Cole had become the unit's punching bag, he was certainly not the one who suffered the most. True to their word, the crew had made Sitra their sworn enemy. While they made no outright attempt to harm her, their tricks were as subtle as they were clever. No one could figure out how, but she had somehow become a magnet to every rodent on the ship. She spent her waking and sleeping hours fighting off rats of varying size and persistence, tossing them overboard or being scared awake by wet noses and scratching claws. Worse than the nighttime visitors was her hourly rush to the toilets. Sitra alone had contracted a crippling malady of the intestines that the crew had dubbed 'bubble gut,' and 'screamin squirts.' Sitra made no attempt to restore peace with the crew, and continued to wear the rifle like a trophy as she waddled around the Firedancer. Cole winced every time he saw her run to the lower decks clenching her backside. Making a silent vow to himself, he swore off all pranks until the end of his days.

As the Firedancer raced towards Oberon, the white powder beneath them turned to a dark mud, which eventually gave way to murky waters. Oberon was now much larger and nearly right above them in the starry sky.

The Firedancer sloshed down into the choppy water, its usual smooth ride shifting to a constant rock and sway. Cole had not seen the captain since the first few days of their journey. He guessed that the salty old man wanted nothing to do with the foolishness going on above him. When the Firedancer neared the shores of the destination, the captain emerged from his quarters, hobbling up the creaky steps and joining the unit on the prow deck.

"This is as far as we'll bring her. We don't have favorable relations with the folk up in the Fangshards." The captain pointed a knife up at the jagged peaks that lined the shore. "I'd offer you one of our ferry boats, but it looks as if you lot are keen to use your Wisdom to carry you ashore."

Valen stretched and flexed his wings. "We will get ourselves ashore, but your offer is appreciated all the same. Should we expect any opposition from the people of the Fangshards?"

The captain shook his head: "No, I don't think so. As long as they don't see you coming from the Firedancer that is. We had some bad blood with them before the banishing, and there's a fair chance they'd recognize a Morthainian ship, so we'll park her right here. We're well on the Dark Side of the world now, far beyond the barrier and our borders. Be quiet about making it ashore and keep to yourselves to the valley once you get there. If you stick to the main pass it'll take you right to Oberon City, and they'll probably not bother you."

Cole didn't feel too assured by the captain's advice. His gaze stretched over the mountain range before them. The serrated peaks seemed to touch the stars and looked as if they'd been pulled from the jaw of some ancient predator. Anyone who could survive in such a place must be tough indeed. Focusing his Wisdom, Cole stretched the lenses in his eyes, zooming his vision and revealing strings of lights and tiny villages sprinkled across the whole ridge. At the foothill was a winding path that cut through the mountains towards Oberon. There were certainly fewer lights around the pass.

"Thank you for the advice, we'll depart immediately." Valen turned, though he was halted by a little cough behind him. "Yes captain?"

"I know relations between the crew and your unit have been a bit… tenuous of late, what with these stupid *prank wars*." He rubbed his hands, wincing slightly, as though the words pained him. "What I'm getting at, or suggesting really, is that if you were to charge up the Firedancer's gratia stones before you left…well it would go a long way to mending things. It would shorten our trip home by a considerable measure, and as captain I would declare you the sporting victors of whatever the hell a *prank war* is. I know your own affairs are priority, but if you could spare a bit of that Passion of yours…" The captain's voice trailed off as he shook his head. "Ahh forget I asked. You lot charged half the fleet back in the docks."

Cole felt a pang of sympathy for the captain and his men. He knew what they were really after was the creature-comforts provided by the gratia stones' power. Hot showers, warm meals, and cold ales were a luxury they had never known while out in the sands. The stones were near empty and they would suffer a bleak journey back if they had to travel by wind power alone.

"Consider it done, Captain," Valen said.

"Are you sure then?" the captain asked. "It's a hard day's march to Oberon City. You'll need your strength."

Eliza approached the captain, placing a soft lavender-lit hand to his jaw. "What Valen meant to say is that you can consider it *already* done. Sitra and I charged your gratia stones earlier today. Do not mourn our strength, for Passion requires none. It merely asks for a moment of kindness and a willingness to heal someone's hurt."

The captain's face slackened when Eliza pulled her hand away. He closed his eyes, smiling as the breeze carried a tear from his cheek.

He opened his eyes, face lit with a child-like glee. "Thank you! Thank you, warrior of The Sill. Thank you all! Should you ever find yourself in the White Sands again look for our sails. You are most welcome in our ranks."

Eliza nodded and resumed her place next to Goran, stroking his white mohawk. Goran sniffed the wind and scanned the mountains with tense, jerky motions. Cole sensed an odd primal urge in his mind. Something about the mountains drew Goran's every thought, as if the jagged peaks called his name. Cole impressed the importance of not jumping overboard, reminding Goran that he was no longer a little mirak, and couldn't swim with his dense new body. Goran whined, gripping the edge of the railing with his curved claws. Cole did his best to soothe the mirak through the link, but his pining drowned out all other thought.

A man shouldered his way to the front of the crew. It was the same man who'd had his rifle stolen by Sitra. "I've a couple words fer the feisty one before ya go flyin off."

Sitra cocked her head and crossed her arms, casting the man a shrewd look. Cole knew she was still sick, but her stubbornness would never let it show. He could hear her stomach squeal and gurgle from a few paces away.

"And what might that be?" she called out to the man, teeth and munisica bared.

"Fiddledust and Riker's Root," he grunted. "They're both a-plenty in the foothills of the Fangshards. Boil 'em up in a tea and you'll be rid o' yer bubble gut."

Sitra's clawed hand dropped to her stomach, which sounded like it was trying to escape. "That it?" she asked, her voice shaking slightly.

"Jus' the one more thing, darlin." He grinned, raising one eyebrow. "Our quarrel's not settled."

"I know," Sitra said. She reached behind her back and drew the man's stolen rifle. With a deft stroke, she heaved the weapon like a javelin towards the man, who caught it with both hands, stumbling back into his fellows. Before the man could say another word she took flight. The rest of the unit fell in behind her.

The flight to the shore was brief. Goran usually loathed being in the air, but as the unit carried them with their collective threads of Wisdom he remained still and tense. Cole had had a difficult time connecting with his friend ever since they came within sight of the spiky ridge. Despite Cole's prodding, Goran ignored everything that was not the Fangshard Mountains. Not even the temptation of food could shake him.

Lileth held Cole tight to her body as her jade wings carried them both towards the shore. Cole wished the flight was longer, withdrawing reluctantly from her embrace as their bare feet splashed into the sandy beach.

"Goran!" Valen cried.

Upon landing, Goran tore into the woodline, sniffing, licking, and climbing everything on his way. The force of his charge had snapped their chains of Wisdom, giving everyone a jarring mental shock.

"He'll be fine, I've still got my link with him," Cole said, rubbing his head. "He's really excited about the mountains. No idea why though. Might have been cooped up too long on the ship."

Cole widened and bolstered his bond to Goran. The mirak's thoughts spilled over into Cole's, making his nostrils flare and heart quicken. Goran felt more like a wild animal than he ever had. Anchoring his focus on the beach, Cole stretched the limits of his Passion and forced a rule upon Goran. Though he yearned to climb the peaks, Goran could go no farther up the foothills of the Fangshards, limiting his reckless wandering to a half mile from the unit. Cole experimented with the leash, giving it a good tug. Goran leapt from the top of a tree and stormed closer until the snapping of branches and enthusiastic snorts were within earshot. Guilt bubbled up in Cole, but for all he knew the Fangshards might hold dangers too great for even a giant mirak. It seemed like only yesterday that Cole was half naked, rescuing Goran from the tendrils of those giant grubs.

"Is Goran well?" Lileth asked as her eyes followed Goran's crashing. "I've never seen him in such a state."

"Neither have I," Cole said. "He's definitely out of his mind, but I can keep him close while we make our way through the pass." Cole winced involuntarily. Through the link he felt Goran tearing into some poor creature. "It's probably better if he's not around people right now."

"As long as he can keep up with us," Valen said, folding his wings and drawing his munisica. "I intend for us to run through the pass without pause."

"Once we get going I'll give him a good tug," Cole replied.

"Then let us be off." Valen turned heel and bolted at a steady trot towards the pass.

Cole drew his munisica and followed, though he kept his Rage throttled to the minimum. Cole sprinted up alongside Lileth, admiring how bits of her hair had become bladed, an achievement that she was perhaps not yet aware of. Cole had difficulty keeping up with his unit, but he needed to control his Rage for the safety of the unit, including Goran. The more Cole delved into the Rage, the weaker his Passion-bond to Goran was. Try as he might, he could do nothing to quell the primal urges of his friend. They had only been running for ten minutes when Goran stopped to savage another creature. The wanton killing bothered Cole on a deep level, as Goran had merely discarded his first kill and not eaten any of it. Cole's disappointment went unnoticed through his mental leash. Cole swallowed back guilty vomit as he gave Goran another pull, causing him to abandon yet another kill. Hopefully the scavengers of the mountains could make use of the corpses.

The beach-sand hardened into a path lined with granite blocks, each embellished with glowing veins of amber. The craftsmanship stood out in stark contrast against the verdant overgrowth that spilled down from the valley walls. The mountains had swallowed nearly all the horizon, leaving only a thin strip of the starry sky and part of Oberon above them. Cole felt a tickling of claustrophobia within the pass. The stale, hot air and steep slopes were an unwelcome change compared to the endless skies and steady breeze of the White Sands. Cole tugged at his link to Goran, who climbed ever higher away from them.

Valen slowed to a cautious jog, signaling for them to do the same. "Something is ahead of us. The trail is far too quiet."

Cole sharpened his eyes and ears as much as his Wisdom would allow. He sensed nothing.

Crouching low, Sitra sniffed the air. "I don't feel it. Liza, do your Passion-thing."

"It's called listening," Eliza said, her voice barely audible. "If you were more diligent in the arts of Passion, the spell would not elude you so. Feeling the life force of other beings can be useful in battle too, you know."

Sitra ignored her, inching forward like a stalking cat. Eliza closed her eyes and raised her chin, spreading her arms wide. Cole felt her consciousness pass over his like a steady breeze.

Eliza's thoughts hummed into Cole's: "*Pay attention. You ought to learn this aspect of Passion as well.*"

Cole pushed back at her mind: "*I'd love to, but right now it's all I can do to keep Goran from running off without tripping over my own feet. I can't be in three places at once.*"

"*I'm not asking you to. Do not try to sing every song. Just listen to the music,*" she replied.

Cole shrugged at her suggestion. While he was eager to learn everything he could about magic, now was certainly not the time to experiment. Though he withdrew from their link, he could still feel her mind vibrating and tingling in his skull. Curiosity nudged one of his own thoughts loose, dipping ever so slightly into the thin stream of their link. He was immediately overwhelmed by the flow of information, and he severed the thought. He would have to try again when he wasn't so taxed.

Eliza spoke without opening her eyes: "There is a spell hanging over the pass. It's keeping the wildlife away. Everything is indeed quiet..." She gasped, eyes snapping wide. "There are people here, just ahead on the trail. They're...massive. Powerful." Her voice dropped to a low hiss as the color drained from her face. "They know I'm listening."

"Should we turn back?" Lileth asked, crouching with Sitra.

"It's no use." Eliza's eyes went to the sky as a shadow moved over Oberon. "They are upon us!"

"Scatter!" Valen hissed, darting up into the sloping forest.

Eliza's apprehension fed into Cole, and through him into Goran. In the mirak's eyes, Cole saw trees bending and branches snapping as

Goran shot towards them like an arrow. Cole slackened the leash, focusing his efforts instead on bending the shadows around him, bathing him in potent darkness. He had never used such Wisdom before, but his urge to hide was so powerful that his instincts made it so. He huddled in between a tree and the slope of the valley, unable to see his own hand in front of his face. He looked around, but there was no sign of the others.

"*Eliza, is everyone invisible?*" he asked.

"*Quiet your mind. She can hear you,*" Eliza replied.

Cole loosened his ties to both links and tried emptying his mind as Chiron had taught him. Chilled Fear bubbled up from his legs as he felt the concussing *thud-thud* of massive wings. Cole covered his eyes as debris buffeted him. The ground shook beneath him as a creature the size of a bus landed on the pavement, claws scraping over the stone slabs. Holding on to his shadows like a blanket, Cole peeked down through the leaves.

Oberon's rainbow glow revealed Alvani hopping down from her winged steed, Gale. She strode towards Cole with a warm smile upon her face.

CHAPTER 12

OBERON CITY

"Shed your shadows and join me, Warriors of The Sill," Alvani called out to the unit, though she kept her eyes on Cole.

Cole waited for the others to move first. Eliza appeared from thin air next to Gale, stroking under the beast's feline jaw. The creature had a feline head as large as Roth's whole body, with wispy ears and a velvety snout. The rest of its body was more avian with golden plumage, black eagle's claws, and wings as big as an aeroplane's. Cole dismissed his spells and approached Alvani as the rest of the unit reappeared.

"It's good to see you too, Gale," Eliza cooed as Gale rubbed his head against her. Gale's head was larger than the whole of her body.

"Master Alvani!" Valen said with a little bow. "Your appearance is most welcome...and unexpected. How did you know where to find us?"

Alvani kept her eyes on Cole. "Roth and I agreed to link our minds with Passion before you left on your mission. He kept me informed of everything you have been through since leaving The Sill, though he has been silent of late. Unfortunately, the Celestial Council has been less than proactive about the information I relay. Apparently, five Colossi loose in the White Sands is of no concern to them. The fact that any of you made it out alive is a miracle." She gave Cole a meaningful look before addressing the rest of the group. "Roth also told me of your struggle in Costas. If his account is accurate, Decreath has taken the one called Kreed as Harbinger. Grotton and Sorronis will likely be seeking their Harbingers as well, which will put their forces in full stride while we remain as segregated as ever. Dark tides creep ever closer. My heart weeps for what we will lose, and what we have already lost. Habbad and Storn…I hoped Roth was wrong."

No one answered. Cole tore his mind from the rooftop where the scene of Storn's death painted itself on the back of his eyelids. He looked around and saw defeated, distant looks on the others. He locked eyes with Lileth, pulling her out of her reverie. She gave him a small, warm smile.

"Storn represented some of the best parts of the unit," Lileth said, her voice trembling slightly. "We will do our best to take up his standards of strength and loyalty. Habbad…deserved better. I mourn for them both."

Alvani spread her arms. "Take comfort in the embrace of the ones you still have. Festering grief will undermine the very foundations of your mind and allow Sorronis to seep through the cracks. The death of a friend is a burden no one should bear alone. Rejoice and be refreshed."

Rosy motes of light poured from her hands, swirling around her as if caught in a strong wind. Behind her, Gale pointed his snout to the sky and chirped a loud song that echoed throughout the valley.

An oppressive weight that Cole had only just noticed came free from his mind and body. He felt as though he'd woken from a perfect night's sleep to a reality even better than his dreams. The rosy diodes spun faster. He laughed, filled to the brim with giddy euphoria. Alvani's Passion rushed through him, bolstering him with the unshakable fact that she loved and truly cared for him. Looking around, he saw the rest of the unit similarly affected, all wearing looks of supreme relaxation and elation.

"You have suffered much," Alvani said to the group. "Let my gift keep your fires burning bright in these dark times."

"Thanks, Master Alvani," Sitra sighed, stretching her arms overhead with a satisfied moan. "I feel like I could run around the world right now."

"Let's start with a little sprint to Oberon City, shall we?" Alvani said, jumping up and throwing a leg over Gale's saddle. "Cole, would you mind riding with me for a bit? I have words for you alone."

"Of course." Cole pulled himself up, sliding into a seat behind his Master. His legs trembled with nerves. "Can you tell Gale to take it easy? I don't like-"

Cole's voice plummeted to his stomach as Gale lunged into the sky. He wrapped his arms around Alvani's middle, latching onto her robes. He leaned his forehead against her back, afraid to see how high they were. Judging by the stars in his periphery, they were already near the peaks of the mountains. Cole felt Gale level out as his flapping ceased to a steady glide. The air around him shifted as a quiet breeze replaced the rushing wind.

"Relax Cole," Alvani said, gently pulling his hands free. "Gale has you now."

Cole unclenched his fingers and buried them in the fluffy feathers behind him. Alvani turned around to face him in the saddle. The air was unusually calm. Upon opening his eyes Cole recognized the glittery sheen of a spell encircling them, keeping the wind at bay.

"Has Roth told you why you are headed to Oberon City?" she asked, leaning towards him.

Cole shook his head. "He didn't tell me anything, just that the Council wanted us all there. The others said they overheard something about a trial. It sounded like I was in trouble."

"I'm afraid the truth is much more worrisome," she said, gripping Cole's shoulder. "I'm sorry Cole, but we have kept you in the dark on some matters. Trust me when I say that it was for your own safety. I cannot tell you everything now, but I will tell you what I can. Chiron has sworn me to secrecy, but he may tell you more. The Council has indeed called for a trial. They seek recompense for the destruction of the barrier, as well as answers for the return of the soul flies and how you are able to Travel. The Sill is also being called into question for our actions in Costas, as the mission was not vetted by the Council. During the trial I advise you not to divulge your mastery of Rage, your bond with Goran, or your ability to Travel out-of-turn. The Council already knows a great deal about you. If they knew the whole truth then you would no doubt be dragged into their politics with no choice in the matter. Your life would no longer be your own."

Cole felt his voice rising with ire. "And what exactly is the truth? What are you not telling me?"

"I'm sorry Cole, I can tell you no more. Chiron has bound my tongue. I assure you he will explain it himself when you get to the capital."

"More secrets," Cole said bitterly. "Well I guess I'll just have to take whatever you'll give me. I Hate this you know, I feel like a dog begging for scraps every time someone hints at what's going on, like I'm not tough enough to know the truth. I may not be as old as any of you, but on Terra I'm not a child. I can handle it, so don't worry about protecting my fragile little mind."

Cole finished his rant, leaving thick silence between them. For a moment Alvani's only response was a look of prolific sympathy and patience, which left Cole's ears burning with shame.

Alvani waited for Cole to look at her before replying, "If I could, I would take your burdens from you, Cole. But I cannot. While my talents allow me to feel the pain that you feel, I cannot understand what it means to live your life. You must live it yourself."

Cole dropped his gaze and played with the feathers on Gale's back. "I'm sorry, Master Alvani."

"Do not apologize for how you feel. Your feelings are the truth as your soul sees it, and one should never apologize for the truth. What you do with that truth is what matters in the end. Your anger has its place. Decide if this is the right one for it."

Cole dropped his gaze and ran his fingers through Gale's feathers. "I never thought of it as a choice."

"You won't have a choice so long as you give your emotions free reign, especially if you're not aware of them rushing up in the first place. Self-awareness is not for the lazy of mind, and a lazy mind is a playground for The Three. If you make a habit of allowing your emotions to govern you, then you leave yourself open to Hunger, Fear, Despair, and Hatred. Have you been clearing your mind as Chiron taught you?"

Cole rubbed the back of his neck. "Honesty I never really understood the whole meditating thing. It calmed me down pretty good back at The Sill, but I haven't been practicing. Our mission in Costas took a lot out of me."

"Before you return to the ground, we will clear your mind properly. It is best for you to learn the process on your own, but events are unfolding faster than we can prepare for them. Do not forget what I am about to teach you."

"I won't," Cole said looking her in the eye.

Alvani's tone shifted from its usual soothing song to one of robotic indifference. "Close your eyes and slow your breathing. Hold your breath just long enough, then exhale just slow enough. You must not be happy or sad. You must not be frustrated or satisfied. You must let go of it all. You are a blank slate."

Cole felt himself slipping into something of a day-dream. Alvani's words no longer sounded as if they came from her mouth, but within his own consciousness.

"Do not force thoughts or emotions from your mind, that is impossible. You must loosen your hold on them. Only when they are ready will they fly from you as sand in the breeze."

A rope of unknown thickness began to unravel in Cole's mind, one strand at a time. He was now within a part of himself he had never been before. He felt himself fumbling in the dark, unable to see where he was going or what was around him. He could feel something tight and massive however. It was very close.

"When you are ready, find your center. If you cannot find it, then build it. There is no wrong way."

Cole didn't know up from down, let alone where any sort of center was. Thoughts and memories swam about him, filling the void with noise and rippling emotions. He shoved them away to rid himself of the distraction, but that only birthed more thoughts and a cloud of frustration.

"Embrace not the hammer, but the wind."

Alvani's breeze caressed its way through Cole's mind, taking with it the clouds and flaking off fragments of his thoughts. The wind felt good. It was the perfect temperature and touched all the right places.

"Create your center."

Cole finally understood. He had never been to the center of his mind before because he had never built it. All this time he had been trying to find a place that didn't exist. He felt a spiky knot of annoyance pop into existence, but the wind persisted, soothing and unwinding him.

Cole had no idea why, but he felt a circular stone room an appropriate place to start. A domed ceiling seemed fitting, so he imagined one into being. There was no need for fancy embellishments or carvings, so he didn't make any. The room was plain, yet the more he focused on it, the more details became apparent; the clarity of the air, the warmth and solidarity of the stone, and the steady breathing that came from above the domed ceiling. Curious, Cole brought his awareness to the dome, noticing a cone of black stone descending from its center. The cone was covered in millions of tiny glass bumps, which after closer inspection turned out to be separate memories playing over and over again inside their teeming shiny marbles. Careful not to lose himself, Cole took a deep breath.

A great rush of air came from somewhere above the ceiling. As he exhaled, a seam appeared around the upper portion of the cone, releasing a blanket of water. The liquid rolled and crawled its way down, dribbling over every memory marble on the way. At the point of the cone it shot down in a perfect line and splattered onto a podium. The room was peaceful and relaxing, but what was it all for?

"Listen to the whims of your soul. There is no wrong way."

Taking a guess, Cole felt that the best thing to do would be to put something on the podium. The water had to be coming down on it for a reason. But what would he put there? He searched the room for clues, though he knew he wouldn't find anything else because he hadn't built anything else. But maybe he didn't need to build this time. He looked back to the stream now pooling on the podium. He approached the center of the room and ran his fingers through the water. It was the best thing he'd ever felt. Aches and itches that he didn't even know he had were massaged away, as though the liquid were a magic all its own. His hand felt light and strong, as if he traded it for a newer, better one. He wanted to bathe his entire being into the water, but there was no way for him to fit his whole body on the podium.

The answer came to him with a flutter of echoing laughter from the domed ceiling. This was his mind, his rules, there was no wrong answer. Abandoning his body, he condensed himself into an ingot of consciousness. He inspected his new form, finding it hot and angry, brittle and blind. It felt as if it were made of baked layers of every bit of stress he'd accumulated over his entire life. Acknowledging the ingot was wearisome, and too hot to hold for long. The room breathed faster as Cole rushed himself to the podium. Steam hissed and howled, filling the room with a dense fog. Cole felt a layer of stress come loose from the ingot. The ceiling exhaled, taking with it his evaporated tension.

With the next breath, the water didn't just creep down, but rather it poured in an eager current, splashing and gushing over his molten ire. The relief was immediate. Now loose, the top layer of stress melted away entirely, peeling away from Cole's mind in another cloud of steam. Another breath and the fog was gone.

Cole repeated the process again and again. Just when he thought there was nothing else, he'd let a little more water down and yet another layer would come loose. It felt as though he had been wearing a dozen layers of too-tight clothes, only apparent with their absence. With each cycle of his breathing, he felt lighter, more open, more aware of himself. He let go of everything that tied him to the world outside his mind. He released not just the negative things, but the positive things as well. He was in such a state of profound neutrality that he could pick up and put down any part of himself that he wished. Now though he would put them all down. He was in his center.

In the blank of his thoughts, Cole felt his curiosity take root like a little flower. It wanted him to leave this place and return to Alvani. After acknowledging this curious part, it was he that decided to oblige it. He was loathe to leave his stone room, but he knew he could return whenever he wanted.

Cole opened his eyes, feeling the gentle vibrations of the wind traveling through Gale's body and into his legs.

Alvani greeted him with a warm smile. "Welcome back, Warrior of The Sill."

"How long?" Cole asked, straightening his aching back.

"If I had to guess, it was more than an hour, but less than two," she replied, unconcerned.

Guilt and worry blossomed in Cole's blank mind. He felt guilty that he had been up here relaxing while the rest of the unit had been running flat out. He was worried about Goran because he hadn't checked up on him in so long. Cole recognized and appreciated each of these parts. They each had their place, and valid reasons for making themselves heard. He assured them that they would be addressed. The parts drifted to the back of his mind, still connected by a strand of significance.

Cole exhaled, realizing he had slipped back into his center for a moment. "That was...I don't know how to describe it. I feel different. More open. More aware...of everything. I don't think I'll ever be the same after that. I don't think I want to be."

"You were a fine person before you joined me on Gale's saddle. Why would you want to change who you were?" Alvani asked, stroking Gale's feathers. A deep purr rumbled under their legs.

Cole could tell it was a loaded question, and he felt a fizzling annoyance rise up because of it. This irritated part didn't much appreciate being treated like a child. Cole acknowledged the needy emotion, coddled it for a second, then sent it on its way. This conversation didn't need that part of him.

Cole noticed how long it was taking for him to respond. "Sorry, I'm just..."

"You are using muscles of your mind that you've never used before," Alvani said, with pride beaming in her voice. "Like anything else, it gets easier with practice. Though the opposite is also true. If you neglect the exercises you just learned, they will fade from your mind as a fleeting memory from another life. This skill will give you immense control over yourself, and can improve every aspect of your life. Decide if it is valuable to you. If it is, then hold on to it. Use it."

Cole took her words with no filter or bias. Her measure of his worth resonated with Cole's own pride, and he instinctively stifled the emotion, worried that it would open a door for other emotions to spill through.

Alvani squinted as she inspected him, leaving Cole with a feeling that she had just sensed him hiding his pride. "While self-regulation is important, there are certain parts of yourself that you may not want regulated. Your pride in well-earned accomplishments for example, ought to be embraced and appreciated. It's not an exact art, and you will only have yourself to answer to. There is no wrong way."

Cole nodded. "I will remember that, but a part of me is worried that I might end up forgetting from time to time. Life on Aeneria is…very busy. I could easily get distracted."

"Which is why you must practice this new skill as often as you can," she said, looking him square in the eye. "As often as possible you must keep yourself in a neutral state. Let the good things fill you without filter. Your other emotions may only enter your mind with your permission. If you can master this art, then you can master yourself. Even the parts that you are ashamed of."

Memories of Cole's Rage flickered, along with the disgrace that he associated with it. With some difficulty, he went into his stone room and poured the cleansing waters over his shame. He emerged from his center after cycling through the process two more times.

He returned to Gale's back finding Alvani waiting with a patient satisfaction on her face. "It gets easier, I promise. Now, if you wouldn't mind joining your unit down in the pass." She turned and patted Gale on the neck. "He's ready, bring him down."

"Thanks, but I'll get myself down," Cole said through a mischievous grin.

Alvani held up a finger, halting him. "I have just one more nugget of advice before you go."

"What is it?" Cole asked, eager and open.

"Do not shackle your bond-brother. Goran is changing, just as you yourself are changing. Let him breathe. Let him grow. Just a suggestion, from one friend to another."

"Thank you, Master Alvani," Cole said, dissolving Goran's mental leash before she finished speaking. She was right. Goran had something in him that he needed to deal with. Cole had no right to restrain his friend.

Cole stood and kicked off from the saddle, leaving Alvani's wind bubble and letting the air crash into him like a waterfall. As expected, his Fear of heights chimed in, which he brushed aside with his confidence in Wisdom. He allowed himself to drop for a moment, feeling something very odd throughout his body. For the first time in his life he was enjoying the rush of freefall. After releasing his morbid Fear of falling, he felt a wild excitement explode inside his chest, filling him to the brim with a reckless rush. Realizing he was holding his breath, Cole emptied his lungs in a long, laughing bellow.

The ground was close now. Spinning, he flipped and wobbled onto his back as his body stopped accelerating, feeling as if he were on a bed of gushing water. He took a moment to appreciate Oberon, whose blooming colors seemed to match Cole's euphoria perfectly. It was odd, how not too long ago something like Oberon would have dropped his jaw to the floor. Lately, however, he had taken the looming jewel for granted, as if its magic and ever-changing hues were as common as the air he breathed.

The mountains on either side of the pass rushed into his periphery. He drank Oberon in just a little longer before flipping onto his stomach. The ground was closer than he expected, but not so close that he was out of options. His first instinct was to use his Wisdom to guide him to a soft landing on the trail, but that seemed like too many steps for such a simple problem. From the center of his mind he called his Rage forth. As if it was waiting for an excuse to explode, his Rage charged at him. Without hesitation it began smashing and shaping his consciousness to fit its own chaotic melody. Cole greeted the Rage, granting it not what it wanted, but what was needed for the situation.

Cole's munisica blinked into existence as the shroud snapped up to his elbows and knees. More than enough to survive the landing. Inventorying his mind, he found Goran high above him on a cliff, still blitzing his way alongside the unit. He felt Eliza farther up the pass. She was so engrossed in her running that she barely noticed him.

Cole collided with the paved trail in an explosion of rocks and sparks, a deafening report echoing throughout the valley pass. Without a moment's pause, he shot out of the rubble and sprinted towards his unit. The Rage sharpened his senses, and behind him he could hear the debris still cutting through leaves and clattering over the pavement. He would have to come back someday and repair the damage.

He gave Eliza a mental ping, letting her know that he would be coming up behind them. Gauging her distance, he realized he was barely gaining on her. Cole uncorked just a little more of his Rage until the shroud crawled up to his shoulders and thighs. Parts of his hair sharpened into blades, bouncing off his scalp with little clicks.

"Must be nice, flying halfway to the city while us commoners slog it down in the dirt," Sitra chided, swiping at him with one of her ebony claws as he joined the unit.

Instead of ducking, Cole brought his own munisica to hers, blocking it with a crack like a gunshot. "Had I known you guys were running this slowly I would have come down sooner. Have you been jogging like this the whole time or are you just getting tired?" Cole took a playful jab at Sitra's legs.

Sitra yelped and darted ahead. "Who lit a fire in your blood? Did Alvani give you some of her liquor again?"

Eliza bloomed into Cole's mind: *"You do feel odd. Your song is different."*

Cole laughed, part of him enjoying their curious glances. "She gave me something better than liquor, though I do feel like I could use a drink. You guys think Oberon City has a pub or something?"

"I wouldn't count on it. Not in a city full of Wisdom followers," Valen said, running nearer to Cole. "Even if they did we are not here for leisure and revelry. We represent The Sill. Not to mention we are awaiting trial. It would not be wise to make fools of ourselves before we meet the Celestial Council."

"Always the pragmatist," Lileth said, meeting Cole's eyes with a sideways glance. "I for one would rather enjoy myself before facing judgment. I will join you, Cole. We shall dance our way to the gallows."

"You're not doing any dancing without me," Sitra butted in. "What if one of the locals gives you some trouble? You'll need someone with some backbone to throw down. Count me in. Liza you're coming right?"

"Oh, I suppose so," Eliza responded in an airy tone.

"Be it on your heads then," Valen huffed, rushing ahead.

The unit sprinted down the trail, teasing and jabbing at Valen all the while. Seeing Valen getting upset, Cole suggested that they dial it back before they digress into another prank war. However, as Sitra pointed out, the angrier Valen became, the faster the unit ran. After a couple hours, the passing trees and rocks were nothing more than a blur as they raced down the pass like five bolts of lightning. Somewhere far above, Cole felt Goran trailing behind.

The captain of the Firedancer had estimated a hard day's march to Oberon City, but he had not known what the unit was capable of. With their Wisdom lightening their Rage-fueled legs and Alvani's Passion trickling down from the sky, they charged through the pass in half a day. The towering valley walls opened up, revealing the other side of the mountain range. They had a good view of the land below them, which was so verdant that it looked as if they now gazed upon a rolling green ocean. Farther out, there were rows upon rows of pyramid-shaped structures with lights running up their lengths. Farther still glimmered a body of water that ran out to the horizon. A massive dark cloud hung just under Oberon, which greeted them with a warm cocktail of ruby and tangerine hues.

The road split into several capillaries leading down the foothills to various suburbs. Valen halted and the unit fell in around him, awestruck by the sights.

"That's the biggest city I've ever seen!" Sitra gasped, summoning a crystalline telescope. "There must be thousands of people living down there."

Concussing thumps sounded from above as Gale's wings masked Oberon from view. The creature released a cheerful chirp before landing on a gravelly patch next to the road.

"There are over one hundred thousand living in the city. And a comparably great number living within the temple itself," Alvani said, floating down from Gale's saddle and joining them. "If need be, the temple can house the entire population of the Dark Side, as it did once in the twilight of the last war. The Celestial Council awaits us at the very top."

Cole scanned the forest out to the ocean. Even after sharpening his vision with Wisdom, he couldn't find the temple. It should be obvious if it could hold that many people. "Sitra, can I use your telescope when you're finished? I want to see the temple."

"You mean you can't see the giant black thing out in the ocean?" Sitra tossed her jade telescope to him. "It's the biggest thing out there, meat-brain."

Cole snatched the lens, then dropped it to the ground. What he had mistaken for a massive storm cloud was in fact a structure. Even from their elevated position he had to look up to see the entire thing. The temple was made of concentric cylinders, the fattest on the bottom and the smallest on top, giving it the appearance of a monolithic wedding cake. It was most certainly taller than the Fangshards. It looked as if it were made from Aeneria's very bones.

"How?" Cole asked. "How can something like that exist? Even with all the technology and magic in this world, something like that couldn't possibly be made by people."

"It was far before my time," Alvani said. "But our records show that it was indeed made by Aenerians, though it was crafted in an age when our magic was wild and raw. Things such as the temple and the floating obelisks are made from an ancient magic that none on the Dark Side could hope to replicate today. Our power comes from the soul flies and the residue that collects on Oberon whilst they Travel. Thanks to you Cole, the soul flies have returned, and so will our strength, though it will take dozens of cycles for Oberon to shine as brilliantly as it once did."

Cole felt their eyes on him, but his attention was on Oberon itself. Even as Alvani described it, he could see clouds of sapphire-blue, blood-orange, and honey-yellow, all drifting steadily towards the opalescent moon above them.

"Master Alvani, did you take part in the Battle at Oberon Temple?" Valen asked, pointing towards the obsidian temple.

"No," she said, gazing out to the temple. "I was but a child when The Three besieged us. I remember hiding in the lower levels with others too young or ill to fight. Roth and Chiron were in the battle, alongside Varka's forces." She turned to Cole, giving him a significant look. "Cole, do you remember who Varka was?"

"He was with the Unbound," Cole responded, confused as to why she was staring at him like that. "Ka Reine told us his story in the Arts District. He won the war or something."

Alvani's eyes were still locked on him. "Varka was the leader of the Unbound and the founder of our entire way of life. The Unbound embraced Rage, Wisdom, and Passion, bringing the full might of our magic against The Three. I remember the battle well. Oberon's forces had all but perished before the Unbound arrived. Even though their numbers were small, their might was equal to the swarms of The Three. Sadly, nearly all of them died in battle when Varka failed to return from the Vault of Wisdom. Roth and Chiron are the only two survivors of the Unbound. If not for their efforts Aeneria would be a very different place."

A heavy silence fell among the group, broken eventually by Eliza: "Master Alvani, have you heard from Master Roth at all?"

"No, child," Alvani replied. "I've not heard from him since he left you in the White Sands. His mind has been closed to me ever since."

The silence returned. Eliza approached Alvani, placing her hands on her shoulders. "Alvani, I am so sorry, but I believe Roth met his end in battle. He shackled us with Wisdom while he took flight and locked munisica with an Alpha Colossus. That was when his mind was lost to you. Roth is dead."

Alvani's chin drooped to her chest, her breathing slow and steady. She brought her head up a moment later wearing a defiant smile that did not reach her eyes. "You may be right, but Roth and I are bonded with a Passion. If Roth died I would die as well, or have a scar like Chiron. I cannot communicate with him, but I can feel him within my soul. Roth is alive."

"You're joking!" Sitra barked, jumping up and down. "Now I can kill him for running off without us!"

"If he is not dead, then he must still be fighting the Colossus," Valen said. "Or fleeing with what's left of Morthain. Either way, the Council must be made aware of what has transpired. It won't be long before the putrid arms of The Three reach their borders. That Colossus was beyond the Rage of Morthain, and as formidable as he is I don't see how Master Roth could defeat such a foe. It may very well be on its way to Oberon City as we speak."

"The Celestial Council has been made aware, and their position is as reactive as ever," Alvani sighed.

"You mean they're just going to sit and wait for The Three to come to them?" Cole blurted. "It's as if they actually want to repeat the past. What if The Sill decides not to bail them out this time?"

"We have considered that path," Alvani said. "When Roth returns we shall deliberate what role The Sill shall play in this coming of the war."

"The more I hear about this Council, the less I like them." Cole scowled, clenching his munisica. "I won't be taking anything lying down, that's for sure."

Alvani flashed Cole a slightly disappointed look. Scolding himself, Cole rushed back to his center and with some difficulty, released his rising fury. How could he forget so quickly?

"You won't be alone," Eliza said, her voice soft and reassuring. "We will all be with you."

"Eliza is right," Alvani said. "The entirety of The Sill is being called into question, so we will all attend the trial. Though we do not identify with any of the Council's laws, we will acquiesce in the name of diplomacy. The Celestial Council has ever been a powerful ally. To lose their hand would only weaken ours."

Sitra crossed her arms. "And what if we don't like what they decide is best for us?"

"We will manage as we always have." Alvani gave Sitra a sideways grin. "Though I hope Roth returns before then. I rather like his ways of compromising."

"He's probably *compromising* the hell out of that Colossus right now." Sitra laughed, grinding her munisica together. "He'd better hurry back. I still need to kill him."

The unit murmured their agreement, though Lileth remained silent. She addressed them all with a pained, worried look.

"This is all very uplifting, but how can we be sure about Master Roth?" Lileth asked Alvani with a brittle voice. "I don't question your mastery of Passion, but I do know it is an imprecise art. I saw the monster he faced with my own eyes. The thing was beyond munisica and magic. It was a true Alpha Colossus."

"You are quite right, Lileth," Alvani said, placing her hand over her heart. Her brow and shoulders sagged, giving her the appearance of a wilted flower. Gale let out a mournful keen behind her. "I must trust in my and Roth's hearts. We are only bonded as long as we both love each other with every facet of our souls. If he was enthralled by his bloodlust, he may very well have died without me in his heart, and I would never know."

"I… I didn't know that," Lileth blinked. "Forgive me Master, my ignorance of Passion has made me a fool. You should not have to explain yourself to a student, especially not with such a private matter."

Alvani closed the gap between her and Lileth in a fluid motion. She cupped her hands over Lileth's cheeks. "You are no student, and you are no fool. Thank you for your concern. I believe Roth to be alive because my heart still burns for him, as I trust that his still burns for me." She then turned and addressed the others. "Now I must leave you, and you must make for the city. Follow the center road all the way in. Despite the stereotypes about Wisdom-followers, there is a variety of entertainment to be had throughout the city. You'll find theaters, shops, inns, museums, and clubs of all kinds. If you hurry you may find a few places still open. Oberon City has no shortage of establishments devoted to indulging your vices. Chiron has asked me to ensure that you all steer clear of these places, lest we risk our already delicate relationship with the Council."

Alvani's robes swished as she spun and leapt up into Gale's saddle. "You may consider yourselves thoroughly warned. On an unrelated note, I will be busy tonight, and won't have time to check up on you. Just make sure you find yourselves on the shore closest to Oberon Temple by late morning."

With a grunting chirp, Gale buffeted them all with his wings before launching into the air. Like a shooting star they flew to the peaks, where Gale banked and disappeared into the pass.

"Where do you think she's going?" Cole asked.

"To find Roth of course," Eliza replied, gazing up into the pass with a dreamy smile. "I do hope she finds him before the trial. As clever as she and Chiron are, I would feel much better facing the Council with Roth at our side."

"Let's go find us a drink!" Sitra grinned wolfishly. "I know I'll feel much better facing the Council after indulging in a few of those vices Alvani talked about."

"You are as stubborn as you are reckless," Valen said, shaking his head as he turned and ran down the center road.

The five warriors raced down the paved road, which was soon swallowed up by towering trees and ferns. Oberon poured through gaps in the canopy with rainbow shafts of light from above. Cole felt alive and excited for the first time since leaving The Sill. The prospects of a night of indulgence swam through his mind, painting scenes of him alone with Lileth. Perhaps tonight he would tell her how he felt about her. Then again, maybe he wouldn't. It wasn't right, it wasn't time. He was still tiny compared to her, not to mention he wasn't the same species. If she rebuffed him then they'd still have to live and work together. Things would be different. With an effort, he released the emotions and brought himself back to his center.

As Cole poured the water over his molten ingot, he was dimly aware of Goran standing on a cliff overlooking the city. Pausing in his meditations, he strummed at their link with his compassion. Cole's reaching thoughts had no effect on Goran. The mirak gave a gruff snort and retreated back up the mountains.

Cole strummed another message through the link: *"I don't know what's up with you, and I won't dig the answer out, but I'm here. I'll always be here."*

Goran paused, giving Cole's mind a rough nudge.

As the unit ran to the city they passed a few locals, each Aenerian greeting them with an offended glare and an upturned nose. Cole laughed to himself, wondering if they were violating some sort of speed limit on the road.

Valen slowed their pace. Even with Rage sharpening their reflexes there were too many close shaves with the growing foot traffic and expensive cars filling the road. The people all looked as if they had just come from a formal dinner, their fine jackets and suits in stark contrast to the rusty cloth armor that the unit wore. The locals had all the warmth and hospitality of ornery librarians. Not a single person said a word or made eye contact, even when Cole almost knocked a frail man over with a clumsy bump of his shoulder. It was unsettling, being surrounded by such a large, silent crowd.

The throngs dwindled enough to reveal a waving veil of light that looked eerily like the barrier Cole had torn down months ago. The wild growth along the side of the road had been tamed and trimmed, giving over to subtle technology and hints of magic. Woven brass machines buzzed overhead, carrying dozens of tiny gratia stones and propelled by little jet engines emitting green light. Planted alongside the road were trees that spun rapidly on rotating podiums. Their branches were adorned with specks of light that formed images as they twirled.

One of the rotating trees spun to life as they passed, showing the face of a dark-skinned Aenerian whose neck was layered with lavish amulets and necklaces. The tree hummed and a regal voice rang out from the branches. "Do not believe the lies carried from primitive lands. Our neighboring barbarians hunger for battle and thrive in strife, but we will not oblige them. Oberon City is safe, and so are your families. The Celestial Council will guard you on our path of peace and progress. May Oberon's light shine on your souls."

"Hungry barbarians are we?" Sitra spat, jamming her munisica into the twirling branches, halting the tree. "Let's see how hungry they are for our help when they have Domina and Corpulants climbing over their walls."

"It's just propaganda, Sitra," Eliza said, sidestepping a weedy man who sneered at their clothes. "Fear is the counter to their cold logic and stiff Wisdom. I don't blame them for trying to keep order, though I do wonder how long the Council will keep them in the dark."

"They're doing their citizens a disservice," Valen said in a harsh tone, looking down his nose at the passing crowds. "Sitra's right. A single Corpulant would wreak unchecked havoc in a city of this size, leaving fields of panicked Despair that a priest of Sorronis could harvest freely. They are woefully vulnerable."

A passing woman glared at Valen, storming off and shaking her head.

The unit pushed on, approaching an arch in the shimmering wall. Just before they passed through, a glass orb wrapped in wire dropped in front of them. The orb displayed a face inside and swung about on a mechanical arm. Cole's eyes followed the arm up, which connected to a robotic thorax and long legs that spread over the entire archway.

"Advance to be recognized," said a bossy voice from within the glass orb.

Valen stepped forward. "I am Valen, from The Sill. Behind me is-"

The face in the orb cut him off. "Enter the city. Next visitor, advance to be recognized."

Valen blinked and moved forward.

"I am Lileth of The Sill." Lileth stepped around the orb before the machine could interrupt her too.

The others checked in and moved through the archway. When it was Cole's turn the machine emitted an alarming tone and flashed red.

Confused, Cole addressed the face within the orb, "Um, I'm Cole...of The Sill. Is there a problem?"

"You are unregistered. Stand by for detainment and verification." The machine's voice sounded rushed and urgent.

"You're not detaining me!" Cole blurted. "I didn't do anything wrong! I'm here on official orders from The Sill, just like the others. Alv-" A hand cupped over Cole's mouth and waist as he was jerked away from the machine.

"Say no more," Lileth whispered into his ear.

There was a flash of light as Cole felt a chilled tingling cover his skin from the head down. He looked down to see his body disappear. In front of him, Cole saw an image of himself facing the machine, talking to it with his voice.

"I apologize," said the mirror-Cole. "I will wait here."

The face within the wire-wrapped globe looked about, suspicious. With Lileth's hand planted firmly in the middle of his back, he followed the rest of the unit through the archway and into the city.

They wove through the crowds, meandering down a less busy street where the judgmental glances of passersby were all the more obvious. After receiving directions from a pompous group of adolescent boys, the unit made their way to a bus stop from which they would be taken to a commercial district that sold clothes 'more fitting for civilized culture.' Pushing Sitra along before she could start a fight,

Valen thanked the boys and made for the bus. None of them wanted to appear before the Council wearing their battle-stained Morthainian armor.

A flying, driverless bus carried them to the markets. The exterior looked like a golden bullet and the interior seemed like it was modeled from a luxury hotel. Unlike the loud, clunky Morthainian vehicles, this bus hardly made any noise at all and the ride was smooth, despite whipping by tall buildings at dizzying speeds. The bus glided to a stop in the center of four pyramid buildings whose walls looked to be made from obsidian polished to a mirror finish. The unit hopped out, admiring the statues and fountains towering about the square. The Sill had its own natural beauty to it, but this place spared no expense with the detail in its architecture. The four pyramids had multiple levels and walkways that framed their exteriors. Delicate bridges of brass vines connected each of the buildings, and there was a soft overtone of dinner music permeating the air. Everywhere they looked there were fine embellishments in the stonework, or mesmerizing kinetic sculptures dancing on jeweled altars.

In the midst of enticing aromas, a sour stench of soiled rags hit Cole's nose. Sniffing around, he felt a breeze coming from a waterfall. Eliza halted in front of it, her dirty armor standing out like a rotten mushroom in a garden.

Eliza gave him an amused look. *"Is something the matter?"*

Cole pinched his nose. *"You are the worst thing I've smelled since the Colossus."*

"Hark who's talking. You were actually inside of one. Why do you think I'm standing all the way over here?" she said, taking another step farther.

Cole lifted an arm and sniffed. His eyes stung and his vision blurred.

"Let's go freshen up, shall we?" Eliza said, admiring the shops scattered throughout the square.

They left the courtyard and found a store with real people modeling clothes in the windows. Having never chosen his own outfits on Aeneria, Cole played it safe and picked out a suit similar to one that Valen chose. When it came time to pay, they discovered that currency in Oberon City was nothing like that at The Sill. After they were scolded by the woman behind the counter, she directed them to a machine called a dispensary, which luckily was not far from the shop. Placing their selections on racks, they left the shop and found the machine.

"I think I get it; we have something like this back on Terra," Cole said, stepping forward. The machine had an uncanny resemblance to an ATM, except instead of swiping a card, there were three gratia stones mounted at eye level. Cole palmed the green one on the left. "Wisdom stones take memories, right?"

"That is correct, but do be careful," Lileth warned. "The memory will be lost to you forever."

"No problem." Cole shut his eyes and attuned his thoughts to the stone. "Goodbye California Gold Rush," he said, dumping an entire history lesson into the stone.

The Wisdom stone blinked twice in acknowledgement. There was a sharp click as a single coin dropped into the basin at the bottom of the machine.

"Is that it?" Cole asked, hefting the light stone. "This won't buy me a pair of socks in that shop."

"Was your memory detailed enough?" Valen asked, leaning closer to get a better look at the coin. "Wisdom stones usually have a higher yield when copious amounts of detail are applied to the memory."

"Well it took me weeks to come up with the guts for that memory, so I think it was." Cole scratched his head. "Ah, of course I can't remember a damned thing from it now."

"Let me try," Eliza said, tilting her head in a curious sort of way.

Eliza hovered her hand over the jade Wisdom stone, but then changed her mind and clapped her palm over the cardinal red Rage stone. She closed her eyes, baring her teeth and munisica. The Rage stone blinked, ringing loudly before a shower of coins poured down, overflowing the basin.

Eliza stepped back, giving the machine a speculative look. "Perhaps in a city full of Wisdom followers, the gratia economy here is saturated with Wisdom. Rage and Passion may be more fruitful for us. Oh dear..." she said, picking up one of the coins.

"What is it?" Valen asked, examining one himself.

Eliza's eyebrows met as she scowled. "These are made from baileen bones. Ribs, I believe. I hope the creatures were dead before these were harvested. It surprises me that such an advanced city would use such a crude form of currency." She took another step back, shaking her head.

"Well if you're not going to take them, I *suppose* I could bear that burden for you," Sitra said, twirling a spell in her hand as the pile of coins shot up into her open bag. "Don't worry, I'll make sure to kiss the next baileen I see. Let's go find some clothes that don't smell like shit and blood. I'm still going out tonight."

Following Eliza's lead, they used the Rage and Passion stones instead, filling their bags to the brim. After paying the Rage stone Cole filled his bag to the bursting point, though he then felt weak and vulnerable. Hopefully he wouldn't need to call upon his Rage any time soon.

CHAPTER 13

A WHISPER OF A HOPE

After paying properly for their clothes, the unit stopped into a cypher shop and picked up a map of Oberon City. Even with the whole of the city now revealed to them, they chose to remain in the quad plaza as it had everything they needed for the night. With their rucksacks bursting with clothes and supplies, they wound their way up to a hotel, which sat perched atop one of the larger pyramids.

The hotel clerk nearly jumped out of his shoes when five shabby Aenerians covered in battle filth entered his fancy atrium. He ran for a wall-mounted device which looked like an old telephone, though Cole thought it might be an alarm.

In a flash, Sitra appeared in front of the man, standing between him and the device he reached for. "If you want to keep that hand then you can put it right back in your pocket. If you want to make some money then you better keep quiet."

The man stuttered, his hand hovering between the alarm and his pocket. "I...I assure you I don't know or want to know what business you have here."

"I think you do," Sitra said, tapping the man in the chest with one of her munisica.

The man rose to his full height, which was still half a head shorter than Sitra. He gave a disgusted sneer at her munisica. "I assure you, I don't. This establishment has a strict policy on how we deal with brigands and beggars. Now, I suggest you take your leave before I force it upon you." He straightened his jacket and added, "I'll have you know that I'm the great-grandson of a Council member. It would not be *wise* to test my Wisdom."

Sitra pouted with mock concern. The clerk smirked, looking as if he were about to say something clever. Before he could utter a word the breath rushed from his mouth as jade ropes wrapped around his middle, yanking him back to the front desk. Lileth dropped her outstretched hand and the ropes disappeared, though the man remained frozen in Fear. Cole upended his rucksack as a cascade of coins poured over the desk and onto the floor. When the final coin wobbled flat, the man's face went from sickly panic to shrewd Hunger.

"You are too quick to judge, great-grandson of a Wisdom Walker," Lileth said. "We are Warriors of The Sill, and more importantly to you, we are paying customers. What kind of room can we afford with this?" She motioned her eyes towards the pile in front of her, shifting her own rucksack higher on her shoulders.

The man seemed to forget he was supposed to be breathing. He tore his eyes from the stack of coins on the desk. "Forgive me, madams and sirs. It seems I did indeed make a grave error in judgment." He took a steadying breath, scanning each of them up and down as if he still wasn't sure if he were being robbed. "In my haste I thought you some band of marauders come to plunder the hotel."

"How do you know we're not?" Sitra asked, appearing next to the man, who jumped and clutched his chest.

"That's enough, Sitra. The man is only doing his job," Lileth sighed. "What is your name, Wise One?"

"Thirsk," he said, picking up a coin from the floor and carefully placing it on the desk. "Er- this payment is a tad...inappropriate for even our hotel. Not to call your intelligence into question," he added, tripping over his words. "You are clearly outsiders. Our currency is no doubt foreign to you. If you, er...feel up to it I could dig up a cypher that would-"

"What, is that not enough?" Sitra asked, hoisting her own heavy bag onto the desk. "Don't you try scalping a profit off us, Thirst. I'll have you know we're all the great-great-grandchildren of bog angels, so don't get testy."

"It's *Thirsk*," he said, rolling his eyes. "And I'll thank you not to accuse me of *scalping* anyone. This sum, which you've unceremoniously dumped on my desk, could pay for every room in the hotel twice over.

Your ignorance has disarmed me, that is all, but we'll set you right in a moment." He settled himself into a chair and summoned a ledger book and monocle from thin air, but the desk was so cluttered with coins that he had nowhere to put the book.

"Sorry," Cole blurted as he scooped an armful of coins back into his bag.

"We are off season," he said, thumbing through his book and flicking his monocle, which changed from clear glass to bright turquoise. "Most of our premium suites are available, as is our top-tier penthouse. Would you like a room each or-"

"How many beds in that penthouse?" Sitra demanded, digging through a bowl of fruit next to Thirsk's desk.

Thirsk watched Sitra in open disgust as Sitra chopped the contents of the bowl with a single claw, blending it into a soup and chugging it with noisy gulps. Thirsk cleared his throat. "Erm, the penthouse sleeps eleven, but more beds can be brought up. It is quite large."

"The penthouse will be fine, thank you," Lileth said. "Take the excess as a tip, or do with it what you will. Don't worry," she added, seeing the look of reluctance on Thirsk's face. "We acquired the coins legitimately. Consider it a token of generosity from The Sill."

"I...I will," Thirsk whispered, his eyes counting out the sum on the table. "Here are your keys." He held his hand up as five brilliant emerald stars shot from his open palm, each burying itself in the left thumb of one of the guests. "The penthouse is at the very top. Just touch the door with your keyed thumb and you'll be right in. And if you need anything else, anything you desire. Just give a ring and I'll come up myself."

"Thank you. We'll see ourselves up. Come Sitra, leave the poor man be," Lileth chided.

Sitra untangled her munisica from Thirsk's coattails, which she had spent the last minute shredding to ribbons. "And I was just starting to like you. Listen for my ring, Thirst. I may have some *desires* later tonight."

He swallowed. "My name is Thirsk."

They took an elevator up to the top floor, which opened to a single door framed with silvery neon lights. Valen pressed his thumb to the door, unlocking it with a ripple. Following the others, Cole pressed his face into the door, sliding through the cool stone and entering the most lavish place he'd ever seen. The main room was large enough to host a party for at least thirty people. Embedded below the center floor was a fish tank curated with various corals and tropical fish resembling those in the lagoon outside The Sill. Carved stone half walls lined the rest of the room, each topped with waving ferns. Hundreds of egg-sized gratia stones hung from the ceiling from brass wires, all cycling through a synchronized pattern of colors like an ocean of little Oberons. An aroma of perfumes permeated throughout, though it wasn't quite fragrant enough to mask the stench of sweat and body odor of the unit.

After a much-needed shower, Cole emerged from his private room dressed in a shale-gray suit with amber filigree on the lapels and sleeves. He joined Valen in the common room, where the Aenerian was busy grooming himself in front of a marble vanity. Cole watched with interest as Valen used Wisdom to cut and style his hair into a fashion resembling the locals down in the courtyard.

"So you're coming out after all?" Cole asked.

Valen hastily dismissed his spells and stepped away from the mirror. "Well someone has to make sure you all represent The Sill with some dignity."

Cole laughed, stepping up to the mirror. He couldn't remember when his last haircut had been, but judging by the werewolf staring back at him he was long overdue. His pride wouldn't allow him to ask Valen how to cut hair, and that resulted in a patchy, rough-cut mess that took far longer than he would have liked. Even after he labored for a half hour in the mirror, the women had yet to emerge from Eliza's room.

Not interested in small talk with Valen, Cole walked around the room, admiring the artwork and statues, and trying out the furniture. Everything looked too expensive to look at, let alone touch. After setting fire to what turned out to be a kitchen stove, Cole stepped out onto one of the four balconies and indulged himself in the view. All of the shops had closed, but the streets below were crawling with people wandering among clubs and restaurants. The liveliness of the city sent giddy sensation wandering up into Cole's chest. He had never so much as seen a party back home or sneaked a sip of alcohol, save for the one time Alvani offered him a pull from her wineskin. Afraid to make a fool of himself, he tried a few bouts of his meditation. He was dreadfully unsuccessful, however. He was simply too excited. Behind him, a door opened, carrying with it Sitra's boisterous laughter.

"What's that burning smell?" she sniggered. "Valen are your pants on fire again?"

Cole returned to the common room. The women looked like a trio of rising stars. Their faces were striking and exotic, with sharp angles, elegant features, and full lips accentuated beyond their usual beauty. They had forgone their usual hair styles, instead adopting silky straight curtains that swept over their shoulders and down their backs. Cole didn't remember them buying any makeup or hair products, but with Wisdom at their disposal it seemed they hardly needed either. Eliza wore a soft, cobalt tunic made from live flower petals. Sitra had cut her cherry-red dress even shorter, showing off chiseled muscles while still flaunting her feminine physique. If not for her warm smile, Cole wouldn't have recognized Lileth in her aquamarine dress. It was cut very low down the back and very high up one of her slender legs. Cole shut his mouth, hoping it hadn't been hanging open too long.

"Shall we go then?" Eliza asked, stepping out onto a balcony. Her hair had been magically lengthened. Instead of a short pixie cut it now looked like a golden river down her back. Taking in Cole's and Valen's star-struck looks, she rolled her eyes. "Well, we may as well make an entrance. I didn't spend two hours getting ready to trudge around in these shoes."

"Right behind you, Liza," Sitra said, snatching Valen's arm along the way.

"I'm only coming out for an hour," Valen said, walking stiffly. "We ought to get some rest before the trial."

"Valen, for one night in your life I forbid you to be responsible," Eliza said, taking his other arm. "Tonight, you are just Valen."

Cole laughed, watching them dip out of sight. He followed, excitement rising.

Someone grabbed his wrist, pulling him back. Lileth hissed in his ear, "Wait."

"What's wrong?" Cole asked as he was spun over to the mirror.

"Let me do you a favor," she said, dragging him back to the vanity. Lileth stood behind him, flicking her hands through his hair, which shaped itself into a tight crew cut. She spun him around, giving a final inspection before patting him on the shoulders. "Much better."

"How'd you- never mind," Cole said, running his fingers through his hair. "What about the stubble?" he asked, raising his chin to the mirror. He had been afraid to shave his face too close with his wobbly Wisdom.

"Leave it. It suits you." She winked, taking his arm as they followed the others off the balcony.

The crowds parted in the courtyard as the unit descended. Cole imagined they looked like a flock of emerald-winged angels. Some voiced their disapproval, scoffing and turning away, though most gawked with wide eyes full of envy.

As Cole was unable to summon wings of his own, Lileth conjured him a flashy pair, which carried him down in slow, graceful flaps. The five alighted in between two fountains, seamlessly rolling into a casual stride as if they had just strolled out from dinner. Their wings shattered in a small waterfall of ethereal shards, clinking over the pavement before vanishing with little cracks.

Following Sitra's lead, they quickly settled into a restaurant that specialized in meat and mead. Waiters and waitresses came and went, arms laden with flagons and skewered roasts. Cole recognized nothing on the menu, but accepted everything. He quickly lost count of how many animals he'd eaten and drinks he'd downed.

Sometime during the second round, the unit was no longer a unit. They were just friends. Their training, their enemies, the trial, none of it mattered. Months of tension melted away like the sweetened steaks that sizzled on their tongues. Valen had long passed his self-allotted hour, lounging dreamy-eyed and content in their booth. Sitra wove a tale about a time she and Storn had been caught stealing food from Roth's bags.

"We were in the rock gardens lugging those stupid boulders, Eliza had broken a nail or something..." Sitra paused, taking a swig from her mug while shushing Eliza with a wave of her hand. "So Storn and me sneaked round the side of the rock gardens where we made camp. Roth had been chewing on that spiced jerky all damned day, so we rifled through his bag looking for the stuff."

"What would possess you to steal from Roth?" Lileth asked through a mouthful of seared fish. "I think I recall this little misadventure. He caught you both, didn't he?"

"Yup," Sitra said, nodding vigorously. "He watched from the shadows. Let us eat the whole bag too."

Valen's mug clunked onto the table. "If I remember correctly, neither of you received a hiding from him. I always thought that odd. He did punish you, didn't he?"

Sitra lowered her voice, making them all lean close. "He didn't say a word to us. But after we finished he popped up like a phantom and then politely asked us to go back to the lesson."

"Really?" Cole asked, taking a gulp of his mead. "You sure we're talking about the same Roth here?"

Sitra cut into him with a questioning glare. "Have you ever had Roth's spiced jerky?"

"Can't say I have," Cole said. "But then again I'd never be stupid enough to steal from Roth. I like my arms just the way they are, unbroken, connected to my shoulders, no extra joints."

"You forgot 'smallest ones at the table'," Sitra added, eliciting a chorus of laughter from around the table. "Finishing the lesson was punishment enough. Storn and I found out the hard way that Roth's spiced jerky was laced with banshee peppers." The chuckling ceased immediately, replaced with pained hissing and wincing. "The Firedancer wasn't the first time I had to deal with bubble gut."

Laughter exploded again, accompanied by slamming fists and sloshing mugs. Valen's laughter rose above all.

Valen dried his eyes on his sleeves, catching his breath. "It looks like you got your hiding after all! I'm sorry Sitra, I shouldn't jest. That must have been dreadful."

Sitra's cheeks flushed as a grin wrestled free from her frown. "The rock gardens wasn't even the worst part. Storn and me had to climb the Endless Wall feet-first when the bubble gut really kicked in."

"Oh, you poor thing," Eliza said, giggling through her fingers.

Amidst the warm revelry, a blooming sadness crept up Cole's throat. Storn should be here laughing with them. He felt a hand slide over his, giving him a gentle squeeze. Lileth's eyes met his, pouring her compassion through the gaze. She looked absolutely stunning.

Gathering himself, Cole stood and raised his mug. The group fell silent. "While we're laughing at the dead, we ought to take a second to drink…to their memory." He paused, his heart quickening and cheeks blazing. This was the first speech he'd ever given.

"Excellent idea!" Lileth said, rising to her feet and raising her mug as well. "To Storn. May he be a thorn in our enemy's backsides, even from the grave."

Eliza stood, gripping her mug with white knuckles as though it might fly away. Blinking a tear away, she raised her trembling mug. "To Deekus. May he be the wind at our backs."

Sitra and Valen stood, raising their mugs and completing the circle.

Cole steadied his nerves and spoke as loudly as his choked voice would allow: "And to Habbad and Lexy. May they…" Unable to think of something clever, Cole settle on something simple. "Well, they were the first people to show me any kindness on this planet. I'll miss them."

"To the fallen," Valen offered.

"To the fallen," the circle repeated.

Five mugs thudded on the table. The silence was broken by a loud belch from Sitra, who wiped the froth from her mouth and gave them all a challenging smirk.

"Let's get out of here. There's a place we need to see up on the second level. You gentlemen will have to cover the tab here, and upstairs."

"How's that fair?" Cole blurted.

"I also fail to see the equality in this proposal," Valen added, voice slurring.

Eliza stood and spun, waving her arms over the length of Sitra's body. "Where do you expect us to hide a stack of coins in these?"

They left the restaurant with their pockets and minds significantly lighter. Eliza and Sitra locked arms with Valen so he couldn't sneak off back to the hotel. Throwing caution to the wind, Cole offered his arm to Lileth, who took it without a word. She still towered head and shoulders above him, but at the moment he felt taller than he'd ever felt in his life.

Cole's head felt as if it were slowly spinning in warm honey. The very air seemed to brim with opportunity and he found the smallest things profoundly amusing. He was part of a group of real friends who were simply enjoying a night out. He felt as if he were right where he needed to be, completely at ease in his own skin. None of the beautiful strangers they passed knew he was human. Even if they did, what would it matter? He was where he belonged. This was his home.

Sitra led them up a flight of winding stairs. Vines crept over the ceiling, and a pleasant, musky aroma tickled their noses. As they ascended, a deep, melodic booming grew louder. When they rounded the final corner the stone beneath their feet began to shake along with the music.

The unit came to an abrupt halt at a set of ebony doors that were twice their height. Standing in front like a pair of matching weapons were two men, each nearly as tall as the doorway. Their skin was rough and scaly, and their fingers ended in white claws. One of them set his elliptical eyes on Cole, raising his upper lip to reveal rows of thin fangs. They were Domina.

Cole's munisica threatened to burst forth. He could feel the shroud crawling its way up his arms and shins. Lileth pulled him aside, burying him in a plush curtain of vines. From in between the leaves and budding flowers, Cole witnessed the others approach the Domina, arms outstretched. The Domina bent down and sniffed each of them, tapping their claws over Valen's suit. A bony, scaled fist banged three times on the double doors, which opened and filled the air with a thin cloud of vapor and thumping music. Eliza, Sitra and Valen disappeared through the doors, which slammed shut, muffling the wild tune inside.

Cole bared his teeth. "But those are-"

Lileth stroked the side of his face, disarming him as his eyes fell into hers. "Not everything is as it seems here. I will explain it to you when you are sober. For now, just have some fun with me?"

Still tense, Cole nodded. "After you then."

"Worry not," she whispered into his ear as they approached the doors. "The vapor in the club will inhibit your Wisdom, but your Rage and Passion will be all the more palpable."

Now he was worried about committing Rage-fueled mass murder. Cole did his best to still the fiery magic while the Domina clicked their talons over his suit. He shut his eyes, opening them again when the doors opened and the music slammed into his chest. Lileth pulled him by the hand into the fog and lights.

The music was deafening. Cole attempted to cast a spell to muffle his ears, but with fuzzy realization he felt the effects of the vapor Lileth had mentioned. It was as if the fog had lifted him beyond his Wisdom, as well as his worries and doubts. His only concern was with the present. Lileth glanced back, her laughter stolen by the concussing bass that jarred his bones.

The vapor thickened along with a stifling heat as they swam their way through the crowds. Cole loosened his collar, bumping into strangers as he tightened his grip on Lileth's hand. She gave him a little squeeze and pushed on. A flash of crimson revealed Sitra's dress. She waved them over, standing over a grate with azure flames tickling up her legs. Eliza and Valen were there as well, circling hand in hand around her. Lileth kicked off her shoes and stepped into the flame. A faint voice in the corner of Cole's mind told him that stepping into a fire was a stupid idea, but a river of euphoria swiftly carried the concern from him.

The blue fire chilled his legs as frozen air wafted up his jacket, the cooling touch a welcome sensation in the austere humidity. Sitra pulled them both closer, her body moving and undulating with the pulse of the music. Cole didn't have the slightest clue how to dance, but he was beyond his inhibitions, just as he was beyond his Wisdom and reason.

Cole lost all sense of time, and even his sense of self. The music mixed with the life that burned in his blood. A limitless sense of wonder stole through him, as if all his dreams were well within his reach. His soul vibrated to the beat of the flesh around him. He poured himself out and drank the energy in. His Rage thundered, fueling his limbs as he danced. His Passion swelled with every crash of his heart. Cole's heart and soul raced each other, leaving his mind far behind.

Amidst the maelstrom he remained intimately aware of Lileth. He felt her body pressing against his, hot and slick with chilled sweat. Wet hair whipped the side of his face as she threw her head back and pulled him closer. Her eyes locked with his, her face bathed in the flickering sapphire. Wild hands pulled and tore at his jacket, ripping it from his body. His shirt followed. Her breath was hot and quick, inching up his neck, tickling the edges of his lips. Cole's mouth yearned and searched for hers, finding it, feeling it, tasting it. Her fingers scratched down the back of his head as her teeth pulled his lips into hers, kissing him deep and hard. Her moan vibrated through her jaw and into his own. Cole wrapped his hands around her back, fingers exploring hard muscle and sweat as he traced his way down the cut of her dress. Lileth quivered, then planted her palm into his chest, pushing him away.

Lileth's face shifted from lusting to stony indifference as she turned and sped off into the fog. Cole swayed, dumbstruck and shirtless in the blue fire. He was suddenly aware of how cold it was.

Cole ran into the fog calling her name as loudly as he could, though the thumping music buried his cries. He collided with a group of people dancing in their own blue fire. They pulled at him, drawing him into their circle. Cole yanked himself free, sprinting back into the vapor. A thin, vertical light cut through the smoke. Cole battered himself against the double doors, throwing them open and jumping out into the clear air. He looked down each end of the walkway, but she was nowhere to be found. Turning back to the doors, the Domina pressed themselves together, creating a wall of muscle and scales as they shook their heads. Ears ringing, Cole spun and leaped off the walkway before his Rage demanded their heads.

His munisica erupted from his hands and feet as he dropped like a rock through the chilly night air. He landed clumsily in the street below, shattering the pavement beneath his obsidian claws. The shredded remains of his shoes landed around him, a large chunk striking a man on a nearby bench. Cole ignored the protests of the gathering crowds, charging through them. He didn't know where he was headed, but the effects of the vapor started to thin. His mind began to clear. A crazed, shirtless, munisica-wielding man tearing up the streets was not the type of attention they needed the night before the trial. Rounding a corner into an alley, he ducked out of sight and made his way back to the hotel.

One glance through the hotel doors revealed a large group of nobles gathered in the atrium. Ushering the crowd along were a pair of men dressed like security guards. Cole darted away from the door before they could catch sight of him.

Hiding his munisica the best he could, Cole trotted around the hotel. He made a left, then another, stopping at the rear of the building. Cole arched his neck, glancing at the peak of the pyramid, where he saw the lights of the penthouse beaming from the balcony. Gauging the height, Cole uncorked a bit more of his Rage until he felt the shroud cover his shoulders and hips. He planted his munisica in a bronze-plated walkway and launched himself into the air. Passing by the third, fourth and fifth floors, Cole realized all too late that he'd overshot. He flew past the sixth and seventh floors, as well as the peak of the pyramid. He gathered what little Wisdom he could and slowed himself to a shaky halt. Struggling through the liquor and vapor, he guided himself down to the rear balcony, sheathing his munisica as his bare feet plopped down on the cool stone.

"Lileth!" Cole's shout echoed throughout the penthouse. He called over and over as he searched every room. She was nowhere to be found. Cole swore, kicking the leg of a heavy wooden table. He swore again, clutching his unarmored toes and falling to the ground. He flexed and rolled his foot, wincing and inhaling sharply as he heard the pops of his broken foot. He tried calling Passion to his aid, but he was too angry. His munisica came back, sending horrible shocking pain up his leg as the shroud moved the bone and ligament back into place.

Cole stood, wondering if he should go back out and try to find her. She probably never left the club in the first place. What had he done to offend her? Hadn't she come on to him? He recalled everything he knew about her, as well as everything they'd shared together. All the long walks and talks, the quiet jokes, the way they always ended up side by side. Everything pointed to her having feelings for him. Not to mention the only times she was ever able to wield Passion was when he was injured. That fact alone meant she had to have some kind of feelings for him. What the hell did he do wrong?

Before he could break any more furniture or bones, Cole punched open the balcony door and stepped outside. He didn't want to go back to the club and he certainly didn't want anyone finding him. He severed his links with both Goran and Eliza before leaping above the balcony, clinging to the wall of the hotel with his munisica. He crawled his way up to the peak, gouging the shiny exterior with his claws. As long as no one looked straight up from the balcony, no one would find him. The peak of the hotel had a nice flat spot at the top, with spotlights facing outwards. He looked around, satisfied no one would see him behind the blinding lights.

Cole laid himself back on the warm stone, determined to repeat his meditations until he was truly in his center. His efforts only rewarded him with frustration, however, as he couldn't find his mental room he'd made with Alvani. He could only vaguely recall its construction, so building it from scratch was out of the question.

"I'm never drinking again," he vowed to Oberon. He stared into the moon, imagining it staring back into him. Oberon now had great swaths of blood-orange swirling amid indigo. His tried to pick a color that best matched his current Rage, muttering to himself all the while.

"Talking to moons now? I hope you haven't lost your mind. You've a rather remarkable one," said a voice right next to him.

Cole bolted upright as one of the spotlights shifted and wheeled around, blinding him. The spotlight flickered and dimmed, revealing itself to not be a spotlight at all. It was the back of a man who looked as if he were wearing a cloak made of the same dark stone as the hotel exterior. The man turned, his cape grinding lightly over the shiny rooftop as Oberon illumined a familiar pair of sweeping eyebrows and the sharp beak of a nose.

"Hello, Cole Carter," Chiron said, greeting him with a polite nod.

"Master Chiron!" Cole blurted. Panic chilled his limbs and set his heart fluttering like a baby bird. He glanced down at his naked chest and bare feet, hoping he didn't sound as drunk as he looked. "I... I didn't see you there."

"It's funny how Rage sometimes does that," Chiron said, placing his hands behind his back. "Though the magic sharpens the eyes, a master of Rage could be very blind indeed."

"I might have a Master's strength, but I don't have a Master's control," Cole said, mimicking Roth's words. "I am no Master."

Chiron frowned thoughtfully, nodding as he paced in circles around Cole. "Wise words, especially given your current state. Did you find the Tunnel Rat to your liking? The artwork in the restrooms is quite charming."

"Uh, the Tunnel Rat?" Cole asked.

"The nightclub from which you made such a ceremonious exit," Chiron said, stopping behind Cole.

"Oh." Cole's eyes dropped to the roof. "We went out for dinner, then Sitra took us dancing. We had a good time."

"It seems so. Though I didn't expect your unit to stay entirely out of trouble, I did hope for a modicum of discretion, what with our trial only hours away. Your unit may be small, but that hasn't stopped you from making a large splash in our capital city."

Shame flooded Cole's cheeks. He wasn't sure if he should stand or not. "Master Chiron, I'm so sorry. Master Alvani told us not to go out. It's our own fault. It's my fault actually. We've been-"

"Inundated with an astronomical amount of stress for weeks on end," Chiron said, cutting him off. "You've seen one of your own fall prey to the worst of our magics. You are the sole survivors of a mission that none of you were ready for. You've been fighting for your lives since you left The Sill so very long ago." His voice softened as he bent down and picked Cole up by the shoulders. "I am the one who owes an apology."

"Master..." Cole breathed.

"I want to tell you it's going to get easier, but this war has only just begun." He gave Cole a gentle clap on the shoulders, bolstering him. "I won't fault you for taking a night to enjoy yourself. The Council might, but I'll see if I can't give them a little nudge towards leniency."

"I hope this stuff wears off in time." Cole rubbed his eyes with the heels of his hands. "I can't have my head all fuzzy tomorrow morning."

"With your recent increase in body mass, I estimate the liquor will run its course long before the trial." He then gave Cole an appraising look. "You have grown like a tower fungus since last I saw you."

Cole laughed, measuring himself next to Chiron. "If I were to go back to Terra tomorrow, I'm pretty sure I'd be the tallest person in history. It's almost as if I'm more Aenerian than human. But that's just another part of the great mystery, isn't it?"

"What mystery do you speak of?" Chiron asked politely.

"Why the Council wants me, why The Three are after me," Cole said, hoping he could pry some answers from Chiron. "Why you won't tell me why I'm special."

"Oh, that one," Chiron said with a casual wave of his hand. "Why that is no great mystery at all, my dear friend. At least not to Masters Roth and Alvani and me. Ka Reine knows too of course. She's the one who confirmed it in fact."

"What do you mean?" Cole asked while silently looking for a trace of a lie on the ancient face.

"I have a theory as to what makes you so special," Chiron explained as though talking about something as mundane as the weather. "Or at least it was a theory until Ka Reine took a peek into your mind. Your actions in Costas further solidified our conclusions. The information is now one of the most guarded secrets of The Sill, as it affects the security and safety of countless souls. To put a blunt edge to it, you are something of a big deal." Chiron flashed a small smile and a wink.

Cole's hands balled into fists. He clenched his jaw to keep from yelling. "You're being vague again. I've been kept in the dark since the day I got dumped here and I'm sick of it. If you know something then I deserve to hear it, all of it, especially since I'm about to be drilled by a bunch of old Wisdom Walkers in a few hours."

Chiron's smile didn't falter. "You do indeed deserve to know. I would give you a torch to light this darkness, but I Fear your drunken Rage will prevent you from accepting it."

Cole's mouth fell open. "Really? You'll tell me?"

"Of course," Chiron said.

"Everything?" Cole asked, cocking his head.

Chiron gave a single nod. "Everything."

"I…I'm sorry," Cole stammered, shamefaced.

Chiron waited a moment with a patient curiosity on his face, as though waiting for Cole to interrupt him. When Cole did not, he asked, "How well do you remember Ka Reine's story?"

"The one she told in the Arts District?" Cole asked.

"The very one," Chiron replied.

Cole was quiet for a moment, sifting through his drunken mind for the memories. "She talked about how the war started over the soul flies' abuse, and the forming of the Council. Then she talked a lot about Varka and his Unbound, who were like the forefathers of The Sill." Cole pulled his eyes away, realizing that one of the Unbound was standing right in front of him.

"I daresay Ka Reine would have waxed on a bit more than you did, but that is the short of it." Chiron paused, waiting for Cole to bring his eyes back up. "Do you remember anything else? Anything about the one called Varka?"

Cole pressed his lips together as he raked through his memories. Ka Reine's story seemed like a lifetime ago. "He was the first one to start using more than one school of magic. He mastered a couple, and helped others do the same. They were the only ones able to hold off The Three before the banishing happened."

"And how did the banishing happen?" Chiron asked, encouraging him.

Cole dug deeper, feeling as if he were taking an exam he hadn't studied for. "Varka went into the Vault of Wisdom to look for answers. Ka Reine didn't come out and say it, but I think Varka was the one who made the barrier, and banished The Three. Which means he was the one who sent the soul flies away."

"That is precisely my guess." Chiron waved his arm out to Oberon Temple, which was so vast that Cole had once again mistaken it for the sky itself. "I was standing guard on one of the lower tiers when it happened. Varka had been inside the Vault of Wisdom for so long that our budding Despair had blossomed in full. Sorronis broke through first, filling our hearts with Hatred as we turned on each other. Grotton and Decreath soon followed, sweeping through our forces like a swarm of starved locusts. Even I thought all was lost. But then, quite suddenly, I was lost. I could see nothing, feel nothing, and hear nothing. In the abyssal quiet, I sensed a shifting of this reality. Someone was changing the rules. When I regained my faculties, The Three were gone, and so was Varka."

"I...I can't imagine... facing The Three." Cole shivered at the thought. "In Costas, I only felt a part of Decreath and it almost killed me. I wished it had at the time. It was the worst thing I've ever felt." Cole fell silent as he waited for his Rage to burn away the memories of his Fear. "But what does that matter now? What does that have to do with me?"

Chiron brought the full weight of his ancient gaze down upon him. "I believe that some fragment of Varka stands before me at this very moment. He is within you, Cole Carter."

Cole's head swirled faster than the liquor. "I...How? How can someone else be inside me?" Even as he asked, he felt the answer approach from the shadows of his periphery. It was *Him*.

Chiron gave Cole a moment to collect himself before continuing. "When Oberon expelled its energies into the temple, Aeneria was in Terra's zenith. The sun had just kissed the peak of the temple as we entered the house of Pastori. I believe that some part of Varka made it to Terra before the banishing was complete. Somehow, that part of Varka made its way into you."

At the edges of Cole's thoughts, he felt *Him*, watching and measuring each of Chiron's words.

"I scoured every inch of Oberon Temple, including the Vault of Wisdom," Chiron continued. "I was certain Varka was not on this planet. Though the banishing prevented me from leaving Aeneria, I had Wisdom enough to probe the aethers. It wasn't until we next entered the house of Terra that I felt the palest shadow of Varka's essence, merely a hint of a hope. I watched Terra very closely for nigh on thirty cycles. Sometimes I could feel him, though other times there was nothing. During his last cycle however, his whisper was so potent it was almost tangible. Then you appeared through the aethers, body and all."

Cole's vision flashed back to the forest outside Costas, to that little cabin where he met Goran. "So...I was brought here...I lost everything...because some stupid alien wanted a ride back to his planet? What, is he in my soul or something?" Cole asked, realizing he was addressing *Him* as well. "Well he's here now, why doesn't he just jump back out and live his own life instead of ruining mine?" barked Cole, snapping his head around, trying to catch Varka in the light.

Chiron folded his fingers together, watching with patient interest. "You speak as if Varka is standing here with us."

"He is!" Cole snapped, jumping and spinning as fast as he could. "He's right here. Can't you feel him? Can't you sense him with Passion or something?"

"I'm afraid I cannot," Chiron said. "I believe you can, however."

Cole swore. "Why would you believe me? How do you know I'm not just crazy?"

"Because you are one of the most resilient and clever young men I've ever encountered. Though I suppose Varka himself may have been crazy at times. I suppose all of us Unbound were." Chiron's eyes drifted past Cole to another life.

Cole sighed, shaking his head.

"It appears I need to do a better job of selling my theory," Chiron said, returning his thoughtful gaze to Cole. "Very well then. The Council will likely be far more difficult to convince than you. Let us consider a few facts, shall we?"

"Go for it," Cole huffed.

"I shall," Chiron said, lips curling into a wry smirk. "When the banishing occurred, four rules were placed on the whole of Aeneria. Firstly, The Three were of course banished to the Light Side, never again to bathe in Oberon's light. Second, the barrier came to be, denying any and all passage between Aeneria's Light and Dark Side. Thirdly, the soul flies vanished, never to dance on our soil again. These rules were set into the very fabric of our reality, and since then have eluded the understanding of the wisest of our kind. Then, as if blown in by the winds of fate, you come along and break these rules, seemingly by accident. But the fourth and final rule has yet to be broken, and I believe it is why both the Council and The Three seek you; you can Travel."

Cole considered his Master for a moment. "Why would anyone care that I can Travel? I'm honestly not even sure if I'm going anywhere. It just feels like a bad dream every time it happens."

"After our first audience, you informed me that you Traveled out-of-turn, back to your Earth. Such a feat was unprecedented among our kind. I have been paying very close attention to the aethers ever since, and there is no doubt that you've been Traveling to Terra. The most recent incident was only weeks ago in fact."

Cole remembered the nightmare in vivid detail. He shuddered, shaking it off. "Yeah. Back in Morthain. I went back to my house on Earth. It was…it was bad. Real bad."

Chiron averted his eyes, allowing Cole a moment to dry his tears. "What you experienced was no nightmare. The truth does not cater to our Fears. All one can do is face it with an open mind and decide how to use it."

Cole had no idea what he was supposed to do with that particular truth. There weren't a lot of ways to use your mother's impending suicide. He changed the subject before his thoughts lingered too long. "So how else do you know that Varka's inside me? I mean, what you say makes sense, but that can't be all, can it?"

Chiron nodded. "There is more of course. I have been to your Earth and studied your people. Varka was quite fond of your race in fact." Chiron chuckled softly, his eyes looking beyond the rooftop. "He said you fought like dogs, loved like gods, and had minds like hungry puzzles. To this day I have no idea what he meant by it, but I do know that humans lack the ability to use our magic, yet *you* can. Humans also do not continue to grow after entering adulthood, and you have grown larger than your species allows. Your undue mastery of Rage comes to mind as well, as Rage was the first magic Varka conquered. Ignoring the fact that humans cannot use magic, it takes a great deal longer than a few months to become fully shrouded in Rage. Not even Roth can don the full shroud, and he is almost as old as I. Varka was the only one to master Rage, Passion, and Wisdom, and he did so in that order. Roth was rather cross with him for the Rage bit."

"That's because Roth probably knows better than to use so much Rage. I'm more of a liability when it happens," Cole said, squeezing his bare hands together. "So Ka Reine confirmed it too? Was it in your tree right before I left The Sill?"

"Indeed," Chiron said. His face darkened somewhat. "Varka and Ka Reine were very close for a time. While he didn't Hate her, he certainly harbored a powerful loathing for her. Ka Reine has a unique gift in the arts of Passion; she can sense all of one's selves as easily as listening to a heartbeat. When she examined you, she saw your selves, as well as Varka's."

"I remember that!" Cole blurted. "Varka kind of grabbed her, like he was going to hurt her. I think he wanted to, but he let her go in the end." Confused, he added, "What do you mean by your 'selves'? Last I checked there was only one of me."

Chiron gave him a reproachful look. "You would do well to learn more about yourself then. You have three selves, and they each affect your life in vastly different and important ways. There is your outer-self, the mediator between your inner-self and the world around you. I am speaking to your outer-self now. This brings us to your inner-self, your internal dialogue that you don't share with anyone without the consent of your outer-self. Deeper still is the subself, the conductor of your dreams. You are never removed of your subself, though it is always there, watching and quietly recording everything you experience. It is in this most core layer that Varka has embedded himself in you."

"How?" Cole asked, his head spinning faster still. "How could he latch onto my mind? I didn't know my father growing up, do you think he and my mom…"

Chiron wove his fingers together as he thought of a response. "When one's magic ascends to the highest orders it can only be understood by the wielder. Varka did things with Wisdom and Passion that I cannot begin to unravel, and I have mastered them both. While it is beyond understanding, it is not beyond possibility that Varka imprinted part of himself on one of your ancestors."

Cole shook his head. "But why would he choose me? Why now? Back on Earth I wasn't good at anything. I'm worse than average."

Chiron didn't answer. He just kept his unblinking, piercing gaze on him.

Cole's eyes fell to the rooftop. Everything Chiron said made sense. Aeneria's cycle was about seven Earth years. His bouts of disappearances had happened when he was three, then ten, then seventeen. *He* was there all along, sitting in the edges of his mind. It was Varka who'd pulled him through the river of soul flies. It was Varka who'd ignited the Master's Rage within him. Varka had seen every thought he ever had, lived through every moment. Varka was even there when Joshy died, pulling him to Aeneria where he would be safe.

The concept of having another man inside the most basal layers of his mind made Cole question everything. Had his choices been his own or had Varka been quietly pulling the strings all along? If he were to jump off the side of the building now, would Varka catch him or stop him before he started? Was Cole the captain of his own ship, or merely a member of the crew?

"This...I don't know what to say. It's too much. I don't want to be used by the Council or The Three," Cole mumbled.

"It is quite a bit to swallow," Chiron agreed, giving Cole a look of deepest empathy. "The key to the aethers is no light burden to bear."

"So what do we do now?" Cole asked.

"That, my dear friend, is entirely up to you." Chiron appraised him, looking him up and down. "You now know the truth, all of it. What you do with it is your choice alone. While The Three suspect that you are the key to the aethers, not a soul knows about Varka, other than who I already mentioned. That truth is your own, we will not use it without your consent."

Cole slapped his hands to the sides of his head. "But I've *no idea* what to do with it! I'm a danger to everyone if The Three catch me. Right?"

"True as the night is long." Chiron nodded.

"So why don't I just turn myself in to the Council tomorrow? I might not like them, but at least they're not evil."

Chiron's face shifted to a pensive frown. "A viable option. You may feel differently after the trial, however."

Cole ground his teeth. "Or I could just kill myself right now. Throw myself off the edge of the building and then no one could use me."

"A very simple answer to a very complex problem," Chiron said, leaning over and peering down the side of the hotel. "But I doubt the fall would kill you. The slope is not great enough, and your body is much more resilient than that of a mere human."

"Then what should I do?" Cole asked. He Hated not having control over his life. Would Varka even let him choose? "Do you have any ideas?"

A warm smile stretched across Chiron's face. "I've been mulling over a few options. Suggestions really."

"You know I'm probably going to do whatever you suggest." A reluctant grin pulled at a corner of Cole's mouth.

Chiron returned Cole's grin with a wink. "A strong possibility, but I wouldn't want you accusing me of excessive hubris. I may be old, but my ideas are not the only ones of value."

Cole laughed. "Yeah but everyone tends to listen to your ideas. Please Master Chiron, may I have your suggestions?"

"Of course." Chiron's cloak changed from polished tile to liquid glass as his bare feet left the ground. "My first suggestion is for you to find yourself a soft pillow and a warm bed. And when you wake, a shower wouldn't be amiss either."

Cole swayed, watching Chiron's silhouette shrink as the elder flew towards the dark mountain that was Oberon Temple.

Chapter 14

The Council's Compromise

"Arise Cole. We haven't much time," said a rushed voice.

Cole felt the blankets pulled from him as chilled air washed over his body. It felt as if there was a tiny hammer bashing the inside of his skull, fighting to keep pace with his heart. His tongue was massive and dry, unable to form words.

"Hurry," Valen said. His voice was far too loud. "We will be late for the trial."

Cole dragged himself upright, swallowing until his mouth could work again. "Did everyone make it back?" he asked, squinting in the dim candle light.

"They are dressed and waiting downstairs. A shuttle will be here shortly. Your suit is ruined by the way. I hope you have something else to wear besides your armor," Valen said, holding up the shredded remains of the dress pants.

"Just give me a minute," Cole said, burying his face in his hands.

"Haste," Valen said, shutting the door to Cole's room.

Cole didn't have any other clothes, and there was no hope of repairing the suit. He pulled his rotten armor out from under his bed.

He nearly lost his stomach in the lift down to the lobby, but that was nothing compared to the shuttle. The vibrations from the flying bus jarred his raw organs and rattled his brittle brain. Lileth wouldn't meet his eyes.

The shuttle came to a halt on a quiet boardwalk. The unit dismounted in a hurry. Cole smiled through his pain, trying to catch Lileth's eye. She walked past him as if he were an empty seat.

Eliza caressed his mind with a feather of thought: *"Leave last night behind you. She'll come around."*

The beach was vacant, but farther down the shore was a multi-leveled pier bedecked with glowing windows. The pier looked like a giant beehive as flying vehicles came zipping in and out of it. Cole's eyes followed one hulking shuttle as it bobbed its way up to the sky and joined a river of cars flowing towards Oberon Temple.

Cole winced, covering his face. Oberon's light stabbed into his already-throbbing eyes. He dropped his gaze to the sand, but that was too bright as well. Silently berating himself, he wrestled with his Wisdom, rubbing his eyes until his spell for night vision fell off. He had grown so used to keeping the spell up that he forgot it was still active. He opened his eyes again, stunned by how bright everything still was. It was no longer blinding, but Oberon's light was still nearly as potent as sunlight.

A familiar shimmering above them heralded Chiron's arrival. Cole watched intently as Chiron's cape kissed the beach, changing from crystalline air to a blanket of flowing sand and shells.

"Shall we be off then?" Chiron asked, greeting them with a warm smile.

"Master, what about Roth and Alvani? Have they returned?" Lileth asked.

"They have not. We will make do without them. But now we must be as quick as thought." Chiron motioned for them to take to the sky.

Wings blossomed from their backs as air whipped up around them. Cole intended to warn Chiron that he flew about as well as a rock, but a whirlwind kicked a pocket of sand up into his mouth. As he coughed, he felt his feet leave the ground as he floated up into open air. He thought he saw Chiron smiling above him.

They rose higher and faster, clothes and hair flapping in the wind. Of all the ways Cole had taken flight, he much preferred whatever spells Chiron used. There was no sense of weightlessness or air buffeting him in the face. It was very quiet and calming, as if he were merely lying in a comfy bed. There was one downside to the relaxing ride, however; Cole now had the freedom of mind to think on the trial. What would he say when they asked about the barrier? Tearing it down must be a crime of some sort. Did they have prisons on Aeneria? What if no one stood up for him?

After they'd flown for half an hour, Oberon Temple had swallowed twice as much of the sky, though it still felt as if they were only halfway there. Cole placed his fingers to his eyes, shooting a spark of Wisdom through them. Zooming, he could make out tiny lights scattered in even patterns up each concentric tier of the temple. There were rough rocks piled up around the base where waves smashed the algae-covered edges of the bottom level. Cole counted ten tiers in all. As his eyes neared the top he noticed a white sheen on the uppermost levels.

"I hope no one minds if I speed things up a bit." Chiron's voice rang crystal clear, as if he spoke directly into Cole's ear.

A white sphere blinked around each of them as their bodies took on a relaxed posture. Emerald wings flickered and faded as they rushed faster over the water. The acceleration was steady, yet unrelenting. Cole's cheeks rippled back from the sheer force of it. Within a few seconds he was moving faster than he had ever flown in his life. Even the baileen wasn't this swift. The power could only be compared to what Cole felt when fully shrouded by his Rage. He could hear the wind tearing around the magical shield, yet the air inside was calm. A concussing shudder jarred Cole's bones, stunning him momentarily, yet the magic accelerated harder still. Looking around, he saw white cones flash briefly around the others. With sobering awe Cole realized they had just broken the sound barrier. Chiron all the while looked as though he were bored and daydreaming.

Within a few minutes they charged up along the temple's ebony tiers, racing their way to the top. The temple's girth now dominated Cole's entire field of view. It was so large that its ringed walls looked completely flat. They were close enough now that Cole could make out little windows with people bustling through hallways and offices. He guessed each tier to be a mile high at least. After what felt like only a few seconds, they slowed near the top layers, which wore a shimmering layer of snow and ice. They approached the penultimate layer, slowing to a violent stop near a snowy ramp lined with large pearly omnistones. Wind and snow pelted against an invisible barrier above the paved walkway.

Chiron's shields dissipated as they passed through the barrier, allowing surprisingly warm air to rush in. They alighted on the black stone walkway. Chiron took the lead, his cape now a rippling, snowy cloud.

A woman approached from the end of the path, her body silhouetted by amber light from the doorway. Her face was as stiff as her walk, and she looked as if she'd never quite learned how to do a proper smile. "Stop right there! You can't enter this way, all visitors must check in with the embassy docks. How did you manage to get through the-"

"Hello Megorien," Chiron said. "I believe we are expected. However, I would be happy to take my number down through the embassies if it makes your day a touch easier."

Megorien shook her head. "No no, that'll take hours. Get in here before anyone else sees you." She walked them to the archway, halting them before a set of stairs. "Fair warning: Arcturus is in a foul humor. The Council just overruled his proposal on taxing Light Side imports. He's been at odds with them all morning over the most trivial affairs. If you ask me, he's stalling in hopes that they won't have time for your trial. I've never seen a Council Speaker cause so much trouble. I wish you'd taken the job when they offered it to you. How many times have you refused now?"

"Twenty-five invitations so far, and twenty-five notices of reprimand for *dereliction of coronation*. I feel my time is better spent cultivating young minds rather than trying to bend old ones." Chiron gestured toward the door. "May we enter?"

Megorien's permanent-frown further hardened into a stony scowl. "They're still deep in it, but I won't stop you. Arcturus will try, though. I might sneak down just to see the look on his face when he does."

"Thank you, Megorien." Chiron gave her a bow and ushered the unit down the stairs.

The stairs took them down to a hallway leading deep into the ninth tier of the temple. Cole peeked around the others, trying to see the end, but there didn't seem to be one. He tried estimating the distance but then Cole felt a dizzying, stretching sensation, as if he had just been sucked through a straw. He didn't know what had happened, but he knew they had moved a great distance. Cole had barely shaken the vertigo when he found himself not in the hallway, but standing on the edge of a round chamber. The walls and furniture were all the same shade of off-white and lacked any embellishments or decoration. The floors appeared to be made of the same dark stone as the outside of the temple. From the ceiling hung an opalescent boulder that looked to be cut from Oberon itself.

There were twenty-one chairs spaced evenly around a table that circled half the room. In all of the seats were Aenerians wearing high-collared white robes and an expression of impassivity. On the opposite side of the rounded table was a man in a raised desk. His collar was the highest, cresting up around the back of his head, and his robes were so bright they made everything around him look dirty.

Upon the unit's entrance into the chamber, the man at the desk did a double-take before casting his surprise into a vicious scowl. His eyebrows were so faint that it was hard to tell if he had any at all. He shook his head, as if shooing a fly. "You have not been summoned. Begone from here, you will know when we are ready."

Without breaking stride, Chiron continued down the steps. "Good morning Arcturus. I do apologize for our early arrival. Please, continue your deliberations. We'll just park ourselves here until our appointment starts, which should be in…" Chiron pulled a timepiece from the depths of his cloak, "One minute."

Chiron walked to the center of the room, standing between Arcturus and the Council. He waved a hand over the empty space, pouring jade light into the floor. Six polished chairs rose from the dark stone in a neat row. Chiron took a seat near the middle, and the rest of the unit fell in around him. Cole slid into the comfy chair. The battle-stench of his armor wafted up his nose, stinging his eyes.

Arcturus flushed the shade of rare meat. He spoke in a voice layered with open contempt: "Did you not hear my words? You have not been summoned! The Celestial Council and I are engaged at the moment. You will wait down in the embassies until our business has concluded. You will be summoned when we are ready for your trial."

Chiron folded his hands in his lap. "While I do relish the thought of exploring the luxuries of our embassy waiting rooms, I'm afraid I cannot afford to idle. We are at war you see, and even as I sit here our enemies maneuver against *and* amongst us. I'm afraid I'll have to hold you to our original commitment. The last correspondence I received from your office indicated that our appointment would take place at this time, so here we are."

Arcturus smirked, his thin eyebrow vanishing in the wrinkles of his forehead. "The affairs within this room change rapidly, a concept you would be familiar with if you spent more time in the capital, and less time stirring up trouble with the Light Side."

"Oh I'm intimately aware of the goings-on of these chambers, Arcturus," Chiron replied in a polite tone. "And if my memory serves correctly, the Speaker's primary function is to *speak* for the Celestial Council, not to act for them. Why don't you ask your colleagues if we should honor my appointment? I must insist that this is one of those 'now or never' scenarios, however. My time is valuable and finite, a fact I'm sure the Council can sympathize with."

Arcturus brought his thumb and forefinger to his brow, pinching and twisting the wire-thin strip of hair as he measured Chiron.

"Oh start the trial already," said a woman's voice from behind them. "We can discuss the finer points of information trafficking later. I want to hear Chiron's account of the war."

Murmurs echoed in agreement around the woman.

Looking as if he had just swallowed a mouthful of dirt, Arcturus pushed a stack of papers off his desk, the papers vanishing in little cracks and flashes of green light. "Very well then, we will start the trial. We are of course not as prepared as we ought to be. The accusations are fairly straightforward, however..." His voice trailed off as he swirled his fingers over his desk, conjuring several stacks of paper as well as a few thick wood-bound books. "Where is the rest of your delegation?" he asked, thumbing through a few pages. "There were three of you, one each Alvani and Roth?"

"My companions are a tad busy at the moment. I believe you received my letter in regards to the recent activities in Morthain?" Chiron asked.

"Yes, I have it here somewhere," Arcturus mumbled, flicking an emerald spark at a stack of paper. A fat envelope shot out into his waiting fingers. He waved his hand lazily as the contents of the envelope shot out, displaying themselves in the air around him. "A fine tale of a Colossus attack. Quite the engaging read. My nephew has taken to writing little stories as well, though his are a little more plausible. This one is almost as good as your epic battle in Costas. That one had a Colossus too did it not? You ought to change the monsters in your fables now and then, lest the reader lose interest." Arcturus swished his hand once more and the floating papers vanished in several fizzing cracks.

Cole's confusion was quickly replaced with rising fury. With each heartbeat his fingers and toes elongated. A firm hand on his forearm stopped his munisica from flaring.

Eliza's voice rang clear in his mind: *"Find your center and stay there! Remember what Alvani showed you."*

Cole swallowed, silently thanking her before retreating to his stone room. He poured the water over himself, keeping just enough of his focus in the Council chamber. Thankfully no one had noticed.

"While my reports deserve a proper accounting, I'd prefer we commence with the trial if you don't mind," Chiron replied, polite as ever. "I alone shall represent The Sill."

"And what of your...troupe? What are they here for?" Arcturus looked at the unit as if they were something that had wandered in from a swamp.

"The Sill is under investigation for our actions in Costas. So here I have done you the service of bringing five eye-witnesses. Their accounts will reflect my reports," Chiron said, motioning to the unit.

"How generous of you." Arcturus's lips curved into a tight sneer. "Your witnesses will be examined by our impartial jury, should we deem it necessary."

Keeping himself rooted in his center, Cole watched as Arcturus raised his arm, extending a finger towards the ceiling. All around him, Cole saw the twenty-one arms of the Celestial Council do the same. Sharp beams of green light raced to the boulder in the ceiling, filling the chamber with an eye-jiggling hum. The buzzing faded after the beams vanished, though the shard in the ceiling remained a swirling display of every shade of green.

Arcturus stood, clasping his hands behind his back. The Speaker's face fell slack and his voice suddenly became a blank monotone. "The Celestial Council is gathered within these hallowed walls to see without filter so that we pass judgment without prejudice. May the words uttered here carry not deceit nor lies, for the Celestial Council will hear only the truth. Under Oberon's light we thrive, by Varka's sacrifice we survive."

The last sentence was repeated by the entire Council. Cole stiffened in his chair. He would definitely not be telling anyone about his soul's tagalong.

"The trial is now commenced," Arcturus said, taking his seat. His voice lost all trace of venom, instead taking on a blank tone of indifference. "The Sill shall now be judged for its actions in Costas. Who here shall speak on behalf of the accused?"

Chiron rose to his feet. "I shall speak for The Sill. The actions taken in Costas were direct orders from me. I accept all charges."

Cole felt a fluttering of relief among his calm. Did this mean he was off the hook? Maybe they had forgotten all about him.

Arcturus nodded. "Let the records state that Wisdom Walker Chiron has identified himself as the accused, and he alone assumes the burden of proving relief from guilt of the following cha-"

"He's not alone!" thundered a familiar voice.

Roth appeared at the top of the stairs, leaning heavily on Alvani. He looked as if he could fall over at any moment. There were sunken purple blotches on his unarmored skin, and he sounded as if he hadn't slept in weeks.

Roth stepped forward, limping down the stairs as Alvani struggled to keep him upright. An involuntary twitch tugged his lip with every step. "Sorry Chiron. Couldn't let you take all the credit. Your cowardly hide wasn't even in Costas at the time."

"Master Roth, your appearance is most welcome." Chiron swept across the room and grasped Roth's other arm.

Cole had never seen Roth accept help from anyone, and judging by the worried faces around the room, no one else had either.

Arcturus's face twisted as his voice resumed its usual tone of disgust. "It is most unwelcome, actually! This is a complete violation of procedure! What's the point in posting a guard at the private entrance if..." His face slackened once more as the Council's magic spoke through him. "The Celestial Council recognizes Bonebreaker Roth and Heartseeker Alvani. Do you wish to represent The Sill in regards to the incident at Costas?"

"I do," Alvani said, helping Roth into a chair that Chiron had just conjured from the stone.

A growl rose and fell from Roth's bared teeth as he sat down. "You damned well better not leave me out."

Arcturus gave a single nod, staring over all their heads. "Very well then. Roth, Alvani, and Chiron, you have identified yourselves as the accused, and assume the burden of relieving The Sill from guilt of the following charges: Treason, fraudulent waste of Council resources, violation of customs procedures, the murders of thirty-eight Dark Side civilians and over two hundred Light Side civilians, and inciting war."

Cole could feel the blood draining from his face. Chiron however looked as though he had expected nothing less. Alvani seemed to not be listening as she fed a steady stream of rosy light into Roth's wounds. The Bonebreaker's eyes were half open and distant. Cole chanced a glimpse at the rest of the unit, who all looked as pale as he felt.

The Speaker pulled a tube of paper from the stack in front of him; the tube leapt from his hand and unrolled itself. He ran a finger along the text near the top of the sheet, highlighting the words in blazing script as he read aloud, "The Celestial Council shall now make its case for the greater good of the Dark Side. The accused, after repeated warnings from the Council, initiated official military operations against the sovereignty of Costas. These actions caused irreparable harm to the relations between the Light Side and the Dark Side. Such aggression will no doubt invite further hostilities from both. Reports indicate over two hundred civilian casualties as well as thirty-eight warriors of The Sill, most of whom were students. The Celestial Council has classified these casualties as murder. Furthermore, a baileen was taken across international borders and used to transport unregistered gratia stones and military assets. Baileens and gratia stones are regulated resources which require Council approval before use, and as with all assets of value, must clear customs before transport across international borders."

Arcturus crossed out a few lines of the scroll. His face was still blank and his voice not his own. The Speaker took a moment to gaze openly at each of them. Cole averted his eyes, trying his best to be invisible in his filthy armor.

"With the recent destruction of Aeneria's barrier, the Celestial Council has worked tirelessly to ensure the mistakes of the past will not be repeated today. In our eyes, the actions of The Sill have been rash and unfitting for the peaceful aims of the Dark Side. The banishing occurred nigh on thirty cycles ago, and the fires of war have long burned to ashes. There have been no hostilities whatsoever from our neighbors on the Light Side, nor has there been any indication that they intended to cast the first stone. The only act of aggression has come from The Sill. You have ignited the fires of war with no regard for the countless souls who will perish in your quest for revenge."

Arcturus vanished the scrolls with a quick jab of Wisdom from his hand. His empty eyes fell in their direction. "As previously stated, we find The Sill guilty of treason, fraudulent waste of Council resources, violation of customs procedures, the murders of thirty-eight Dark Side civilians and over two hundred Light Side civilians, and inciting war. Rothael Bonebreaker, Alvani Heartseeker, and Wisdom Walker Chiron, you may now speak on behalf of the accused and attempt to defend yourselves in this open forum."

Alvani rose first, leaning Roth into Chiron's arms. "It saddens my heart when I think of the suffering that has yet to come. Evil is at your borders whether you choose to see it or not. The Celestial Council is the most influential force on all of the Dark Side. You have the power to stanch this suffering before it is too late. Please, open your minds and your hearts. Join us join in our efforts against The Three."

Arcturus's face lit with amusement as his usual sneer returned. "Is that all?"

"It is," Alvani replied, holding her chin a little higher.

"Not much of a defense, but your words are your own," he said. "Who is next? Make your case so we can move this along."

Roth stirred, shrugging off Chiron's arms.

"Master Roth!" Sitra gasped.

Placing one clawed foot in front of the other, Roth approached Arcturus's desk. Cole winced as Roth's mottled, half-healed wounds stretched and ripped. Gobs of clotted blood smacked to the floor, uncorking a fresh crimson flow.

Arcturus raised a palm. "I assure you, I can hear you perfectly well from where you are. There's no need to come close enough for me to smell you."

250

Roth ignored him, limping his way to Arcturus's raised desk. Without word or warning, Roth planted a foot and speared a bladed hand into the white-marble desk, sending chips and sparks flying in every direction. Before the debris had touched the ground, Roth heaved, sending the desk whistling to the chamber wall, where it cracked neatly in half.

Cole flinched, covering his face. By instinct alone he drew his munisica, opening his eyes to see Roth standing over Arcturus. Roth shuddered in pain, speckling the Speaker's pristine white robes with fresh blood from his cuts.

Arcturus fell back in his chair, falling backwards and scuttling away. He raised his hand as emerald sparks fizzled and sputtered from his palm. He shook the failed spell from his hand and tried another, but to no avail. Eyes darting about the chamber, he cried aloud, "Chiron! Chiron, restrain your dog!"

Chiron did not reply. He remained in his chair, tapping his fingers in quick patterns in his lap as though listening to music.

Munisica aching for action, Cole rose to his feet, unsure of what to do. The rest of the unit rose as well, turning towards the Council with claws and magic at the ready. Without taking his eyes off Arcturus, Chiron shook his head ever so slightly, indicating that they should stand down. No one moved a muscle.

Arcturus cried out again, "Someone, do something! Any of you, this man is about to murder me! Debaiti, Callum, Haphalus, help me!"

A woman from the Council table replied with a voice that almost sounded amused, "We cannot aid you, Arcturus. Alvani Heartseeker blocks our Wisdom."

Cole moved his head slightly, stealing a quick glance at Alvani. Her face was set in relaxed calm, though her eyes blazed with cold fury.

Roth prowled after Arcturus as he scooted back against the wall, his eyes wide and searching. Roth bent low until his face was an inch from Arcturus's nose. He spoke with a voice of rolling thunder: "You Speak to me now, Speaker."

"But...but how? My Wisdom..." Arcturus whined as another spell fizzled in his hands. His eyes darted to Chiron, begging for assistance.

"Don't you fucking look at him. Look at *me*." Roth's voice was slow and deliberate, as if he tasted every word before engulfing Arcturus with fire of his tongue. "I have not passed through fields of death and shit to trade quips with you, coward. If I wanted your lip I'd pull it off your face, and if I wanted you dead there's not a soul in this room who could stop me." Roth jerked his arm forward, sinking two claws on either side of the Speaker's neck and into the wall. "Chiron and I were among the few who voted your ancestors on to that throne, and we're the only two who can knock you off. There's no rule or regulation that can save you from us. Don't forget where you came from, and don't forget what we are."

With a practiced motion, Roth flicked a single claw to Arcturus's arm, snapping the long bone with a muffled crack. The Bonebreaker had left his mark.

"Now get up and do your job." Roth pulled his claws from the wall and turned, dropping down from the dais and shaking the entire chamber as his munisica collided with the floor.

Arcturus's face was as white as the unsoiled parts of his robes. Cole couldn't help but stifle a laugh, seeing the Speaker scramble to his feet, utterly disheveled and intimidated. If Cole's own arms hadn't been broken by Roth so many times, he might have felt bad for the Speaker. Even so, Cole admired how Arcturus had kept face, letting no grain of agony betray him as his arm dangled uselessly at his side.

Roth turned away from Arcturus and stood to his full height, speaking directly to the Celestial Council: "I, Rothael Bonebreaker will now make my case. It's easy to decide what's best for others when you're not the one who has to bleed for those choices. I've led every echelon of military force from simple strike teams to entire divisions. Throughout my service I've worked with the good and the sour, both above and below me. I've treated them all the same so long as they pulled their weight. I voted each of you into those cushioned chairs with hopes that you might make a scrap of difference in this second coming of The Three. It's been nearly thirty cycles, but I have not forgotten what it's like to bleed *with* the ones I lead." The Bonebreaker pointed a jagged claw at each Council member, splattering his red life across their perfectly white chamber. "When was the last time you bled for your people?"

The Council stiffened in their seats, as if to show that they were not all that comfy. Cole felt his Rage yearning for an outlet, but in the quiet of his center he could hear his Wisdom calling, telling him that Rage was not the answer. He poured more water over his molten ire until he could hear his Passion as well, showing him the open Fear in the faces of the Council members. In the quiet of his center, Cole could hear strange echoes of emotional clamor bouncing throughout the chamber. There was a general sense of unease, an anticipation of impending doom coupled with tones of revulsion. Louder than all were the keening screeches of Arcturus's Fear and shame. Cole attuned himself to it, both disgusted and intrigued. It may have been his imagination, but Cole felt as if he could draw out the Speaker's Fear. He could amplify it. Feed on it. It would be all too easy, instinctual even. The feeling reminded him of when he last tasted Decreath at the Devotion, only now he could bring that unbridled Fear upon another.

Joshy sprang unbidden to the fore of Cole's mind, carrying his stupid pin-striped fedora. Cole could see his little arms reaching, offering the hat to Arcturus in aid, as if he were about to make everything all right. The Speaker's eyes found Cole's, and in that gaze Cole poured his Passion into the broken man, letting him know that everything was indeed going to be all right.

Cole shivered and dropped his eyes to the floor. Why would Joshy appear to him now? What worried Cole on a deeper level was his sudden interest in the arts of Fear. Shelving his confusion, Cole resigned himself to delve at a later time into what had just occurred in his mind. He was eager to see what other parts he might recognize in the quiet of his center.

Roth grunted, his teeth half-bared in a savage grin. "Decreath has taken a Harbinger. I saw it myself. It's Kreed, the oily bastard-child of turncoat Elites. It won't be long until Grotton and Sorronis find their own Harbingers, and you'll be here begging us to pull your asses out of the Hatefire once more." Roth spat on the floor, limping back to his seat.

Arcturus shuffled back to where his desk used to be and righted his chair, taking a seat while cradling his broken arm. He appeared more composed, though certainly diminished. His eyes met Cole's once more, but only for a blink before the Council spoke through him once again.

"We have no tangible evidence that The Three have taken footholds or Harbingers. As you are all accused of heinous crimes, your testimony is inadmissible. Furthermore, since the barrier fell, Kreed has only shown the Dark Side complete cooperation and confidence. Even after The Sill's assault on Costas, Kreed continues to extend the hand of friendship. Kreed is no enemy of this Council."

Cole's mouth popped open. He couldn't believe what he was hearing. Were they talking about the same Kreed? The same psychopath that burned souls by the thousands and kept Corpulants as pets? They really had no idea what was going on in the rest of their world.

"They don't believe us!" Cole's Rage thrummed into Eliza. *"Everything we went through in Costas, everything we saw. Storn's dead! They don't believe a word of it!"*

"And your Rage won't change that." Eliza pushed back, dousing his Rage with cooling Passion. *"The Celestial Council is governed by logic and facts. We will have to win them over through their means."*

Roth slumped into his chair, his face wincing more loudly than his voice would allow. Alvani immediately set her pinkish glow upon his wounds, stilling their flow.

"If Rothael Bonebreaker has concluded his defense, then may the final representative make his case now," Arcturus said with the Council's words.

Chiron waited for Alvani's nod of approval before standing and facing the Council. "Please, let down your guard and resume whatever spells you wish. You now have full use of your Wisdom."

Cole noticed Alvani relax somewhat, pulling Roth into her shoulders as she nuzzled into his bladed hair. There was a collective sigh of relief amongst the Council as emerald hands glowed and clouds shimmered. Speaker Arcturus made a few quick swipes of his hands, resuming his own protective spells.

Chiron waited for the chiming magic to cease, then said, "I apologize if our display frightened you, but it was necessary to gain your collective attentions. You all represent the wisest of our kind, yet as you plainly see, we few of the Unbound have disarmed you as easily as a parent would a child. But alas, as we have been your better, just one of The Three would make short work of everyone in this chamber." Chiron paused, as a tide of indignant muttering rose around him. "As you are all Masters of Wisdom I will make my case as practical and concise as I can. Decreath, Grotton, and Sorronis are still the masters of our ruin. At least one of them has taken a Harbinger and the others will quickly follow. Join us in our efforts to cull the swarms before they take flight, or, simply stay out of our way. You have our response to your charges. Do with it what you will."

Whispers wafted about the chamber. Cole's Rage-sharpened ears picked up most of it, but none of it seemed overly alarming. After a moment the chamber grew quiet and somber. Arcturus stiffened in his chair, blank-faced and distant-eyed as the Council once more took control of his tongue.

"We recognize your defense and find it to be inadequate. The charges still stand. Oberon's Nations will not join you in your engagement against The Three. The criteria for war has yet to be met and there is no evidence to support your claims. Not even your memories would be admissible, as Wisdom Walker Chiron has the ability to alter the recollections of the accused. We find your actions unjust, and warranting punishment. While we recognize that the Celestial Council lacks the means to enforce the punitive actions our laws require, we do hope you will be amenable to a compromise." The Speaker fell silent, inclining his head.

Roth's pained laughter rumbled throughout the chamber.

"State your terms," Chiron said, hushing Roth with a raised hand.

"The Celestial Council cannot be unresponsive to your crimes. Such passiveness would diminish our integrity and undermine our authority among the citizens of the Dark Side. Nor can we enforce the penalty of death or imprisonment, as your likely resistance would result in our deaths. Our proposal is thus: The temple shall be your prison and you will remain confined here indefinitely. The remaining citizens of The Sill will not be punished so long as they do not follow in your wake. Should you decide to leave the Temple, all of The Sill shall be expelled from the nations of the Dark Side. The Sill will be excluded from all trade, travel, and communications. Also, the Human will be transferred into Council custody after his trial. Do you accept our terms?"

A chilly flicker of panic lapped at Cole's insides. They hadn't forgotten about him. With some effort, he distanced himself from the emotion, though it did not dissolve entirely.

Chiron's face darkened almost imperceptibly. "Your compromise is reasonable enough, though I will sorely miss watching the sunrises from atop the temple. The sight is truly breathtaking."

"Are you implying that you will not stay within the temple?" Arcturus asked.

"Oh heavens no," Chiron replied. "There is too much to be done, and I shudder to think of what nightmares The Three will bring to your borders if we dawdle here too long. No, I intend on leaving after the human's trial, with the human. I will make it quite plain however, that should you set yourselves against us, or see fit to align yourself with The Three, our actions in Costas will be the least of your concerns."

Arcturus blinked in acknowledgment. "We assume that your compatriots are of the same mind?"

"Of course," Alvani replied, giving Cole a warm smile.

Roth sat up higher in his chair. "I'll stick around for the next trial at least. Someone needs to make sure you bureaucrats don't rake our only human over the coals."

"Very well," Arcturus said. "We will remind you that you hold no authority over the human. The Sill has no jurisdiction in regards to undocumented Travelers."

Roth chuckled. "And we'll remind you that you can't stop us."

Arcturus paused for a moment, but otherwise ignored the not-so subtle threats. "Your position brings us grave disappointment. We hope you will reconsider, but we must accept your stance. This will conclude your trial. Do you have anything else to add?"

"Only a request to know when the human will be tried," Chiron said. "I must insist that it be sooner rather than later."

"The human's trial will take place tomorrow at the start of the day. You did bring the human with you?" Arcturus asked.

"Certainly." Chiron extended an arm behind him. "He's right here, and his name is Cole."

Arcturus's face fell into open shock as excited talk broke out among the Council. Cole stared at the floor as he attempted to scratch off something that had dried to his armor. He could feel each one of their eyes on him.

"You're joking!" cried a Council member on the far end of the room. "He's no human, look at the size of him. What trickery have you brought before us?"

Cole turned slowly. The man leaned over his crescent table, stretching his neck to get a better look at him. He looked older than most of the Council, but his eyes were calculating and his features were keen and pointed like a fox. Cole kept his mouth firmly clamped, unsure if he should speak or not.

Chiron smiled, walking over to the man and placing a hand on his shoulder. "Cole, meet Wisdom Walker Larkin. He is Terra's representative for the Celestial Council."

"Um…Hello…Sir," Cole said with a weak smile.

Larkin jumped, as if Cole had just slapped him. "Come now, Chiron. You know as well as I do that *that* is no human. I don't need to be Terra's Walker to see it. He'd be a freak among freaks to his own people."

Chiron gave Larkin a gentle pat on the shoulder. "I'm glad to see your eyesight remains undiminished by the passing cycles, but I'm afraid the evidence is against you on this. Ka Reine herself confirmed the boy's species. You can check for yourself, if young Cole permits it that is."

Larkin scowled, waving his hand dismissively. "Bah! You know how the Council operates. We haven't the time for the paperwork required. Perhaps I'll come find the boy after-hours. I will however be reaching out to Ka Reine before the day is out. I wouldn't doubt if her mind's been permanently clouded by all those plants she smokes."

"You may be right," Chiron said, turning back towards Arcturus, whose impatient frown indicated he now spoke for himself. "By your leave, Arcturus."

"Begone, all of you," Arcturus spat as he began preening the blood from his robes with steaming emerald pulses from his fingertips. "And make sure your little troupe makes less noise than they did last night."

Following the others, Cole left the room through a tall liquid-stone door. Cole shuffled his way closer to Lileth, trying to catch her eye, but she sped off and took a place at the head of their queue. His head throbbed, but his heart hurt worse.

Cole lost all sense of direction as they twisted and wound their way into the temple's core. Chiron led them to a lift that took them deeper still. After what felt like half an hour the lift shuddered to a halt, opening to a copse of thick, towering trees. There were winding ramps that walked up the trunks and gleaming gratia stones embedded in the bark. Above them the ceiling opened to a blanket of inky black sky pocked with stars. The place looked oddly familiar.

"Either I'm losing it or we're back in The Sill," Sitra remarked, punching a nearby tree with a hollow *thunk*.

Chiron pointed to the sky as a pack of sun-lily leaves rippled above. "I thought these accommodations would be most comfortable for you all."

Eliza's face was full of wonderment. "It's perfect, Master Chiron. Oh-" A soul fly fell out of a tree, halting before Eliza's face and shrinking into a violet orb the size of a deka seed. The soul fly inched forward, zapping her on the nose before darting off into a flowering bush. Eliza blushed. "This can't be The Sill, can it?"

"This place is called the Everglen, and it's as close to The Sill as one can find here in Oberon Temple. The Unbound created the Everglen before the banishing. It was a comfy place to rest our heads in-between Traveling. The Everglen should have everything you need if you look hard enough. I hope it will be much harder for you to offend the citizens of Oberon City in here."

"Not all of us were so bawdy, Master Chiron," Eliza said, throwing an accusatory glare at Sitra. "Some of us were perfectly content to enjoy a quiet night of relaxing discretion."

Sitra crossed her arms but didn't seem to have the energy to respond. Judging by the bags under her eyes and the sour misery painted on her face, Cole wasn't the only one nursing a hangover.

Valen cleared his throat. "Masters, what exactly is our intent? Will we defy the Council and leave? Surely there will be repercussions."

"We will leave after Cole's trial, and yes, the Council will be a salty thorn in our side until the end of our days," Alvani said, massaging Roth's arm. "They are cunning, and if their logic dictates that they act against us then my heart will weep for them. Their combined Wisdom makes them immensely powerful, but to us they will be a mere thorn as I said. I see worry in your eyes, young Valen. Give voice to it."

Valen looked up. "I am not eager to defy the Celestial Council."

"Neither am I," Sitra croaked. "It feels wrong."

"I would rather not run afoul of the Council," Lileth said, her voice quiet. "There must be another way."

Eliza swept closer. "Since we're all in such a sharing mood, I too have no desire to break the law. Nor do I wish to wait in a prison while The Three creep ever closer. I'm with Lileth. There has to be another path for us to take."

All eyes fell on Cole. He stood as tall as he could. He tried his best to speak from his center. "I'm not going to jail. They weren't at Costas. They didn't see... They didn't have to watch..." Cole twitched involuntarily as Lexy's burning, deathless corpse flailed before his mind's eyes. He forced himself back into the Everglen. "The Three have to be stopped. I'd leave right now if I knew where to go. Or what to do."

For a moment no one spoke save for the symphonies of insects and birds around them. Chiron broke the silence. "There will come a time in each of your lives when you will lead, and be led by those whom you disagree with. Though Roth, Alvani, and I are much older and much wiser than each of you, I still expect you to question us and defend your own morals. As clever as we think we are, we are still vulnerable to bias. If your morals bring you down a different path than our own, then we must accept your choice and make do without you. We won't stop you."

Sitra let out a raspy chuckle. "But you'll twist us inside out if we decide to go join the Council's peace-parade against you. We're not stupid, Master. You know we won't oppose you, we just don't want to break the law."

"As I said, I expect you to abide by your own sense of right and wrong," Chiron replied. "From the day a person is born they rely upon their senses and memories to build their own reality around them. No two people sense the world in exactly the same manner, just as no two people share the precise sequence of experiences. Thus, no two people live the exact same reality. People are flawed, and people make laws. I would be ashamed to think any of you would follow someone blindly, whether it be the written laws of the Celestial Council or my own advice. I told each of you the day you joined that you may come and go as you wish. The other elders and I will depart tomorrow after Cole's trial. You may join us or seek your fortunes elsewhere. If you choose to count yourselves separate of The Sill, then may we depart in the highest esteem. Personally speaking, I think you all heroes for your service and sacrifice in Costas, and I wouldn't dare ask any more from you."

Roth made to speak, but doubled over in a hacking cough, spraying dark blood over the shiny grass at his feet. He wiped his mouth. "Personally, I think you're a bunch of petal-hides who need a good kick in the ass. I go to fight. Join me or not, just don't let me catch you hesitating when it comes time to choose."

"The only place you're going is to bed, Rothael," Alvani said, tucking her shoulders under his arm. Roth was too weak to resist. "You're at the door to death's house and you know it. I need to work on you. Chiron, we won't be joining you tomorrow. Not right away at least."

Roth let out a weak laugh. "I suppose you're right. It would be much harder to kill The Three if I'm floating in the aethers. Not to mention my death would likely break the spirits of our whelps here. Let's go, Alvi." He nudged his feet along towards the lift, leaning heavily on Alvani.

"I think I'll come along as well," Chiron said, sweeping along and grabbing Roth's other arm. "That is Colossus nest-venom bleeding from you. It will take the two of us and half the stock at the temple's apothecary to keep you from dying." He turned back towards the unit.

"We will return in the morning. Keep your minds open. More importantly, keep your noses out of mischief."

"Wait! Master Roth!" Sitra cried, clutching her hands. Her eyes were eager and shining. "What of the Alpha Colossus? Did you take it down?"

Roth turned his head, only one black eye and the corner of his grinning mouth visible. "You know it."

The door to the lift closed behind the elders, leaving a seamless boulder in its place. For a moment the unit stood in silence as they listened to the familiar chorus of forest life. Sitra wandered off, sniffling. Cole turned towards the others. With a pang of heartache he saw Lileth was already gone.

CHAPTER 15

GROTTON'S PROMISE

"I won't," Habbad said in a quiet voice.

Kreed flinched as if dodging a fly. "That's so odd, perhaps I've had too much to drink. For a teensy moment, it sounded as if you had just defied me. Please Habbad, say it again, won't you?"

Habbad waited a full minute before repeating the words. "I won't."

"Oh?" Kreed shifted on the pillow, his pale, hairless thigh slipping from his satin gown. "That's...what I thought you said." He rose to his feet, making Habbad feel like a frightened rodent beneath the giant Aenerian. Kreed took a step, tripping on the tassels of another pillow. He regained his balance as he stepped in front of the window, gripping the rusted metal bars with his lotioned hands.

Habbad stared at the pillow below him, feeling the weight of his actions crashing down. What had he done?

Kreed ran his fingers through his hair, muttering to himself as his gown swayed about his legs. "No no no, don't. Such a sweet boy. He's not ready. Ready? Yes...get ready for it. Get ready for all of it. No no no! Is he though?" A dark silence fell over the room.

A squeaky giggle hissed from Kreed's lips.

Father Kreed took a deep breath, turning and walking back to Habbad with the loping grace of a drunken lion. Kreed bent low, scooping up Habbad and the pillow he was perched upon. They were now eye to eye. Habbad choked, swallowing the vomit that crawled up his throat.

Kreed's voice dropped to a rich, husky rumble, like oiled leather worked by strong hands: "You know this will cost you."

"I know…but still…I can't…I won't." Habbad bit his lip to stop its trembling, finally meeting Kreed's eyes. There was no trace of anger in Father Kreed. Instead, the Aenerian looked as if his most gratifying fantasy were being served on a gilded platter.

"I am proud of you, my son," Kreed said, leaning close and placing a wet kiss on Habbad's forehead. "So brave. You grow quicker than a starving shadow, but I think you're ready now to grow just a little more."

Dripping, crippling anticipation stole Habbad's voice as he tried to tell Kreed that he *would* do the thing, but his breath lacked the conviction to utter so much as a whisper. He felt himself descend to the floor as the pillow room swirled about him. Frozen, he sat gazing at a mural on the wall as Kreed used magic to conjure his day clothes.

Fully dressed, Kreed approached the door, pausing before it. "Get in," he ordered, pointing at a chest that had not been there seconds ago.

Habbad snapped upright and ran for the chest, throwing it open as if his life depended on it. He turned to Kreed, looking for affirmation that he was doing it correctly, but Kreed was gone. Heart hammering against his little ribs, Habbad squirmed his way up into the chest, flipping and landing painfully on the bottom. The lid crashed shut, shrouding him in complete darkness. Habbad reached up and pushed, but the lid may as well have been made from solid rock. He punched and scratched at the chest, skin flaking off his knuckles. The air seemed too thick, too hot. He couldn't breathe. Habbad kicked, and thrashed, breaking himself upon the crate as invisible hands seemed to close upon his throat and chest. His screams went unheard by anyone who might care.

Why? Why would he defy Father Kreed? Father Kreed did the worst things to people who disobeyed him. Why should he think he was any different? What would his mother and father say if he lost his apprenticeship? Would Lexy look at him the same? Underkin never got a chance to use magic or be anyone important. Habbad knew he'd just thrown it all away. If he even survived the punishment, he would have to return to his district a shamed mess, a poor excuse for a son, useless. Kreed was probably running through his workshop now, looking for the perfect tools for torture. Or maybe he would come back and fill the chest with wriggling, burrowing insects, the kind that wouldn't stop digging until they found marrow.

Habbad's breath shocked him with uncontrollable gasps. He shuddered as he recalled the various ways he'd seen Father Kreed punish people. However, in his panic he remembered that he was not entirely useless, not yet anyway. Kreed had taken him for a reason. Habbad was valuable. Habbad could use Wisdom.

Little hands shaking through wracking sobs, Habbad focused with all his might, tapping his fingers together as Father Kreed had taught him. Green sparks flew between his fingertips, bringing flickering light to the darkness. As terrible as his situation was, he found solace in the little control he had. The failed spell brought his gusting breath to a gradual, steady rhythm as he tried over and over, each time getting closer. Finally, a minute candle of olive flame danced in between his little hands.

Fluttering giggles slipped into Habbad's whimpers as he hugged the little flame, rubbing and pressing it against his cheek. He was not alone. Nor was he unable to breathe. The chest had plenty of air for him. The suffocation was only in his mind. Locking him in here was probably just a test, just another way to bring out more of his Wisdom. That must be it.

Wiping his nose and eyes on his wrappings, Habbad stilled his mind just as Father Kreed had taught him. He was going to be punished, of that there was no doubt, but it wouldn't be too severe. Father Kreed had invested too much time and effort in him. He was too valuable.

Habbad inventoried every spell he knew, recalling the extreme measures that were used to bring the Wisdom out of him. The first time he had altered gravity came to mind. Habbad had been placed in a pit in that instance, the walls too slippery and tall for him to even scratch the top. Father Kreed had dropped Habbad into the pit; his only instruction was to 'stay alive.' Father Kreed had then emptied a barrel full of blood crabs into the hole. The creeping, armored bugs had clutches of sharp legs and a lamprey's mouth made for scraping and sucking. Alone, the blood crabs had been of little threat so long as he didn't stray within leaping distance, but there were far too many in the narrow pit. Within seconds, several of the parasites had latched themselves deep into his legs and back. In the panic his Wisdom had presented itself, causing himself and his attackers to float out of the pit. Habbad had survived, but the crabs had taken too much, their sacs full and firm with his blood as they bobbed like balloons. Father Kreed had been there to catch him, to save him. He was proud of his son.

The pillow room was eerily quiet now, all the better for Habbad to focus. He snuffed his candle and shifted his Wisdom to his ears instead, sharpening them further than he had ever done before. His heartbeat suddenly became the loudest thing in the room. It took a moment for the gushing pump in his chest to become white noise, but when it did the rest of the room seemed illuminated by his augmented hearing. Habbad experimented, rapping his bloody knuckles against his prison. Through the echo, he could hear the softness of the pillows, hear the smoothness of the walls. It was an odd sensation, though somehow it felt natural. Habbad smiled in the dark, reveling in his control over the situation. He would make Father Kreed proud. He would make his family proud.

Hours seeped by and Habbad eventually grew tired. He was afraid to sleep, afraid to miss anything important. Father Kreed could not be disappointed again. The slow and steady rhythm of his heart lulled him, beckoning him to rest his mind. Habbad had never kept a spell up for so long, and it taxed him dearly. Eventually he gave in, confident that even the faintest whisper would wake him as easily as a banshee's scream. Gently tapping his knuckles on the chest, he checked the room once more before succumbing to his lethargy.

Habbad was woken by a hail of popping so loud that he feared a thunderstorm had broken in through the window. The final *POP* was much louder than the others.

"Please, come on in and make yourselves at home," Father Kreed's voice rang through the room, jarring Habbad's skull. "And I must thank you all again for coming, young Habbad is going to flourish like you wouldn't believe."

"We live to serve, Father Kreed," said a familiar voice. "My family is honored to be of assistance to you, Sir. Might I ask where my son is, however? I thought we were going to help him."

"Don't you fret, Mr. Sermund, Habbad is in a place where he can hear everything happening in this room," Kreed replied. "I'm afraid it won't be appropriate for you to see him, however. It would hinder the boy's prodigious progress. I tell you he's blazing along like a little meteorite! We wouldn't want to slow him down now would we?"

"Oh no, no, just a father missing his son is all," Sermund said, laughing jovially.

"Perfect," Kreed gushed, clapping his hands together rapidly. A tiny, deadly giggle fell from Kreed's lips. Habbad knew that giggle. "You're going to help him more than you'll ever know."

Fear, potent and pure fell over Habbad. His heart stopped beating. One, two, three seconds. Then it doubled up, crashing against his ribs like an icy fist. The sound of it echoed painfully off the walls of the chest. He could hear their hearts too; his mother, his father and...

"Beautiful Lexy!" Kreed exclaimed. "Why don't I perch your cute little bum right up here on this chair. Give you a prime seat for the show. How does that sound?"

"I live to serve!" Lexy squeaked. Habbad heard her fluttering heart sail across the room as a muffled *thump* landed atop his prison.

Habbad jumped, pushing and battering himself against the lid of the chest. "LEXY NO! DON'T LISTEN TO HIM! RUN AWAY NOW!"

"That's a good girl," Kreed said with an audible grin. "Sweet Lexy, may I ask you a favor?"

"Of course, Father Kreed!" Lexy replied, her heels bouncing merrily off the chest. "This chair is comfy!"

"I'm glad you like it," Kreed said. His voice then dropped to a whisper, though every syllable stabbed into Habbad's ears. "Lexy, I need you to watch what's about to happen, I need you to watch very closely. Would you mind if I placed just a few spells on you, just so you can see it better? If you do a good job then maybe I'll find an important spot for you one day, just like Habbad."

Habbad threw himself against the lid, smashing his head over and over. "LEXY RUN! HE'S GOING TO KILL YOU! RUN AWAY NOW!"

Lexy giggled. "Yes yes! Please use magic on me! I *love* magic!"

"Father Kreed," said a woman's voice who could only be Habbad's mother. "I'm not so sure I feel comfortable with you...with magic and Lexy. She's so small, you're sure she won't be hurt at all?"

"Not a hair on her beautiful head. You have my word, Mrs. Dainis," Kreed hummed.

"Oh all right then," Dainis sighed. "Be brave Lexy. Be brave for Habbad."

"Okay mommy," Lexy said in her most adorably obedient voice.

Habbad plunged his fingers into his ears. He did not want to hear this. He could not. Reaching for his Wisdom, he released his spell. He pulled his fingers from his ears, but he could still hear every heartbeat, every breath, even the swishing and scraping of their clothes. Cursing, Habbad tried again, but his hearing was just as acute as ever, perhaps even more so. His stomach flipped as he realized that the spell was no longer his own. Horror tickling him, he felt Father Kreed's spell layered seamlessly over his own. Habbad was meant to hear everything, just as Lexy was meant to watch.

"Hold still now Lexy-sweet," Kreed said, his voice grating like a hungry predator's.

Habbad could hear Lexy tense, feel her tiny heart thrum faster. Her squeaking voice sounded like an animal caught in a snare. "No no no…I don't think I like this. Father Kreed I can't shut my eyes. I can't move. Please let me go-let me go! Get it off me!"

Footsteps. Swishing legs. Father's voice. "What is this Kreed, you didn't say anything about tying her up with the magic. No, we're stopping this right-"

Father's Groan. Mother's scream. Lexy's squeal. A clinking glass hammer sounded, bashing into Habbad's ears.

tink

tink

tink

tink

Five hearts, four in the room and one in the chest. Together drumming a horrible symphony, each battling as if to see which was loudest. Four ran with fevered abandon while one chased with lustful intent. Mother and Lexy wailed in tandem. Habbad felt their souls unravel with wild Fear. He coiled into a ball at the bottom of his prison, eyes shut tight in the loud darkness. The sounds painted a scene that Habbad's eyes were blind to.

tink

tink

tink

tink

Skin snapping. Sinew popping. Make it end. Wet flesh stretching, slapping to the pillows. Slow. Too long. Make it end. Father's heart still beating. Air still whistling from a torn whole. Screams rising. Make it end. Let him die. Big footsteps. Pillows kicked aside. Mother gasping, swishing legs kicking. Clothes tearing. A soft thud striking. Nakedness. Shame. Make it end. Mother's screams changing, rushing, rising. Pain. Slick, slow sliding; a blade on skin. Tearing, wrenching, squelching. Too slow. Move faster. Make it end. Let her die. Mother's heart slogging, unyielding.

tug-rip

tug-tug-rip

tug-rip

tug-tug-rip

"Let them die," Habbad babbled into the darkness. "Kill them. Please make it end."

With a final yank Mother's screams ceased, though her heart did not. Her breath came and went, in and out, scratching alongside Father's ragged whistling. Something heavy and soaked fell to the ground as a steady *tap tap tap* beat against the pillows. Lexy's screams discovered new levels of horror, making sounds that no child ought to know how to make. Father Kreed's footsteps clacked nearer.

Habbad sprung to his feet, wrestling his Wisdom into submission. He had it. Focusing with mortal intent, he readied a spell that would kill Lexy. He brought his hands together and willed a tiny sphere of volatile gravity into existence. It didn't need to be large, or strong. The sphere was immaterial, made of nothing but twisting thought. It would pass through the lid of the chest, bending and twisting space along the way. Confident the spell would hold, Habbad thrust the sphere towards Lexy's pulsing heart.

"NO!" Habbad bellowed as he woke, leaving the chest and returning to Kreed's present-day Library. "Again," he growled.

"Impressive," Kreed replied. "You're mighty brave now that you've taken a Domina, though I worry you may start shedding fur or start clawing up the furniture. Ugh, and I'd probably have to get you fixed should you take another feral mirak."

Habbad ignored him. Rising, he walked across the embroidered carpet to a serving table, where a platter of food had been thrown together. Habbad sprung onto the table and tore into the food with savage gusto. Crumbs and scraps fell to the floor about him.

Kreed watched with disgusted interest. "You'd better choose your next Domina with care. Grotton won't take you as Harbinger if you're more animal than not. And you're going to have to clean that up by the way; the Aenerian servants just quit."

Habbad stuffed a hunk of meat into his mouth. Standing upright, he cradled a goblet in one hand while pointing a finger down at the spilled food, incinerating every bit with a flash of white flame. "I think your definition of *quitting* is a little loose," Habbad replied, still chewing.

"Hardly," Kreed scowled as Habbad chugged a goblet, spilling milk down his front. "They stopped doing their jobs adequately, so I considered that their resignation. What happened after was no less than what they deserved. If the damned Underkin weren't so good with these menial tasks then perhaps the general public would have learned how to cook a simple fillet. It's a shame there's none of your kind left."

"So what's next then?" Habbad demanded, dropping his goblet with an obnoxious clunk. "I have other memories we could use."

"No, we're done with memories for today. It's been awhile since you've taken a Domina, why don't you give some thought to your next thrall?" Kreed asked. He walked over to the table and considered the food, which was now a complete mess. He shooed Habbad back onto the floor.

"Domina bore me. The one I have already only whines about wanting to go back to its clan. I don't see the benefit of having a host of complaining souls bickering on all day. Are you going to eat any of this?" Habbad asked, placing his chin on the edge of the table.

"Not anymore," Kreed sighed. "You'll be on your own for the rest of the day. Decreath and Sorronis have business that will keep Talin and me occupied for some time. I want your candidates for your next thralls first thing in the morning. No excuses."

"You've been spending quite a bit of time with Talin lately," Habbad said, grinning darkly up at Kreed. "It seems you've taken favor with him."

"The business of Harbingers is of little concern to you, my budding apprentice. Talin has a big job coming up and we've got a few things to sort out before he crosses over to the-" Kreed cut himself short as his face contorted with disgust. "Wait, why the hell am I explaining myself to an Underkin? Get out of my sight. Now."

Habbad stuffed his pockets with food before darting out of the room. Kreed may have been more lenient since Habbad proved himself a worthy candidate for Harbinger, but there was no need to provoke his creative side. Habbad knew he could survive any sort of punishment, but Kreed's punishment could take valuable time away from Habbad's personal endeavors.

Popping out of the library, Habbad indulged himself in a wild burst of speed, just one of the fruits that his mirak Domina provided. The halls of Kreed's home passed by in a blur. Even with Wisdom he never could have run as fast as he did now with the mirak augmenting his limbs. Grunting, he leaped up to the base of a statue, launching himself up once more to the second-level balcony. He had no intention of leaving through the front door. He despised walking among the rabble.

He slid the glass window open, sniffing the air. Perfume. Alcohol. The theater must have just let out, releasing its hordes of drunkards all too eager to aim a kick at the last Underkin. They had no idea what power Habbad now wielded, what he could bend and break within their minds. If Kreed allowed it he would make an example of just a few. Habbad fantasized about replacing a few of their memories with waking nightmares, or syphoning off their best qualities into their most bitter rivals. Kreed, however, held every citizen of Costas in the highest regard, serving each of them as if he had nothing better to do. For now Habbad would satisfy himself with a simple, traceless act of rebellion.

He rubbed his thumb and forefinger together, and a sticky indigo ball no larger than a raindrop appeared. He leapt from the window and landed as soft as a shadow on a slate roof across the street. Following a pack of raucous voices, Habbad crept to the edge, finding his target. A man, broad-shouldered and handsome, walked arm in arm with his sweetheart. There were others, but Habbad only had eyes for the cocky man. The man bragged to his group, showering himself with accolades and exploits of his work in the soul fly harvesting business. Apparently he'd just fired half his staff for not exceeding this month's demands. Habbad rolled the spell a little larger. This man's head was so big he would need an extra dose. Taking aim, Habbad flicked the spell down to the idiot.

The spell collided with the bridge of the man's nose, startling him as it flashed into a vapor and seeped into his eyes. He looked around for the source, but the spell was already well underway. Habbad scuttled back, jumping to the next roof as he laughed to himself. Under his spell the man would gradually lose his ability to create memories. They would leak from him before they could collect, like a barrel with a rotten bottom. But the second part of the spell would be the sweetest. The gaps in his memory would be filled with an overwhelming urge to defend himself, taking every word and gesture as an act of aggression. If Habbad were very lucky, he would read about a drunken murder in tomorrow's paper.

Setting his sights on to the taller buildings, Habbad skirted the main thoroughfares and scaled his way towards his destination. He would set aside his concerns over Kreed's lesson. Instead, he would move onward in his search for power, which didn't entirely deviate from Kreed's orders. He would indeed find a second thrall, and this one would change everything.

After an hour traversing the rooftops, Habbad craned his neck, gauging the height of the building he was about to scale. It was a flashy luxury apartment that only the most affluent could afford. Habbad scurried from window sills and up drain pipes, working his way steadily up the skyscraper with the mirak's agility. Kreed himself had a room here, or rather the entirety of the two uppermost floors. Habbad was never allowed up there, and while his Hunger demanded to know why, he stopped several floors short. Swinging himself from a marble gargoyle, Habbad sailed into the open window of his destination.

He had never been in Florien's home, but he had talked with and known the doctor well enough to deduce where he lived. The stench of shrikeshard dust and alcohol confirmed his deductions.

Habbad landed on a plush fur carpet, making as much noise as he could. The lump in the bed made no reaction whatsoever. It continued its unsteady rise and fall, spewing horrible smells from the night before. Habbad checked the time. It was near midday, a little early for Florien to rise. He knew the doctor needed all the sleep he could get. Habbad busied himself with a lengthy perusal of the apartment. Florien was a reclusive, bottled-up sort of man, never revealing too much. Other than the time he spent at work, stitching and swapping body parts like a mechanic, the doctor shut himself up in his apartment nearly all the time. There were not-so-quiet rumors however, that the doctor would indulge and revel to such excess that some thought him indestructible, or perhaps chosen by Kreed. Habbad knew the reason behind these rumors to be nothing more than Florien's mastery of pharmaceuticals. Continuing his tour, Habbad found crushed pills peppered over every table, and shriveled bags of shrikeshard littering the floor.

There was one odd thing about the apartment that Habbad's train of logic couldn't reveal. Scattered throughout all the opulent sculptures and expensive gadgets were the most horrible paintings Habbad had ever laid eyes on. They looked as if a child had been left unsupervised for a moment in front of a canvas, just long enough for a vague mess. Whoever the artist was either didn't care for the craft or lacked the eyesight to know what everyday objects looked like. Conversely, however, the canvas and oils themselves were of the highest quality. The materials were equal to what one would find in the most prestigious galleries. Habbad was at a loss, and the unanswered question gnawed at him like a dog scraping at a long-clean bone. There was something to those paintings.

After glossing over a few books that looked as if they had never been touched, Habbad decided it was time to wake Florien. Jumping up to the foot of the bed, he drew upon his Wisdom, compressing a large volume of air into a needle point. He released the spell, jarring the room with a teeth-rattling explosion. Several paintings crashed to the floor.

The blankets continued to rise and fall.

Habbad kicked at the lump, raising his voice: "That is why you shouldn't prescribe to yourself, doctor. If I meant you harm there would be nothing you could do about it. Not that you could stop me if you were lucid."

The lump was utterly unresponsive.

"Let's see if you can sleep through this then," Habbad said, readying another spell.

An emerald web fell over the pile of blankets, tightening into a solid veil that squeezed every inch of the lump. Habbad crossed his arms, waiting. Before long the breathing became rushed and desperate.

"No!" Florien wailed, throwing the blankets off and shattering Habbad's spell. His mouth gaped like a fish's. With Fear etched over every line of his face, Florien dove for the floor, falling to his hands and knees as he sucked in as much air as his lungs would allow. Eventually he calmed himself, clutching his chest and leaning back against his bed.

"Good morning, Doctor." Habbad smirked, standing above him on the night stand.

"What!" Florien bellowed, shooting across the floor and snatching a shoe, brandishing it like a weapon. His puffy eyes squinted up at Habbad before furious recognition lit in his eyes. "What is this? Get out of my apartment, Underkin!"

Habbad jumped down to the floor, striding over until he was standing in between Florien's sprawled legs. "Don't be rude, doctor. I'm a guest. Offer me food."

Florien dropped the shoe, slapping his hands to his face and rubbing his eyes. "I don't keep food in the apartment," he mumbled through his fingers. "I never kept any food here. What do you want, Habbad?"

"I came to talk with you," Habbad said.

"Well, I've nothing to say, not to mention I'm not fit to entertain guests." Florien's hands drifted to his stomach, holding it in as if it were about to explode. "Get out of the way."

Habbad sidestepped as Florien scrambled to his feet, shooting like a wayward javelin towards the kitchen sink.

"Something from last night not agree with you?" Habbad asked, following him to the sink. "Try some foreign cuisine?"

Florien heaved and belched, a shaking hand wrenching the nozzles on the sink. When he finished he ran the water over his face and hair. Habbad tossed him a towel. Florien took it without a word and cleaned himself.

Dabbing his eyes, he turned his wobbling frame to face Habbad. "You woke me too early. I hadn't slept off the nauseating effects of the depressants."

"Perhaps you should learn to sleep without them," Habbad replied. "For such a smart man you ought to recognize a crutch when you see one, or when you eat them by the cart-full."

"The crutches I use are for good reason, and of no concern to you!" Florien spat, opening a drawer and pulling out a small balloon of shrikeshard dust. "What do you want?"

Habbad watched Florien as he stabbed the balloon with an ornate golden straw that he pulled from nowhere. Intrigued, he waited until Florien finished huffing the entire bag before he spoke. "I want to know about the person who made these paintings."

"Why would you care about that?" Florien asked, rubbing his nose.

"These painting are the worst thing I've ever seen, and I've seen two Devotions," Habbad said, pointing to a glob on the wall that looked like dried meat stew. "Every single one was crafted without thought, without care. It's as if whoever made them had nothing left of value, not even the time to put in any effort."

Florien scowled. "Did you break into my apartment just to insult me? No, that can't be the reason. You've never seen the paintings before, so why would they interest you? Wait, is this not the first time you've been here?" Florien's white knuckles gripped the countertop, looking as if he were trying to tear it from the base.

"Calm yourself, doctor. This is indeed the first time," Habbad said in a bored voice. "I didn't know it until now, but I believe that these paintings are exactly the reason I'm here. What can you tell me about the person who made them?"

Florien's anger turned to a sharp suspicion. "He's a man under my employ. I value his work and pay him well for it. That is all you need to know."

"Bullshit," Habbad replied, jumping atop the counter so he was eye level with the doctor.

Florien glared, dropping his voice to a harsh whisper. "Prove it."

Without turning away, Habbad whipped his arm back, pointing a gnarled hand at the glob of stew on canvas. The painting smoked and curled, turning soot black before falling from the wall in ashen flakes. Habbad kept his eyes locked on Florien, whose look of offense took a little too long to show.

"Does that bother you?" Habbad asked.

Florien's eyebrows crammed together. "Arrogant little blighter. I long for the day Kreed discovers you are no different than any of your kind. Impulsive. Unintelligent. Breed like rodents. You are lesser beings. It won't be long until the Underkin plague is finally wiped from the world."

Habbad dove forward, wrapping his legs around Florien's neck and yanking his face close.

"WHAT THE HELL? GET OFF ME! " Florien's hands wrapped around Habbad's tiny arms, wrenching them. Habbad's grip was unyielding, however.

"You can't hide your shame from me, Doctor," Habbad said, summoning the Fear needed to dive into Florien's mind. It didn't take long to find what he needed. Habbad twisted out of the doctor's grip, landing back on the counter with a savage grin.

"Get out. Get out now. Kreed be damned I *will* kill you… using that foul magic on me!" Florien sputtered, opening another drawer and yanking out a sweeping, serrated blade.

"What's that for? I thought you didn't keep food here, Florien," Habbad laughed. "You know a knife is of no use against me, even in your capable hands. You'll need magic to kill me. Seeing as you're about as magical as that bit of steel in your hand you may want to choose your words more carefully. I may take offense and choose to defend myself."

Habbad's eyes flashed green and Florien yelped, waving the knife as if it were trying to stab him. Sizzling, popping sounds came from the doctor's clenched hand as he tried to release the blade. Smoke rose from his hand, filling the kitchen with the stench of burnt meat.

"Please! Let it go! My hand's on fire!" Florien wailed.

Habbad watched with mild interest as Florien picked and yanked at the blade with his free hand, burning and cutting himself. He slammed his burning fist down on the counter over and over. Even his breaking bones wouldn't release the scalding knife. Florien fell to the floor, weeping and defeated.

Habbad jumped down, landing on the doctor's chest. He released the heat from the blade, but not Florien's grip. "Ready to tell me about Dirken?"

Florien shook his head, crying softly. "Please, I'm begging you. He's a good man. Beautiful family. Don't harm him."

Habbad grinned, flicking his fingers along the serrated edge of the knife. "How noble. Even a monster such as yourself isn't without some redeeming qualities. Don't fret doctor, your shame is safe with me, and so is dear Dirken. I won't make him do anything he doesn't truly Hunger for."

Habbad took the lift down to the streets of the Cloud District, stopping at a bakery near the bottom to wet his throat and fill his belly. When Habbad mentioned he had just come from Florien's apartment, the owner was all too helpful, hailing him a cab and foisting sweets and pies upon him. Eating at a proper restaurant while wearing a fine suit scratched his Hunger in all the right places.

The back seat of the cab was supple, yet firm. It was by far the most luxurious thing Habbad had ever sat on. He couldn't decide if the best part was the feeling of high status, or the sour look on the driver's face that plainly stated his disdain for carting around a mere Underkin.

The cab hummed to a stop outside the Wind district, a slummy trade port where all goods came in and out of Costas. Habbad forced a heavy tip on the driver, knowing full well that the man's prejudice wouldn't stretch far enough to refuse the money. The Hunger in the Man's eyes told Habbad he would keep the extra money for himself and not share it with his coworkers, nor even tell his wife. He would tell her he was working late, then make a beeline for Florien's night clubs in search of an outlet for his most basal desires. The fact that an Underkin's money would make this all possible pleased Habbad to no end.

Hopping out of the cab, Habbad smoothed out the front of his crimson suit before striding out into the Wind district. The air reeked with the stench of briny fish, and every surface was somehow covered in a wet sheen. Habbad's shoes clacked along, drawing the attention of the surly locals as he strutted through busy streets. Voices fell into hushed whispers as he neared and crowds parted for him. Could word of his importance have spread this far?

Heeding Florien's directions, Habbad followed the main road down to the docks. Cargo ships bayed across the port, heralding the arrival of goods from other lands, or moaning a farewell as they set out to sea. A quick hop brought Habbad atop a thick wooden wall that kept the sea in check. Darting along, he quickly left the commercial district of warehouses and slaughterhouses. The torchlight gave way to polished gates and crisp lawns of the upper-class residentials. The rustic, boxy architecture gradually softened to a comfy neighborhood with clay-shingled roofs and walls of happy blues or yellows. He was getting closer. Hunger urging him, Habbad dipped into his Domina blood and bolted faster down the wall, dropping into a four-legged sprint. Before long the flashy mini-mansion of Florien's memories came into view. The house stood alone on its very own pier as if to distinguish itself as a notch above the usual upper-class. Habbad followed the wall up to the crisscrossing framework of the lower pier, scaling beams as easily and quickly as walking up the front stairs.

Habbad sniffed the air and sharpened his ears with Wisdom. Dirken had to be in there somewhere. In this moment Habbad regretted not having put more of an effort into his lessons at The Sill. He recalled how one of the females could use Passion to detect the life forces of nearby creatures and people, a useful trick that had saved them from many surprises. Habbad would make do with his other skills, however.

Habbad sent a wriggling tendril of Wisdom into the latch of the back door, clicking it open while casting another spell to muffle his feet. He stepped into a darkened room. The smell of acrylics and wood shavings permeated the air. He couldn't see well, but he didn't need to. There was enough ambient noise for his sharpened ears to make out the corners of tables and clutter on the shelves. Habbad thought he could hear the steady drumming of a lonely heart dripping through the floorboards above.

Habbad took a deep breath, calling from the darkest reaches of himself and drawing upon his most foul memories. He filled himself with Decreath's gift, bathing in the Fear until his blood threatened to freeze solid. Exhaling, he promised the Fear a fresh victim, one lonely and willing. The Fear rushed from his mouth, filling the room with a noxious olive cloud. Closing the door behind him, Habbad darted from shadow to shadow, listening as his Fear searched every crack and crevice for a timid soul. Panicked rodents scurried and scratched beneath the floorboards, snuffing themselves dead before the touch of Fear. Habbad pushed the cloud out farther, but there was not a soul on the first floor. The Fear mixed with his Hunger, climbing and racing up the stairs. Habbad followed.

As he approached the landing of the second floor, a jerking terror caught his attention, like an insect caught in a spider's web. Habbad pulled in the slack, attuning himself to the frightened creature. Shame. Worthlessness. Despondence. These were the qualities he needed, the hallmarks of a malleable soul. Habbad drew the shadows about himself, listening to Dirken's every concern from the corners of the artist's own mind. When Dirken's perseverating thoughts began to loop back upon themselves, Habbad injected yet more Fear into the layers of the broken mind. Silent as a shadow, Habbad entered the room.

Dirken was curled up on a mauve sofa, wrapped in a laced blanket and shaking with empty sobs. The fireplace was lit, but only minutes from dying. Strewn about the bookcases and desks were pictures of Dirken's family, their faces set in forced smiles that did not reach their eyes.

"Something the matter, Dirken?" Habbad asked, revealing himself at last.

"Gods above!" Dirken screamed, his whole body jerking as he pulled himself upright. He shot off his couch, backing away with one arm raised while the other searched blindly for a weapon. "Who are you?" he demanded, grabbing a fire-poker and swishing it about like a sword.

Habbad dropped his gaze to the floor, rubbing his hands. "I'm sorry to frighten you. I felt you crying from the street and thought I might come see what was the matter. I'll leave now, Father Kreed is expecting me anyway." Habbad turned to walk away.

"You!" Dirken cried. "I've seen you! You're the Underkin that's been scurryin' about with Kreed! How'd you get in here?"

Habbad glanced back, forcing a look of deepest shame upon his wrinkled face. "I'm Father Kreed's apprentice," he offered, shrugging his shoulders. "Father Kreed taught me magic so that I might help people as he does. He's so busy these days that he can't be everywhere at once. I thought I'd come down to the Wind District and see if there's anyone here I could help. I see I was wrong. I'm so sorry, Dirken. I'll leave now, trespassing is illegal." Habbad rushed himself from the room with a rapid pitter-patter.

"How do you know my name?" Dirken asked, lowering the fire-poker.

Habbad paused, inching back into the room. He gestured with an open palm. "I'm Father Kreed's apprentice. I know many things. I know that your heart hurts, and that you've been betrayed. I know that you are a talented artist with potential for so much more, though no one else can see it. You are not appreciated as you ought to be."

Dirken set the fire poker back in its stand. "What else do you know?"

"Many things," Habbad replied, hugging the door frame. "Dirken Sir, can you put some more wood on the fire? I'm very cold."

Dirken blinked, his words rushing from his mouth: "Of course, of course, please grab yourself a seat. I'm the one who should be apologizin'. Had no idea you were Kreed's boy. Habbad, right? Can I get you some food or somethin'?"

Habbad struggled his way onto the Aenerian-sized couch. "A drink would be nice. A strong drink if you have some."

Dirken tossed a log into the hissing fire, sending a cascade of sparks up into the chimney. "Got a bit of Galdebrean brandy in the hutch here, but ain't you Underkin not supposed to drink? Ain't it illegal?"

"I won't tell if you won't," Habbad quipped and grinned.

Dirken returned the grin with a sad smile. "'Course I won't. You come up here of your own goodness, trying to do old Dirken a favor. It'd be bad luck to turn on you. Bad in the gods' eyes too, and I can't afford to miff them any more." Dirken pulled a matching set of crystal glasses from a sturdy oaken hutch. He thunked them down and filled them with amber liquid from a plump wooden cask. He carried the drinks over and sat next to Habbad. "Take it nice and slow now. This'll set your toes on fire if you gulp it down too quick."

"Thank you, Dirken," Habbad said, using both hands to grab his glass. Habbad waited for Dirken to take a sip before bringing his glass to his pinched lips. With a silent spell, Habbad transported a sip of his own glass into Dirken's. Habbad pulled an appropriate bitter face, nodding at the quality of the drink before inclining his head towards the pictures on the mantel. "That is a beautiful family you have, but where are they now?"

Dirken's eyes fell back to his glass as he took a bigger sip this time. Habbad matched him, refilling his glass once more. "They're off seeing to their own affairs. My boy's gone to work with a church of Sorronis out in Amoskeag, and my girl's taken up with some puffed-up pin head on the other side of town. Writer or somethin'. Neither of them visits much. Can't scrape a few hours a month to spend on their old man. No thanks at all for the fortunes I've spent on their fickling fancies. Ah, but all kids leave the nest don't they? They'll come back around someday. The gods test our resolve now and again to make sure we're deservin' of their graces."

Habbad sat in silence for a moment, watching Dirken drift into a daydream. He feigned another sip from his glass, triggering Dirken to do the same. "What of the woman in the pictures? She's stunning."

Dirken's face soured, but his eyes remained in the fire. "She's my...that's Raiya. We were bonded once, still are as far as the law's concerned. She's busy with an affair of her own."

"What do you mean?" Habbad asked. "A wife's place is by her man's side."

"So it was until she found the side of another more suitable than my own." Dirken suddenly looked as if he were about to be sick.

"Impossible," Habbad scoffed. "How can another man have more to offer than you?"

"Other men can use magic," Dirken growled, his face twisting into a knot of fury. "Magic grants you power and status, opens doors for you. Raiya wants for a man that has that power. Even my own children have the gift. A barren man such as myself has nothin' to offer them."

"That is the most foolish thing I've heard in my life," Habbad exclaimed. "You've cared and provided for your family, more so than most by the look of your estate. You must be the wealthiest man in the Wind District." Habbad's voice rose with enthusiasm, eking out a reluctant smile from Dirken. "I've been all over this city and you're better looking than most, not to mention you have an artist's heart. My friend Florien is the most illustrious surgeon in Costas and he adores your work. Every corner of his apartment is covered in your talents."

Dirken's eyes popped wide. "You know Florien the Generous?"

Habbad smiled. "I do. Would you like to know a secret about Florien?"

A greedy shadow fell over Dirken's face. "I would."

Habbad waited a moment, studying the man's eyes, tasting his Hunger. "Florien can't use magic either. He's as fallible and flawed as you are, yet he is a man of status. Of power."

Dirken's expression changed from yearning to shock. "That's incredible. You'd never know, what with the way he carries himself, the way that others treat him. He's somethin' of a celebrity down here in the Wind District. He's the one that discovered my art in the first place, made me popular among the local galleries. Everythin' that I have I owe to him." He fell silent, his face scrunching as a tear rolled down his nose. He spoke in a shaking whisper: "I Hate him."

Habbad allowed Dirken a moment to collect himself, patting the man on the knee. "Why would you Hate a man that has given you so much? Didn't you just admit that you owe everything to him?"

Dirken bit down on his trembling lip, forcing it still. "Everythin' I have I owe to him, but everythin' I've lost is because of him. When Florien discovered me, I was but a poor dock hand fightin' tooth and nail for my Raiya and the babes. Florien found a bit of my art floatin' somewhere and demanded I accept payment. It wasn't worth nothin' and I knew it, just a stupid drawin' for the babes to look at. Florien offered me a fortune, and bein' an honorable man of the gods, I refused. Then he increased the offer by tenfold, and I took it. I took it all. More than I was due, more than I was worth. What's worse is he demanded more of my work. Made me promise to have another piece ready in a week. I took it all like a starvin' dog."

Dirken wiped his nose, taking another sip. Habbad refilled his glass once more. "It sounds as if your gods were taking favor with you. You went from a poor laborer to paid artist overnight. Perhaps it was their intent for Florien to discover you."

Dirken grunted, shaking his head. "That was their intent all right, but the gods was only testin' me. A test that I failed good and hard. Money corrupts, especially when it's not deserved. My art's shit. Worthless garbage. My life, all of this is just a lie. Florien the Generous took notice and paid me boatloads. I didn't trust him. I knew there'd be a catch for takin' more than my worth, but the money had already started workin' its magic on me. Raiya was happy at first, and I was too. I could treat every day as if it was her birthday. We moved out of our home, snubbed our old friends and family as though they was nothin but rats lookin' for a bite of our cheese. It changed us. The money gave me power, made me important, and Florien made me valuable to others. The money and status gave my sweet Raiya a life she had been dreamin' of since she was a girl. We mingled in different circles and it wasn't long before other men began to catch her eye. Men with real power, real value, real magic. She knew my art was shit, that my money was fake. Can't blame her though. Her greed's just as powerful as mine."

"Dirken please, don't say any more. You've been through enough, my friend," Habbad cooed.

"Nah, got to get it out while the wound's open. I shut it up for too long and now my seams is burstin'." Dirken rubbed his raw eyes and blew his nose into his shirt. "Hey Habbad, I think I just figured somethin' out. I can make peace with what the money did to me and my Raiya, but what doesn't settle is what the money did to my kids. Grew up never havin' to work for nothin'. They expect all of life's fruits brought to them, though they won't put so much as a nail in the dirt for it. They treat everyone like ghosts or worse unless there's somethin' to gain. We raised them wrong we did. And now it might be too late. Too much Hate stacked against me now. I've no worth, no value. Nothin' to offer my wife or my own kids."

Habbad moved his gaze respectfully into the fire, which no longer sputtered. The flames crackled and lapped their way up the fresh logs, as though driven by a Hunger of their own. Habbad's heart quickened. He was very close now.

Waiting for Dirken's sobbing to wane, Habbad offered another careful measure of sympathy: "Your story is a sad one friend. Is there nothing you can do? Any way at all to get them back?"

Dirken released a shaky sigh. "You're a sweet boy Habbad. No, there's nothin at this point. Suppose I just take the gods' spankin' and just be thankful I didn't lose no more." He took a deep pull from the brandy, waving it about with a flourish. "Though I bet a bit of magic would set a few things right. I'd love to boil the guts of the struttin' rooster that my Raiya's fuckin' nowadays. Sorry for cussin'," he added, his words melting together under the effects of the brandy. "Drink brings it out of me. Makes me thirsty for unsavory things. Shouldn't be drinkin' like this. But then again, this stuff's expensive. Drink up Hubbard."

Habbad threw his empty glass back, both hands shaking with anticipation. He was so very close. "Dirken, do you know the miracles of Father Kreed, of his work with The Three?"

"Course I do," Dirken sloshed. "The most powerful man in Costas workin' for the most powerful gods of our world. Kreed's a hero to us all."

Habbad nodded. "Yes he is powerful, but he is also generous. Even more so than Florien. He helps people realize their true potential, gives them the hand they need to take back what is truly theirs."

"Go on then," Dirken grumbled, Hunger burning visibly in his eyes.

"It's no accident that I happened upon the Wind District today," Habbad said, slowing his words, allowing Dirken to drink in every syllable. "As Kreed's apprentice, I've become attuned to the suffering around me. It's a heavy burden, but the worst part is that I can't help everyone. There simply aren't enough hours in the day. So I spend my time helping those who need it most. You have been wronged by Florien, by your family, by the gods even. Yes, the gods Dirken. I have touched them with my own soul, and I assure you they are not as perfect as the church would have you believe. You're a good man, and good men deserve a second chance to put things right."

Habbad paused. Dirken slumped from the couch and onto the floor, kneeling his way closer with his fingers entwined in prayer. His eyes were round and begging, his lips wet and thirsty. He was rock-still, as if afraid the sound of his own breath would betray him.

Forcing his own breath to continue its steady, confident cadence, Habbad stood on the couch. Dirken's eyes followed. "Dirken, will you allow me the chance to help you?"

"Yes," Dirken whispered. A mixture of Hunger and Fear spread across his face. "But I've nothing to give. Nothing of value."

Habbad placed a hand atop Dirken's bald head. "You have something very valuable, my friend."

"Name it!" Dirken squealed. "Name it and it's yours!"

Habbad allowed himself a sigh of relief. Dirken was his. "Soon, my friend. We will set things right when the *time* is right. But now you need sleep. We both do. Rest your eyes and we shall continue when you wake."

Without another word Dirken threw himself upon the couch, asleep before his head hit the cushion. Habbad hopped over Dirken's legs, landing on the table and then the floor. He trotted his way through the house, making his way to the front door. They had talked through the night. Kreed would be expecting him for lessons in only a few hours, though Habbad had no intent on going. Habbad was doing the work of a god. He was about to serve Grotton in a way that was unprecedented in all of recorded history. Kreed couldn't hope to comprehend it, nor would he allow such a violation of one of his subjects. Habbad knew he must do this alone and in secret. There was still much work to be done, but if he were very lucky he would be the first person to take an Aenerian Domina, a sentient being.

Habbad reached the front door, opening it slowly. The front yard was empty, the guard safely asleep at the front gate. Habbad then noticed something on the steps in front of him. Soft as a shadow, he darted from the doorway and snatched a newspaper off the steps before retreating back into the house. Closing and locking the door behind him, Habbad opened the paper, reading the headline.

MAN MURDERS FRIENDS IN CLOUD DISTRICT, REMEMBERS NOTHING

Habbad grinned, hugging the paper into his chest. His Hunger purred, ready for another meal.

Chapter 16

Bonds Broken

Cole explored the Everglen with Valen and Eliza, making a game of finding all the similarities to The Sill. They walked from tree to tree over footpaths of braided roots, careful not to stray too far as there seemed to be no end to the place. Conversation was unusually light and superficial, never straying too close to the Council's sentencing or the machinations of the elders. A deep worry budded within Cole. He had a horrible suspicion that he would be leaving the Everglen alone.

Cole fell silent, slowing behind as Valen and Eliza debated over which starscape the Everglen displayed. He drifted into his center, cleansing his wayward thoughts and emotions into the stone room. Once he was confident there was nothing more, he was struck with a sudden yet profound lack of purpose. Taking a deep breath, Cole began to explore what his purpose ought to be. He felt parts of himself rise up to answer. The first and loudest part told him he needed to fight The Three and stop their evil from spreading. But why? Why did he need to fight? This was not his world. Another part arrived at his center, nudging harder than the first. It was the same part that didn't like his Rage. This part didn't want him to be defined solely by violence; a life of constant fighting was no way to live. He was more than a warrior, but what exactly, he didn't know. Unable to wring any answer out, he emptied his mind once more and asked himself the question again.

Eliza's distant belly-laugh brought another part of him to the surface. His Passion answered this time, showing him everyone he cared about. He hadn't lived on this planet long, perhaps barely a year in Earth-time, but here he had real, meaningful relationships. Outside his immediate family he had never known such wholesomeness. His Passion hummed again, wetting his eyes as he thought about how much his new friends meant to him. They had been through so much together. The feeling was difficult to label and impossible to pinpoint. It was as if his friends had made new parts of him grow and flourish, parts that changed him into a better person. His appreciation gushed alongside memories of every moment of shared victory and loss. The Passion waxed, illuminating this strange feeling in such an obvious way that Cole laughed aloud. It was simply love.

The magic acted of its own, pulsing so forcefully that upon his next exhale Cole's feet lifted an inch from the ground. Beams of lavender shot from his swelling chest, striking Eliza and Valen, halting them as their faces lit with euphoria. Cole's breath took an alarmingly long time to leave his body, though he had no desire to breathe. The lavender light dimmed as his lungs finally emptied and his feet reunited with the woven root path. Eliza and Valen turned slowly, surveying Cole with looks of gratified wonder.

"What was that?" Valen asked. He glanced down at his own body, checking and patting himself.

"I... I don't really know," Cole said, wiping his face quickly. "I was just going over some stuff in my head. The Passion came out of nowhere."

Valen tilted his head, curious. "As long as you're well. Thank you for that, Cole," he added.

Eliza gave him a knowing, sly grin. *"Been practicing I see. You are growing faster than a rising sun, little human."*

Cole made his apologies, then his excuses so he could be alone. Dodging a flock of eager soul flies, Cole made his way over to where Sitra had discovered the sleeping quarters. His Passion clung to his thoughts as he walked, offering other answers to his question of purpose. He felt a powerful desire to rescue Habbad, though his Wisdom told him that his friend was lost forever. Cole wanted to save him, but thoughts of another disastrous rescue mission curdled his bravery. Habbad belonged to The Three now, just as Lexy did. Brother and sister bonded in the vilest of magics. Cole paid silent tribute to his friends, remembering their toast from the night before. After a while,

Cole's mourning brought about another depressing thought; his love for Lileth.

He spent the remainder of his walk trying to discern his feelings for her, but more important was her actions towards him. When he reached his tree, however, his forking thoughts only led to more questions and a slippery ire that evaded all attempts to soothe it. He trudged up the ramp of the tree he'd picked out, resigning himself to a foul mood as he forced Lileth from his mind.

Popping through the door, he delved into his foggy Wisdom and produced a glowing jade orb barely bright enough for him to see. Focusing another spell, he locked the door behind him, ignoring Eliza's twangs of concern through their link. Fumbling in the dim werelight he found the smooth surface of a fist-sized gratia stone. Cole brought his eye close, but couldn't guess what type of stone it was through his dim light. Growling in frustration, he forced his Rage into the glassy surface.

The stone roared to life, filling the room with bloody red hues. The tree gave a gentle shudder as soft white lamps flickered to life and running water gurgled inside the walls. Much like his room at The Sill, this one was sparsely decorated. There was a simple bed, nightstand, and armoire, all blending with the floor as if grown from the tree's ringed interior. Cole threw his bag down and sat himself on the end of the bed. The momentary distraction allowed his concerns for Lileth to branch like creeping vines, now blooming with their own desperate answers.

Cole shook himself, gripping his hair until individual strands snapped free. He knew he was being stupid. He had placed more value on a simple kiss than he ought to have, but whenever his mind relaxed she pulled at him like a riptide. His heart and stomach seemed to be twisting themselves into a heavy knot, eluding every meditative trick he tried. He punched the wall, leaving deep gouges leaking with sap.

Opening up the armoire, Cole found an entire wardrobe stocked for him. There were several outfits, all singlets with thickened armored sections and verdant, flowing designs worked into the trim. There were no shoes or gloves, though there was a bandoleer and a short, over-the-shoulder cape. The material was stretchy and patterned more like earthy camouflage. From Cole's limited experience with Aenerian fashion, he guessed these outfits would suit him just fine at either a formal dinner or a fight for his life. He might look like some kind of ridiculous comic-book hero, but it was certainly preferable to the Colossus-stained rags he currently wore. He closed the armoire, wondering if he was perhaps about to wear Varka's old clothes. He waited for it, but there was no response from his subconscious tagalong.

As he suspected, the apartment wound around to a bathing room similar to his tree at The Sill. Without bothering to take his clothes off, he stepped into the abrasive shower ring and allowed the magic to disintegrate his armor and filth. He did another pass for good measure, leaving his skin raw.

After his shower Cole was too tired for much else, even food. Weariness from the night before crashed over him, dragging his eyelids shut and pulling him towards the bed. He didn't bother checking for undergarments, instead crawling into bed naked. With a lazy flick of Wisdom, his timepiece flew from his bag and thwapped into his palm. He set the device to wake him long before his trial, which ought to be more than enough time to recover and get ready. Perhaps he would find Lileth in the early dawn and tempt her with breakfast, just as friends.

Cole's dreams seemed unable to make up their mind. He was in the hallways of his high school, trying to find the quickest way to Roth's lesson. Arcturus's voice came over the intercom, beckoning him to come to his office, but then he wouldn't be able to visit Joshy like he'd promised. Bumping through tall shoulders and mean glares, Cole fought his way to Arcturus's office. The throngs were too thick and the people around him seemed to be getting taller, or was he shrinking? He was going to be late. The crowd pushed him along as though he were a log floating down a river. Cole eventually broke free near winding stairs that led to Arcturus's office. The stairs were empty, though something echoed down to him, enticing yet haunting. Cole lunged up the steps, taking them two at a time. The bell rang; he was definitely late now.

The steps became a wooden ramp, its grainy slats wet with spilled oil from those that had climbed ahead of him. He peered over the edge of the ramp, taking in the riotous debauchery below him. He was exhausted and the bag of odium made his arms burn, but he had no choice but to trudge on; he was *chosen*. Cole followed the line shuffling ahead of him, which had mercifully stopped near the very top. Leaning against the tower, he hoisted his bag of odium to his shoulder and indulged in a little break. After he'd enjoyed a moment of peaceful reflection, something slammed into his gut, pulling him tight to the tower and taking the air from him. He could barely breathe, but that didn't matter. He couldn't die. He was special. He was *chosen*.

An overwhelming desire seemed to move his limbs for him. He twisted the cap off his bag, pouring the odium over his head. It was warmer than he expected, and sweet. His tongue wandered over his lips, savoring the tang of the oil. A scent of cooking meat wafted up from far below. He sniffed eagerly, only now aware of how ravenous he was.

Cole's eyes snapped wide, bringing him back to his tree-top apartment. The lights had shut themselves out, though the Rage stone bathed the room in a bloody glow. He was cold. The blankets had fallen off, leaving him completely naked. He must have kicked them off during his nightmare. Breathing a quivering sigh of relief, Cole sat himself up to find the blankets. To his confusion however, he hadn't moved an inch. He was still lying like a corpse upon a mortician's table. Dimly disoriented, he tried again, only to find himself utterly stuck to the bed. He had no control over his body.

Something buzzed near his ear, passing over the murky light of the Rage stone. It landed on him, stinging and biting. Cole swatted at the thing, but only in his mind. His arm lay still, and to his horror was covered with flies. They had been there all along, crawling and pinching. Another landed on his cheek. Cole watched helplessly as the little out-of-focus wings twitched their way to the tip of his nose. His body useless to him, Cole grasped at his Wisdom, igniting a spell that would burn the entire tree down. But his Wisdom wouldn't come. He couldn't find it. Cole's mind was occluded with something thick and rancid. With a brittle heart he recognized the touch of Fear.

The bed shuddered. From the very bottom of Cole's periphery, he saw a spindly bone-white hand groping at the footboard. Another hand joined the first. Something heavy slid from under the bed as a hooded figure ascended between the two hands. Even in the shadows of the crimson light, there was no mistaking the purple-tinged lips, the mouth far too large, the curtains of wrinkled skin jiggling under a bony chin. The Corpulant rose, its knees and spine popping and snapping its way to full height. More flies dropped from its bulky sleeves, taking flight before they hit the ground. The bone-stick fingers moved towards Cole's bare feet, twitching with anticipation. Long hands enveloped his ankles like snakes of ice. The Corpulant's chin dropped, its purple lips stretching against the dried mucus that glued them together. The lips split at a corner, making a sticky, peeling sound as the gap ran to the other cheek. Cole watched paralyzed as his feet were lifted from the bed.

Cole's screams echoed in his mind as his toes inched towards the twitching maw. The mouth popped ever wider, as Cole knew it would. His toenails touched first, scraping and snagging on the ribbed upper palate. The Corpulant's breath slid like cold oil over his legs, tickling the hairs on his shins. His feet were gone now, sliding along the chilly wetness of its throat. The gangly hands crawled up to his knees as the Corpulant dragged itself up onto the bed. The maw continued to widen as Cole's shins and legs passed through. The chapped lips began to crack and bleed as they wiggled wider over his naked thighs. A hand wove its way around the back of his neck, the other under his back, lifting and pulling as the lips scratched over his genitals. The Corpulant worked its head back and forth, side to side, its jaw cracking wider as the mouth worked its way up Cole's stomach.

From the depths of the fleshy tube, Cole's lifeless feet met something sharp and alive. The thing recoiled and struggled, gnawing and cutting into him like an animal backed into a corner. Cole was moving quickly now, sliding like a foot into a slipper of dank meat. The lips passed over his arms, scraping and bleeding over his nipples and shoulder. The Corpulant swallowed and shook, making more room within its gut for him. The thing that bit at Cole's feet was now wedged between the walls and his buttocks, thrashing and slicing in renewed panic.

The hood fell back, revealing a head with sparse, wiry hair and a shiny scalp pocked with liver marks. Its deep black eyes came up to Cole's as its nose bumped his. Its upper lip squirmed and clamped over Cole's, filling his mouth with a rancid stench of old vomit.

• • • •

The walls of the Council Chamber echoed with a bevy of excited questions and shrewd warnings. The chamber was full; however, every seat was empty. Each member of the Celestial Council was locked in debate with one of many circles discussing the same thing from different angles.

"Wait a moment, what time is the trial? We should push it back a few hours. We're not prepared," said a portly man, his belly resting on a table as he searched his pockets.

"Preposterous!" a vulture of a woman replied, jabbing her beak-like nose to the man. "It's no *trial* at all, we're merely asking the boy a few questions. And you know as well as I do that Chiron won't hold out another minute. The old tyrant is likely waiting outside our doors as we speak! You did lock it didn't you?"

"Yes, yes, we're quite free of him for now," the man said, waving a stubby arm towards the main door. He pulled a timepiece from a deep pocket of his robes. "We've still a few hours anyhow. Chiron won't show up *that* early. Still think we ought to push this off a bit. Or perhaps get the boy up here alone?"

Arcturus approached the Speaker's dais and slumped into his desk, which showed no sign of the previous day's violence. His injured arm was secured to his chest, immobilized with a lattice of green crystal. With a flourish, he conjured an emerald hammer and matching bell, each hovering in the air on front of him. Arcturus nodded to the hammer, and it tapped the bell, filling the chamber with a concussing gong. The conversation sputtered and faded as everyone took their seats.

Arcturus cleared his throat ceremoniously, adjusting the neck of his white robes. "I hear a lot of excellent ideas being exchanged, but as usual, you're all sprinting in separate directions. We'll get nowhere if we don't bring consensus to our efforts."

The vulture woman let out a chuckling hiss. "Perhaps when you contribute something of value to this Council your ideas will have some pull as well, Speaker."

There was a smattering of agreement at which Arcturus could only scowl. He silenced the rising din with another ring of the bell, sending the Council grumbling to their seats around their crescent table.

Keeping his bell and hammer at the ready, Arcturus waited until all eyes were on him before speaking. "Our appointment with the human is scheduled to start in two hours' time. It is my intent for the Council to reach consensus before he arrives. Lamnar, why don't you lead us off with your concerns."

A bald man stood, addressing the entire Council. He twisted his sleeves and spoke with shaky confidence. "As Wisdom Walker for the house of Allias, I have a number of concerns regarding this human. Chief of which is the security of the aethers. While there is no evidence of aggression from The Three, we cannot assume they won't fall into their old habits. Travel to the local planets still eludes the Council, so it can be assumed that The Three are as stationary as we. The human is obviously the key to Travel, and must not fall into the arms of The Three."

"Thank you Lamnar," Arcturus replied, scribbling rapidly across a fresh scroll. "Your concern has been added to the consensus. Next Wisdom Walker?"

The portly man rose from his seat as Lamnar took his. He cleared his throat with a series of neat little grunts before opening his mouth.

An explosion shook the chamber. Council members jumped, hiding behind each other or diving below the table. Wide eyes jolted to the only door in the room, which looked as though it had been knocked crooked. Another bang followed the first, sending dust and chips sprinkling from the edges of the door frame.

Arcturus peeked up from below his desk. He flinched as another bang sent his hammer and bell falling to the floor, where they shattered and vanished. He rose silently, taking a timid step towards the door before glancing back to the Council. Hushed murmurs urged him on. He held his palm in front of him, and a crystalline shield flashed to life. He approached the door, holding his shield high with a look of forced bravery. The banging stopped. Arcturus dismissed his shield, reaching to unlock the door as the Council members behind him readied offensive spells. Before his fingers touched the smooth stone, the door gave an ancient groan as it tipped forward. Arcturus dove to the side as the massive slab crashed to the floor.

Standing in the door frame was a figure shrouded in a black so complete that it seemed to darken the space around it. Bladed hair clinking, the figure leaped onto the fallen door. In its munisica appeared to be large, bloody mess of blankets. The figure stalked into the chamber with such confidence that not a soul in the room dared speak or loose a spell for Fear of provoking it. Dragging the bloody bundle along, the figure painted a swath of ruddy purple along the onyx floor. The figure cast the lump across the chamber, where it landed in a wet heap on the crescent desk of the Celestial Council.

• • • •

Cole's Rage seethed, begging him to take action as he stood before the Celestial Council. He ground his armored teeth. Now was not the time. Not the place. He capped his Rage before it could burn any hotter, halting the growth of his munisica. He savored the dread and shocked faces that surrounded him, reveling in their weakness.

"Identify yourself, Rage Follower," demanded a woman with a beak-like nose. "You are surrounded by the most powerful Wisdom-users on Aeneria; we will harbor no lies or threats here."

Cole shut his eyes, inhaling the electrified scent of ozone as his ears picked up the zapping of fingers readying spells. He wanted them to attack. When nothing happened, he exhaled, opening his eyes as his Rage-shrouded voice filled the room. "I am the human."

Befuddled gawking was his only reply. Cole raised his chin and opened his arms to them, inviting their attack, but none came. Instead, the Council's eyes slackened, unblinking and sightless, though their spells remained coiled in their hands.

Speaker Arcturus broke the silence with the voice of the entire Council: "Your appointment is not for another two hours. You will leave and return at the assigned time. Tread carefully human, further acts of aggression will be taken as open threats and we will react accordingly."

Cole grinned, not bothering to look at Arcturus. He had no intention of leaving. Not before he had his say. He watched with savage pleasure as the two Council members in front of him lost their stoic composure, coughing and gagging as the stink of the corpse on the table struck them. They swatted flies away with flaming hands.

"And take this rotten thing with you," the woman closest to him said through the crook of her elbow. "What is this anyhow? Wait, is this a body?" Her elbow dropped as she snapped to a look of alarm. "Was this a person?"

"That is evidence," Cole said, joining the claws of his hand, pointing them like a broad dagger. "That is your proof that The Three are still your enemy."

"That's a Corpulant!" the man next to her wailed, shoving the corpse away from him. Flies took flight at the jostling. "The human has brought a Corpulant into Council Chambers!"

The chamber erupted with contentious shouting. Those nearest the Corpulant pushed themselves away, while those farthest inched closer for a look. Cole stood like a burning tree in the middle of all of it, doing his best not to lash out at the lot of them.

A moment later, Eliza and Chiron skidded over the fallen door, relief flooding each of their faces. Cole was only just now aware of her Passion battering against his Rage-hardened mind.

"Cole!" Eliza rushed forward, looking unsure if it was safe to touch him or not. She stopped just outside reach of his claws, speaking with a shaky voice. "I was awoken by Fear and death! I felt you slipping into the void, but the Fear clouded you from our bond. Oh Cole, I thought I was too late!"

She reached forward and wrapped her arms around his shoulders. He could barely feel her touch.

Chiron pulled Eliza away, his eyes scrutinizing. "Are you in control?"

Cole's lip twitched. "Barely."

Chiron nodded. "Then let us leave. You've made your point."

"No, I haven't," Cole growled, turning and stalking towards Arcturus.

The Speaker cowered behind his desk, ringing a conjured bell as though his life depended on it. Cole stopped before the dais, catching Arcturus's eyes with the full weight of his Rage.

Cole forced the words out so hard that his voice drowned out all else, including the gonging bell. "Hear my words, Speaker. Hear them for the whole Council, because I'm only going to say them once."

Arcturus dropped his bell as silence fell over the chamber.

Cole lowered his voice: "That is a Corpulant that just attacked me in my sleep not ten minutes ago. Within this very temple. The Three are acting against you as we speak. That is your proof."

Cole turned to walk away before he said more, but his growing Rage immolated his inhibitions. He stopped and spoke over his shoulder. "I am a human, and I have Traveled both in and out of turn. And though I have no idea how, I destroyed the barrier and allowed the Soul Flies to return. I can use your magic. All of it. These things are possible because part of Varka is inside me. Believe it or don't. I'm leaving to go fight The Three."

Without another word, Cole left the chamber in ringing silence.

Cole was dimly aware of Chiron and Eliza joining him on the lift. He knew they wanted to talk, but at the moment he didn't much care. He was busy debating whether or not he should dig his way out of the temple and run away. The lift hummed and started its descent.

"You may want to release the shroud," Chiron mentioned in an offhand tone. "The sight will cause unnecessary excitement throughout the temple. Even more so than what you just did."

"I'm naked," he replied, holding his eyes forward.

"Well that's an easy fix," Chiron said, tapping Cole hard on the shoulder.

Through the shroud, Cole felt the slightest shift in weight as gray Underkin's cloth wrapped itself around his body. Cole glanced down, making sure it covered the necessities. The lift began to slow.

"Need a little help?" Chiron asked when Cole did not dismiss his Rage.

"Yes," Cole admitted, grinding his shrouded teeth. It was all he could do to halt the spread of the Rage. Releasing it was still beyond him.

"Eliza, if you would be so kind," Chiron said, taking a small step back.

"Of course," she said in an assertive tone. She wheeled around to Cole's front and slapped her hands to his cheeks, one eyebrow curled as she bore into him with a motherly sternness.

Cole stared back into her with his blackened eyes, resisting both her Passion and the urge to kill. To his surprise, his Rage echoed into a seemingly limitless ocean that was her compassion for him. His Rage surged again, but he felt the red magic tapering into comfort, as if removing a heavy pack after a long march. The shroud receded into his munisica, and a heartbeat later they vanished as well. The lift stopped as the doors opened.

Cole exhaled a sigh of relief, gazing into Eliza's wholesome smile as he retreated into his center, dousing himself with soothing waters. The Rage was gone.

Eliza flashed him a clever wink as their Passion link rang high and clear. "*Welcome back.*"

Cole said nothing, pressing his lips softly together as shameful tears stung at his eyes. She was too good to him.

"Eliza, please give us a moment. I'd like to talk with Cole in private," Chiron said as they stepped out of the lift.

"As you wish, Master Chiron." Eliza gave a little nod before turning and starting down the braided root path. Cole watched until her flame of blond hair vanished behind a stout tree.

Chiron's hands flexed gently as a spell shimmered about them. "There. Now we can speak without worry for prying ears."

"The others wouldn't eavesdrop on us," Cole said, knowing full well that they all were probably sharpening their ears at this very moment. Eliza would pick up traces of it through their link as well.

"It is not our own ears that worry me. Oberon Temple is not as friendly as I was foolish enough to assume. No one should have been able to access the Everglen without my permission, let alone a mere Corpulant. Speaking of that little mess, how are you?"

"I'm fine," Cole replied in a hard voice.

Chiron gave an understanding nod. "I am very proud of you, Cole. To defeat one of Decreath's minions without help takes true

297

mastery of one's self. If it is not too much to ask, I would appreciate a more detailed account of the ordeal."

Cole ground his teeth. He'd known this was coming. Cracking open his Rage, he trickled a tiny stream of the red magic into his center. Just enough to keep the Fear at bay. Cole described the ordeal with pragmatic detail, as though it had happened to someone else. However, when he started to explain the inside of the Corpulant not even his Rage would steady him. He stammered, unable to find the words to describe the horror.

Chiron placed a hand on his shoulder. "Why don't you skip to the part where you escaped?"

Cole let out his sick breath. "I, I mean Varka pulled me out of it. He pulled me out of the Fear. I could feel him in there with me. He was inside me all along. It was like he lit a fire made of Rage, and it burned everything away. It was so…strange. One second, the Fear was the only thing I was, then the Rage replaced it, ate it. Varka saved me, just like he saved me at the Devotion."

Chiron drew his fingers over his chin as his eyes ventured into the distant reaches of the Everglen. "I thought as much. This confirms a few suspicions, though it tempts a few questions. One certainty is that The Three have wormed their way into the heart of our capital. I suspect they had help from within these very walls."

"You mean there's a traitor within the temple?" Cole asked.

"*Traitors* more likely. A Corpulant never could have made it this far without assistance. They are too single-minded, too easily distracted by their next meal. It had help."

Cole's eyes wandered unbidden to the shadows around him, searching for another ragged, lumpy figure. "There could be more of them out here! What about the others? Have you checked, is everyone safe?" His heart sank as he thought of Lileth. He wished he could just see her.

"They are safe. Roth and Alvani cleared the Everglen after you left," Chiron reassured Cole, gesturing towards the apartments. "They are still asleep in fact, and I have no intention of robbing them of a good night's rest. Something that I'm sure you are in dire need of as well. Take my tree, and rest assured that you will be the only living thing inside it." Chiron waved his palm towards a stubby tree closest to them.

At the mention of sleep, the weight of the past week returned to Cole, pulling heavily at his eyes and mind. "I think I will, but my mind's still going crazy."

"Anything I can do to put you at ease?" Chiron asked, giving him a look of warm compassion. Cole knew Chiron would do anything within his power to help him.

"I can't believe I told them about Varka!" Cole blurted, unable to hold it in any longer. "I'm sorry, I know you told me not to, but the Rage... I don't want anyone getting into trouble because of my stupid mistake. I'll go back to the Council and face the trial alone." He brought his eyes to Chiron, wincing as he prepared himself for reprimand.

Chiron gave a slow nod. "What's done is done. The choice was yours, and you only have yourself to answer to. But don't worry yourself overmuch. The Council won't bother the others while Roth and Alvani are here."

Worry crawled its way up Cole's gut. "You make it sound like they're all staying here. I thought we were all going to fight The Three."

"We are indeed, but you know as well as I that the rest of the unit will not follow us." Chiron's words rang with both reason and finality.

Cole's eyes fell to the knotted roots at their feet. "I know. I'm still going to try and get them to come. Offending the Council is the least of our worries."

"I would have to disagree, respectfully of course." Chiron flashed him a small, uplifting grin. "They may seem a hindrance to us, but the Council is an invaluable asset. We may yet be able to placate them while furthering our aims."

"But how?" Cole asked, but he didn't want to hear the answer. His heart gave a sudden pang for Lileth.

"That remains to be seen," Chiron said, turning as his cape of woven roots creaked behind him. "Get some sleep, Cole. I'll be back after the sunrise tonight."

"We're moving into a different house already?" Cole asked. It seemed like the last sunrise was only days ago.

"As this day dies, we will leave the house of Dunhaven and enter Rhunam. I rather like Rhunam." Chiron stared dreamily up through the canopy. "It has more stars than any other local planet. I advise you to find yourself a nice spot to watch the show. The sunrise from beneath Oberon is quite a treat. Now, go rest." He waved his hands towards the fat tree before disappearing into the double doors of the lift.

Cole leaped up into the entrance of Chiron's tree, which had no ramp leading up to its second-floor doors. He pushed through the liquid rock door, popping into a room that looked very familiar. The walls were lined with turquoise mushrooms whose roots chased down to the floor, soaking up a runnel of water that trickled under his feet. The room was sparsely decorated, with a single bookshelf, a table for one with matching chair, and a sleeping mat. Flicking on a few of the mushrooms, Cole plopped himself down on the mat. As he lay his head down, the room's familiarity became clear to him. It was almost identical to the cabin where he'd met a much smaller Goran. Instinctively, he groped the reaches of his mind, trying to find his brindle-furred friend. However, the mirak's mind was nowhere to be found. He could feel Eliza's fraternal link, quiet and waiting to be strummed. Cole scoured every corner of his mind, but still Goran evaded him. He would try again with a clearer mind when he woke. Goran couldn't be gone.

Eliza's link flickered as if struck by a gentle feather. *"Need some help falling asleep?"*

Cole replied with a sad grin, *"Yes please."*

"Go to your center. I'll follow you there," she replied in a soft tone.

Hours later, Cole woke feeling light and refreshed, though his body was sore and stiff. Rage always took a toll on him, as if every moment spent fully shrouded were a marathon for his entire body. Standing and stretching out his weary muscles, he left Chiron's tree and made for his own.

When he popped through the door to his room, the stench of death and gore assaulted him. The Rage Stone was still thrumming, bathing the room in a bloody glow. Flicking on a few of the white lights, Cole found pieces of the Corpulant spackled on every surface of the room. A few flies still buzzed about, searching for warm flesh.

Drawing a bit of Rage to steel himself, Cole snagged a shirt from the armoire and wrapped it around his face to block the smell. Then he drew upon his Wisdom and pulled heat from the rest of the tree into the room, roasting the flies as sweat beaded and poured from him. With all the flies grounded and dead, he fumbled with the liquid stone door, using his Wisdom to nudge it to open. The door obliged, sinking into its frame and allowing fresh air to rush in through it. Cole cleaned the rest of the room with his munisica and a wet shirt, calling upon his Wisdom to move the bigger chunks to the drain hole in the shower room. After an hour the apartment looked as if he had never been there. Cole took another double shower before tearing off the Underkin wrappings and donning a wardrobe from the armoire.

Leaving the door open, he hopped off the ramp and felt for Eliza.

"I hoped you'd be ready soon," Eliza said. *"We were waiting for you to watch the sunrise. Hurry to me, the others are eager to see you. Especially Lileth."*

Cole was about to ask where she was, but he felt her presence tugging him deeper into the Everglen. He drew his munisica and tore off into the forest. After running a quarter of an hour he found her with the rest of the unit against a dense wall of vines and bushes.

"'Bout time you showed up." Sitra greeted him with a rough hug. "You look pretty damn good for someone who passed through a Corpulant. Looks like you got taller again too."

Cole hugged her in return, noticing his head was now level with her shoulder. "So you heard?"

"Only after you were snoozing in Chiron's tree. Roth told us what happened and then had us search the entire Everglen," Sitra huffed, releasing him. "He'd already scoured the place with Alvani, but we still had to climb every tree and look in every pond and cave. We were at it for hours! You had it easy. Probably ripped that Corpulant in half in about two seconds."

"Master Roth likely wanted to keep us busy," Valen interjected. "The elders are up to something."

Eliza and Sitra murmured their agreement, though Lileth kept her back to him as she gazed out through a gap in the vines.

"So how'd you do it? Did the Corpulant try to swallow you?" Sitra asked, looking both disgusted and intrigued.

Cole stifled a gag, wrestling his throat in to a dry swallow. "I was all the way inside it before I could fight my way through the flies' venom. Rage saved me."

"Ha!" Sitra boomed. "Rage gets results! See that Val?"

"It certainly did in this case," Valen replied. "I'm glad to see you made it out unscathed, Cole. We all are."

Cole thanked him, but his heart and thoughts drifted to Lileth, who hadn't said a word. She still wouldn't meet his eyes. Casting his doubts aside, he strode towards her and spun her around, hugging her. Her hands crept over his lower back and pulled at his shoulder cape. Cole felt something wet drip down the side of his neck.

"You nearly died," she whispered into his ear.

Cole squeezed her tight. "I've never felt more alive."

He held her for a moment longer, forgetting the others around them.

Sitra gave an obnoxious cough. "Sorry to break up your romantic reunion, but we've got a sunrise to catch. I'll be damned if I'm going to miss this one. It's not every day you get to see one from Oberon Temple."

Lileth withdrew, giving him a weak, wet smile. "We should be going. I'll carry you, but you'll need to make yourself lighter. You've had another growth spurt."

"Why would you have to carry me? I thought we weren't allowed to leave." Cole followed Lileth's gaze to the gap in the leaves. There was a glow of such a vibrant pink that he mistook it for a Passion Stone.

The gap was a window to the outside world. Cole pushed the branches aside, revealing a blazing horizon and shimmering ocean. A cool salty breeze whispered through the leaves, caressing over Cole's hair.

"Is this a window?" he asked, squinting as he tried to make out toothy mountains on the far side of the water.

"Found it during our search," Sitra replied, sidling up next to him. "And I found us a place to watch the sunrise. Keep up will you?"

She flashed him a wolfish grin before diving out the window. A second later a pair of emerald wings rushed up as she cut her way up towards Oberon.

"Better hurry!" Eliza said with a bit of childlike eagerness. She took a galloping leap and followed Sitra.

"Indeed," Valen added, hopping onto the ledge and shooting off like a winged spear.

"I hope you still trust me after our drop into Costas," Lileth said as she bent to pick him up. "Ready?"

Cole flashed her a mischievous grin. "Catch me."

Faster than she could react, Cole dug his munisica into the dirt and launched himself out into open air. Seconds passed as the roaring wind pulled the laughter from his mouth. He waited until he felt strong arms wrap firmly around his chest before he called his Wisdom to action, reducing his weight by magnitudes. As light as he was, he still felt his face droop with the force of Lileth's emerald wings as she willed torrents of air to carry them higher.

Cole shivered. The upper tiers of the temple were covered with a thick blanket of snow and ice. The air was frigid and thin. He could feel it icing the insides of his nose and throat. Lileth pulled him closer.

Freezing minutes passed in rising agony as Cole attempted a few spells to warm him, but he was only capable of summoning a meager windshield in front of his face. He tried pulling heat from around him, but there simply wasn't any. They continued their ascent for another ten minutes until Lileth finally slowed, revealing their destination.

The others landed ahead of them at the top of Oberon Temple. They wasted no time working spells over the surface, melting snow and erecting wind barriers. Cole's breath rushed in and out in panicked gasps, trying to pull the thin air into his burning lungs. He hoped one of their spells made the air more breathable.

As Lileth carried him through the barrier, warm air rushed down his throat, alleviating his headache and soothing his lungs. His icy feet clapped the top of the warm temple stone, which felt like it had been baking in the sun for hours. Lileth released him as he wobbled over towards a fire Sitra had conjured in the center.

"Those flames will ruin our vision," Valen said, warming his hands. "May I?"

"Go for it," Eliza replied.

Valen caressed his fingers over the fire as silvery water fell from his hands. The fire seemed to douse and vanish, but the steady hiss of the flames and radiating heat remained. Cole stumbled close to the invisible fire, his limbs thawing instantly as his breathing returned to normal.

Lileth pulled his hands into hers. "Never mind your frozen fingers, it has started."

She guided Cole to the edge, where the others were huddled. A brilliant golden aura beamed from the horizon, its center white and pure, a beacon heralding the end of a long day. The halo reached up to the sky, painting the clouds with swaths of supple pinks and feathery reds. The stars were invisible now, washed out by the imminent sunrise. Such a mundane event reminded Cole of Earth, hitting him with a pang of longing for his previous life. Remembering Habbad's explanation of the local planets, Cole swung his gaze away from the rising star to the darkened sky opposite. There he beheld a swirling marble of salmon and azure floating just above the horizon; the planet Dunhaven. Teeming rivers of soul flies pulsed their farewell to the inky canvas as they raced through the aethers back to their home. Multi-hued dust drifted from the snaking rivers, flowing and collecting above them on Oberon's ever-watchful eye.

The others turned, following his sudden twist.

"I always forget to look for the local planet," Sitra said in a dreamy voice. "It's like a little bowl of soup."

"Look at them all!" Eliza gushed. "All those dreamers spiriting through the aethers! I couldn't begin to guess their numbers. It's too bad they have to wait another cycle to visit again."

Valen hummed his agreement. "The greater tragedy is the number of souls tainted by The Three during their spell here. How many monsters have we released upon Dunhaven?"

No one answered. They contented themselves to embrace the sad beauty of the scene.

Cozy sunlight kissed the back of Cole's head. He turned back around and saw the crest of Dunhaven's star. Squinting, he threw an arm up to block the light, which ran down his body in a neat golden line. As soon as the starlight met the black stone, the star flashed so brilliantly it appeared to have exploded in a supernova. Just as quickly as it flared, the star was gone, and so was Dunhaven.

For a few eerie seconds Aeneria was in between worlds, in between realities. They were in utter darkness. Cole whipped his head about, unable to see even his nose. Above him, Oberon had the faintest glow, like a half-remembered ghost against an infinite backdrop of nothingness. Tiny winking dots began to poke through the blackness, few and far apart. Cole moved his head around and rubbed his eyes to be sure he wasn't just imagining them. More came, timid and sparse, flickering to life next to their fellows that had been brave enough to appear first. Soon there were swirling arms arching across the entire sky, each filled with puffy star clouds and twisting galaxies. The wondrous spectacle eventually roused Oberon. The rainbow moon returned brighter than before, as though refreshed from a quick nap.

While the others were occupied with the newborn starscape, Cole wove his fingers through Lileth's and tugged her out of earshot. She followed without a word. Cole shut his mind so that not even Eliza could hear him.

Whispering over his beating heart, Cole found her eyes in the starlight. "I'm leaving soon. Will you join me?" He felt himself laid bare by the question. His words carried more weight than their meaning alone.

Her eyes remained locked on his, long enough for him to drop his gaze. The silence gave him the answer before she opened her mouth. "I won't go with you, Cole. Though part of me longs to."

Even though he had braced himself, the words still struck him like hammer blows to his gut. He knew she wouldn't reveal much, but he needed to know more. He hadn't much time. His hope flared perilously within his chest, begging and pleading for something to light his way.

Swallowing the bitter reality, he tried to meet her eyes once more, but his gaze rested cowardly upon her shoulder. "Lileth, do you have feelings for me? Do we have something real?"

Her hands cupped his cheeks, bringing his face to hers. Her voice was empty and careless. "I have real feelings for you, Cole. But there are many reasons that we cannot be together in heart and flesh."

His hope curdled like sour milk. "Tell me then. Why can't we be together?"

With a mixture of guilt and satisfaction he saw his words sting her. A lonely tear escaped from one of her clamped lashes. His jaw trembled in her hands.

"I am an Aenerian. You are not." She wouldn't look at him, but her voice was framed with cold reason. "We are students fighting for something much greater than the both of us. Mixing our hearts together would only distract us from what needs to be done. Bury your desires elsewhere, Cole. They will find nothing but sorrow should you sow them within me." She released him, nodding over his shoulder. "I think Chiron would like to speak with you."

Mouth dry and face numb, Cole took a step back. "You're wrong and you know it." Fighting the tears back, he turned and found Chiron floating off the edge of the temple. The elder ignored the others, looking at Cole with an air of significance. It was time. Cole held his breath and walked towards Chiron.

As he neared the edge of the temple, Lileth called out to him in a desperate voice, "Cole wait! When are you leaving?"

Cole bit his lip and looked up at Chiron. The Wisdom Walker gave him a heavy nod. Cole drew a deep breath and looked back to Lileth, wondering when he would see her again.

Grim recognition passed over Lileth's face as she fell to her knees. The others shuffled to her side, apparently unaware of Chiron's sudden appearance.

"Where in Oberon's backside do you think you're going?" Sitra hollered, looking both angry and confused. "We're staying here to train, you can't go fight The Three by yourselves!"

Cole didn't answer.

Eliza wore a weak smile and glassy eyes. She pressed her mind against Cole's, embracing him through their fraternal link. *"I will always be with you in heart and spirit, brother."*

Valen stepped closer, shaking his head as if there had been some minor misunderstanding. "Master Chiron, we discussed this. We are going to train here at the temple and wait for the Council to come to their senses. Surely you're not taking Cole anywhere. Are you?"

Chiron's snowy cape fluttered in the wind. He extended an arm, beckoning Cole onward. He locked eyes with the Wisdom Walker and found the strength he needed to step off the ledge and leave his friends.

CHAPTER 17

TABULA RASA

The air rippled and exploded as Cole and Chiron tore through the sky. Chiron's Wisdom cradled him in open air and had them moving faster than Cole could guess, though the blurry speed wasn't enough to outrun what he left behind. Lileth's face remained burned in his mind's eye and the baleful protests of the others still rang in his ears. It felt as if he were leaving his entire life on top of Oberon Temple.

At least he still had Eliza. They would stay in touch, and she could keep him up to date on all the goings-on at the temple. Even now she fed him a steady stream of comfort through their link, sharing the burden of his pain.

Another pang of loss stung at him. He'd never said goodbye to Goran. Cole scrambled through his mind, crying out for his friend, but there was nothing to find. Goran was gone. Cole had felt the waning of their bond since they separated at the mountains, but he had hoped it was just a phase. Now he couldn't feel the dimmest trace of his first friend. Cole glanced over at the toothy mountain range, guessing where Goran might be now. He blinked tears out of his eyes. They fell from him, spattering upon Chiron's invisible shield before freezing into salty snowflakes.

Cole could sense Chiron's concern as he hovered above, but neither of them spoke. A burst of silent speed pulled Cole's face back, and within a few minutes Oberon City was beyond the horizon.

They flew for what felt like hours. Having emptied his eyes of every tear he could eke out, Cole finally broke the silence.

"Where are we going anyway?" Cole croaked. His voice was raw from the long silence.

"The Sill," Chiron replied.

Cole wobbled himself around and faced Chiron. "Why? I thought we were going to fight The Three."

"Do you feel ready to face them now?" asked the Wisdom Walker.

Cole felt his Rage rearing up to answer, but his Despair felt like a rotten, unstable bog that his entire being now rested upon. Sorronis would cut him down like a wilted sapling.

"No," Cole grunted. "I'm not ready to face *anything* at the moment. Decreath was bad enough. The Three would probably kill us both before we even had a chance to fight back."

"Without a doubt," Chiron remarked. "That is why we are going to The Sill. You need some proper training and my full attention if we are to draw out whatever gifts Varka has bestowed upon you."

"But why couldn't we do this at Oberon Temple?" Cole could feel the heat in his words. His voice trembled with restrained ire. "The Everglen had everything that we needed, and the others could have trained with us. Why would you take me away from everyone I cared about?"

Chiron's face remained flat and calm, burning Cole's temper ever hotter. "Find your center, Cole. Go there now and ask yourself those same questions. When you are ready, we will talk."

Cole whipped his back towards Chiron and crossed his arms. After a moment's stubborn silence he attempted to enter the stone chamber in his mind, but it was locked to him. He used Rage to force his way in, but upon entering he found the room masked with heavy clouds. His roiling emotions occluded everything. Groping his way through the fog, he felt for the pedestal and the cone above, willing tiny droplets of the soothing water down onto himself. The little beads sizzled and joined the steam filling the room, completely impotent. Taking a deep breath, Cole tried again, wringing a few more drops out this time. Slowing his breathing, he repeated the process over and over until the water came in a steady flow and the room revealed itself to him. Eventually the weight of his emotions fell from him, bit by bit, until he truly was in his center. He embraced himself for a time, re-evaluating each unruly thought without all the noise. When he opened his eyes again the landscape was entirely different, and Oberon was low in the sky behind them.

Cole turned back towards Chiron. "The Everglen isn't a viable option."

"Oh, and why is that?" Chiron asked without looking at him.

"The Council knows about Varka. They won't just sit by and ignore that while I'm a few floors below playing with magic. And if someone snuck a Corpulant in there, there's a good chance they'll do it again. Or something worse. Also, if whatever Varka imprinted on me is our best chance at stopping The Three, then I can't afford to be distracted by..." He almost said her name, but let the words drift away unfinished.

"Those are my thoughts exactly." Chiron gave him a nod of appraisal, saving him from elaborating. "Though I would like to add that some of your lessons will be practical, with real effects on this world. This cannot be done from the confines of a stone cage."

"Practical huh?" Cole thought on his last practical exercise with Roth. There was no way they could be that tough. "These *practical* lessons wouldn't happen to place me in harm would they?"

Chiron smirked. "I beg your patience, but I won't reveal all my tricks just yet. However, I will promise you that your definition of what's dangerous will be very different before long."

"Great," Cole huffed.

Hours passed in silence as the lagoon and The Sill came into view. Cole could make out little gratia stones winking up to him from their coral husks in the shallows. He made a mental note to stop by Deekus's grave for Eliza.

Instead of flying over the walls, they came to a lurching halt just outside one of the thick gates. Chiron set them both on the warm dirt and dismissed his shield. Cole wobbled somewhat after spending so many hours weightless. As expected, Whind, the Master Gatekeeper, melted from the hulking tree, greeting them in his airy voice.

"Greetings, Wisdom Walkers." Whind extended a reedy arm as wire-thin vines spread from his fingertips to the knotted roots of the gate. "The Sill welcomes you."

With an ancient groan, the trees cracked themselves up by their roots and revealed a tunnel lined with gratia stones. Cole followed silently behind Chiron, remembering the tunnel to have seemed much bigger the last time he passed through. He glanced back to Whind, who stood at the mouth of the tunnel like a solitary tree in his leafy garments. Cole gave him a weak smile and a wave, which went unreturned. He missed his friends very much.

Chiron led Cole through the familiar route he had taken on his first walk through The Sill. They came upon the markets, which were unusually bare. Only a few proprietors rushed about with arms full, looking as if they were running several shops at once. Cole was indeed much taller than he'd been when he last set foot in the markets. He remembered the constant worry of being trampled in a sea of legs, but now he wasn't even the shortest one. A shopkeeper carrying a basket full of plump mushrooms nodded up to him and Chiron as they passed. He silently hoped he wasn't done growing, and that he would perhaps be as tall as Chiron one day, or even Roth.

"I've never seen the markets so empty. Where is everyone?" Cole asked, peering through a darkened window.

"The battle at Costas taxed The Sill heavily. We lost a great number of our warriors, a loss felt not only in our hearts but our economy as well. Many shopkeepers brought their businesses elsewhere. You will still find most of what you need, however."

"That's good. I was looking forward to seeing what I can afford now that I've mastered Rage," Cole said, eyeing a shop full of glowing gadgets and whirring instruments.

"I'm afraid you won't have much time for recreation once your training starts," Chiron said, beckoning Cole onward.

Cole tore his eyes away from a glass display of sleek formalwear, picking up his pace. "I assume we're starting nice and early tomorrow?" Cole asked, resigning himself to a meager night's rest.

Chiron interlocked his hands behind his back. "No. We will start now. Do you know where my home is?"

Cole swallowed, quelling his indignation. "No, Master Chiron."

"It stands in between the Necropolis and the Dancing Gardens. Your first task is to make it there before I do." Before Cole could so much as mutter a question, Chiron rose into the air, his transparent cape flapping behind him as he shot off into the treetops.

Stunned, Cole broke into a run. He'd imagined himself getting some food and some sleep before they really started. He glanced up at a passing clock. It was already mid-evening and he was still exhausted from the night out in Oberon City. Hopefully the first lesson would be quick.

He drew upon his Rage, his shrouded legs pumping rapidly and effortlessly as he cut across The Sill, only touching the ground every twenty feet or so. He knew he couldn't beat Chiron, but he didn't want to be embarrassed. As he ran, Cole felt a barren melancholy in the air around him, as if The Sill had lost some of its vitality since he left. The winding ramps and walkways were covered with a layer of old leaves, as if no one had walked on them in months. Doorways that once glowed with full gratia stones were nothing more than darkened holes in the sides of trees. Not a single sun lily leaf flew overhead. The air felt empty and lifeless, save for a few stars that twinkled through the canopy.

The trees grew thinner and closer together as Cole passed from the residential districts, slowing him somewhat. He brought his clawed feet to a sloshing halt as he splashed upon the edges of the Necropolis. Resisting the temptation to visit Deekus's grave, he veered off towards the dancing gardens.

Cole had never been to this part of The Sill before. The trees were much skinnier than the hulking towers he was used to, but they were just as tall and grew in endless rows, as if planted in a grid. He whipped his head about, searching for anything that looked like a house. Chiron had not said what it looked like, but surely it would have stood out from the never-ending rows and columns.

Chiron's house did not stick out, however. There was no break in the patterns as far as Cole could see. He ran to the edges of the dancing gardens, where the skinny trees were replaced by fruit-bearing vines that snaked their way over every rock and rolling hill. Darting out, Cole snatched a cluster of green fruit from an unsuspecting vine, which rattled in protest before rearing up and galloping away.

He somehow felt even hungrier after the snack, but decided against looking for more. He didn't want to keep Chiron waiting. Setting off again, Cole took a different angle into the massive grid of trees, aiming for a more systematic approach. This time he ran straight until he came upon the outer walls of The Sill itself. Swearing into the empty rows, Cole ran the entire border of the odd forest, then up and down every column until he found the old gouges in the dirt from his first passing. Rage swelling, he allowed the shroud to spread until his hair tinkled like glass with every step. After what felt like hours, the entire grid had been torn by his munisica and the day was certainly over. He had failed.

Roaring mad, Cole stabbed his munisica deep into a trunk which he had passed several times. Bark and insects rained around him as the tree wobbled. Whining cracks splintered up its length as the tree tipped and crashed its way to the forest floor. The ground shook beneath Cole with a satisfying thud. Before the thought of tearing down the entire forest became too enticing, Cole rested himself on the broken tree and gazed up through the hole he'd created. With an effort, he released his Rage and retreated to his center.

The starlight poured through clouds of pollen and falling needles, drawing Cole's gaze up to the sky. An idea suddenly struck him. Cole drew his munisica once more and leaped up, sinking his claws into the bark. He climbed his way up in quick, cat-like strides. In his eagerness, Cole had only searched the floor of the forest. There was still the entire canopy.

Cole shimmied his way to the top, stopping when the tree started bowing at his weight. The reedy branches revealed something large and solid not too far off. Shifting his body weight back and forth, he leaned the top of the tree over to the next, reaching over and sinking his claws into it. In this awkward manner, he made slow progress to the object, which now seemed to be moving away from him.

Relaxing his munisica, he stilled his Rage and drew instead upon his Wisdom, making himself as light as a bird. Cole hopped his way across thin branches until his fingers met the edge of a sturdy platform. With a slight tug, he hoisted himself up and found Chiron sitting at a small table outside a small round hut. Chiron sipped at a steaming mug, seemingly enthralled by the stars.

"You could have told me your house was on *top* of the trees," Cole grunted, brushing pine needles off his uniform. "I searched every leaf and rock in between the Necropolis and the dancing gardens."

"Did you now?" Chiron asked, pulling his eyes from the sky. "And what did you learn on your quest?"

"That your house is somehow floating on top of the canopy, quite *unlike* every other structure in The Sill. I also learned that it takes me about three hours to run up and down every row in this weird little forest. Master, why didn't you tell me? I wasted the rest of the day."

"Would you have me pander to your every inadequacy? Hold your hand and give you every answer forthright?" Chiron spoke in a voice of quiet calm, yet the words were still scathing. He sipped from his mug, holding Cole's gaze.

"Of course not!" Cole stammered. "But what's the point of being vague if I'm going to waste precious hours figuring out some stupid puzzle? The Three grow stronger every minute and I'm here running laps."

Chiron set his mug down and drummed his fingers on the table. Cole had no idea if his Master was inspecting him or trying to think of the right words. A minute passed in silence. If Chiron wasn't going to answer, then Cole certainly wasn't going to bother asking another question. Tired of the staring contest, Cole plopped himself down upon the deck and stared at Oberon's shifting colors. Sleep pulled at his eyes and slowed his breathing. He withdrew to his center to keep from dozing.

Time passed. How much, Cole couldn't guess. Chiron may have left his chair and gone to sleep in his house for all he knew.

"Patience is a skill that requires practice. Obstinacy, on the other hand, is a reflex that merely requires a perceived wrong. Both have their uses, but I'm glad to see you landed on the better of the two."

Cole jolted upright. Chiron was still in the chair, cupping the mug with both hands. A yawn wrenched Cole's mouth open. "Master, I don't know how much I have left in me. It's late."

"Why did you fail in your task?" Chiron asked as if Cole hadn't said a word.

Cole shook himself, forcing his eyes to stay open. "I didn't have all the information for starters. There's no way I could have known your house would be up here. I've never seen anything like it. And you can fly faster than anything I've ever seen."

Chiron's face remained expressionless. "You're right, I didn't tell you *exactly* where my house was, but you certainly had the ability to find it a shade sooner than three hours. As for how fast I flew, it was no quicker than you could run, even without your Rage. I even made a stop along the way to pick up some fertilizer for my garden. Now, tell me the reason for your failure."

Coles broke his eyes away, staring a hole through his bare feet. "Besides what I already told you, I don't know...Master."

Chiron waited for Cole to look up before responding. "You failed because your mind is as flexible as Morthainian glass. Remarkably strong of course, of that there is no doubt. Your actions in Costas and your current mastery of Rage are iron-clad testaments to the strength of your mind and soul. However, as the Morthainian glass is strong, it is just as unyielding. It has its limits. You on the other hand, need only accept the limits you impose upon yourself."

"What do you mean, Master? What limits have I given myself?" Cole asked, hiding his shame behind a mask of curiosity.

Chiron raised a hand, flexing it casually into a branch of ebony knives. Cole had never seen Chiron summon munisica before. "Rage will always get results, as Master Roth is apt to tell you. It may not be the most efficient, or the most desirable, but Rage will always get results. You mastered the red magic first, just as Varka did. And, like Varka, you have used it as a crutch ever since. When you're faced with a problem you can't solve by mundane means, your Rage pops up like a reflex. It has made you formidable of body, but stiff and stale of mind."

"Just like the glass," Cole said, feeling the softness of his unarmored hands.

"Precisely," Chiron said, dismissing his munisica with a lazy flick of his wrist. The Wisdom Walker rose to his feet and walking over to Cole, clapped his palms on Cole's shoulders. "Now, what other tools might you have in that toolbox?"

"I'm junk with Wisdom, and my Passion is unreliable. I don't even have my bond with Goran anymore," Cole admitted, mushing his lips together. Saying it aloud hit him with a sense of crushing finality.

"Ah but you *do have* them. Do not disregard one of your tools just because it is a little dull. Sharpen it," Chiron said, curving an eyebrow. "You have another tool at your disposal, one that requires neither magic nor inherent gifts, though it may be the hardest one to sharpen."

"What is it?" Cole asked, intrigued.

"It is your power of reason. Logical deduction. When wielded by a fluid mind, this tool can work through any quandary."

"So you're saying I need to be smarter?" Cole asked, feeling not so smart at the moment.

Chiron crossed his arms behind his back. "Think of your ability to reason as your hands. Your magic, memories, relationships, assets, these are your tools. Your hands must know how to use each tool, and more importantly, *when* to use them."

Cole imagined himself with stubby, rough hands. Hands calloused from years of swinging a simple hammer and nothing more. Other tools were in his toolbox, but he wielded them like a child would, clumsy and lacking finesse.

"How am I supposed to learn how to be more clever? I'm still new to this planet and I've only seen a small part. I'm just as likely to be killed going for a walk as by our enemies," Cole said, thinking of the White Sands. If not for the unit he would have drowned in the insubstantial powder.

"You are confusing critical thinking with wisdom - the non-magical wisdom of course. Experience begets wisdom, but critical thinking only requires a flexible mind and a situational awareness. Wisdom without reason is as useful as a ship with no crew." Chiron rolled his sleeves, stretching his fingers. "But to answer your question, the path to cleverness is traveled by those who do not shy from the unknown. When an answer is veiled, one must use every faculty at hand to lift the veil. You, Cole of Terra, must learn what to do when you *don't* know what to do. Are you ready for your next task?"

Cole blinked, taken aback. He was nowhere near ready for another task. What he was ready for was a hearty meal and a warm bed. Chiron's next lesson was likely to tax him to his limits, and he hadn't the clarity of mind or the strength in his bones for anything more. Still, he could tell by the lack of sympathy on Chiron's face that things were not about to get any easier for him.

"I am ready, Master," Cole said, wishing he hadn't.

"Very well," Chiron said, tapping an emerald fingertip to Cole's brow. He then swung his chair around and sat Cole into it. "Your first task is to tell me if the chair you sit upon is real."

"Okay, that sounds easy enough." A nervous laugh escaped Cole's lips as his hands reached unbidden to the seat under him. There had to be more to it. "Are there any restrictions?"

"You may use everything within your power to deduce the validity of the chair." An ominous shadow fell over Chiron's eyes. "The challenge is that you must complete it without the aid of your senses."

Cole's heart seemed to trip over itself. "Without my senses? What does that even mean?"

"That is the veil that you must lift." Chiron took a step back and settled himself into another chair.

Cole sat still as a statue. He resisted the urge to reach between his knees and grip the seat, just to keep it from going anywhere. When would Chiron's magic take effect? Had it already? He ran his tongue over his teeth and cheeks, unsure if he tasted anything. He sniffed, wondering if there was anything to smell in the first place. Cole's eyes stung and itched, but he was afraid to blink. What if he opened them and there was nothing to see?

For a moment nothing seemed to happen. He was quite ready to blurt out the answer while he still could, but something odd made itself plain to him; he could no longer feel Oberon's warmth on the back of his neck. Cole swung his hand back, slapping the skin, but felt nothing. He dragged his fingernail sharply over his neck, but there was no pain. Fumbling, Cole examined his fingers. There was blood running from his nails, but no sensation of warmth or wetness. He brought the blood to his mouth and licked it, tasting nothing. He couldn't even tell if the finger had made it to his mouth. Cole rocked in the chair, snapping his fingers and clapping his hands, producing no sound whatsoever. He knew his heart was kicking like a mule, but there was no sign of it. He stretched his dry eyes as wide as they would go, watching the rapid rise and fall of his chest, though he had no urge to breathe. Never in his life had his sense of sight felt so inadequate a thing to view the world with. As meager as it was, he wailed inside himself as it too began to fade. The last thing Cole saw was Chiron's steady eyes watching over him.

Panic became him. Where was he? What was this place? Could it even be a place?

Cole flailed with no body, screamed with no lungs. There was nothing to reciprocate the commands of his brain. He was trapped in a void absolute, unable to quell the sickening dread that shocked and pulled at every corner of his limitless prison. He was powerless. He was nothing.

He struggled with everything he had against infinite openness. When nothing happened, he fought harder, gradually coming to the realization that he had no idea what he struggled against. With utmost caution, he eased up and released some of the tension. The panic relented, but only barely. The result gave Cole a shred of confidence. He had elicited a reaction upon whatever this environment was, using nothing but his own will.

There was no immediate danger, nothing at all causing him direct harm. With satisfying recognition, Cole identified each of his unleashed emotions wreaking havoc around him. He may not have his senses, but his emotions were certainly something he could feel. He now knew exactly where he was. It was a place he had never left; his own mind. The knowledge bolstered him. With every ounce of willpower he possessed, he shed the crushing Fear of non-existence. The tumultuous ocean stilled and slowed to a quiet eddy. Cole watched passively as each of his wild emotions retreated beneath him, dragged away by his cackling Fear. With his mind quiet, Cole took a deep mental breath.

Instinctively, Cole drew himself to his center. Finding the stone room was no trouble at all. It was easy in fact, and clearer than ever. The conical stalactite and the pedestal were there waiting for him, the water already flowing. Cole placed himself beneath the clear rope of water, reveling in how soothing it was. The stress melted from him, and to his very pleasant surprise, he heard his own laughter echo above the chamber. The water was perfectly cool as it rippled over him. He could feel things here, if only in his imagination. His laughter thundered to him from above the domed ceiling.

On a whim, he willed his body into the room. As he reached out, a vague concept of his naked hand swam in front of his vision. He had legs too, but only a fuzzy idea of them. He could have focused more on the details, but then the room would have faded. He rather liked having a place to be. Cole moved weightlessly over to the cone, running his fingers over the little marble orbs of his memories. The cascading water followed his fingers, running down his arm in a wandering line and soaking his clothes. Cole laughed, amused by what he was now wearing; jeans and a hooded sweater from Earth.

He pulled at the clothes. They felt real enough. The cotton of his sweater was a little rough from too many washes, and his jeans were loose and breathable, perfectly broken-in.

One of the little orbs on the stalactite glinted to him. Cole dug his nails in and pried it from its nest, bringing it to his eye. Inside, a memory played for him. It was his first moments in the forest outside Costas. He was in his hospital gown, yanking his foot from the squishy, fake rock. Cole replaced the marble, clicking it into place. As he did, he felt something else click into place, granting him a sense of much-needed orientation.

He was in his mind, of that there was no doubt. He knew his body was on the deck of Chiron's house, where he was in the middle of a task; determining the validity of a chair. As if waiting for him to remember, an exact copy of the chair in question appeared next to the pedestal. Just as his clothes and body, this too was merely a fabrication. Still, it would make a nice place to sit.

Cole slumped into his newly imagined chair and considered it. He had no means of interacting with things outside the stone room, but that didn't mean he was powerless. As Chiron had instructed, he inventoried his toolbox. Curious, he reached for his Rage first. His munisica flashed into being upon his illusory hands. Something else flashed from his periphery. A red toolbox rested against the wall of the room, a crude mallet sticking out of the top drawer. Cole's laughter echoed above the chamber. Rage and hammers would be of no use to him here.

His breath caught in his throat and he jolted upright. The water ceased its flow from the cone. If his Rage worked in here, surely his other magics would.

"Eliza!" Cole hollered as loudly as he could.

Her mind spiked from his excitement before lulling back to the gentle strumming of a harp. *"You scared the shadows off of me! You feel odd. What's wrong, Cole?"*

Cole poured his affection through the bond. *"Eliza! I never knew how good you could feel. Wait a second, this means you're real!"*

She responded with bubbling amusement. *"As far as I know, yes. What brought about this revelation?"*

"Well, if I'm real, then you must be real too," Cole said, feeling the matter settled.

She went utterly silent, though Cole could feel a drip of annoyance staining their bond.

"Eliza!" Cole nudged.

"Cole, what is it?" she shot at him. *"I'm in the middle of a lesson with Roth. If you wish to play games with me then you'll have to wait."*

Cole's excitement mounted, as the breathing above the ceiling quickened. *"It can't wait, I'm sorry but I'll explain later. I need a favor."*

"What is it?" she asked as echoes of a sharp pain rang through their link.

Cole infused their link with a sense of importance. *"I need you to use my body. Look through my eyes and do something for me. Tell me -no, show me what you see. I need everything."*

"This is ridiculous," she said, withdrawing somewhat.

"I know, I know, but can you do it?" Cole pleaded.

She sighed, stepping closer to the link. *"Of course I can. I just wanted to hear you say it."*

Cole faded from his center. He needed to be as clear and open as possible for this to work. The fraternal bond widened and thrummed as a few blurred images and hollow sounds came to him, distorted as if watched through a TV with a bad signal. The bond hardened and Cole grasped it with everything he had. The scene became crystal clear, though he still had no control.

Chiron peeled a long dark fruit, meticulously choosing each leaf before prying it open as if picking the wrong one might spoil the whole thing. His eyes went up, peering into Cole's re-transmitted vision with mild interest.

"Ah, I see now." Eliza beamed with realization. *"You are disconnected. Oberon's light, you are entirely disconnected! How is this possible?"*

"Chiron did it, it's part of a lesson," Cole said, his excitement bubbling over into her. *"Eliza listen, I need you to use my body and show me what I am sitting on. Say it out loud, with my mouth."*

Her reluctance was palpable. *"Cole, that is…a most intimate thing to ask. Are you sure?"*

"Please," he begged.

Cole felt the bond creak and strain. This was pushing the boundaries of what their Passion was capable of.

His five senses came through disorganized and unsynchronized. His sight was most clear and transmitted first, followed sluggishly by his hearing and then his sense of touch. It was unnerving and nauseating, inducing a sort of inverse vertigo within him. Cole struggled to keep his symptoms from spilling back into Eliza.

He watched as his body stood, turning slowly. The scuffing of his feet came next, then the sensation of movement. Eliza forced his hand down, tapping his finger against the high back of the chair. A moment later, he felt the vibrations in his throat as both his and Eliza's voices played into his mind.

"It's just a chair," they said together.

The fraternal bond waned as his organic senses waxed. His sight, touch, and hearing harmonized in perfect synchronicity. He was back in his body.

Standing upright and breathing on his own, Cole rubbed against Eliza, feeling another jolt of pain from her end.

"That was perfect. Are you all right?" he asked, wincing.

Agony shot through their bond. *"I will be once Roth finds somewhere else to stand besides my neck. I too am in the middle of a lesson."*

Cole offered his wordless apology.

"Think nothing of it. Now go learn what you can. Do not disappoint Varka." She winked out of his mind before he had a chance to apologize, leaving behind an unbreakable golden strand.

Flexing his arms and legs, Cole embraced control of his body and met Chiron's gaze. "It's just a chair."

Chiron set the fruit down. "Explain."

"Reality is relative," Cole said, kicking his toe against the chair's leg. "Here and now, this chair, that house, the trees below us, they are all real. You are real. But only to me, and only right now." Cole fell silent for a moment, waiting for the right words before continuing. "Without my senses, the entire world ceased to exist. I wasn't connected to any of it, so it didn't matter, it wasn't relevant. None of it was real."

"You must have felt trapped inside your own mind, no?" Chiron asked.

Cole frowned. "At first, yeah. It was terrifying, but not the worst thing I've ever been through. After I got ahold of myself it didn't seem like I was trapped. It was more like living in a dream."

"Indeed. And now that you have returned to this reality, what do you make of the chair?" Chiron asked, nudging his eyes towards the chair.

"It's just a chair," Cole said with a nervous giggle.

"Of course it is." Chiron snatched the fruit off the table and continued peeling it absentmindedly. "So, how did you know Eliza was real? How can you be sure that you're not still imagining all of this?"

"I, I'm not sure," Cole stuttered. Concern washed over him as the implications loomed up from the shadows of his mind. "I didn't think about it at the time. She...she felt real. And I knew that I was real." Cole resisted the temptation to call upon her again just to check.

Chiron chuckled, finally easing the tension between them. "You did very well, Cole. A sight better than your first task, though I suppose you didn't set the bar very high."

"Really?" Cole exclaimed. "I didn't fail?"

"Aethers no!" Chiron swatted his hand dismissively. "The only failure is one that you do not learn from. Now let us move on from this lesson! There is much for us to cover."

Cole's heart sank along with his hopes. He was dead tired. That lesson had taken the last bit of his reserves, and now that it was over, his lethargy was back heavier than ever. His stubborn pride wouldn't carry him through another minute, let alone another lesson.

"Master Chiron?" Cole said, unable to mask his desperation any longer.

Chiron inclined his head in answer. "What is it?"

Cole forced his eyes open half-way, "I can't take any more. I need sleep." He knew he was starving too, but next to his exhaustion even his clawing hunger wasn't a priority.

If Chiron was disappointed, his face didn't show it. He rose from his chair and offered Cole the peeled meat of the dark fruit. Cole took it with no intention of eating.

"We all have our limits, and they are there for good reason," Chiron said, his eyes piercing through Cole's droopy lids. "However, we do not have the luxury of indulging our limits when sailing the oceans of consequence. When you are ready, eat the fruit. It is called a blackstout, and it will nourish you for days on end. However, as for the limits of your need for sleep, there are but two solutions."

Cole tried to ask what they were, but could only manage an unintelligible mumble.

"You can sleep, right here and now. You will wake fully rested and ready for another day's lessons. However, every breath spent dreaming is another inch of ground The Three will take from us. Each passing moment, countless soul flies will be tortured and broken beyond repair, who will then return to torment their kin. Every hour another warrior takes his last breath. All while you sleep."

Storn's primal wailing echoed hauntingly up from the bowels of Cole's nightmares. Cole swallowed back the revulsion, and the bile.

"What is the second option?" Cole asked, his vigor returning somewhat.

Chiron raised his chin, appraising him. "In the markets there is a shop called the Cordial Compendium. Do you know it?"

"Yes," Cole replied. Storn had taken him there on his first day at The Sill.

"On the top shelf of the Passion section lies a cypher labeled *dreamsource*. Take it into yourself and you will never sleep again. Being top-shelf it is among the most expensive cyphers, and rightly so. It will affect you for the rest of your life. I do not expect you to make the choice lightly, but I must now ask you to leave here and make that choice. I will await your return, whether it be in an hour or a day."

Cole's heartbeat thumped into his ears. He was sorely tempted to simply fall from the tree and let his dreams take him before he hit the ground. He wasn't even sure if he could make it to the markets.

Chiron gave his shoulder a gentle shake and grin. "Now would be a perfect time to ask your Rage for assistance."

Cole nodded drunkenly, turning and stepping to the edge of the deck. To his surprise, the house was no longer above the patterned grid of trees. It was now above the necropolis. Too tired to ask questions, Cole bared his teeth and called upon his Rage. The magic was there, but invoking it was as hard as asking fire of wet wood. He could feel his fingertips sharpening, but he needed another good push to really get the Rage burning. Casting aside his caution, Cole stepped off the deck into open air.

His Rage lashed out from its cage, enveloping his entire body in the ebony shroud before crashing into the ankle-deep water of the necropolis. Cole's Rage purred at how powerful and jarring the impact was, daring him to try again so he might plough right through the planet.

Cole allowed his Rage another moment of indulgence before releasing a portion of it. He only needed enough of it to keep him awake for a bit longer. Looking up he could see Chiron's house was already moving on, wandering over the treetops like a passing cloud.

Smelling something sweet, Cole raised his hand curiously. The blackstout was mashed in between the knives of his munisica. Careful not to cut his naked tongue, he ate what he could. The fruit itself was tasteless and unsatisfying with the sticky consistency of peanut butter. The effect of the fruit was immediate however, giving Cole the sensation of swallowing a lead brick. His whining stomach ceased all protest, as if it couldn't recall how to be hungry. It was not a satisfying meal, but he knew he wouldn't need to eat again in the foreseeable future.

Blazing his way into the markets, Cole gazed up at the network of ramps and walkways. He couldn't remember exactly where the Cordial Compendium was, and the excitement of his Rage didn't help matters. It wasn't until now, however, that he thought on the repercussions of never sleeping again.

He turned off the main thoroughfare and found a bench facing a darkened shop window displaying an array of crystals. Cole slid into the bench, ignoring a passing woman who gave his munisica a wary look.

Why should he give up sleep? He would have more time in his day of course, but his body must have needed sleep for good reasons. Sleep was essential for repair and recovery, but Passion could do that even better. There surely were some mental benefits of a good night's sleep, but they were unknown to him. The thought of losing part of his life was unnerving. Sleeping was something he enjoyed and indulged in, something he would never be able to look forward to again. He loathed to have it taken from him, just as he would loathe losing the ability to see color.

A bubble of sorrow rose from him, bringing a cold fact to the surface; if he never slept again, then he would never see his family.

His dreams were the only place where he could hold his mom and tell her he's coming back. Only in his dreams was Nana Beth still alive, imparting her sagely advice and strength onto him. His dreams still had Joshy, whole and untouched, giggling up at him from the couch where he watched the Spanish channel on mute. His dreams were his last anchor to his life on Earth. Without them, part of him would cease to be.

Cole sighed, losing himself in his half-reflection in the shop mirror. His hair was wild, though not unkempt. The skin on his face was tanned and tight. His shoulders were wide, each larger than his head with matching thick arms. He decided he liked his eyes most of all. They dropped with lethargy, but they were also dangerous.

Checking to make sure no one was looking, he twisted and flexed his arms, appraising himself in the window. His chest, once narrow and shapeless was broad, tapering down to a slim waist. It seemed like just yesterday he was the chubby, pale child, fumbling to keep up with giants.

Lights flicked on inside the shop, revealing a magenta-robed man who had apparently been enjoying Cole's posing routine. Cole adjusted himself awkwardly, trying to play it off as if he were only just trying to scratch his back with both hands. The shopkeeper laughed, shaking his head. He flicked on another light and disappeared into a back room.

Flushing, Cole stood to leave. Something in the shop window caught his eye, however. A jagged pair of olive crystals danced for him in the window, clinking shrilly off their glass container. A skinny brass label on the shelf read *FOCUSING SHARDS*.

Cole pressed his forehead against the window. On his first trip into the markets Storn had purchased all of his cyphers for him, and Cole had promised Storn a set of focusing shards in return. Un-sticking his forehead from the window, Cole wheeled around and entered the shop. He pocketed the focusing shards and made for the door.

"Hey! You have to pay for those!" the shopkeeper hollered, stumbling out of the back room with a stack of boxes. "I don't know who the hell you think you are but those shards are worth more than..."

The shopkeeper's voice trailed off as Cole slid his hand from an omnistone set on a pedestal near the door. The stone blazed lavender and emitted a powerful humming sound that rattled a nearby shelf full of jars. Cole wiped his eyes and left the shop before the shopkeeper could thank him.

Cole's mind was set. He would take the dreamsource into himself and sleep no more. He would spend every moment he had working against The Three. Anything less than everything he had wasn't acceptable. Storn deserved it.

After only getting lost twice, Cole found the Cordial Compendium tucked away in an obscure corner of an upper causeway. The cyphers appeared untouched, though someone had replaced the ones he took months ago. Having just spent a good portion of his Passion on the focusing shards, Cole slapped both hands on the red gratia stone. His Rage was fuzzy and tired, but it was still there. He just hoped it would be enough. Cracking open his reserves, Cole's body hardened as the shroud snapped over every inch of him, sharpening him into a living weapon. The gratia seemed to suck his munisica in, taking all of the red magic from him. Cole could feel the shroud receding, and fought back against it, but to no avail. The more he gave, the more the stone took.

He watched from the corner of his eye as the invisible barriers shimmered along the shelves. The bottom and middle shelves were already unlocked and the upper shelves were currently opening. The very top shelf maintained its shimmering veil, however. Cole knew he had the Rage to unlock it, but it would leave him utterly drained and defenseless. Groaning, he heaved the last dregs of the red magic into the stone.

Cole fell to the floor, weak and feeble. Both his Passion and Rage were spent. He couldn't remember the last time he'd felt so weak. Without his Rage to stay his drowsiness, he relied upon sheer, mundane human will to resist the urge to shut his eyes. Moaning, he pulled himself to his feet and dragged his eyes over the top shelf of the Passion section. It was there waiting for him, perched in a cutout behind a brass label that read *dreamsource*. As Cole plucked the cypher from its nest, the magical shields flashed on every other shelf, locking the displays. The cypher was immensely heavy for being no larger than an egg. Within its confines, white smoke chased itself in little tornadoes, emitting shocking pink sparks like little fireworks.

Cole grasped the cypher and shut his eyes. His family waited for him behind his eyelids, tempting him into dozing for one last goodbye. He lifted the cypher to his mouth and kissed his fingers. A tear leaped from his cheek, crashing over the cloudy orb.

"Goodbye," he whispered.

CHAPTER 18

STRENGTH AND HUMILITY

The passing weeks inched by with all the speed of a creeping glacier. True to its description, the dreamsource cypher relieved Cole of his need for sleep. The effect was not immediate or all that noticeable. He expected some sort of buzzing stimulant, as if drinking an entire pool of black coffee. His lethargy clung to him for days with sleep eluding him all the while. When he tried dozing, it felt like trying to walk up a hill of smooth ice. He would take a few steps towards sleep, only to have his feet yanked out from under him as he slid rapidly back to the waking world. After he'd spent a week as a walking zombie, his drowsiness left him entirely. Cole had to rely upon his ever-fading memories to visit his family back on Earth.

Without him taking breaks for food or sleep, Chiron's lessons drove on without interruption. Cole learned something new every hour, but to his silent annoyance the lessons never covered any practical use of magic. He and Chiron spent a great deal of time in the library combing through sections Cole had never been to. Chiron lectured him the lore of each of the local planets, as well as how Aeneria had influenced them by preventing wars, harvesting endangered species, and nudging technology along. Though the Wisdom Walkers agreed to guide the local planets with subtle hands, many couldn't resist interacting with their charges. The Wisdom Walkers were exalted as gods among ancient civilizations, unintentionally shaping legends and widespread religions that lasted to this day. Cole took great interest in Aeneria's recordings of Terra. The meddling of the Wisdom Walkers coincided with the epics and deities that wove the tales of Earth's religions.

Another topic covered at length was anatomy. Cole learned that the Aenerians were made of nearly all the same parts as humans, though there were slight differences that required drawn-out explanations. The anatomy lessons were tedious and never-ending; however, Cole took deeper interest when Chiron mentioned that the knowledge was necessary for certain aspects of Passion to work properly. He couldn't quite grasp it yet, but it sounded as if a mastery of Passion would allow him to modify any part of not only his own body, but those of plants and other animals as well. He couldn't wait to try out a few of these tricks.

A portion of every day was spent going over the vast number of governments and tribes on Aeneria, to include their economies, relationships, magical dispositions, and locations. It was interesting enough, but the subject only added to Cole's growing annoyance that they had yet to learn anything to help fight The Three.

One night while the rest of The Sill was asleep, Chiron brought Cole into a cave at the edge of the lagoon. The wall of the cave was lined with an ore comprised of rare metals that would illustrate a chemical reaction they had just covered in an earlier lesson.

"We have chemistry classes back on Terra you know," Cole said, fumbling through the shallow water of the cave. "I didn't learn much then either. I don't see how learning about atoms and bonds is going to help me. Maybe I could bore my enemies to death with lectures and quizzes."

"You've all the tact and creativity of a bog angel," Chiron replied, walking on top of the water. His cape trailed behind him as a blanket of algae-covered pebbles. "Chemistry may very well be the most useful thing you'll learn. Surely you can think of at least few reasons as to why the subject is important."

Cole swore after wrenching a toe on a slimy rock. "It's for Wisdom right? If I understand the true nature of something I can change the rules. There's just so much of it to learn, and who knows what elements make up everything here."

Chiron slowed, waiting for Cole to navigate a particularly tricky cluster of rocks beneath the water. He wasn't allowed to use any magic outside of Wisdom for this lesson, and the lack of munisica slowed him considerably. He waited for Cole to catch up before replying, "The chemistry of Aeneria is quite the same as your Terra. In fact, every local planet is made of the same basic elements, which follow the same rules for how they interact. The subject is an immense one. You will likely never know every nuance of every combination of atoms, but the more you know, the more tools you will have at your disposal."

"It makes sense," Cole said in a hollow voice. "I just hope I do better this time around. I nearly failed out of my last chemistry class. Master, can I put on a light? I can't see a thing and these rocks are tearing me up."

Chiron considered him for a second. "Use whatever Wisdom you have at your disposal."

Cole swung his arm up, pointing two fingers to a spot just above his head. A tiny bead of white light popped into existence. His eyes were already magically augmented for night vision, so he kept the light as dim as possible. The spell was simple, but it still drained his focus, making mundane tasks like walking and talking just a little harder.

Chiron raised an eyebrow. "Tell me how you just cast that spell."

"I just messed with the air a bit." Cole rubbed his chin. "I don't know exactly how it works. Lileth taught me a while back, but I didn't understand the finer details."

"I thought as much," Chiron said, stopping them. "Effective, but inefficient. Do you know what light is?"

Cole dug through his memories of every science class he'd ever had, but nothing came up. He hoped he hadn't dumped that memory into a Wisdom stone at some point.

"I've no idea," Cole admitted.

"Light is nothing more than the emission of photons, which occurs when there is an interference in the path of an atom's electron. When you 'mess' with the air, you are altering the orbits of the electrons in a given space, causing photons to release themselves." Chiron grasped his hands behind his pebbly cape. "Would you like me to repeat that?"

Cole felt a sudden shift in his magic. It was as if his spell itched, and Chiron's explanation gently scratched it. "Say it again, slower this time."

Chiron gave a knowing smile and repeated himself three times. With each passing, Cole's understanding bent and widened, allowing new concepts to form. The weight of the spell lessened considerably, taking only a sliver of Cole's focus to maintain. It was as easy as snapping his fingers.

"That was incredible!" Cole blurted, marveling at his pin-prick of light. "I think I can change the color too!"

With a twist of thought, the little star drooped to a more comfortable cherry-red. Cole's laugh echoed throughout the dripping cave.

"Chemistry," Chiron stated, urging Cole deeper into the cave.

With his mind less occupied, Cole wove another spell to lighten himself, allowing for a pain-free stroll over the rocks. He thirsted for more tricks to make his Wisdom more effective, wondering how Chiron made the water strong enough to walk on. More questions sprouted in his mind, though he decided to save them for the walk back. Chiron didn't like it when he asked too many questions before a lesson.

A hail of clicking joined the chorus of dripping water echoing off the cave walls. Cole jumped as a crab ran over his foot, scuttling over shiny rocks into a deeper pool. Chiron stopped, guiding him onto a dry slab as the tunnel opened to a wide chamber. Oberon's light poured through cracks in the ceiling, creating shafts of rainbow in a pond that filled up the entire chamber. Cole dismissed his marble of cherry light as his eyes drank in Oberon's familiar glow. He retreated into his center, releasing every thought and emotion that clouded him. He was ready to learn.

The start of Chiron's lessons was always silent, allowing Cole time to attune his mind and make observations on their surroundings. Having cleared his mind, he opened himself to his environment, casting quiet spells to sharpen his senses. He had to dial back his sense of smell, as a slight odor of rotten eggs became a rancid hurricane. Something in the room stunk terribly.

Shifting his focus to his sight and hearing, he noticed hundreds of crabs nestled into every crack and crevice of the walls and ceiling. For the most part they looked like normal crabs back on Earth, though each sported a horn longer than their bodies. Squinting, Cole zoomed in on a fat purple-tinged one, watching as its blunt claws scraped and chewed on an edge of a boulder. That explained the clicking. His sharpened hearing also revealed clouds of insects swirling about on unseen currents of ocean air.

After a quarter of an hour of Cole listening and watching, the chamber revealed nothing else to him. He opened his mouth to mention this to Chiron, but a raised hand from the elder hushed him.

Chiron spoke in a captivating whisper: "Just a moment longer, the tides are about to shift. Then the lesson will begin."

The previous day Cole had learned that Aeneria's tides were not caused by Oberon, as the moon did not orbit, but by shifting currents in the molten metal of the planet's core. The predictable seasons of the core's magnetic field affected the ocean water, which was heavy with its own metals and caused the tides.

The concept of magnetism tickled Cole with more questions regarding Wisdom, though he pocketed them with his other curiosities. He didn't want to miss a thing. A minute later, something chilly tickled against Cole's toes. He glanced down to find there was a lot less of the slab for them to stand on. The tide was indeed coming in.

The briny water rose up his ankles and shins, continuing up past his navel. A moment later Chiron laid himself onto the surface, looking as though he lounged upon a comfy leather sofa. Cole resigned himself to treading chilly water.

As the water slowed its ascent, the crabs clicked and scuttled their way up along the ceiling, converging in throngs around the rainbow shafts of light. A powerful stench of spoiled eggs rushed into Cole's nose and stung his eyes. Through his blurred vision something along the ceiling caught his attention. Pale violet sparks began crackling from the horns of the crabs, creating an illuminating drizzle bright enough to compete with Oberon's beaming waterfalls.

Attracted to the flashing sparks, insects fluttered about the crabs' dense swarms. The crabs chattered with excitement at the arrival of the bugs, but otherwise did not react. Cole bobbed closer to Chiron, no longer able to contain the questions boiling up inside him.

Chiron silenced him with a stern look, pointing towards the cracks in the ceiling. "Watch."

Cole clamped his mouth shut.

A flapping noise came from the ceiling, followed by a flock of bat-like creatures pouring down from the holes. The creatures broke Oberon's light as they chased after the insects. Cole's eyes sharpened as he zoomed in as far as he could. The flying creatures were not bats at all, but winged lizards dancing madly as they snapped at the bugs.

A thunderous crack split the air. One of the crabs emitted a violent purple explosion from its horn. A lizard fell limp, caught in a pair of outstretched claws. The tiny hunter charged through its fellows, carrying the lizard like a trophy before disappearing through a dark hole.

The lizards dispersed briefly, but the fat cloud of insects was too tempting. A few seconds later another lizard fell in a purple explosion, caught by the waiting claws of another crab. Cole deadened his hearing after he caught a permanent ringing in his left ear. He wondered what sort of spell the crabs might be using against the lizards, guessing at how he himself might create such a force. Cole had become adept at transferring heat from one object to another, albeit in a slow, methodic manner. However, these crabs were creating powerful fireballs that rivaled even Valen's and Lileth's talents. How could mere crustaceans conjure such explosive fire?

After a half hour the lizards dispersed as the crabs' supply of insects dwindled. Chiron eventually nudged Cole and gave him a patient nod, indicating the end of the lesson.

"Why don't we go find a comfy spot to reflect on what we just learned," Chiron said, gliding back out of the chamber. Cole propelled himself through the murky water with his Wisdom.

Outside the cave, Chiron led him up a jagged wall of rock to the roof of the cave, which was thankfully covered in a bed of cushy blue moss. They stopped at a flat spot nestled just above the chamber they'd just vacated. A moment later a much smaller flock of lizards swirled up from holes in the moss, chirping and chasing each other towards the forest of the mainland. When their flapping and squeaking faded, Chiron sat himself cross legged, drawing his now mossy cape around himself like a blanket.

"Can I ask questions now?" Cole blurted before Chiron could get too comfortable.

"Oh I suppose so," he said as he pulled his cape tighter. "Let's have them."

"How is it that the crabs can use magic?" Cole asked, peeking down a hole. "I thought only intelligent creatures could wield it."

"Nothing you witnessed in the cave involved magic," Chiron said.

Cole gave him a sideways grin. "Not even your little walking-on-water trick?"

"You caught me," Chiron sighed. "I reserved a bit of hope that you'd figure that trick out on your own, but that is a lesson for another time. Would you like to know how the candle crabs put on such a lovely show for us?"

Cole plopped into the spongy moss, casting a spell to draw heat into himself. Steam rose in swirling wisps from his wet clothes. "I find it hard to believe that those little bombs were just crabs being crabs. But please, enlighten me."

"The funny thing about nature's magic is that it exists whether believed or not. Do you remember what the crabs were doing before their prey joined us?" Chiron asked, raising a winged eyebrow.

Cole peered down the nearest hole, then back to Chiron. "They were chewing up the walls, weren't they?"

"They were," Chiron replied with a nod. "Can you think of why the crabs would eat something of no nutritional value?"

"Nervous habit?" Cole guessed.

Chiron's hand slid from his mossy cape and dug into the rock below the moss, wriggling a tiny piece loose. He swirled another finger above the chip. The rock vibrated and shrank, releasing a cloud of gas that smelled horribly like the rancid eggs from the chamber below. Chiron then yanked a handful of moss from his side, wringing a few drops of water onto the rock. The pebble sizzled, then exploded in a flash of pale violet, startling Cole.

Chiron rubbed his hands together, brushing off the ashes. "The candle crabs were eating the walls, which are leaden with a substance called arcanite, or to use its proper chemical name, potassium sulfate. The crabs ingest the compound, and through their own biological systems, isolate the potassium into their horns. The potassium is then mixed with water and weaponized for use against their prey. The remaining sulfur is expelled in gaseous form, treating us with that pleasant, eggy aroma."

"I'm starting to understand why chemistry is so important to Wisdom," Cole said with a grin. He felt as if he'd taken a tiny step closer to understanding Wisdom. "If a crab can learn how to turn rocks into bombs, then I ought to be able to turn wood into gold, right?"

"The path of Wisdom can be perilous," Chiron warned. "In the wrong hands, an intimate knowledge of potassium can devastate entire legions with a well-placed spell."

Cole perked up. "How so? Those explosions were so small. Wouldn't that take a huge amount of…what was it, arcanite?"

"Potassium is a common element that permeates much of our food as well as our bodies." Chiron's voice dropped to a grave tone. "Our bodies are comprised in no small part of water. With the right twist of thought…" He squeezed more water onto the rock chip, producing a series of crackling explosions.

• • • •

With creeping profundity life began to take on a sense of timelessness for Cole. Without the need for sleep, the passing of hours held no significance to him. He simply lived from one moment to the next. His time piece lay forgotten at the bottom of his rucksack, unnecessary since he never had appointments to be punctual for. His meals were replaced by a quick snack of blackstout fruit, which nourished him for days on end. He made infrequent trips to his tree on the short breaks that Chiron demanded he take, but Cole would only use his room to bathe and change before heading back out again. His bed had become a shelf for storing jars of various metals, salts, and oils he would experiment with on his time off. When his experiments overflowed onto the floor, he persuaded Chiron to show him how to shape plants with Wisdom and Passion. Every wall from ceiling to floor lined themselves with cubbies and shelves before long. Cole even gave himself a cozy loft in his apartment.

As Cole suspected, Chiron had also relieved himself of the need for sleep. He kept up with Cole for weeks on end, not even pausing to eat when Cole's stomach squelched for another blackstout. Cole made a game of trying to catch him in some mundane act, but the elder drove on ceaselessly like some ancient ghost, never sleeping, never eating. Cole couldn't remember if he ever saw his Master blink, let alone scratch his nose. Chiron rarely showed interest in topics outside of Cole's education. They only stopped when he insisted Cole's overloaded mind take a break, or when Chiron made abrupt trips by himself to aid in a nearby battle. Cole stopped asking to join Chiron after his third trip, leaving his Rage aching and restless. They had yet to practice with the red magic.

Cole's education broadened over the passing weeks. Though none of it was the flashy spells he expected from one of the Unbound, they did at least cover some basic magic. Chiron gave him a chart of every element that existed naturally on Aeneria, as well as a spell that would allow him to identify them in nature. Cole recognized most of the chart, as it followed the same progression as the periodic table from his science classes.

To combat the negative effects of his everlasting waking hours, Chiron guided him through a meditation laced with Passion, granting him the boons of a full night's sleep in minutes. When the soul flies visited, they met with the creatures, attuning themselves to the colors of their individual songs. The process was insightful and invigorating, leaving both parties glowing with a shared wholesomeness. Unable to remember his last dream, Cole relished the dreams of the soul flies as they leaked into him. With a nudge of Passion he was able to amplify their fantasies and brush away nightmares.

When not working with magic or diving in books, Chiron took Cole far beyond the borders of The Sill, showing him different landscapes and tricks of every plant and animal along the way. Chiron's education was unlike anything Cole had experienced. Cole soon realized there was something to gain from observing just about anything, whether it be a competition between shrubs battling for Oberon's light, or the odd relationship between cave moths and candle crabs. Cole was content with the lectures, though a growing part of him yearned for the fervor of battle. He belonged at the fore of the fight, not mired in meditations and toiling in libraries.

Though his lessons demanded most of his focus, a portion of Cole's mind dragged his thoughts to Lileth. He had hoped the time away would make things easier, but she permeated both his mind and his heart, seeping up through the gaps in conscious thought. If even the slightest lull presented itself, his heart would stop and skip a beat, only to return in a fevered tattoo of panicked thought. He felt as if he were sailing through a squall in a too-small boat. Each wave was a widowmaker, crashing over him with precious memories or terrible speculation of what she and Valen might be up to. He found himself spying through Eliza's eyes, feigning interest in her lessons while catching glimpses of Lileth when he could. He wished there were some way to send a private message to her.

The next sunrise came and went, bringing Aeneria from the house of Rhunam to the house of Wulfmont. Cole hadn't expected the month to pass so soon. What troubled him the most was that he still had yet to learn anything to make him any better off against The Three. Where were the roaring firebolts and crackling lightning? Or invisibility and shielding spells? The day came when Cole decided he'd had enough. Cole resolved to demand a more practical exercise from his Master.

Cole hoisted himself up onto the deck of Chiron's house, which he found floating atop the pines near the Arts District. The Wisdom Walker sat in his chair, showing no reaction to Cole's arrival as he gazed up at Oberon.

"Master, I'm sick of climbing up these trees," Cole said with stony determination. "Teach me how to fly."

As Cole expected, Chiron did not respond for a time, or break his gaze from their rainbow moon. Cole moved and stood in between Chiron's face and Oberon, forcing the elder to look him in the eye.

Chiron sighed. "Cole, I have reasons for the pacing of your lessons. A tree that grows too quickly will have its branches cracked by a harsh winter. I have already asked you a number of times, but I will ask it of you again; please trust my judgment."

Cole shook his head. "Master, I trust you with my life, but I know what's out there. You've been going out for your little 'diplomatic assistance' trips more and more lately. I know what you're doing. You reek of blood and death every time you return. The Three are gaining ground every day. Would you have me wait until they come knocking at our doors to have me tested?"

"If it were in my power, you would *never* face The Three, and I would spend the rest of time teaching you everything there is to know about the universe. Even then I worry you may never learn the value of patience." He flashed Cole a chastising glare.

"It's not impatience that drives me," Cole said, his voice rising. "Morthain has fallen. Three more Colossi found the city yesterday, each of them even smaller than the one I took down. The fact that I know this means you must have known about it for at least a few days. We could have done something. I could have saved them. Instead, I've been here, learning about the lifecycles of plants and fungi." The harshness of his tone was in no small part fed by the guilt of leaving Milette in Morthain. Not only had he taken her hands, he'd sentenced her to whatever undeath that Sorronis's priests had brought upon the city. If dreams were still possible, nightmares of her fate would have haunted them.

"I see you've kept yourself busy during your time off. Not only have you been keeping up with current events, but by the looks of it you've been keeping up with Roth's lessons." Chiron reached up and gave Cole's upper-arm a squeeze. "You are filling out nicely."

Cole shrugged off Chiron's hand. "Eliza told me about Morthain. And your lessons never come within a mile of Rage. Since you won't teach me, I've been taking matters into my own hands."

"And how exactly have you been doing that?" Chiron asked, a glint of amusement in his eye. "I haven't exactly given you an abundance of free time."

"You've given me enough," Cole said defiantly. "I've been watching Eliza's lessons. I pick up what I can in between turning pages, and while running around trying to find your house every day. I pick up what I can, but I can only half-pay attention. Like right now I know they are all practicing aerial combat, but I still have no idea how they summon wings."

"I sensed that you've been learning more than what I've been teaching you, but that doesn't quite explain how you've bulked up so much," Chiron said, appraising Cole's shoulders.

Cole spoke through a grin: "One *practical* thing I learned was how to manipulate gravity. I've been using it for months now to lighten myself. Really came in handy in the beginning when I was too short to climb up your stairs. But now I've been using it to make myself heavier, and when you leave I follow along with Roth's lessons the best I can. My Rage can't sit still too long."

"I was wondering who cleaned out my entire crop of blackstouts. Those are supposed to fuel a strong Aenerian for nearly a week."

Cole shrugged. "Well, sometimes I do a week's worth of work in a day. Don't worry, I'll get my own food from now on."

"No matter." Chiron brushed his hand through the air. "Today we will go over Passion's uses for invigorating plant growth. You'll have the blackstouts bearing more fruit than you could ever eat, even with your monstrous appetite. Come, I'll show you now." Chiron's cape swished behind him as he made for the edge of the deck.

Cole didn't move.

Chiron paused, speaking without turning. "You are determined?"

"Master, I had a prisoner. Her name was Milette. I forced her to stay in Morthain, and she's dead or worse because of me. The first day I came here you told me that I could stay as long as I wanted, that I was free to come and go as I please. If you don't start teaching me something useful, I'm going to leave and learn it on my own."

Chiron was silent for a moment. When he spoke again his voice lost all traces of polite cheeriness. "Follow me then."

Chiron floated from the deck. Cole waited to see what direction he flew in before taking the leap himself. As he fell, he guided his descent with Wisdom so that he would miss the buildings below, landing instead on a grassy lawn. Chiron flew with uncharacteristic haste, forcing Cole to delve into his Rage so that he could keep up. He had a feeling where Chiron was leading him.

As their trail suggested, Cole trotted to a halt at the three trees where he'd had his first lesson with Roth. The middle tree towered over the others, the gratia stone still glowing a pinkish lavender from his contribution.

Chiron began to disrobe, shedding his tunic and his magical cape, which fell to the grass in a clump of green stalks. He turned, facing Cole with his shirtless body. Cole's eyed flicked over Chiron, sizing him up. The elder's body carried no fat, and little muscle, giving him the appearance of a long-distance runner who missed one too many meals. His features were striking, but the most shocking was the scar. The deformity was white and shiny, crawling down his neck, where it stretched as wide as a handprint over his torso before tapering into a neat spiral around his navel. The scar glowed and pulsed, as if touched with lingering magic.

"Your Rage demands use. Draw your munisica and bring the full weight of it to bear against me. You may use whatever magics and skills you have." Chiron bent his knees slightly, taking a relaxed fighting position as he tied his storm-grey hair back.

"You want me to fight you?" Cole asked, dumbstruck.

"Consider this one of Roth's lessons," Chiron said, crouching his spindly body even lower. "I want you to try to kill me."

Cole felt blood rush to his face. It was uncomfortable as it was unnerving to think of hurting Chiron, but if this was to be one of Roth's lessons then he wouldn't hesitate. Cole disrobed, stripping down to just his pants. It seemed unfair that he should wear armor while his opponent fought naked. Cole was as tall as Chiron now, and more than twice as thick with his recent growth. So long as the elder didn't resort to Wisdom or Passion, Cole thought he might earn an easy victory.

Balancing between caution and confidence, Cole ran not at Chiron, but at a tree root where his feet would find solid purchase. As he uncorked just a bit of his Rage, the shroud gifted him his wicked blades. He kept his eyes on Chiron, his feet caught the root and he lunged for his Master, one arm outstretched in the shape of a spear. As Cole guessed, Chiron hopped out of the way. The old Wisdom Walker was fast, but Cole had only just begun. Digging into the grass, Cole rounded for another attack. Chiron waited for him, his expression detached and limbs entirely too relaxed. Halfway across the span, Cole summoned more of his Rage, bringing the shroud all the way up his shoulders and upper thighs. This was Cole's favorite place to be, dancing the line between precise violence and wild bloodlust.

This time his claws found something, but only a glancing blow, deflected and harmless. The weight of Chiron's hand against his told him that the attack was expected, simple.

Instead of allowing his momentum to carry him away, Cole used Wisdom to halt himself inches from Chiron, well within reach. He made another simple knife-jab at Chiron's ribs. The strike was lightning-quick and would at the very least show Cole what the elder was capable of. A probing attack, as Roth had called it.

To Cole's utter astonishment, Chiron's torso bent back in an impossible angle. He moved just enough to dodge the munisica, his naked skin resting against Cole's shrouded forearm. Chiron's legs spread wide as he wove his arms around one of Cole's, cranking it into an awkward position. Before Cole knew it he felt himself yanked forward. He teetered off his feet in a flash. Chiron released him mid throw, sending him sailing and spinning. Cole knew he would land badly, likely sprawled out in a vulnerable position, but that was not what worried him. It was Chiron's deceptively immense weight coupled with the ease of his counter attack that gave him pause. The fact that Cole sensed no magic from the elder troubled him more deeply still.

Cole ploughed into roots and dirt, but not before he wrapped his back and chest in the shroud. His Rage surged. He drank in the bloodlust, allowing it to fill him and replace his reason. Chiron's passive indifference threw yet more fuel on his Rage fire. Cole grinned, baring his teeth, and his bladed hair lengthened, prickling the back of his neck. The old Master was fast, but when was the last time he had meddled with a true master of Rage?

"Don't sell yourself short now," Chiron said. "There's no point giving half measure here. Let's have it all."

"You know what you're asking for right?" Cole shut his eyes, immolating himself with Rage. Before Chiron could answer, the shroud enveloped him full and true, blackening every inch of him inside and out. Cole was Rage incarnate.

Cole laughed to himself. Chiron had no idea that Cole had been handicapping himself with thickened gravity all along. He had intended on waiting until later in the fight to dismiss the spell, but as his Rage swelled the magic fell from him like a lead coat. There would be nothing slowing him now.

While Cole gave himself fully to the red magic, it did not consume him as it once had. Ever since his flight with Alvani he'd kept part of himself anchored in his center. Every action was of his own choosing. The Rage merely provided the means.

Instead of lunging towards Chiron, he walked with steady grace towards his enemy. The wise one was reactive, so Cole would force him to make the first move. The shroud protected him from any conceivable wound, so he could afford to take his time. Cole stopped in front of his Master, boring a glare of midnight fire into Chiron. Raising a single hand, he slowly wrapped his dagger-fingers around Chiron's shoulder.

As the obsidian tips grazed over Chiron's skin, he moved ever so slightly, rolling the shoulder away while bringing the other closer. He obviously wasn't afraid of the proximity. Maintaining eye contact, Cole lashed out with a kick that would have cloven an anvil in two. His foot met air, though his body twisted on the follow through, just enough for Chiron to wrap around to his side, inching ever closer.

A deep growl rumbled in Cole's armored throat. He continued his kick, shifting and gripping the ground with his planted foot as he wheeled around. Though he moved faster than a cracking whip, Chiron's increasing proximity rendered Cole's kick harmless. Cole was dimly aware of Chiron's soft hands sliding around his back, pulling his right arm into a useless angle. Knowing his attack was now for nothing, Cole brought his kick to the ground and jumped as hard as he could.

There was an odd weight to his flight. Somehow, Chiron had attached himself to Cole's back, still trapping Cole's arm behind his waist. They flew up alongside tree branches, spinning and struggling all the while. Cole changed his tactic in midair; he embraced their closeness and pulled Chiron in tight, intent on making the elder strike the ground first. However, the wise one evaded his munisica once again, bending and twisting in extreme angles while using Cole's trapped arm for leverage all the while. Cole's face struck the ground first, cranking his neck with the full weight of both their bodies. The impact was harmless, but infuriating. Cole allowed himself to slip from his center, giving every facet of his mind to the Rage. He would kill the old man.

Cole thrashed and whirled, striking and lashing indiscriminately. He would not stop. He would not relent. He needed to feel bone and blood. His free hand and both feet cut and clouted everything they met, the munisica doing exactly what they were designed for; bringing ruin upon all things material. He was only dimly aware of his arm still trapped behind his back. The restraint was the only thing telling him that the old man was still alive, the only thing telling him to keep fighting.

The ground gave way beneath them as Cole's munisica passed through root, rock, and dirt as if swimming through water. Cole's vision darkened as they dug deeper into the ground. His arm was still somehow trapped. Chiron was there, clinging like a fluid magnet as he exploited Cole's every movement. Cole attempted to shift his pattern of slashing and carving, using the subterranean boulders as a means to scrape Chiron off him. He hammered his free limbs every which way, but he eventually ran out of boulders to push and patterns to weave. His imagination drove his munisica wild, but Chiron flowed along with them, unharmed and unyielding. Cole halted, seething.

They were beneath the ground, covered entirely in dirt and broken rock. Cole pushed his munisica blindly through the dark, hoping to find something for leverage. There was none to find. Chiron was still wrapped all around him, just waiting for him to move. Gripping the loose guts of Aeneria, Cole focused all of his strength and Rage into freeing his trapped arm. Crackling power hummed through the ground. Chiron had the mechanical advantage over his chicken-winged arm, but Cole's Rage had pushed beyond the limits of bone and muscle. His arm broke free.

There was another desperate tornado of claws and dirt as they dug deeper into Aeneria's crust. For the first time, Cole felt hot, wet flesh through his dragon claws. He didn't know where or how, but the old man had been wounded. Cole pulled and roared into the dirt, reveling in the violence. After a moment's struggling, however, he became disoriented once again. Before Cole knew it, his other arm as well as a leg were twisted uselessly behind his back.

"I give up," Cole huffed through a mouthful of mud.

Cole felt himself pulled by unseen forces. Chiron rose behind him, keeping a firm grip on Cole's ankle and wrist. When they emerged into open air, Cole dismissed his shroud and munisica. He may have lost, but at least he had victory over his Rage. Months ago he wouldn't have been able to accept the defeat. He would have kept fighting and digging until one of them eventually stopped breathing.

Chiron set him down gently on a patch of soft grass. Cole shook out his hair and glanced down the hole, which was twice as deep as he was tall. The area around the hole was covered with fresh dirt and clean-cut rock.

Cole winced at the sight of his Master's leg. There were five deep gouges torn in his shin, exposing muscle and a clearly broken bone. Blood ran in a steady dark ooze in between flaps of pale skin. Without a word, Cole made for his Master's leg, hands lit with lavender Passion. It took him a bit longer than he would have liked, but his recent lessons on anatomy proved invaluable. For the first time his Wisdom blended with Passion. Skin had different layers that needed accounting, muscle needed to be woven in certain patterns, bone must knit in a tunneled lattice to allow for marrow to flow. The finer points of the nervous and vascular systems still eluded him, but Cole prodded and coaxed everything back into its proper place. Once satisfied, he ceased the flow of Passion and looked up to his Master, who was thankfully smiling.

"How sporting of you," Chiron said, putting weight back onto the leg. "Good as new. *Better* than new, actually."

"Your muscle and bones are as dense as metal," Cole remarked. "How is that?"

"There are ways of combining our magics," Chiron said as he inspected his leg. "As you just combined Wisdom with Passion, Wisdom and Rage can be mated as well. We will progress to it eventually, if your patience will allow us to get there."

"I *knew* it!" Cole blurted. "I *knew* you were using magic!"

Chiron's winged eyebrows went up with mild indignation. "I did no such thing. Your Rage was the only magic I detected after you released your Wisdom-induced handicaps. Very clever by the way."

"You did all that without magic? That's impossible." Cole shook his head, unable to wrap his mind around the concepts. "I took down a decent-sized Colossus by myself."

"Of course I did," Chiron said, twisting Cole's arm in a gentle demonstration. "With the proper application of leverage, a weaker man can easily subdue a stronger one. You are one of the strongest and fastest combatants I have ever witnessed, and that's including the Elites of old. We might still be down there if I hadn't offered you my limb for two of yours. However, as strong as you are, you lack flexibility, technique, and most importantly, creativity. Having a touch of those qualities at my disposal, I exploited your absence of them. If I may assume your thick skin extends to your ego, we need to address your atrocious flexibility. Can you touch your toes from standing?"

Cole hid the shame that rushed to his cheeks. He didn't have to try it to know he couldn't. "No. I can't touch my toes."

"Fortunately that weakness is the easiest to remedy," Chiron said, walking around Cole and appraising him with a sharp eye. "Your muscles are too large. They affect your range of motion more than anything else. You will have to shrink them if you ever want to be more nimble than an ox."

Cole rubbed his arms absentmindedly. He didn't want to lose his muscle. Even without his Rage, his strength and physique had been earned through hard months of training and fighting for his life. He loathed to go back to the days of being the chubby kid who couldn't make first cut.

"Can't I just do some stretches?" Cole asked. "It took me a long time to get as strong as I am now. I don't want to give it all up."

"I said nothing about losing strength," Chiron said, finished his second loop around him. "What I'm referring to is called a condensing. The condensing will alter the anatomy of your muscle, bone, and all of your connective tissue. Your body is too thick in places, so you will make it denser. Without your Rage I am many times stronger than you, though I am much smaller because I have been through the process several times in my younger years."

"That explains why you're so damn heavy," Cole said with a laugh, resisting the urge to give Chiron a shove. "It felt like you were made of lead." A thought popped into Cole's mind. "Master, has Roth been through a condensing? He's massive, but I've seen how he moves in battle. He's definitely not lacking in flexibility or finesse. Looks more like he's dancing."

"Rothael is an anomaly," Chiron admitted. "He has been through a condensing every cycle of his life, but his body can't compress much more. How he has maintained flexibility and finesse is beyond my understanding of the process. I may have some talents with Wisdom, but when it comes to the dance of death, Rothael is wise beyond reason."

Cole remembered Roth dueling with Captain Seive, looking more like a ballroom dance than a battle to the death. He also recalled the unrestrained ferocity with which he'd disassembled a Colossus. If Roth thought condensing a good idea, then he should too. Shrinking his muscles didn't seem so unnerving a thing to him after giving up his ability to sleep. He could always train and grow himself bigger again.

"All right then, when will you show me this condensing?" Cole asked, feeling the tightness of his hamstrings and shoulders.

"Right after you fix the damage you did to this sicara tree. Your arbitrary thrashing cut several of the load-bearing roots on this side. It will develop a permanent limp if not remedied today." Chiron stepped to the edge of the hole, cocking his head. "That's quite a bit of work for a less than a minute's scrapping. I shudder to think what you'd be capable of with the proper technique."

• • • •

After his match with Chiron, Cole was allowed an hour a day for fighting so that his Rage wouldn't distract him from lessons. Chiron never sparred with him again. Instead the elder suggested Cole work with some of the other warriors still residing in The Sill, as it would expose him to different fighting styles. Cole never felt comfortable enough to use much of his Rage fighting with others, and as a result he lost every single bout. The other warriors had cycles of experience with the fighting arts. They exploited every one of Cole's glaring weaknesses just as Chiron had. He learned quite a bit however, and the condensing along with guided stretching from the other warriors remedied his flexibility.

It took Chiron a full day to teach Cole every step of the condensing, and another day for Cole to perform it. His Rage needed to be present but passive so his Wisdom could take control. Cole found that the green and red magic wouldn't mix readily, but with Chiron's guidance he got there in the end. When every muscle, tendon, and bone had been altered, Cole retreated to his room to assess the damage. He half-expected to look emaciated and skeletal, but to his relief he looked more like a lean runner. His strength remained undiminished and he could finally touch his toes, but he would still have to labor for Chiron's flexibility.

To Cole's relief his training took an aggressive pace ever since confronting Chiron. They still spent a good portion of their time in the library, meditating in meadows, and discussing the day-to-day activities of creatures such as spring-heeled mice. Now though, the monotony was broken up by practical magic.

Cole learned other aspects of Passion, many of which were useful in battle. Plants could be fed and coaxed into a riotous state, twisting with bone-breaking roots or biting with venom-filled needles. Whind was particularly adept in the art, which made sense to Cole as the gatekeeper always had seemed more plant than person.

Chiron also showed Cole how to listen with his Passion, allowing him to sense the living essence of other beings around him. Chiron would take his sight for days at a time, forcing Cole to navigate The Sill by Passion alone. It was terribly disorienting at first, but eventually Cole's bubble of awareness stretched from just arm's reach to over ten paces. After a few weeks he could even differentiate between the vital songs of plants and animals.

There were other aspects of Passion that Cole flat out refused to take part in. Chiron tried time and again to expose him to creative exercises, but Cole had neither the interest nor innate talent to make anything worth his time. In Cole's eyes, every second spent crafting a wonky poem or carving out a dreadful sculpture was another second he could use for battle training. The Arts District was captivating and never ceased to entertain him, but Cole never fancied himself a creator. He was perfectly happy with observing and enjoying other people's work.

Long weeks of lecture and observations had granted Cole greater control over his Wisdom, allowing him a broader range of flexibility and efficiency with the magic. After learning the majority of the common elements and how to find them, Cole started experimenting with alchemy and crafting solutions. Chiron confiscated his entire stock of ingredients after finding Cole unconscious in his apartment from a failed experiment. All alchemy experiments were closely supervised thereafter.

Apart from his other studies, Cole took zealous fervor with the flashier, more destructive spells. Despite Chiron's visible irritation, he took every opportunity to summon a gout of fire or a bolt of electricity. It seemed nearly every day Cole picked up a new piece of Wisdom. Some spells were silly and useless in his eyes, such as changing the color of a spoon or making ice hot. No matter the application, Chiron impressed the significance of expanding his catalogue of spells, as there was no telling when a piece of magic might save his life.

When Chiron deemed Cole was ready, they dabbled in the more costly applications of Wisdom. Chief among the weighty spells were the conjuration of material objects. It was the same magic that the others used to summon their emerald wings and telescopes. Creating something from nothing took constant, unwavering focus and an explicit understanding of the item. Cole immediately understood why Chiron had delayed these lessons. After weeks of practice, he could barely summon a passable replica of his old dagger, an object he knew better than any other. His main issue was that his focus was too fine, too specific. The blade of his crystal dagger would have all the right angles and hardness, but the hilt and handle would come out vague and mushy. Cole took his creative exercises in the Arts district a little more seriously from then on.

Another month flew by, taking Aeneria from the house of Wulfmont and into the house of Jindaere. Cole was so engrossed in a Wisdom lesson that he barely noticed the sunrise. It didn't bother him much however. There would be others for him to see.

He kept in touch with Eliza, talking with her most nights before she drifted to sleep. Cole never had too much to share, but Eliza would fill him in on how the others were doing and what was going on around Oberon City. The Celestial Council had stood firm on their rulings, confining the others to the temple and stacking an ever-growing list of violations against Cole and Chiron. Envoys had been sent across Aeneria's Light Side, carrying open invitations for peace treaties and trade agreements. To Eliza's knowledge, none of the envoys were heard from after they crossed over. Cole asked every day, but Eliza hadn't seen or heard any trace of Goran, even after taking several covert trips out into the mountains. Cole rested on his faith in Goran's toughness and ferocity to protect him.

Though Cole eventually stopped asking about her, Eliza's reports on the others would reveal hints on Lileth. Through the fraternal bond it was impossible to hide his elation or dread when conversation drifted towards her, though Eliza was tactful enough to pretend not to notice. Cole knew that his feelings towards Lileth were not about to change anytime soon, but he had grown accustomed to the pain of losing her. It was as if his heart's skin had thickened, or Lileth's knife had dulled. There was always a chance that when next they met she would see him in a different light. That chance, however slight, gave him hope. With that hope rooted deep in his heart, Cole resolved to master all of Chiron's lessons so that he would become the most desirable Aenerian she'd ever laid eyes upon.

CHAPTER 19

SHADOW TIDE

"Where. Have. You. Been." Kreed's voice was deadly quiet, as if teetering between restraint and rampage.

Habbad strolled into Kreed's office, admiring the paintings on the walls. Half of the artwork depicted scenes of detailed torture, while other works displayed captivating landscapes. It was certainly better than he could do, even with his newly acquired skills with the brush. Habbad recognized the style and stroke patterns, but he wondered where the artist had sourced the acrylics. He took his time inspecting a few others, but a sudden increase in Kreed's disquiet told him that he'd better humor the man before blood was wasted.

"Aren't you happy to see me?" Habbad asked, unable to hide his pleasure. He was now the same height as Kreed. "Notice anything different?"

"You're a hair away from having your skin removed from the toes up. Answer my question." Kreed's tone went even lower as intent flashed in his eyes. His haggard glare cut into Habbad like a kinked blade dragged over silk.

"I've been keeping busy," Habbad replied, glancing down at Kreed's desk. He ran his fingertips over the blanket of letters and maps. "It looks as if you've been busy yourself. How's Talin? Or should I call him *Sorronis?*"

Kreed snapped at last. He wheeled around the desk. The snow-white arm of his suit rippled through the air as a letter opener gleamed in his fist. His hand came to a slapping halt as Habbad's fingers clamped around Kreed's wrist.

"Come now, Father Kreed," Habbad warned. "We mustn't put action before reason. You ought to hear me out before burying that piece of metal in my ear. Aren't you the least bit curious to learn what I've been doing for Grotton over the last two months?" Habbad gave Kreed's wrist a satisfying squeeze, marveling at his new strength over his old nightmare.

Kreed wrenched his hand free, rubbing it as he took a seat in his high-backed chair. His face sagged with a weariness that made him look old for the first time in Habbad's memory. "There's more to Grotton's magic than acquiring a few Domina, but you've piqued my interest. What silly animal did you lie to for the height?"

"A man down in the Wind District found himself wanting for power. I gave it to him, for a price. Florien took offense to our contract, but it's not like he lost his friend. He just works for *me* now." Habbad stretched himself as tall as he could, admiring the view. He'd never looked down at Kreed before.

Kreed's mouth fell open. "You took an Aenerian for Domina?"

"Obviously," Habbad said, waving his hands over his Aenerian-sized body.

"Habbad…" Kreed drifted off, his eyes scanning the walls as if a fitting response were scribbled on one of his paintings. "Habbad my sweet, that's impossible. Such a thing has never been done, yet here you are!" He jumped from his chair, lunging at Habbad once more, only this time with a joyful embrace. His eyes swam with happy tears as he gripped the arms of Habbad's crimson suit. "You incredible, jewel of a boy! At first I didn't think you had the makings for Harbinger, but here you are delving into uncharted pools of Grotton's magic. How, how did you do it?"

Habbad waited for Kreed to loosen his grip and grant him some personal space. "It wasn't easy. I had to find a man broken by life and show him that Grotton's gifts were his only salvation. Now he's happy, inside me. I helped his revenge bear fruit, and granted him a life of significance." Habbad placed a solemn hand over his chest, feeling where Dirken resided. "Once I learned how to bend the will of one, the others folded easily enough. Everyone has a price, even you."

"Others?" Kreed asked, worry tugging at his smile. "How many?"

"I know you have a duty to protect your people, but trust me when I say they all gave themselves freely. I didn't take a single one that didn't want it."

"How many?" Kreed repeated.

Habbad ran his tongue over the inside of his lip as he skimmed through his catalogue of memories from the last two months. "I don't know, I lost track after ten. Twenty? Perhaps thirty or forty? What does it matter?"

"It matters to *me*. They were *my people*. You had no right." Kreed wrung venom into every word. His hands dripped with shimmering black Fear as they gripped the edge of his desk.

Habbad felt Decreath rising from the depths of Kreed's essence. Invisible clouds of Fear permeated the office, dimming and freezing his limbs as a sound not of this world howled from the shadows. Habbad may have amassed a measure of power through his host of Aenerian Domina, but he was still no match for one of The Three. Not until he proved himself a worthy Harbinger. Grotton had yet to bless him with Hunger's true grace.

His Fear-chilled veins creaking with every step, Habbad rushed over to Kreed, placing a hand flat on the Harbinger's chest. "They are not gone, Father Kreed. They are within me, willingly and gratefully serving The Three with every pulse of their souls. I am but a tool, a messenger to bring about the second coming of our lords. I have already done much to further their aims. Even as we speak, my webs weave themselves across the Dark Side. Oberon City will soon feel the ripple of my influence."

Habbad's words seemed to go unheard. Kreed's eyes filled with infinite blackness as his broken grin released an endless breath, his head rolling back slightly. He wrapped a ginger hand around Habbad's, pouring the crippling Fear into him.

Habbad knew he was at Decreath's mercy. With all his Domina aiding him, he prayed to the god of terror, promising every favor within his power. The Fear pulled him deeper, tearing memories with feral indulgence from every mind within Habbad's control. Though it was excruciating, he fed the black god, wading his naked mind through fields of razor grass in hopes of appeasing him. Before he knew what was happening, Habbad fell from himself, from the present. He was back in his stone prison, watching Lexy burn at the base of the tower. Not even Kreed had brought him here, as the awesome Fear of that moment had all but killed everything he was. His sanity slipped on the edge of a knife. Decreath gripped him just a little tighter before finally fading away.

Habbad gasped, sweaty and somehow on the floor. He rose back to his feet, finding Kreed's eyes watching him with condescending disdain.

"Cocky little shit, aren't you?" Kreed said, throwing a handkerchief to Habbad. "Your every breath is a gift from Decreath. Don't you ever forget that, or I'll shove you back in that stone tub and you'll watch sweet Lexy burn ever more. Now clean yourself up and convince me why I shouldn't reunite you with your sister."

Habbad wiped the sweat from his face and flattened out the front of his coat. Shaking the residual Fear from his bones, he took a steadying breath. "Over the last two months I built a network of sorts. With Grotton's arts I garnered a wealth of knowledge with every Domina in my employ. With this knowledge came an understanding of whole industries, economies, political ties, all given willingly from Hungry minds. Most important of all were the secrets. Old, forgotten secrets, which I then used for our advantage. There were little things too, such as your head of transportation cheating on her husband. But then there were other secrets so juicy that they may as well have been keys to the city."

Kreed raised an eyebrow. "And what might one of these juicy secrets be? I find it hard to believe that anything significant could have slipped past my own informants. My priests are most adept with trading Fear for information."

"But who is keeping your priests in check?" Habbad asked, a measure of confidence returning to him. "One of Decreath's own, a priest by the name of Jahdiic has been siphoning your stock of Underkin for the past three cycles. It seems the man had a change of heart after falling in love with a female Underkin. If Jahdiic had not betrayed you, there would have been enough livestock for another two towers in this last Devotion. The Colossi that attacked Morthain would likely have been strong enough to capture the human."

A shadow fell over Kreed's face. For a moment Habbad Feared another lashing from Decreath. "Jahdiic will pay with his sanity, and then his life. Perhaps I'll hold another Devotion, just for him. His own children will contribute to the next Colossus."

Habbad slapped a hand down on Kreed's desk. "Don't. Fear of your priests wasn't enough to keep him from betraying you, but his Fear of reprisal is a boon to us now. The Underkin he spirited away have flourished over the cycles. Their numbers are staggering, the vast majority of which lie within the city of Dorada. Recently Jahdiic has been most cooperative in harvesting and moving the stock for us, and thanks to your head of transportation the first shipment will arrive within a week. We can sustainably draw dozens of Underkin every two weeks, and within a cycle the population will be equal to the pre-Devotion levels. Your house could do with a proper cleaning, and you know the gardens have been running wild."

As Habbad made his case, Kreed's scowl lifted to his old, manic grin. "Habbad you wonderful, *wonderful* boy! No, *wonderful man!*" Tears welled once more as Kreed seized Habbad and hugged him close. "Do you really mean it? We'll have all our Underkin back within a mere cycle?"

Habbad raised his chin. "Judge me by my results, not my words."

"I'm so sorry my boy. It seems I mistook your confidence for arrogance." Kreed released Habbad, appraising him with newfound respect. "So what does this make you now, a secret-slinger? A bribery-broker?"

Habbad shrugged. "I prefer Underking. Or at least that's what citizens have taken to calling me. I have yet to reveal my identity in a transaction, so I've retained my anonymity while weaving my networks."

"I wonder, how far does that web reach? Did I lose my mind for a moment or did you say that you had influence in Oberon City?" Kreed's voice resonated with genuine Hunger. Habbad held back Grotton's temptations to capitalize on the opportunity.

"I have hands in every city on the Light Side, and the majority of the Dark. By your grace I won't reveal how, but I have tugged a few strings within the walls of Oberon Temple itself." Habbad finished, savoring the effect his words had over the Aenerian.

Kreed hung off every word. It became increasingly more difficult for Habbad to refrain from drawing out his Hunger.

"Trust must be earned, my sweet," Kreed admonished as he waggled a finger. "But, I'd say you've earned a sliver of mine. You've accomplished so much off the leash, it would be a shame if I tied you up now. I want to see you *fly*. There's no limit to the value of a well-guarded secret, so you may keep yours for now."

"Thank you, Father Kreed. Though you may not be privy to the minutia of my operations, know that the information market is nestled safely under the wings of The Three. That being said, I have no intention of leaving you entirely starved."

"Oh?" Kreed's eyes flashed with the Hunger again.

Habbad picked up a heavy pen from the desk, twirling it in the light. "As I said before, everyone has their price. No one, not even the Celestial Council is immune to that fact."

Air rushed through Kreed's teeth, visibly filling him with questions. However, he shut his eyes and released them with a long hiss. "You sure know how to wet a whistle, Habbad. I yearn for every little detail, but heavens do I love surprises. The Celestial Council fell first to Grotton you know. It's most fitting they taste his honeyed-words once more. Words crafted from the lips of the Underking no less." Kreed shut his eyes and moaned, "Momentous things are on the horizon. I can feel it in my marrow."

"I've heard tell of a few of these momentous tidings." Habbad laid a heavy gaze upon Kreed. "You plan to move on Oberon City. When?"

Kreed shook his head, smiling. "Now now Habbad, secrets lose their value if bandied about like candy. I have my own little information economy to maintain."

Habbad waited for Kreed to finish giggling. "That's well and good, Father Kreed, but I can do more with the information than you can. I could find out on my own, though I'd rather not taint certain knowledge pools. So please, indulge me."

Kreed sighed, "Oh you're probably right. Depending on reports from Morthain, we could be ready to move within a week."

"Morthain has fallen. The Colossi razed the city yesterday," Habbad said.

"But of course you would find out before me!" Kreed whipped his arm out, sending the letter opener whirring through the air. It buried itself in the wall with a twang. "I'm only the fucking chief of every department-head in Costas. How on Oberon's backside am I supposed to bring about a revolution if I'm not kept up-to-date? Is there anything else I should know about?"

"As a matter of fact, yes. The reason for my visit was to bring you a gift. You'll have to follow me outside to meet them, however. Your guards wouldn't let them in the house." Habbad motioned for the door, beckoning Kreed. "Come, take a break from your labors and see the fruits of mine."

Kreed massaged his forehead in little circles. With a groan, he stood to his feet, clapping his hands together. "Show me what you've wrought. I could use the fresh air and sunlight."

"After me then," Habbad gave a curt nod before popping out of the office.

Kreed's shoes clacked along with Habbad's as the Underking led the Harbinger to the stairs leading to the roof.

"The cabana huh?" Kreed asked, keeping close behind. "There's a trick at every turn with you, my friend. What manner of gift might this be?"

"One that will change how this game is played," Habbad replied, quickening his pace. "I'll let them introduce themselves. They are eager to meet you and I doubt my description would do them justice."

Kreed giggled, clapping his hands together rapidly. He urged Habbad faster, nudging them into a run. They skipped up the final flight and popped through the door. The light from Jindaere's golden sun splashed across their faces.

A vine-covered pergola shaded half the rooftop cabana, while a marble patio and winding pool took the full strength of the seasonal sunlight. They each cast their own spells to deaden the harsh light, rubbing the magic into their eyes. Kreed walked up to the bar, leaning his elbows on the dark oak surface.

"Kevan! Where the hell are you?" Kreed leaned over the bar, screaming down the hall to the staff room. "Kevan! I need a drink!" Hissing, he turned back to Habbad. "That shipment of Underkin can't come soon enough. Not once did any of those little bastards abandon their post, or show up less than half an hour early for their shift.

For what I'm paying Kevan he should live up here for Decreath's sake. I'm too damn soft on the Aenerians. Perhaps I should start placing the derelicts on probation..."

"I sent Kevan and your other staff away for the hour," Habbad said, hopping over the bar with the agility of a mirak. He rummaged through shelves high and low, collecting various ingredients required for Kreed's favorite drink. In seconds he whipped up a pair of fizzing cocktails in copper mugs. "It wouldn't be appropriate for them to witness this. Here." He slid Kreed the mug.

Kreed took a noisy sip. "This cocktail is superb. Did you take a bartender for Domina? No, never mind, I don't want to know. So where is this gift then?"

Habbad inclined his head towards a shaded corner of the patio, which looked entirely too dark in the bright sunlight. The shadow bent into three looming figures, their outlines hazy and intangible. As they stepped into the light the shadows melted from them, revealing three skinny figures that looked like walking skeletons. Their dark robes were wispy and frayed, as though made from storm clouds. The material seemed to consume the surrounding light with each flowing strand, shrouding their forms as if coated with liquid shadow.

The tallest approached Kreed and peeled back a hooded shawl, revealing a face that appeared to have been semi-digested in the belly of a nightmare. Its nose, lips, and ears looked as if they had been chewed off by something with dull teeth. The features it did have were sexless and pale, like a skull bleached by starlight. If not for a slight bust and feminine gait, there would have been little differentiating the thing from an emaciated corpse. It pulled its lipless smile into a wild, demon's grin, showing off a cluster of thin, crowded teeth that looked more like a bundle of dirty fingers.

The thing inclined its head, staring down at Kreed through a translucent ash-grey bandana. A sultry female voice somehow glided out of her misshapen mouth: "Greetings, Harbinger."

Habbad cleared his throat. "Father Kreed, may I introduce-"

"The Cold Crows require no introduction in my house," Kreed interrupted. His eyes were wide and apprehensive, though his mouth curled in disdain. "What brings you here, shadow-witch?"

The Crow's neck twitched as she clicked her cluster of teeth. Her half-lips wormed together in a scowl. "We come to serve the Unholy Trinity."

Kreed leaned back as her breath hit him. "I'm aware of that. I'm also aware of how easily your loyalty sways with your vagaries. Decreath has no use for mercenaries who play turncoat when tempted with a few sweet promises."

The Crow pulled her cheeks back into a grin. She slid around Kreed, her twitching fingers flowing like water over his shoulders. Kreed's eyes closed as she worked her hands gingerly over his shoulders and chest. The Crow brought her mouth to his ear: "We serve *all* of The Trinity, Harbinger. Even you. We may be hired blades, but we only take contract with the blessing of the gods. We may further the lusts of a god other than your own, but you mustn't be greedy, Harbinger, that is Grotton's treat. Keep in mind when Grotton and Sorronis gain, Decreath *swells*." Her hands wandered down Kreed's stomach and grasped at his crotch.

Kreed's face snapped to stone as he clapped his hands over the Crow's, whipping her around and throwing her from him. "Your arts hold no power over Decreath, witch. Make your case to the Dread Father or begone."

Black smoke leaked from the corners of Kreed's mouth. Habbad took a step back before the Fear could touch him.

The Crow twisted around, clutching her wrist with a wicked grin as she fell into her siblings. The other Crows stiffened as the shadows swirled around them like coiling snakes. She assuaged her sisters with a tender stroke before addressing Kreed again.

"As we said, we come to serve the Unholy Trinity. At the moment they are scattered and weak. As powerful as you are, *Harbinger*," she offered the appellation with a derisive curtsy, "You remain weakened while Grotton's Harbinger remains uncrowned. You are unable to fulfil the entirety of your duties."

Recognition flashed almost imperceptibly across Kreed's face. The falter was not lost on The Crow.

"Yes Harbinger, we know your truth and your shame. We bathe in the Shadow Tide. We know of your power and your weakness.

We've been watching you, Kreed. We swim in the wake of your dreams. We watched you fight alongside the Unbound during the siege of Oberon Temple. We wrapped you in Hope, watched you clutch it like a blanket. With the blessing of Sorronis, we buried you in your own Despair, then filled you with the Hatred you needed. We tempted you with Grotton's promises, and by Decreath's graces we infected your mind. You wield Fear like your favored blade, but it is the very thing that will be your undoing. You Fear those whom you betrayed so long ago. You Fear the Unbound."

More black smoke poured from Kreed's mouth, filling the rooftop with acrid Fear. Habbad wrapped himself in the minds of his Domina, throwing their sanity into the fray while protecting his own.

Kreed threw his head back and screamed like a child, wrapping his arms around himself as he released an endless breath. The otherworldly sound rose from the depths of his body, rising to a tight plateau before he cut it short. Steadying himself, he faced the Crows with murder in his blackened eyes. Decreath's influence faded as he resumed control of his body.

"I mastered my Fear!" Kreed spat. "Decreath crowned me Harbinger! His approval is all that I need."

The Crow bowed her head in acknowledgement. "The Dread Father's trust is well-placed, but as you know, no mortal is perfect. You have your flaws, though you have fulfilled the duties of Harbinger to the letter. Not one soul in this world is more deserving of Decreath's graces. You even gifted Sorronis a Harbinger, a feat beyond what is expected of you. And with your guidance, Grotton is sure to coronate your young associate here." The Crow stilled her twitching fingers and pointed them at Habbad.

Habbad swallowed, drawing upon the bravery of his more cavalier Domina to maintain a stoic demeanor. He forced his eyes into the Crow's sheer bandana. Judging by the size and sheen of the orbs behind the cloth, her eyelids had been removed in the same manner as the rest of her features. He gave her a nod, breathing through his pursed lips so that he wouldn't have to smell her breath.

Kreed coughed, hacking a black mass of phlegm onto the marble tiles, which began to fizzle and smoke. He shot Habbad a disdainful look before addressing the Crows again: "That settles the matter I think. As you just admitted I've been making out fine on my own, and I certainly don't need your lot creeping over my shoulder. The Three will have their second coming and I will be the conductor of the black orchestra. I will personally see to it that the remaining Unbound and their offspring are dealt with."

The Crow's lips stretched over grey gums as she clicked her teeth. Her oily voice spoke with unwavering certainty. "You will fail."

Habbad leaped over the bar, standing next to the crow and braving her breath. "Listen to her, Father Kreed. Listen to *me*. My ears stretch to every corner of this world. The Unbound learned too much from the last war. They've adapted. There are rumors of the human as well. Wild rumors that I'm reluctant to believe, but they grow more valid by the day." He took a step closer to Kreed, locking eyes with him. "A portion of Varka lives within him."

Air hissed into clenched teeth as Kreed ran his fingers through his hair. He swore, then spoke in a slow, defeated whisper. "I Feared as much. Decreath felt Varka's presence in the little bastard during the Devotion. We tried, but we hadn't the power to snuff his Rage. There is no need to persuade me further. This news confirms my own suspicions." Kreed shook himself and took a long breath. "What do you propose then?"

A sigh fluttered from The Crow's chattering teeth. "The Unholy Trinity are scattered and weak. They must be reunited. We know the ones who hinder their revolution: Alvani, the Flame of Passion; Roth the Mountain of Rage; Chiron, the Light of Wisdom. Together they form the antiforce to The Three. All is not lost, however, for we see all from the eddies of the Shadow Tide."

"Explain," Kreed said, taking a step closer.

The Crow brought a skeletal hand to her chest with a little bow. "We are but artists. Ripe souls are our canvas, our blades are the brush, the snuffing of souls is the art. We desire not for money or power. Those who do are desperate, lacking a proper muse. They *need* the job. As true artists, we possess ardor for the kill, we make it beautiful, we make it our own. We pour ourselves into the craft, which gives it value. You will pay for our art. The Unbound are nothing more than a canvas, which we will gladly paint, for a price."

Kreed swiped his drink from the bar and downed it in a long draught. A measure of calm returned to him. "Name your price."

The three Crows clicked and stirred in unison, excitement building as their shadows deepened around them. The Crow looked up with her lipless grin and veiled eyes. "We demand Varka, and the human, Cole."

CHAPTER 20

ENTER EVIL

Cole's bare feet padded over a rooftop slick with dew. He leaped, clearing the street below without the aid of magic. He gazed upon Oberon one last time before crossing the roof and dropping to a paved alley on the other side. Though the drop was a little over three stories, Cole resisted the urge to slow his fall with Wisdom. Brimhallow Village appeared vacant, but there was no telling what might be hiding nearby. Domina had sharp ears, and Corpulants could smell Wisdom from a block away. Cole was entirely alone on his first mission. The slightest miscalculation would leave him to deal with the consequences without his giant magic-wielding friends. He had to be his own hero today.

Cole landed roughly, his legs buckling as he sprawled painfully over the stone pavers. The condensing prevented his bones from snapping and tendons from tearing, but the impact left him bruised with bloody palms. He slumped up into a crouched position, shuffling behind a stack of wooden boxes, where he could wait and see if anything had heard him. After five minutes there was no sound besides the chattering of exploring rodentia. Guessing he was safe, he stalked away from his hiding spot and made for the side streets.

A week prior, Earth's Wisdom Walker, Larkin, had contacted Chiron with an urgent message. Larkin had curried favors with the rest of the Celestial Council, awarding Cole a sanctioned mission. The mission was to investigate the village of Brimhallow, which recently had gone dark on all communications. Brimhallow was a village comprised of Passion-followers, and had reported harassments from Domina. Though the mission was beyond the scale of a single student, the Council saw it a fitting task for one who claimed to be Varka's second coming. Larkin insisted that Cole take the mission without aid, as its success would go a long way to mitigating his offenses. Chiron hadn't pressured him to accept the mission, though nor had he opposed it. He'd left the decision entirely up to Cole. Cole thought on it for a few days, eventually concluding that he lacked the training for such a task. However, when Chiron had left for a mission of his own, Cole's Rage had urged him towards the challenge.

Cole spent an entire day circling and observing Brimhallow from the surrounding treetops, though after only an hour he had a good measure of the fate of the village. Now that his feet kicked up flakes of dried blood, there was no doubt. Brimhallow had been razed.

Cole darted through the alley, listening and watching without the aid of magic. It was difficult to discriminate between an echo of a footfall and the dripping of a gutter, or the flapping of a clothes line and evil laughter. Something in the atmosphere felt wrong. Cole slowed to a quiet halt. He shut his eyes and chanced his Passion, reaching out into the buildings around him. There was no living thing larger than a cat within two blocks. Cole opened his eyes and drove deeper into the village.

As he explored, he peeked through windows both low and high, but there were no bodies to be found. Signs of death and struggle were painted over every surface, however. Murky brown stains soiled beds and walls, while hunks of shiny flesh black with rot clung to the furniture and stairs. Cole imagined the assault must have been so swift that the residents hadn't even had time to get up from dinner. Dropping from a second-story window, Cole noticed deep gouges on the partially-torn doorframe below. He ran his fingers through the rough cuts, unable to touch the bottom. Nothing short of a Domina or munisica could make claw marks like that. Cole kept his eyes wide and threw a rag over his mouth. The stench of death thickened as he plodded on.

Cole was not entirely walking through the unknown. Chiron had taught him the general strategies The Three used for places like Brimhallow. Their forces moved from town to town like a virus comprised of a small, yet dynamic force. As this had been a town full of Passion followers, priests of Sorronis likely had set a cloud of

Despair over the village, weakening the civilians with crushing depression and murky lethargy. Thus weakened, the victims would make easy prey for the Domina, who would normally be susceptible to the empathetic facets of Passion and lose their thralls. Brimhallow was not a small town, but Cole judged that perhaps two or three priests could have taken it with the aid of no more than a dozen Domina. With grim admiration Cole acknowledged the efficiency of The Three. The strategy made sense to Cole, but he kept his mind open to all possibilities. For all he knew this was all an elaborate trap set by some unnamed horror he had yet to encounter.

Cole wandered deeper into Brimhallow, chancing the main roads here and there. He was careful to maintain part of his mind within the stone confines of his center, where he could observe the rest of himself objectively. Still, he wasn't entirely sure whether the Fear that tickled him was born of his own dread or seeping from an external source. He wished he'd had more training, or at least another person with him. Eliza's bond had to be suppressed to an insubstantial hair of thought to avoid rousing the attentions of Sorronis's Priests.

As he crept by the shattered remains of several homes, Chiron's lessons coincided with his observations with increasing solidarity. There were no bodies to find because it was custom for the priests to have them consolidated in a larder and prepared for harvesting. The priests of Sorronis would take parts to repair their Colossi, while Decreath's priests would feast on their Fear-ripened souls. Whatever was left afterwards would be quartered out by Grotton's priests and fed to the Domina. The system left no part of the victims to waste. Cole went over the facts with a steely pragmatism that shed light on the unknown, easing his Fear. With quiet confidence, he poked his head around the final corner to where his reconnaissance told him the temple would be.

Cole swore, his curse echoing throughout the temple square. The temple, once a place for worshiping love and life, was now a totem of desecration, a profound insult to innocence. Covering every inch of the two-story building were the skins of the Brimhallow residents.

The Three's minions hadn't spared child or elder from the grisly quilt. While flies and birds picked at remains throughout the rest of the town, not a single creature fed upon the temple's bloody coat. The entire area was devoid of any life or sound. It was as if the bloody light spilling from the temple windows poisoned the very air, mixing with the sweet tang of rot.

Cole fell against the wall of a house, slumping down and panting as he clutched his knees. This was real. This was not training. This was beyond life and death. He had stumbled upon a demon's nest. Should he enter the temple no one would ever know what happened to him. Sickly heat flashed up his face, soaking his forehead with cold sweat. Fear had him now.

From his center, Cole drew upon a thin stream of his vast ocean of Rage, careful not to overdo it. His sprinting heart didn't slow, but its cadence changed from fluttering panic to hammering fury. The Fear sizzled and puffed into irrelevance.

Taking a steady breath, he rose to his feet and strode out into the open street. He had to go in. He had to kill the ones responsible. If he left now the monsters inside would spread like a blight, stronger and hungrier for the next town. If Cole walked away now then the skins of every man, woman, and child would be on his head.

The horrible smell hit him harder with every step as he approached the main door. A childhood memory of finding bad ham in the fridge came to him. These people were nothing more than meat to The Three. Cole's toes clacked over the crusted steps as his munisica spread over his hands and feet. From the quiet of his center he could feel the Fear pouring into him, threatening to choke and freeze him. The dark magic permeated from the temple itself. He loosened the leash on his Rage, just enough to burn the Fear away faster than it could blossom. Holding his breath, Cole pushed aside a gently billowing drape of Aenerian hair and passed through the threshold, entering the demon's nest.

There was an empty foyer cast in the same bloody light that seeped from the windows. The light had no source and cast no shadows, giving the impression that the hall was submerged in wine. The silence from the exterior had carried inside, making Cole's burning heart the loudest thing in earshot. Scattered about in messy heaps were broken statues and torn paintings, as if the priests had wanted to make sure no aspect of Passion would ever be found.

Unsure of where to start, Cole decided to treat the temple like a maze. Keeping a mental hand on the right wall, he followed it as he slinked to the first room, creaking open the door.

Inside the chamber was a hospital bed resting upon a framework of bent brass and broken gratia stones. Cole crouched and snatched a shard of gratia from the floor, unable to guess its color in the red light. He threw the piece onto the bed, where it plopped on the remains of the ripped cushions. His heart hammered on.

The next room was near the end of the hall. He passed over every door on his left, keeping his mind's hand on the right wall. The shadowless light began to wear on him, diminishing his sense of depth as he crept deeper. A whisper tickled his ear.

Cole snapped his head about, searching for the source. He heard it again, unsure if he was imagining it or not. Shaking between Fear and Rage, he pulled more of himself into his center.

The next few rooms were similar to the first, each with hospital beds and gratia stones. It was a shame to see such waste of a facility that could have helped so many people. The desecrators had opened every single drawer and cabinet, mangling everything from intricate medical tools to children's toys. The minions of The Three had taken meticulous care to ensure that the temple would never be used for Passion again.

After clearing the first floor, Cole made for the second. He planted a clawed foot on the landing, stopping when he heard a sickening wail beneath the floorboards. It was the cry of someone tortured beyond all reason, someone who had long earned the solace of death.

Swallowing, Cole turned from the second floor landing and found a heavy wooden door set into the floor. The area around the door was clear of debris and muck, looking as if it had only just been closed. Cole bent and wove a clawed finger through the iron latch, jumping as another scream cut the blood-soaked air. The door opened smoothly and silently, revealing a spiral staircase devoid of light. Whispers crept up from the deep black, warning yet tantalizing.

Without the shadowless red light, Cole relied upon his Rage-sharpened ears to guide him down the steps. The air was dank and stagnant, somehow worse than the smells above. Cole wandered blindly, hoping there was more than one exit from the lower levels.

As he continued blindly underground, sounds of scuffling and slapping skin wound their way up to him, replacing the monotony of his heart's tattoo. The noises grew louder, their sources multiplying as if they were something vast and many. Cole stopped at the corner of the very bottom. Whatever things made the noises were right on the other side of the pitch blackness. He needed his magic, Corpulants or not.

His entire body vibrating, Cole jumped from the bottom landing, casting an orb of pure white light above his head as he charged forward.

He stopped abruptly, nearly running himself face-first into a wall made from hundreds of charred, groping arms. The limbs flailed, desperate and eager for anything that might come within reach. The ones nearest Cole stuck straight out, twitching and stretching for him. Cole took a step back as the cold hand of Fear tickled his guts.

There was an echoing rumble from Cole's left. He crouched, baring his claws as the body of a woman fell from a rusty chute, flopping lifelessly at the base of the wall. Waiting hands found her face and hair, pulling at her with the tenderness of a mother holding a newborn. The arms out of reach of the body slapped and clawed at the stone floor, tearing fingernails and flesh from their tips. Just as quickly as she came, the woman's body disappeared through the bundle of limbs.

Cole knew what he had to do. He called to his Wisdom, casting an invisible barrier around his skin branded with a simple rule: Nothing shall touch him. Tugging his floating star along, he inched himself into the wall. Maintaining his barrier, he allowed the arms to pull him in. Thankfully, he didn't feel a thing, though he could hear the drumming of hundreds of fingers on his magical shield. He held his breath as he passed through.

A claw ripped through the air, bouncing off Cole's head and shattering his barrier. The broken spell jarred his mind as his eyes blurred. He ducked instinctively as a follow-up blow whooshed above him. Guarding his face, Cole thrust his floating star into the face of the Domina. The creature howled and stumbled backwards. Cole followed it with a bladed kick, cleaving its furry kneecap open. The Domina dropped, exposing the back of its broad neck. Blinking the tears from his eyes, Cole jumped on the Domina's back, landing blow after blow to the top of its spine until the beast stopped moving.

Wheeling around, Cole flexed his starlight brighter. He was in a circular room with a single hall branching off opposite the wall of arms. Grunts and clanging weapons echoed, rushing louder and closer. Dashing to the side of the threshold, Cole pressed himself flat against the cool stone wall. He left his starlight floating above the prone Domina. A few breaths later, a dozen more of the beasts rushed into the room, barking their garbled language as they brandished wicked blades and axes.

The Domina ran past Cole and approached their fallen comrade, hesitant and confused. Cole wove his Wisdom and raised the woman's body from the ground, making it look as if she stood on her own accord. One of the Domina bellowed in alarm, jabbing a clubbed fist at the woman, who now stumbled towards them. Cole sneaked around the distracted Domina, careful not to touch the wall of arms. There was a scuffle of cloven feet and hacking weapons as the Domina attacked the woman.

Quick and light, Cole hopped onto the wire-haired back of a Domina, digging his bladed feet into its hips. Clamping his fingers into a blade, he drove his munisica into the base of the beast's skull. Before its body flopped to the ground, he leapt to the next one, dispatching it just as quickly. Masked by the commotion at the front of the group, Cole felled three more before the remaining Domina took notice.

Releasing his spells on the woman's body, Cole dimmed his starlight to an almost invisible granule, simultaneously casting another spell to dilate his own pupils. The remaining Domina gnashed their teeth and weapons blindly. One drifted too close to the wall of hands, bleating madly as it tried to free itself. Tip-toeing through the chaos, Cole snatched up a thin sword and stabbed it into an eye, an ear, a neck. The blind Domina fell in heaps, leaving only the one still fighting against the choking arms.

Cole approached the final Domina, restraining his bloodlust and focusing instead on the stone room within himself. Determined not to rely solely on Rage, he attempted to infuse the struggling creature with empathetic Passion so that he might release its thralls. The smell of releasing bowels and gore filled Cole's nostrils, stunning him. The scene was simply too horrific, too inhumane for him to invoke Passion upon. With a few sharp jabs to its chest Cole silenced the squealing beast, watching with disgust as the wall of arms proceeded to yank and twist it apart.

Cole was sure the commotion had grabbed the attention of everything in the temple. He dismissed his starlight and donned a few spells Chiron had taught him. If there were Corpulants nearby he would have his Rage at the ready.

After a few minutes working, Cole drained roughly half his focus into the enchantments. His body was light, though his munisica were heavier and thus deadlier. His senses were sharpened, tuned to specific sounds and smells while masking white noise. He stomped a heavy munisica on the stone floor, chipping and sparking pieces off without making a sound. Every few seconds a blast of Passion pulsed from him, detecting any living thing within ten paces. Finally, he placed within his throat a filter, which would hopefully block any noxious Fear gases. The spells took a constant effort of will, but Cole had spent sleepless weeks with Chiron practicing and perfecting the juggling act.

Cole left the room and his fallen enemies, plunging deeper below the temple to a hall filled with ghostly blue light. His self-generated Fear was quickly replaced with a sense of apprehension and confidence. The fact that he'd just killed over a dozen Domina on his own bolstered his resolve. Surely there couldn't be anything more dangerous than that.

The hall wound deeper in a wide spiral. Azure flames rippled in sconces set into walls covered in a sheen that mirrored the cold sweat on Cole's forehead. Every so often he would tap a munisica on a step, checking to make sure he was still muffled. He considered casting another spell to shield his skin as he had when passing through the wall, but he was already nursing a light buzz from his current efforts. Tapping further into Rage would be ideal, as the shroud would cover him inside and out, but he didn't want to make himself easy prey for a priest of Grotton. He needed balance.

Rooms sprouted from the sides of the spiraling hall. His Passion detected no living things within, but he checked them anyway. Each room was a small library, or they had been at one point. Books lay split and burned throughout or chopped up into heaps. From the covers that still had words on them, it appeared they were a collection of healing spells, songs, artwork, recipes. The subjects reminded Cole of the Arts District.

The stairs leveled out and widened to a wooden archway curtained with strings of glassy beads. Through the strands, Cole saw figures striding about a large chamber. There was a lack of a sense of urgency in their movements, hinting that they might not have heard the commotion upstairs. Or perhaps, they assumed the Domina were still indulging in whatever had wandered in. Just as Cole had waited and watched Brimhallow from the outskirts, he crouched behind the curtain listening to what the voices within might reveal.

There were three people within the chamber. One was female, her sandpaper voice humming a sort of lullaby. Her hunched figure worked over a statue set upon a dais in a far corner. The other two circled around, busy with whatever was on the tables at the edge of the room. Large objects hung from the ceiling, dozens of them all twirling slowly while rattling with twitches. Cole inched closer until his nose kissed the glassy beads, his eyes squinting through the gaps. The hanging things were bodies. He was at the larder.

"What's taking your Domina?" said a man in a strained voice. He was tall and freakishly skinny, his shoulders and elbows poking through his robes like tent poles. "I can't shell all this marrow on my own. My fingers are getting raw."

"How should I know?" replied another man from a chair. His portliness was audible through his voice, as though his tongue was several times too fat for his own mouth. "Once they take a second thrall they don't respond to anythin' that doesn't involve hot meat. Probably feastin' on that runty Domina as we speak. I knew she wouldn't last a week."

"You're one to talk," the taller man grunted as a snap rang throughout the chamber. "We can hardly get you to do anything unless there's a reward of warm flesh. Where will you stick it now that the women have gone cold? Pass me that, would you?"

Something flew through the air, clapping into the skinny man's waiting fingers.

"Oh I suppose I'll make do with the little ones here." The fat man kicked at something on the floor. "Shame they can't wake up. Maybe I'll keep one around, grow it into somethin' worth my girth."

"Girth? Bah!" the skinny man let out a wheezy chuckle as he scooped something into a bowl. "I'd be surprised if you felt anything at all with the grown women. I see the way they laugh at you. It's no *small* wonder that you have to force your *girth* upon them. Now if you're quite through flattering yourself, get your dogs back down here. We're running out of time."

The fat man rose from his creaking chair, crumbs falling from his rotund belly like a waterfall. "What's the rush? The odium hasn't even been blessed yet. Megdalina's still workin' on the little ones." He jabbed a thumb towards the woman at the dais.

At the mention of odium, Cole zoomed in through the gloomy torchlight, noticing huge vats lining the walls. He also saw what the woman kneeling on the dais was doing. She was placing squirming infants into a row of open cadavers. Chilled, sickly Fear pulled him to the floor, shaking his spells loose. Cole slapped his hand over his mouth, biting back vomit.

"Ah, well that makes sense then," the skinny man said with rising inflection.

"Wah? You're actually agreein' with me?" asked the fat man.

"Of course not, fool." He turned from his table, slowly wiping his hands and rolling his sleeves. "The Domina haven't returned because they've been killed, and the person responsible is lurking on the other side of that door." His eyes fell straight upon Cole as his thin lips stretched into a sneer. "Come on in and join the party then."

With a lurch, Cole felt his grip loosen as some invisible force pulled him into the room. He bumped through the hanging bodies, coming into full view of the two men. His spells and munisica faded, replaced by rancid Fear.

The skinny man's smile widened, revealing a large gap between his front teeth. He approached Cole, fingers outstretched. "What a handsome lad. So young, so brave, so full of fire!"

Cole was utterly frozen. Some microscopic part of him remained cowering in his center, but the man with the grin had him now. He felt as if he were back in the stone tub watching the Devotion. In fact, the priest of Decreath was currently pulling that very memory to the fore of his mind, indulging and amplifying it. In a matter of seconds the priest sifted through his worst moments as easily as skimming through a book.

"How can you tell he killed my Domina?" The portly man yanked Cole's chin, locking his gaze into the man's black marble eyes. "Did you kill my pets?"

Cole could only manage a gagging whisper.

"Look at his munisica, dolt!" Decreath's priest snatched Cole's hand, bringing it up to eye level. His shroud receded to his fingertips, then vanished. "Do you think he just skipped his way past thirteen Domina?" He dropped Cole's hand and licked the blood from his own fingers. His face twisted into a disgusted scowl. "Those are your dogs for certain."

The fat man jerked Cole's hand up, popping a finger into his mouth. Cole could feel his tongue swirling and sucking around it. He popped it out, an evil smirk pulling across his face. "Oh I'm gonna take my time with you laddie. We're gonna get real intimate, you and I. Rage user huh?"

A fluttering moan slipped out of Cole's mouth.

He pulled Cole closer. His breath smelled as if all the reek from the temple had been condensed into his enormous tongue. "When you can't take no more go ahead and call that Rage of yours. I can see it in there." He tapped a stubby finger into Cole's sternum. "Like a little bomb itchin to go off. I'll have it sooner or later, but try your best and stay strong. Grotton loves the chase."

Cole tried in vain to pull himself from the man's grip. The priest's fetid breath hammered him like a fire hose. His heart felt as if it were trying to escape through his chest, but a chilled hand of Fear held it fast. He receded to his center, but could no longer find it. The Fear had him. His Wisdom was frozen solid by it. He struggled to keep his Rage in check. The red magic snarled at his side like a rabid dog on a leash of dried twine.

"A Rage-wielder changes things a bit," Decreath's minion said, raising an eyebrow. "I hear they make for a most delicious meal. He can't have much of it though. It shouldn't be this easy for me to hold him with Fear. Nevertheless, he'll make a nice addition to the Colossus. When Megdalina finishes with the base stock we'll see if she won't make him chosen. If we do it right we won't even need the odium to strip him of himself."

Both men looked to the woman kneeling at the dais. Her head rolled about with closed eyes, as if she heard music no one else could. Spit frothed and dripped from her mouth as she worked. Cole tried not to watch what she was doing, instead bringing his gaze to the dais. There was a huge open basket of sharpened bones perched behind the bodies. It was a Colossus's nest.

She finished sewing one of the cavities on the headless cadavers, urging it awake with a flash of purple light from her palm. The body crawled its naked form up the side of the nest, impaling itself on the bones. Fleshy tubes wriggled out of the nest, and wormed their way into every open wound and orifice of the body.

"She'll be a minute by the looks of it. Sorronis's arts tend to take a while, 'specially as she's doublin' up on the nest," Grotton's priest said. Hunger blazed in his black eyes. "She won't chafe us for indulging a bit. We're doing her a favor anyway."

"I believe you're right," Decreath's minion said, scraping a length of curved metal from his table. "Let me have him first. Take him for Domina when he breaks, but only when he breaks."

"Be it your wish," Grotton's minion replied, dragging a too-small chair close to Cole. He stuffed himself in between the armrests as the chair screamed in protest. "I like to watch anyhow. Tickles my grittles like you wouldn't believe. Just don't go breaking him too quick."

"Please, this is art." Decreath's priest slapped the tool into Cole's shoulder, poking it through the armor. "The art will dictate the pace. It will not be fast, or slow. It will be perfect."

His eyes narrowed as he dragged the hooked tool down Cole's chest, cutting through the armor with an effort. He continued the blade down Cole's stomach before crossing over and repeating the movement from the opposite side. Clamping the tool between his teeth, the man jerked Cole's armor open, exposing his chest, which now bore a great, crimson 'X'.

Repeating the motion on Cole's backside, he stripped the armor from Cole's torso and sleeves. Cole hung there, frozen like a scarecrow left out in winter, unable to muster the courage to move. It was all he could do to keep his Rage from breaking loose and betraying him.

"We'll start small then, if it pleases you." Decreath's priest returned to his front, the tool back in his spindly hands.

The point of the hook stung into one of the scratches in Cole's chest. Spiking pain jolted across his skin, making Cole's arm twitch involuntarily. The priest pulled and yanked the tool with careful precision, ripping the cut wider as he worked his way down. Cole's Rage barked all the while, its leash fraying and snapping as a low moan slipped from his lips. A minute later the priest finished his tracing of the first cuts.

Air whooshed into the priest's mouth as he fiddled with the center of the 'X'. He dug his nails in and yanked a corner of skin from Cole's chest.

The leash broke. Cole's Rage flared, his munisica ringing clear in the dank air.

"Tut tut little warrior," Grotton's priest hissed from behind, pressing a soft finger into Cole's lower back. "Not so fast now."

The Rage hit an impenetrable wall. It shriveled and siphoned out into the Hungry mind of Grotton's priest. Cole shook, weak and powerless. Decreath's priest brought his hands to the flap again. Cole saw bits of his own flesh hanging in small chunks from the nails.

Something wriggled loose from Cole's center, bright, wholesome, and soothing. Passion flowed from him. Rosy light blared from his wounds, knitting and closing them together.

Decreath's priest flinched, his face twisting in disgust. "Flowery filth...how can this be? Come round and look at this."

The chair creaked as Grotton's priest scrambled to his feet and waddled to Cole's front. "What's that now? Passion?"

Decreath's priest ran a bloody nail down the freshly healed skin. "It seems so. It's not common to wield dualities in their magics, is it?"

"Definitely rare, but not unheard of. Can you stop it?" Grotton's priest asked as he rubbed his stumpy fingers over his collection of chins.

"No, only Megdalina can. But this does make the game more fun," he replied with a grin that showed every one of his gapped, fuzzy teeth. "I want to see if he can fix it faster than I can pull it apart."

Before Cole could even draw breath, the sickle tool thwapped into his shoulder. Decreath's priest worked the tool like a knife, wriggling and burrowing it deeper. The point of the hook suddenly struck a nerve that not even the Fear could stifle. Cole screamed on his invisible crucifix.

Decreath's priest uttered a lustful shudder, twisting the tool deeper, bathing in the agony. "Go on, look at it," he said, sliding his tongue over his lip.

Jaw trembling, Cole reluctantly brought his eyes to the wound. The tool was hooked entirely under his collar bone, its needle end and handle protruding from either side.

Cole had received worse in training from Roth, but this was different. This was deliberate, careful, and purposeful. The husky breathing and perverse bliss on the priest's face was nauseating. No one should take pleasure in such things. This was evil.

"Please…" Cole breathed.

The priest's eyes went wide. His voice was gravelly and wet. "Oh! There it is! You don't like that do you, you want it to stop? What will you give me to make it stop? Show me your jewels, warrior."

With the hooked nail of his pinky finger, the priest waggled the tool in little circles, striking the nerve with each turn as spurts of ruby blood shot onto his face. Cole's wailing rose and fell with each rotation of the tool.

Still working the tool, the priest brought a gnarled hand to Cole's face. Putrid Fear poured from his palm in an olive cloud. With every scream Cole's Fear deepened and widened as he sank further into the black trench. The room flickered, then vanished. The Fear was too much. Cole would have driven the tool through his heart to escape it. He was drowning.

The dark magic subsided, bringing the room back into focus. Decreath's priest shuddered, taking a long ragged breath in between his thin teeth. The priest swelled like a balloon. The sunken gaps in his robes puffed out as his face filled with tone and color. He looked decades younger, and his body was no longer reedy, but stout and healthy.

With a snarl, he tightened his grip and yanked the sickle straight out, snapping though bone and flesh as easily as ripping the hook out of a fish's mouth. Cole screamed as loudly as he could. When his lungs were empty, he refilled them and screamed again.

Every drop of agony filled Decreath's priest with renewed vigor. His shoulders broadened as thick knots of muscle bulged under his robes. He waited, panting and grinning.

Cole didn't know when he'd started weeping, but now he couldn't stop it. This was what they wanted. They wanted to see him cry, to break him. Reluctantly, he wrapped himself in Passion and set to healing his wound. Warm lavender glowed from his collarbone, bathing the priest's wicked visage in the light of the magic. From behind, Grotton's priest let out a high, hacking chuckle. A minute dragged by and Cole healed his wound, though he could no longer feel his arm. Chiron had yet to teach him how to mend nerves. He couldn't keep this up for long.

"Marvelous." The word rolled off the tongue of Decreath's priest. His voice was deeper, stronger. "A lover as well as a fighter. I'm sorry friend, by the looks of it we have the time for only one more. Megdalina will be done soon." He glanced at Sorronis's priest. She waved her arms over the nest, which rattled and glowed a dark raisin color. "Once she gets a whiff of that Passion there won't be anything left for you. No, we'll have to push this along." He strode back to the table, hefting a heavy, rusted saw. "It's crude, but sometimes the most beautiful solution is the simplest one."

"Leave his giblets!" Grotton's priest bellowed. "I'll need those if I'm taking him for Domina!"

Decreath's priest cast an appraising glance over Cole's midsection. He smirked, then brought the saw to the side of Cole's stomach, its ragged teeth catching and pricking.

It was now or never. The miniscule part of himself that hid in his center had been hard at work, scouring over every aspect of magic that might help in the slightest. Wisdom and Rage were of no use. He was out of time, out of ideas. In a final act of desperation he aligned his Passion with a memory, hoping he could trick himself into working the magic into the priests.

"Keep walking, Joshy," Cole whispered.

Decreath's priest faltered, confused. Then, his face lit with alarm as lavender light flooded from Cole, filling the entire chamber. Cole's feet left the ground as tears chased each other down his cheeks, glinting like diamonds. The tears rushed down his chin, flaring in blinding white light before swirling off. The sparkling magic rained over the two priests like a hail of starfire. As soon as the Passion appeared, it vanished, leaving the chamber in flickering torchlight.

Both priests frowned, clutching their chests. Grotton's priest looked over his vast belly, taking inventory of his faculties. Giving his stomach a pat, he nodded as the worry fell from his face. His eyes met Decreath's priest, who was similarly elated.

"You know, I think there might be some merit to the lover's art." Grotton's priest jumped to his feet, stretching and flexing. "I feel ripe as a Pastori sunrise!"

Decreath's priest let out a reassured chuckle. "My word, that *was* a powerful bit of magic. My thanks, lover-warrior. That was delightful, but don't think your gift changed your fate. There are more fruits to pluck from your gardens." He lifted the rusty saw, deadly intent etched upon his face.

Cole panted, Fear replacing the warm light of his Passion. Had it worked? He was sure it had, but why were they still standing? He groped through his mind, searching for his center. It was gone.

Baring a savage grin, the Priest of Fear slapped the saw to Cole's naked skin once more, sending a thousand rusty lightning bolts into Cole's side. The priest gritted his teeth and pushed, cutting a jagged trench into Cole's oblique. Cole held his breath, biting so hard that a tooth cracked in his mouth.

The saw fell to the ground with a wonking clang. Decreath's priest shuffled sideways, clinging to a hanging body to support himself.

376

The paralyzing Fear lifted from Cole's body and mind. Regaining control of his body, he took a step back and shook the remnants of Fear from him. Gasping, he replenished himself to his center before they could attack again.

"I…I feel so…famished." Decreath's priest slid down the hanging body, panting as though he'd just sprinted a mile. "Why am I shaking so?" His eyes went out of focus as he fell to his back, chest rising and falling in shallow hics.

Grotton's priest waddled to his comrade, squatting low and running fat fingers all over him. The back of the fat priest's neck had as many chins as the front. "What in Grotton's graces did you do to him? Answer me, worm!"

Cole grimaced, brushing lavender light over his wounds. His skin shimmered as his Wisdom returned. He glared at the fat man. "Passion. A healing spell used to quicken the body. Helps with sickness. You're too fat though, so it'll take longer to kill you."

"Healing spell? Then why's he doing the death rattle?" he said, a slight tremble sneaking into his words. "To hell with it, I'll rip the knowledge from you when I take you for Domina!"

Grotton's priest sprung from the ground and charged with astonishing speed, pulling a fine white blade from his robes. A hanging body snapped free of its bonds, glowing with a dull emerald light as it collided with the priest, sending his hulking mass careening into a vat of the unrefined odium. The barrel split in half, soaking the priest in sticky pink liquid.

Resisting the urge to free his Rage, Cole called his Wisdom once more. He thanked Deekus under his breath before casting the spell.

Spitting mad, the priest clambered to his feet, wiping the odium from his eyes. "I'll have you boy! Let's see you trick your way out of this!" His hands dripped with magenta light as his blade stretched itself into a long, snaking whip. With Hunger in his eyes, he raised the ribbon blade, ready to strike. The priest set back a foot, which slipped on a puddle of frozen odium that had not been there a moment ago.

He regained his balance, giving Cole a murderous glare. "Ah, Wisdom. Your magics will see better use in *my* hands. A puddle of ice though, tut tut. Maybe I shouldn't take one so stupid for Domina."

He shook his head, odium jiggling down his chins as he cracked his bladed whip.

Cole rolled the sickle tool in his hand, which was now glowed white hot with the heat he pulled from the floor. Without a word, he tossed the hunk of molten metal to the priest, who tried catching it and dodging it at the same time. The hissing tool struck the odium-soaked gut of the priest, igniting him.

The fire spread slowly, creeping over the front of the priest in curious fingers. The priest dropped his whip, slapping his chest and stomach, igniting his hands. Panic stretched his features as he waved his hands, fanning the flames into a steady blaze that licked up over his chins. Gasping, he broke into a charge, heading straight for Cole.

The man was remarkably fast for one so large. With his Wisdom unhindered, Cole lightened himself and darted to the side. The priest blew past, rounding on Cole and charging again. This time his movements were labored and clumsy. He slowed midstride, unaware of the flames that now crackled over his round cheeks. His breathing took on a ragged, desperate pattern, gradually thinning into shallow hics. The Passion had taken its toll at last, multiplying the man's metabolism by magnitudes. Grotton's priest teetered on his feet before falling face-first to the ground, sizzling and burning like a massive torch.

Cole waited for the priest's breathing to cease altogether before allowing himself a steadying breath. The smell of burning flesh mixed with the other rank odors of the room, bringing hot bile up into Cole's mouth. Shaking, he rounded on Sorronis's priest and the grisly scene splayed out before her. The headless bodies covered the bone nest in a morbid embrace. Cole pushed through his revulsion, ignoring his instincts to flee from the temple and run to the farthest reaches of Aeneria. He was grateful that sleep was no longer a part of his life, as the nightmares before him would haunt him to the end of his days.

Sorronis's priest rose to her feet, now steady and coherent. She turned, the dreamy smile falling from her as she beheld Cole. She opened her mouth to speak, possibly to beg and bargain for her life.

Before she could utter a word, Cole plunged his munisica through her chest, feeling her heart and spine give way under his ebony blades.

Seething Hatred erupted from the light that faded from her eyes, fueling Cole's Rage. He knew he shouldn't, but he clung to her Hatred, leaning on it like an addict tugging on his vice. The Hatred dulled his emotions, dimmed his awareness of the atrocities around him. Taking a final pull, he threw her corpse into the blazing pyre that was Grotton's priest.

Cole felt the shroud crawling over his skin. Rage blended with Hatred, hardening him into a potent, single-minded weapon. He looked around the chamber billowing with acrid smoke. Cole Hated this place. He Hated the priests. He even Hated the victims. They were too stupid, too weak to embrace other magics that might have saved their lives. They deserved their fate.

Considering how best to destroy the temple, Cole set his eyes upon the headless bodies clinging to the bone nest. Their stomachs kicked and squirmed like a pregnant mother's. The babies inside had been chosen by the priest, and like the other unliving corpses about the chamber, they could never die. Not unless someone skilled in Passion freed them of Sorronis's taint.

Both the Hatred and Rage melted from Cole, leaving him with a sick, unwholesome pit in his stomach. His Passion filled the pit, soothing and erasing the Hatred. There was no place for such evil in his heart.

Tears streamed from Cole's eyes as he approached each of the bodies on the nest, casting the necessary Passion to erase their tortured minds. The cadavers and their tiny passengers ceased their thrashing as their suffering could no longer fuel the evil magic. Sobbing, Cole freed the rest of the victims, granting them solace in a true death. After the final victim had been freed, Cole shook the tears from his cheeks and stormed over to the vats of odium, kicking them towards the growing bonfire in the center of the chamber. As he heaved the final barrel, he noticed something very odd behind it.

A baby, sound and whole, slept in a thick bundle of burlap rags. Its cheeks were flush with life and a shock of ginger hair poked out of its perfect little head.

Cole scooped the babe into his arms, casting a filtering spell around them both to keep the smog out. The child opened its almond eyes and shook him with the purity of her innocence.

• • • •

"Hey! Is there anybody home? Open up! It's an emergency!" Cole was back in The Sill, standing outside what he hoped was a healer's house. Cole hammered the door again. Above him, the embedded Passion stone flickered and threatened to fall from its perch. "Open your door or I'm going to break it!"

An offended shout accompanied a clatter of pans from inside the home. Cole sighed with relief, checking the baby tucked under his arm. She was still fast asleep.

"Hurry!" Cole hollered. Again he clubbed the door, which now had a series of knuckle-shaped dents.

"I told you to wait a blasted moment!" cried a wispy male voice.

The door rippled and the head of an old man popped through its middle, nudging into Cole's chest. Cole stepped back as a pair of glasses fell to the wicker door mat. A narrow set of shoulders and nearly naked body followed as an old man hobbled out to retrieve the glasses. He was bald and lean and covered from neck to ankle in tattoos. One hand gripped a small towel preserving his modesty.

Adjusting his spectacles, he blinked rapidly at Cole as though he could only view the world through snapshots. His raspy voice sounded as if his vocal cords were made from sandpaper. "What on Oberon's backside are you doing, lad? It's the middle of the night."

"I'm sorry sir, it's an emergency." Cole gently moved the girl into his view. "Are you a healer?"

"You're Chiron's boy, the human creature aren't you?" the old man asked. "Go find your Master, lad, he's the best healer on Aeneria."

"Chiron's not back yet. Please..." he pleaded, holding the girl out for the man to see.

"What am I supposed to do with that then?" he asked.

Cole nudged the girl closer. "Please, just take a look at her. I found her in Brimhallow village. The entire town was slaughtered. A priestess of Sorronis had her."

At the mention of Sorronis, the old man's face turned to wrinkled stone. "Get her in here," he wheezed before disappearing through the door.

Cole followed. Once inside, he was assaulted by a torrent of perfumes and earthy fragrances. The old man was nowhere to be found. Fluffy furniture occupied the first floor of the home, though none of it looked set up for hosting as nearly every surface was covered in clutter. Dusty books were stacked high on the seat of an armchair, and the dining table was covered in clay pottery. A warm fire of acid green and turquoise flames danced from a basin set in the center of the room while Passion stones of every size lined the walls. With a wheezy groan, the old man trudged up from a staircase in the back of the room. He was garbed in a massive fur gown, despite the stifling temperature of the room. How he didn't sweat to death in such an outfit was beyond Cole.

Darting to a tall oak cabinet, the old man threw the doors open, revealing rows upon rows of potions, powders, and countless drawers. He pulled a bottle of clear solution from a lower shelf and squirted it over his hands, briskly rubbing them together as a cloud of steam erupted from his palms.

Clapping his hands, he rolled his sleeves and gestured towards the tub of dancing flames. "All right then, place her in the fire."

"Put her in the fire?!" Cole withdrew the baby and took a step back.

The old man waved a hand dismissively. "It's not that kind of fire. Now do as I say or let me get back to my sleep."

Frowning, Cole approached the basin, running his fingers through the odd fire. The flames were warm, but not hot. They were tangible, wrapping and supporting Cole's hand, caressing it. Scabbed cuts on his palms tickled pleasantly as the wounds erased themselves. Reassured, he placed the girl in the fire. The flames converged on her, removing her bundle and revealing a chubby, dreaming baby beneath.

The old man gave Cole a swift elbow and hovered over the girl, dancing his glowing fingers above her as if playing an invisible piano.

"What's your name?" Cole asked, rubbing his ribs.

"Naythan. Now be quiet." He wheezed.

"Sorry, I didn't mean to distract you." Cole clamped his mouth shut.

Naythan gave a derisive chuckle. "You couldn't distract me if you tried. Annoying me is what you're doing. You've a voice like a screech hawk, and I'm still miffed about being pulled out of bed." He poked the girl in the belly button, which blared with a pink shimmer like a jewel. She woke with a kick and a coo. "Pulled me out of bed for nothing, I should say. There's not a thing wrong with the babe. Where'd you say you got her from?"

"Brimhallow," Cole replied. "The Three sacked the town. She was the only survivor."

In a fluid, practiced motion Naythan scooped and wrapped the girl with a fresh swath of golden silk. "How'd you get her here?"

"I ran," Cole stated.

Naythan's eyes inventoried Cole's bare chest and feet, which were riddled with travel filth and numerous cuts and bruises. He smacked his lips and set the squirming girl on a puffy pillow. "Looks like you ran through hell on the way. Did you meddle with the girl's mind or was it Sorronis's witch?"

"I'm not sure what they did to her, but I sifted through her memories and took just about everything into my own mind." Cole looked around the room for something to vomit in. The girl only had a couple months' worth of memories, but they were enough to curdle his stomach.

Naythan mashed his lips together and gave Cole an inquisitive frown. "I'd say you had no right, that you just committed an act of moral thievery on an innocent, defenseless child. I'd say that you ought to be put to death for it. I'd say those things, but I trust that as a disciple of Chiron you had good reason."

Confused, Cole looked the old man square in the eye. "Explain."

Sighing, Naythan set a finger on the girl's brow. "Removing memories is not something you do with a young mind. She wasn't ready, and you did a poor job. The babe's developmental progress will be handicapped for the rest of her life. To put a blunt point to it, she will be intellectually retarded, but I trust you knew that as well."

The blood drained from Cole's face. He threw a hand out, grasping the back of a chair to stop the room from spinning. He had no idea. "I, I can put them back! I have to." Even as he said it, he knew it was impossible. He hadn't the skill.

"Boy, look at me." Naythan poked Cole in the stomach and glared up at him. "I know what Sorronis's priests are capable of. I know what they do with angels like this one here. She's better off without those memories. What she would have become if they festered inside... well, she would have given Sorronis another priestess, that much is certain. You gave her a clean start."

Cole bit his lip, looking at the girl through watery eyes. Her pouted lips and winged brows gave her a regal countenance, like a tiny queen. She was asleep again, but what could she be dreaming of? Her only memories would be of several hours of trudging through the woods. Cole hoped that bird song played in her little bean ears. He imagined starlight twinkling behind her silken eyelids. The feather of ginger hair that fell over her brow was the same color as Joshy's. He tried imagining her growing older. If she ever developed a capacity for Hatred, she would Hate Cole with all her heart. He'd condemned her to a limited life, just like Joshy's.

"Will you take her?" Cole asked.

Naythan coughed, wrestling a choking fit in his wheezy throat. "What, you're just gonna dump her on me? She's your bastard-shame, not mine!"

"I'll pay you," Cole said.

Naythan crossed his arms. "Listen to me, lad, unless you somehow plan to pay me with three cycles worth of time, then I'd say you're stuck with her. You've already taken a night's sleep from me, I won't lose another-" His words fell unfinished as every Passion stone in the room blazed to life.

Cole took his hand from the gratia stone above the doorframe. "Naythan, I'm not asking this of you to shirk my responsibility to this child. I intend to care for her the best I can, when I can. But I am a Warrior of The Sill. If I don't help in the war then everyone, including her, will suffer a fate we can't even imagine." Cole paused, wondering if he should trust the tattooed old hermit. "Aeneria needs me.

Everything I've got. Part of Varka lives within me and I'm our only hope in defeating The Three."

To emphasize his point, Cole let his Rage off its leash. The shroud snapped fully over him as his munisica sprang to life, raising him several inches taller. His bladed hair scratched the ceiling as he brought his black eyes down to Naythan. "I need your help, Naythan. Aeneria needs your help."

"Stars above." Naythan flinched, scooping the girl up and clutching her to his chest as he backed away several paces.

Cole leashed his Rage and shrank back to his normal size, which was still two heads taller than the old man.

Naythan collected himself, the dread falling from his face. He held onto the girl, bouncing her slightly. His raspy voice smoothed into an almost normal one: "I will help you, Wisdom Walker. I will take the babe."

Cole faltered at the title, but decided against correcting Naythan. He had Traveled of course, but it was Varka's doing, not his. "I have to go find Chiron. Do you need anything? Anything at all?"

Naythan's eyes flicked to the dozens of Passion stones, which were all humming with energy. "When do you think you'll be able to fill those again? I have enough work to drain them within a week, but it would take me several months to fill them as you just did."

Cole smiled. Naythan may have been a man of Passion, but he had the eyes of an entrepreneur. "It will take me two or three days to replenish. I'll come back when I can. If they're empty, I'll fill them."

"Then we have ourselves a contract." Naythan's wrinkled hand shot out.

Cole shook it. Leaning in, he gave the girl a kiss on the forehead before disappearing through the semi-solid door.

Cole left Naythan's house, which was on the secluded outskirts of the Arts District. He made for his tree in the barracks. Though he was eager to clean the filth from himself, he didn't call Wisdom or Rage to speed him along. He needed the time to think.

Back in his tree, Cole ran the abrasive laser-shower over himself until his skin was rashed and raw. No matter how many times he ran the shower, he couldn't seem to wash the lingering taint that clung to his thoughts. He felt dirty on the inside. The girl's memories kept swimming to the fore of his thoughts, sickening his mind and his heart. His own memories were no better, as his thoughts of Joshy had somehow broken free from where he'd locked them. He may have been bigger and stronger, but by Earth-reckoning he was barely an adult. Most people go through their entire lives without seeing the horrors that he'd seen. There were so many bodies. So much agony. No one should have to see what he saw. It was too much. Cole resolved to find the nearest Wisdom stone and dump everything he could.

Rummaging through his closet, Cole found an old set of armor to replace his ruined one. When he'd strapped the last buckle into place a sudden jolt struck him, baring his teeth and igniting his munisica.

Another mind rushed into his, familiar and fierce. The room faded before him as Cole saw the world through Goran's eyes.

He was high in the Fangshards outside Oberon City. Wind and sleet bore down on him, but he was unaffected by the biting cold. Goran stood sentinel on an icy peak, gazing down to the ocean below. Horns blared over the mountains' howl as torches flickered to life. Domina stirred on boats, crying out orders and scurrying about like angry ants. Sniffing deep, Goran's nose beheld the cocktail of scents from the waves below. Hunger. Sweat. Bloodlust.

Crunching through the snow, Goran turned to the other side of the mountains, towards the shimmering lights of Oberon City. Filling his vast lungs with mountain air, Goran roared. It was a call to arms, a herald to the impending battle. The dogs of war had come.

CHAPTER 21

CONFRONTING THE SWARM

"Greetings Cole. How fared your mission in Brimhallow?" Chiron greeted Cole as he pulled himself up onto the decking of the floating house. The elder appeared to have just returned from his own mission.

"Why didn't you tell me?" Cole demanded.

"Tell you what?" Chiron asked, politely perplexed as he set a heavy satchel down on his table.

"That The Three are at the borders of Oberon City. If I could find out then so could you. Surely you must have known." He widened his link with Eliza, making sure he had her attention.

"Did you know about this?" Cole jabbed the question to her.

"I know about it now," she replied, ignoring his accusation. *There are battle horns blaring throughout the city as we speak. Now that I think on it, this explains why Roth has been so chipper. He must have known as well."*

"Keep the bond open. Wide open." Cole flooded her with what little Passion he had built since leaving Naythan's.

She responded without a word, but poured her own Passion into him, replenishing a good portion of what he'd spent.

Chiron seemed not to have noticed the silent exchange. "The Three's swarms were bound to break upon the temple before long. Though you are learning at a prodigious pace, let me assure you; you are still quite as vulnerable to Thee Three as when you first arrived. There was no use distracting you from your training," Chiron said, casually plucking a blackstout from his satchel and offering it to Cole. "You look dreadful. Are you hungry?"

Cole's stomach clawed at itself, but he declined. Try as he might to keep an even tone, anger simmered through his words. "And what about the others? My unit? Roth and Alvani?"

"All perfectly capable of handling themselves. Best not to let Roth hear that you've been worrying about him. The man nearly took my head off last time I wished him *safe travels*." Chiron leaned back in his chair, memories swimming in his eyes.

Checking his renewed bond with Goran, Cole drew images of the thousands of ships the mirak had seen swarming up the coast. Countless bobbing sails waded through the waters, all heading for the mountain pass to the capital city. How could Chiron sit there and joke at a time like this? This was no small skirmish, or even a large battle. It looked as if every Domina and priest were packed on those ships. This could very well be a swift end to the entire war.

Cole swallowed hard, pressing his gaze to the ancient Aenerians as if staring into the sun. "Master Chiron, I'm going to Oberon City."

Chiron bobbed his head in a pensive manner. "Well of course you are."

"I...I am?" Cole stammered. "I mean, you're not going to try and convince me not to?"

Chiron shook his head, rising to his feet. "I wouldn't dream of it. I've been force-feeding you an ocean of knowledge through a straw, some of which has no practical use in battle whatsoever."

"I knew it!" Cole blurted. "You've been stalling me on purpose!"

Chiron raised a palm, silencing Cole. "My intent was to teach you everything Varka knew. I hoped to attune your conscious-self with your subself, in hopes of bringing you closer to Varka's state at the time of the Banishing. While you've made enormous progress, more than any other student as a matter of fact, I feel in my heart that you are no closer to uncovering Varka's secrets."

"How much more training would I need to match what he knew?" Cole asked, afraid of the answer.

"Considering your current rate of learning and the fact that you no longer require sleep," Chiron flicked numbers off his fingers, "I'd wager another six or seven cycles would do the trick. Keep in mind, Varka had been to every local planet, most more than once. The man was a lodestone for knowledge."

Cole faltered. He wasn't ready. The incident at Brimhallow had nearly killed him and that was only a couple of fledgling priests. How could he hope to make a difference now? If just one of The Three made an appearance he'd be worse than useless. He'd be a liability. Perhaps that was why Chiron had kept him in the dark, so that he wouldn't get captured and used against Oberon's forces. Cole could feel Chiron's eyes on him, quietly observing and calculating. From within, he could feel Goran and Eliza's trickling curiosity from their separate bonds.

Cole broke the silence after a lengthy pause: "Brimhallow was a disaster. I was too late."

"I would hear your tale. Unless you are in a hurry to get to the capital?" Chiron offered Cole the blackstout once more. This time Cole accepted.

Cole recounted every gruesome detail, feeling as if he were heaving a sickness from his mind's gut. He left nothing out, watching Chiron's reactions all the while. The Wisdom Walker showed no surprise or even the slightest change in his passive demeanor, even when Cole spoke of the infants. When Cole finished, he felt no better. In fact he felt as if he needed another shower.

"Master Chiron, I don't want these memories," Cole said, rubbing his knuckles into his forehead. "I can feel them eating at me. I'm afraid of what's going to be left after they've had their fill. The little girl's memories alone are enough to break me."

Chiron turned his gaze to the stars. "When I was young and full of self-righteous ambition, I made my first trip as Wisdom Walker to Allias. There was a world-war that the Unbound intended to resolve. The people were primitive, but their capacity for malice seemed all the greater for it. During my time there I witnessed atrocities that shattered and sickened my heart. We were successful in the end, but the sickness clung to my soul like a virus. When I returned to Aeneria, I found the largest Omnistone I could and filled it with every unwanted memory from my visit."

"Do you regret it?" Cole asked.

Chiron's face remained a stony mask. "Every time I look upon one who has survived evil. My cowardice was an insult to their suffering. The survivors had to live with their burdens to the end of their days, while I carried on with no trouble at all. I tell you this not to persuade you one way or another, but to give you the perspective of a very old man. You are young, and must carve your own path through this beautiful madness we call life. You answer to no one but yourself in the end."

Cole walked to the edge of the decking, resting his arms on the railing as he gazed out towards Naythan's house. He would answer for what he did to the girl, of that he was sure. His first step in making things right wasn't going to be dumping her only memories into a cold, uncaring rock.

"I will bear the burden. She deserves it," Cole said.

"That is very brave of you." Chiron patted Cole on the shoulder with a soft hand. "And I wouldn't worry on the babe overmuch. There is no telling what damage has been done until she is much older. By then you very well may have discovered a means to alleviate the infirmity. In the meantime, Naythan will take perfect care of her. He's been alone far too long anyhow. I daresay he has the most to gain from their relationship." He gave Cole a squeeze and turned him so they were face to face. "Now, how does Varka's only descendant intend on getting himself to Oberon City?"

"I hadn't thought about that part yet," Cole admitted. "I could run there, though even with my Rage it will take me weeks. I don't suppose you're ready to teach me how to fly?"

Chiron beamed at him: "My dear Cole, you've known all along. I shall ferry you to the capital, only this time I want you to pay closer attention to my spells." He laughed, seeing the eagerness in Cole's face.

Cole bounced on his heels. "Are you serious? I'm going to have wings like the others?"

"Heaven's no." Chiron gave a dismissive wave of his hand. "Wings are dependent on one's control of the wind and air, though they do grant superb low-speed maneuverability. Here, this is much more efficient." Chiron swept his hands over his shoulders and removed his cape, which changed from slats of wood to flowing glass. "This was Varka's. I give it to you now."

"Master Chiron!" Cole gasped, taking the cape into his hands. It felt like warm, flexible glass. "Thank you, but how will you fly?"

"I learned the secrets of this garment long ago," he said, helping Cole fit the cape around his neck. "I was merely holding on to it for safekeeping. Now if you would give attention to my spells. Let us see if what lies at Oberon City can't coax a little more of Varka's charms from you."

After filling his pockets with the rest of Chiron's stock of black-stouts, Cole opened himself to Chiron's spells. Through Passion they formed a temporary bond so that Cole could feel exactly how it was done. To his astonishment, the spells were not nearly as complex as he'd thought, they simply required a mind-boggling amount of focus.

Their feet left the decking, floating in the same exact manner that Cole might levitate a small object. The difficulty was in trusting the magic, and not letting worries or stray thoughts interrupt the spell. Cole wished they had wings. Then at least he could feel the wind under him holding him aloft. This empty floating was disorienting.

As they gathered speed, the wind quickly became unbearable. Cole's cheeks rippled as the air howled painfully in his ears. Chiron's next spell was a bit more complex, but then again it was nothing he hadn't done before. Cole had woven a similar spell about himself to keep the wall of hands from touching him back in Brimhallow. Chiron spun a hull of thought all around them, crafted by a simple yet ironclad idea: No air shall pass through. The web was long and frictionless, ending in an infinitely sharp point, and once it solidified, their acceleration took on new fervor. It was like an invisible fuselage had formed around them.

Two spells, two rivers of focus to maintain. Cole sensed Chiron shift his attention, ready to hand off the reins.

Chiron pressed the ideas into Cole. *"You saw how I did it. Now I shall pass the spells off to your mind. Maintain the air-shield and keep yourself moving. Do not worry about me."*

Cole hesitated. *"What happens if I slip? I've never done this before."*

Chiron let out an audible chuckle. *"Then you will have to manage a fall into the water, though I would advise against it. At this speed the waves may as well be boulders. Do not forget the cape."*

"But how is a cape supposed to-" Cole's stomach lurched.

Chiron released the spells, letting the ideas run wild through Cole's mind. Before they could flutter off, Cole grasped them with every bit of focus he had. His sight dimmed to nothing as his hearing faded to mute. He hadn't even the focus to spare for his senses. He drifted from the world as the spells took more and more from him. The two concepts dominated him, became him. As his sense of touch began to fade, he felt Varka's cape flap over his back. How was he supposed to use it?

Just the thought of the cape caused something to click into place. It felt as if Chiron's ideas were a foreign language, and the cape translated them to better suit the workings of Cole's mind. Cole had no idea when it happened, but the cape was suddenly inside him, as if his very consciousness was wearing it as well. It tickled him with a sense of wonder, daring him to try the impossible.

As his senses returned, he beheld Chiron, a look of pride on the old Wisdom Walker's face.

"That truly is your cape," Chiron said aloud, leaving Cole's mind entirely.

Cole was slow to speak, as the spells still took a good measure of his focus. "I think I'd still rather have some wings. They look cool."

Chiron chuckled and nodded. "I'll surrender to that argument. There is still time for me to show you that aspect of Wisdom before we arrive at the capital."

Excitement threatened to unseat Cole's spells. He quieted himself, putting a larger portion of his mind in the stony room of his center, where he could better conduct Wisdom. He spoke in a passive, subdued tone: "That would be great, Master. Varka's cape should make it a breeze. Why didn't you give it to me earlier? I could have learned so much more."

"You weren't ready to learn *how* to learn," Chiron replied, holding out his palm and conjuring a crystalline version of Cole's dagger.

Cole reached out, grasping the familiar phantom. Aside from being crafted from glowing emerald magic, the dagger was identical in every way to his own. Cole recalled the moment when he'd received it many months ago. It was his first gift from The Sill.

Cole hefted the blade, drawing the original from his side and comparing the two. It had the right weight and balance. It was sharp too. Cole was about to test the edges against each other when Chiron's phantom dagger twisted itself into a little emerald bird. The creature flapped out of Cole's hand and flew alongside them.

Chiron kept his eyes in Cole's: "The summoning of objects requires an act of direct focus. You are bringing forth your own thoughts into the mundane. These are the most costly of spells. Once mastered, your conjurations can take on a life of their own."

To demonstrate his point, the crystalline bird sprouted azure feathers. Its beak painted itself yellow and its eyes black. It was no longer translucent, but solid, completely indecipherable from a real bird. The bird dove through the air shield, swirling and twisting about.

The concepts began to take shape in Cole's mind. He nodded to Chiron, ready to learn.

"Now, join minds with me once more. Allow the cape to attune my Wisdom to yours," Chiron said, floating around Cole with his arms crossed.

By the end of their flight Cole was able to conjure small objects without fail. None of them had the detail Chiron was capable of, but he could create a crude copy of his dagger without dropping the idea. Cole was confident that had he not been so taxed by maintaining the flight spells, he could have crafted a marvelous pair of wings that would certainly catch Lileth's eye.

Oberon temple came into view first, a gargantuan monument piled to the heavens. Oberon loomed close above as if drawn to its snowy peak. Cole only just now realized that the temple shouldn't exist at all, based on Chiron's lessons on geology and physics. The structure was several times larger than the planet's crust could support, and should have collapsed under its own mass. He couldn't fathom the Wisdom required to defy so much gravity.

As the city's lights winked up from the horizon, Cole felt Goran tugging him towards the Fangshard Mountains. The toothy ridge wasn't as tall as Oberon Temple, but its jagged peaks were still well above breathable air. Goran was still perched somewhere in the snowy summits. The mirak felt different in Cole's mind. His thoughts were no longer sharp and instinctive, but methodical and patient, like an ancient tree that cares for nothing less than the passing of seasons. The change was alarming and invoked a deep worry in Cole. Even though he was reconnected with his furry comrade, he'd never felt more distant. Goran was only dimly concerned with Cole's imminent arrival. What could have caused such a change in him?

Something else pulled at Cole's thoughts as he approached the city. Even though he was incapable of sleep, his waking dreams had been filled with nightmares of Lileth. Worries mated with memories and surfaced in between gaps of conscious thought. A mixture of his own Fear and Despair crafted a pallid quagmire that part of him couldn't escape from. Brooding thoughts branched off into solid possibilities of her seeking the attention of other men. Eliza tried to hide it, but Cole was acutely aware of every time the unit spirited themselves from their prison to indulge in the city nightlife. From Eliza's periphery, Cole spied Lileth dancing with reckless grace at clubs, an open invitation for other suitors. The behavior was very much unlike the Lileth he knew. Nearly every time he tuned into Eliza's training he found Valen paired up with Lileth. He was never too far from her side. Cole wondered if she would even bother telling him that she and Valen were an item, or if he would have to figure it out on his own.

"Focus on the facts, Cole. Do not give dread to mere possibilities." Chiron's smooth voice shook him from the silence.

Cole blinked, unaware that his mind had drifted. He forgot that he was still linked with Chiron. "Right. They're at the foothills of the Fangshards, city-side."

"Lead the way," Chiron said.

Cole aimed the air shield lower and urged himself faster, attempting to reach the speeds Chiron had them at on the trip to The Sill. Try as he might, Cole was unable to match the elder or create the rippling sonic boom.

With the outskirts of the city now below them, Cole dove for the foothills. He let Goran know that he would be right up shortly afterwards; however, the mirak barely acknowledged his presence. Goran merely fed Cole his constant awareness of the enemy forces, which now beached themselves on the other side of the Fangshards.

They zoomed lower. Cole could make out individual windows and rows of crops painted with Oberon's fickle hues. Farmers cried out in alarm as they passed. One woman working a rolling combine actually cast a bolt of fire at them, which Chiron graciously did not react to. Cole scrambled up a hasty counter to the spell. Without time to prepare, Cole summoned a crude wall of thought branded with the rule, 'no fire shall pass.' The spell worked, but only barely. The flaming bolt splashed over his counter and robbed him of most of his focus, shattering both the flame and air shields. Amid a violent buffeting of wind, he re-conjured the air shield and flew a bit higher. Cheeks flushed, Cole ignored Chiron's silent judgment.

He followed Eliza's fraternal bond, and his eyes found a clearing at the city-side of the mountain pass he and his unit had run through many weeks ago. The grassy alcove was empty. Curious, Cole sent out a pulse of Passion and detected dozens of life forces scattered among the trees, all glowing like a garden of candles. Flashing Chiron a wild grin, he slowed and dismissed his air-shield. Bringing his Wisdom into the mundane, a pair of emerald wings erupted from his shoulder blades. The razor sharp tips snapped into his periphery. Cole flexed the wings, giving them a couple test-flaps. Satisfied, he folded the wings and banked into a steep dive.

They alighted upon the hissing grass amid a swirl of loose flower petals and leaves. A thundering voice shook the rain from the surrounding trees: "Of course! Arrive in the final hour, *after* all the hard work's been done. You know I Hate logistics." Roth's towering figure shimmered and appeared. The Bonebreaker shook the ground with every step as he cut through the waist-high grass. His eyes drilled into Chiron's. "You're dealing with the bureaucratic shit-storm after this mess is settled. Had to chew a few Council hides to stir this lot into defending their own borders. Got a decent force stacked up, but between us-" he dropped his voice to a low rumble, "-their odds look about as good as the last time The Three crawled through here. It's a damn good thing you two showed up."

"You never fail to light a fire in me, Rothael," Chiron beamed. "It has been too long since we've drawn magic and blade together. I would pity our foes, but at the moment I find such compassion beyond me."

Chiron brought his gaze towards Oberon. His eyes hardened as the white scar on his neck took on an opalescent glow.

The rest of the unit dismissed their shadows, blinking to solid forms in the grass around them. Eliza's slender frame sparkled into view as Sitra's long braid bounced from side to side. Valen greeted him with a look of genuine appreciation. Cole was acutely aware of Lileth's athletic grace striding from the edges of his sight. Her raven hair was tied high in a practical bun while rebellious strands framed her face. Cole glanced at her feet, unable to look her in the eyes. He flexed his wings once more, suddenly reminded of Storn's showboating. With a restrained smile, he dissolved his wings in a cascade of green sparks.

Cole felt the weight of Roth's gaze fall over him. The Bonebreaker gave him a savage grin. "I told you when we first met that you would become a living, breathing weapon. Looks like I sized you up properly. You are now a weapon."

Cole raised his chin, realizing he was now almost as tall as Roth. "I'm at least a little more deadly than I was."

"Indeed you are, Human," Roth grumbled, closing in until his nose was a hair's breadth from Cole's. "Try to kill me."

Alvani shimmered into view next to them. "Really! The tides of war are coming in as we speak and you need to wrestle with the boy now? Find your senses, Rothael! Now is not the time."

"Now is the only time. I need to know if he's gone soft in the last couple months." Roth looked back to Cole. "Are you hesitating?"

"No, Master Roth," Cole said, setting a foot back. He wasn't scared, but Roth never failed to intimidate him. The rest of the unit backed away, giving them space.

"Be quick about it then!" Alvani stormed off, shouting over her shoulder, "Don't ask me to fix whatever you break!"

Roth ignored her. He stood with his hulking arms crossed, tapping a clawed foot in the grass. He flashed Cole a look that told him his window of hesitation was about to close.

Cole drew his dagger. It seemed childishly small in his hands, but it felt fitting that he use it now. With a nervous grin, he strode towards his Master, unshrouded. He would hold his munisica back for now. Roth didn't know Cole had been through a condensing.

Cole lunged from several paces away, aiming for Roth's chest. The feat of strength and agility failed to elicit even the slightest reaction from Roth, other than a casual flick of his clawed hand. The dagger met with his munisica in a flash of sparks and smoke. Cole followed through with a kick to Roth's inner thigh, but his bare foot collided with a shrouded shin as Roth blocked the blow.

Ignoring his possibly broken foot, Cole made a series of jabs and slashes with the dagger, each producing a hard clink of sparks as Roth deflected them. Cole could feel the dagger flexing and threatening to snap with each strike. Just like his newly condensed body, the dagger wasn't nearly enough to pose a threat to the Bonebreaker. Feigning another kick, Cole cast the dagger at Roth's face as he finally drew his munisica. Continuing his would-be block of Cole's kick, Roth spun and sent the dagger spinning away with his bladed hair.

Knowing Roth would expect a swift follow-up, Cole leaped high above their grassy battlefield, drawing the rest of his Rage as he flew. Like an obsidian bird of prey, Cole descended on Roth with all four munisica bared. He fell too slowly, however. His claws snapped upon open air.

Roth was simply too quick and too clever, dashing out of the way before Cole's munisica could find his neck. Cole landed, roaring loudly enough to send a ripple through the surrounding grass. He shot after Roth and their claws met at last in a flurry of blows. Cole held nothing back, striking at Roth with every ounce of his Master's Rage. Roth staggered back, but he still appeared in control of the fight, drawing Cole back around to where they'd started. The blows were hard enough to cleave Morthainian glass, but had no effect on Roth's munisica other than an ear-stabbing report. Around them, the others plugged their ears or summoned little green shields over them.

Cole struck at Roth with every attack he could think of. He even tried a few underhanded tricks such as pretending to slow and tire, or leaving himself wide open for counterattacks. Though Roth clearly put forth an effort, Cole failed to land a single blow or catch the Bonebreaker in any of his traps. Being fully shrouded, he was both stronger and better-armored than Roth. But as with Chiron, the Master's experience proved a boon against Cole's lack of technique and flexibility.

After using the same attack for the third time, Cole sensed a wall of redundancy to their dance. He considered calling Wisdom or Passion to his aid, but didn't want to provoke Roth into doing the same. Out of sheer frustration, Cole allowed his Rage one last kick, which sent Roth flying back in a graceful flip. Cole stilled himself and released the Rage as he returned to his center.

"I don't remember telling you to stop," Roth growled, striding over the torn grass.

Cole retrieved his dagger with Wisdom. The dented blade spun through the air and slapped into his naked palm. He sheathed it behind his back and turned to Roth. "What's the point? I couldn't even scratch you, let alone kill you. And I'm pretty sure you couldn't hurt me either," he added, raising his chin a little higher.

Roth shook the ground as he stepped to Cole. Cole couldn't tell if the fire in his eyes was pride or fury. He kept his Rage at the ready just in case.

With a grunt, Roth slammed his forehead into Cole's, holding him there with the strength of his glare. Cole saw stars, but to his relief the Bonebreaker was smiling.

Roth's laughter thundered into Cole's chest. He leaned back and slapped a clawed hand jovially on Cole's shoulder. "You've got Varka's spirit in you all right. Definitely not his talent in battle, but the spark's there. After we have our little party with The Three, you and I are going to hone that technique of yours."

"I would appreciate that, Master Roth." Cole grinned. He could feel Varka's cape shifting into a blanket of itchy grass over his back.

Chiron's pacifying voice caught both their attentions. "Now that you've got a good measure of Cole's skill with Rage, allow me to show you what he's done with the other magics." Chiron rolled his fingers together, producing a flowing web of jade light.

Roth grunted, closing his eyes and letting his head fall back. Chiron brought the wispy light to Roth's forehead, where it flowed into his eyes and ears. Roth's eyes snapped open as he appeared to search the stars. After a few seconds he nodded slowly, then returned his gaze to Chiron.

"That all?" he demanded. Cole thought he heard an eagerness to his voice. Or was it worry?

Chiron flashed a clever smile. "No, but I'll leave Cole to tell you about his journey in Brimhallow."

For the first time since Cole had known him, Roth's stony demeanor softened. He looked relieved. Cole was in no great hurry to retell the events, not unless Alvani knew some form of Passion to heal the sickness that clung to his heart.

"Maybe after," Cole blurted before Roth had a chance to question him further. "So what's the plan? They must be close to the valley by now. I've reconnected with Goran by the way. He's watching from the peaks on the other side of the Fangshards. Last I checked it looked like there was an entire army coming through."

"Megorien can speak on that," Roth grunted, flicking his eyes to a figure approaching from Cole's left. "Her scouts are posted up on the shore."

Megorien joined the circle. She wore battle robes that billowed without breeze and shimmered with green light. In her hand was a conjured staff that towered over her head, crowned with a leaf-shaped blade. Her demeanor was hard as stone, yet lined with traces of Fear. "The human is right. They are nearly at the other side of the pass. I'll fill you in as we walk. The scouts on the coast went dark about a half hour ago."

Chiron gave a bow. "Lead the way, Battle Matron."

Cole trailed behind the elders, sharpening his ears so he could hear every word. He wanted to be close to Lileth, to show her how much he'd grown. He was certainly taller than her now, and he was competent with all three schools of magic. There was no way she could still see him as just a human. Casually dropping back in the crowd, he tried to meet her eyes, but her stoic gaze was locked straight ahead. Dejected, he glanced farther back and beheld a sizeable formation trailing behind them. They all wore the same battle attire as Megorien and carried a variety of conjured weapons. It suddenly dawned on Cole that he was at the head of an army marching into battle.

Something hard and sharp clapped him on the shoulder, snapping him out of his brooding stupor. He jerked his head to find Sitra beaming up at him.

"Damn you got tall! Skinnier though." She raked her eyes up and down the length of his body. "I bet I can wrap my munisica around that little waist just like when you were a wee human. I'm surprised you gave Roth such a good show with these sticks." She squeezed Cole's upper arms with her munisica.

"Unless I'm mistaken, Cole's been through a condensing," Valen said, giving him an endearing bump on the opposite shoulder. "I'm glad to have you back, brother."

"I'm glad to *be* back," Cole replied, grinning as Eliza approached from behind and poured a measure of Passion into his shoulders with her hands. His anxiety melted from him.

"This won't be like Brimhallow. You are not alone this time." Her soothing voice echoed throughout his center.

"Thank you, Eliza."

"So, Varka-two, what was it like going off on your own mission?" Sitra asked, skipping with excitement. "Bet they weren't expecting a master of Rage."

"Eliza told you already?" Cole asked. Eliza's hands suddenly withdrew from his shoulders.

"You never mind our sources." Sitra cuffed him in the ear. "So tell us, did you tear them to pieces?"

"I couldn't use my Rage." Cole shifted uncomfortably, trying to stifle the memories before they could bubble up. "One of them was a priest of Grotton." Cole felt the man's hot, fetid breath on the back of his neck.

"How in Oberon's backside did you get out of that one?" Sitra gasped, inspecting her munisica. "Wisdom?"

"No. Decreath had a priest working on me too. Sorronis's priest was busy." Cole's stomach flipped, threatening to release the blackstouts from the flight over. Sitra looked all the more excited now.

Cole felt another gush of Passion ease his discomfort as Eliza spoke for him: "He used Passion of course. A very clever bit of magic too. Perhaps he'll show us sometime when we're not so busy. I think we'd better let Cole listen to the Elders and get himself caught up."

Sitra cut her off, planting a clawed hand on Eliza's chest. "You didn't tell us he almost died. I know you two have your own private link, but next time Cole's almost killed how bout you give us a little more detail?" She shot Eliza a venomous glare.

"He survived, that's all you needed to know," she said plainly. "I assumed Cole would rather speak for himself, if he chooses to. Besides, we don't share everything. I never told him about the time you sneaked out and landed yourself in a tavern brawl and spent a night in jail."

Sitra's eyes rose with her voice. "That little scrap isn't quite on the same scale as Cole taking on a triad of priests by his damned self. That's life and death!"

"You fought the whole tavern, Sitra," Eliza reminded her in a gentle tone.

Their bickering rose in tempo. Valen caught Cole's eyes and urged him towards the Elders. "You really ought to get caught up. I don't know what Goran's shared with you, but from what I've gathered this doesn't bode well for us."

Cole nodded. He turned back and gave Eliza a look of gratitude. Ignoring Sitra's tirade, she flashed him a warm smile and nudged him forward. Cole sped up to the front of the formation, noticing that Lileth's eyes were now on him. She looked as if she wanted to say something, but drifted away when his eyes got too close. He followed her, but Roth's booming voice cut him off.

"Cole, get your skinny ass over here and get your brief!" Roth shouted, beckoning him with a bladed hand.

Cole trotted over, passing through some invisible barrier that had been blocking Megorien's words. He stepped on the paved path, his cape becoming measurably heavier as it shifted to a sheet of stone.

"Varka's descendant huh?" Megorien appraised him with a look of incredulity. "If I hadn't seen you wear a Rage-Master's shroud then I wouldn't have believed it. I hope the rest of you can live up to his legends. Anyway, here's the situation as it stood a half hour ago. Our scouts are probably dead now, but they did give us a good measure of what we're facing. There's near a thousand Domina and not a single one of them carries less than three thralls. By that alone we can assume they have another small army of Grotton's priests to control them all. We counted a good number of Corpulants too, between one and two hundred. Roth, your lot will have to deal with them. And Decreath's priests."

Roth grunted. "That's a tall order, Battle Matron. We'll do it, but you know you're going to lose a good number on the ground. I wouldn't bet on even half of your little Wisdom-squad walking away from this one. At least it will be easier to convince the rest of this city to adopt other magics after a hundred of their kids get eaten."

"That's a... practical way of looking at it." Megorien faltered for a moment. "Moving on, we haven't seen much representation from Sorronis, which is either very good or very bad. It's safe to assume he's got a few dozen priests at least. There's been no sight of Colossi, but we can't count them out either."

"And the Harbingers?" Alvani asked. "Do you know if they've crowned any more?"

"I was hoping one of you could answer that." Megorien's eyes shifted towards Chiron.

"Sorronis has taken a Harbinger," Chiron said. "And I'm afraid the winds carry whispers that Grotton is soon to choose as well. We may very well be facing the full measure of The Three in this valley."

Silence fell over the group. Cole had known Kreed would be here with Decreath, but Sorronis and Grotton too? Doubts blossomed into dread flowers within his heart.

"I Feared as much," Megorien replied in a quiet voice. "But that doesn't change our course. None of us have experience fighting The Three, so I'll defer to your judgment."

"Alvani, Rothael, and I will see to The Three and their Harbingers," Chiron said. "They were Aenerians once. At least some fragment of their black hearts still is. They are not invulnerable."

"Agreed," Alvani said, a soft pink glow emanating from her body. The light bathed Cole like a welcome sunrise, invigorating him. "However marred their souls might be, they cannot evade our grace entirely."

Roth let out a rumbling chuckle. "The Harbingers are creatures of flesh. Flesh can be broken."

"We have not been idle these last thirty cycles," Chiron said in a hard tone. "Though our numbers are few, The Three cannot best all of us in open combat. A stalemate perhaps, but they will gain no ground once we find them."

"Your confidence is bolstering," Megorien replied, holding her chin a little higher. I wish the Celestial Council saw things that way."

"Any word from the mountain folk?" Roth asked, casting his eyes up the steep valley walls. "Their asses are on the line too. You'd think they might want to pitch in."

"Not a word." Megorien shook her head. "Our emissaries are chased off with bolts of ice whenever they get too close."

Roth took a deep breath, sniffing the air. "I'll have a little chat with the mountain-cowards when we're through here. Do you have a battle plan, Megorien? Or is that on us too?"

"We have several. But I wouldn't be doing my job as Battle Matron if I didn't ask to hear yours, Bonebreaker. You do have a plan, don't you?"

"As a matter of fact I do, and it's the one we're going with." Roth stopped, halting the entire procession. "Since your lot can't handle a bit of Fear without wetting yourselves, you'll take the Domina. All of them."

"But those are fool's odds!" Megorien cried. "You expect us to take on one thousand triple-thralled Domina with only one hundred of our warriors?"

"Like I said, I expect at least half of your number won't make it. Should have pleaded your case to the Council before marching off to battle. Maybe then you'd have yourself a proper army. Take heart Battle Matron, for you only get the beggar's share of this meal. We take the King's plate. There's only eight warriors from The Sill and we'll be handling the Corpulants, the priests, and whatever Harbingers might be joining the party."

Megorien looked to the other elders. When they didn't object, she gave Roth a grim nod. "Forgive me, Bonebreaker. I know not of strategies of large-scale battles. The Council should not have elected me as Battle Matron. I am too young."

Roth stepped forward and gave her a solid brow-to-brow thump. She staggered, but held her ground. Roth tapped a claw to her breast. "I might have my differences with the white robes up in the temple, but they chose well. You are clever. The Domina are strong, but stupid. Use your Wisdom as a weapon and they'll fall for every trick you throw at them. Fangshard Valley is too steep for the Domina to climb easily. It makes no difference how large their numbers are, they're going to be forced to squeeze through this little pass. You take the ground and own it. Don't give them an inch. We'll take to the sky and pinch them from up there."

"Thank you, Bonebreaker," she replied in a stronger voice.

Chiron placed an arm on a shoulder of each, his voice light and pleasant, as if they had been merely discussing dinner plans. "A fine plan! I suggest we put it into place before our enemies delve any deeper into the pass. Best of luck to you, Megorien. Come Rothael, spread your wings with me." Chiron blinked slowly, looking up to the stars as his feet left the ground.

Megorien nodded and stalked away from the elders, barking orders to the front of her formation. Cole heard the clinking of conjured wings as the rest of his unit took flight. After a moment it was only him and Alvani left on the paved road. She held him with her eyes.

"You don't need to live up to Varka. In just a few months you've accomplished things beyond any student. You are a marvelous person Cole, and I'm better for knowing you." She gently pulled his head down and kissed him upon the brow. She withdrew, raising an arm to the sky. A series of concussions battered the air as Gale came from nowhere. He flapped to a halt and took her hand in his feathery paws, carrying her up into the valley ceiling.

Cole smiled to himself, looking back at Oberon and indulging in its balmy glow one last time. Alvani's words soothed some deep-rooted concerns that he wasn't actively aware of. Varka had been inside him, and likely still was, but he only appeared in the strangest of times. There were countless occasions when Cole could have used his help, only to be left scratching at the dark to figure it out on his own. Varka may have provided a nudge here and there, but it was Cole who dragged himself through the worst of it. At the moment he couldn't even recall the last time Varka had showed himself. What did it even matter? This was Cole's fight now. This fight was for today's Aeneria. Varka's time had come and gone.

Cole turned from Oberon and peered down the empty trail. Rage tingled up the back of his neck and lit his munisica with fiery wrath. The shroud enveloped him inside and out, strengthening every fiber of his body with undiluted Rage. Cole threw his shoulders back and filled his lungs, releasing a primal bellow that echoed down the valley.

To his chagrin, Cole felt Varka's cape working over the processes of his mind. It was far easier to partition himself. He kept a coherent portion of his consciousness firmly embedded in his center. While still fully shrouded with Rage, it was no hard task to call Wisdom to his aid. His feet left the ground as the stone cape melted to flowing glass. He surged upward to his comrades.

Roth was in the lead, his great sweeping wings easily three times the size of any other. Cole fell in behind them, noticing his lungs beginning to ache and quicken. The air was too thin at this altitude, too weak. Maintaining his Rage, he cast yet another spell of Wisdom, compressing the air around him. The task was more taxing than he had anticipated. He released a small portion of his Rage and the shroud receded from his torso.

They were only two-thirds the elevation of the Fangshards, but Cole could see both ends of the valley. At one end the meager army of Oberon City cut its way in with little specks of emerald weapons. Cole saw a few of their soldiers take higher ground, lining the steep banks of the pass just ahead of the front line. They progressed aggressively and confidently.

Cole gazed down towards the coastal end of the valley, unable to discern anything from the vague shapes that splotched the landscape. After a moment he realized something was off. Cole enhanced his vision to the limits of his Wisdom, zooming miles down the valley. What he had taken for a great swath of trees at the mouth of the valley was undulating, moving. It was the Domina. Cole didn't have to count them to know their numbers were several times that of Oberon's army. Megorien's estimation of one thousand was an absurdly conservative number. He considered flying down to tell her just that, but Roth's arching wings banked hard to the right, leading the rest of the unit to a flat alcove.

Munisica and bare feet crunched into the rocky ledge. Gale's hulking claws made a prominent statement as his paws collided into the stone. He chirped and folded his wings as Alvani hopped down and joined the others. Her feet and hands were no longer gentle and pale, but wicked, black weapons. Cole had never seen the Passion-Master draw munisica before.

Cole fell in close to Roth, who considered the scene before him as a jeweler might inspect an heirloom of questionable value. The group was silent for a long while, merely watching the two armies progress towards the middle of the pass. After a quarter of an hour it became painfully apparent how hopelessly outnumbered Oberon's army was. The elders remained still as statues the whole while, though the unit began to stir as unease spread over the ledge.

Valen was first to break the silence. "Masters, please enlighten us. I know you have assigned the Domina to Oberon's forces, but should we not help them while we sit idle? We could eliminate a good portion before they ever reach the front lines. Give us the order."

The elders didn't respond, though every ear was poised and ready. Eventually Roth rumbled an answer: "Your orders are to watch and learn. The Wisdom Warriors are more capable than they let on. They might need to see a few of their friends take their last, but they'll find their rhythm soon enough. Watch the Domina, watch how they move. See what animals they've taken for thralls. Consider them, but do not let your eyes neglect what crawls up the coast behind them."

All five heads of the unit snapped to the right while the Elders maintained their passive sweep. Cole peered through his own sharpened lenses while others conjured their crystalline telescopes. It looked as if a great flock of birds flapped their way into the valley. They appeared drunk, barely able to keep aloft. A quarter of an hour passed, bringing their figures close enough so that there was no mistaking them. Oberon illuminated their sagging abdomens and gaping maws, their thin wisps of hair and gangly hands. A swarm of Corpulants devoured the sky, hobbling through the air on stubby wings.

"Well that's a new trick," Chiron remarked.

"I bet they still come apart just as easy," Roth said.

Cole swallowed hard, stifling a gag. The Corpulants were already the vilest things he'd ever seen, yet somehow they had managed to make themselves even more repugnant. He wished he could burn the lot of them with fire, but the horrors were bred from Fear, making Wisdom invalid. Passion wouldn't do either. There was nothing about them that he could remotely relate to and sympathize with. It would have to be Rage. He glanced down the line, seeing munisica stretching, aching for use.

Gale chirped with unease, trotting in place as his great amber eyes glared at the flock. Alvani stroked his neck feathers with a rosy hand, soothing him. She looked to the unit with a sly grin. "Valen, would you be so kind as to take your unit and rid this valley of that swarm? I would do it myself, but Gale doesn't like Corpulants and I'd rather not clean the mess from his plumage."

"With pleasure, Master Alvani." Valen looked each member of the unit in the eye, exchanging bloodlust in a moment's gaze.

"Wait till they're over the front line," Roth hissed. "I don't want them balking and fleeing the way they came."

"And don't forget about their flies," Chiron added, crossing his arms behind his back, inspecting the Corpulants with a scholarly interest. "Other than their poor interpretation of wings, they appear to be the same…" His voice faded as he squinted. Then his eyes widened slightly in surprise. "Oh, no I was wrong. Their throats are unusually engorged. Be mindful of that little detail. I'm sure it's not insignificant."

"Thank you Masters." Valen's munisica clutched the sharp edge of the escarpment. He poised himself in a low crouch as his emerald wings uncurled like blooming lilies.

Over the next half hour, the front lines of both ground armies met. First blood was drawn by the Domina. Their sluggish progress belied how fast they were in close quarters. Roth's prediction was accurate; once a few of Oberon's number had fallen, the others tightened their formations and retaliated with terrible efficiency. Summoned shields broadened into an impenetrable wall as spellcasters hurled their magic into the legion of Domina. After a few minutes of skirmishing, a wall of the fallen beasts had piled high enough to halt the oncoming flood. Oberon's warriors continued to rain down a storm of offensive magic upon the Domina, who were too busy navigating their fallen comrades to notice the attacks.

Cole observed the exchange with passive interest. Good people were dying down there, but he detached himself from that idea.

Passion had its place, and his Passion wanted him to jump off the ledge and heal the warriors before death became them. From the calm of his stone room he could see the situation clearly. He would save a far greater number by analyzing the Domina for a moment, as well as sticking to their plan. The Corpulants were nearly at the front line now. Decreath's Fear would change the tide of the ground-battle within seconds.

Something familiar caressed the edges of Cole's mind. It felt pure and wholesome, and carried with it echoes of every memory he had from The Sill. He checked his bond with Goran, but the mirak was still watching the mouth of the valley from some far-off peak.

Eliza joined the gentle touch, urging it into Cole's mind. *"I'm widening our bond so the whole unit can communicate. It's not as acute as what you and I share, but it will allow us to work together as a cohesive whole. Accept it."*

Without a word, Cole opened himself to the myriad of swirling minds. He could feel each mind of his unit as a separate thrumming strand that wove them all together. The connection was ambiguous and crude, like the first time he connected with Goran. He felt a moderate drain on his Passion, but nothing too worrisome.

Fire.

Flight.

Rage.

The concepts came from Valen's rigid strand. They were simple, yet made perfect sense with the context of his desires. One at a time, the unit flexed their wings as a churning whirlwind of fire spiraled around their bodies.

Cole had never summoned fire in such a manner, but now Varka's cape nudged his grasp on the necessary Wisdom. Using the familial bond, the cape translated the spell into something Cole could easily understand. Grinding his teeth with effort, Cole ignited his own flame-cloak. He opened his eyes with a jolt. The rest of his unit had already taken flight.

Alvani's voice rang out clear and powerful, "Go blaze a trail for Terra."

Cole nodded to her through the rippling flames. He took a steadying breath to solidify himself in his center, pouring the cooling waters over his consciousness. Eyes snapping wide, he locked on to his unit and dove from the ledge.

Varka's cape fluttered over Cole's backside as it shifted to liquid glass. He dropped several stories, indulging in the thrill of the fall and the rushing of the wind. On a whim, he summoned his emerald wings instead of moving himself with direct Wisdom. The air rushed into the crystal wings, filling them with tight control of the winds. As Chiron had mentioned, the conjured wings gave him much better low-speed maneuverability. He did a few sharp banks and experimental rolls, but he was quite sure he could fly circles around the hobbling Corpulants. Decreath's horrors looked as if they could barely maintain flight with their ramshackle wings of baggy skin and crooked bones.

Cole filled his wings and swooped up to join his unit's formation. Through their unit-bond they agreed to assault the Corpulants from altitude. Without a spoken word or thought, they folded their wings and shot into a steep dive, five blazing meteors of Rage and Wisdom tearing through the valley.

Cole picked his target and surged faster; a fat Corpulant chundering along with a labored gait. His Rage wanted to dive straight through, but his Wisdom knew he would lose too much momentum. Shifting slightly, he opened a wing and with a sharp *thwack*, cleaved the head of the first Corpulant. The monster dropped like a sack of soiled laundry.

Opening his wings, Cole looped back up to the fray, coming head first with several more of the misshapen horrors. They circled around him. Tugging at the gill-like flaps on their torsos, they shook clouds of stinging flies towards him. The insects flew straight for him, only to crackle and pop as they buzzed against his flame cloak. Cole hung in the air for a moment, watching the Corpulants flap closer as morbid curiosity took hold of him. One Corpulant edged nearer than the others, its jiggling folds rippling as it worked its mouth open. Surely it wouldn't be foolish enough to try and swallow him?

The Corpulant's maw snapped open, sending a levered appendage hurling towards Cole, clouting him in the face with alarming force. Cole snatched at the thing before it could retract, squeezing and severing it with his claws. He banked up and away from the Corpulants, checking his face to make sure the shroud had protected him from the blow. Once at a safe height, he inspected the severed appendage. It looked like a ball of bleeding gums with a leathery arm at its base. At its tip was a yellow horn as long as his forearm. Clear liquid oozed from little holes along its length like some great needle. Cole shared the information through the unit-bond, warning the others.

Not willing to take any chances, Cole dismissed the flame cloak so that his Rage could fully shroud him. The emerald wings took a greater effort to maintain and he knew he wouldn't be as agile, but then again he didn't need to be. The Corpulants were slow and sloppy, and their tongues and flies would have no effect on him. Once above their flock, he dove through again, more slowly this time. With careful deliberation, he plucked at their heads with his munisica, crushing and killing eight on his way down. Flies and spiked tongues battered his shroud all the while. He wove his way three more times through the flock before the Corpulants began to scatter. They never made it down to the front line. Cole glanced down at Oberon's warriors. Their jade shields had been bolstered, covering the entire formation in a seamless hull. The Domina's progress had not only been halted, but reversed. The tides of battle were quickly flowing in favor of Oberon's army.

When the unit couldn't find any more Corpulants, they made for the rear flank of the Domina before the beasts could escape from the valley. A savage giddiness took hold of Cole as he imagined himself using the full measure of his Rage against so many foes. The unit was about to land when a thundering mind exploded into their unit link.

"*GET YOUR ASSES BACK UP HERE NOW!*"

They all winced, looking to each other for an answer.

"Why the hell would he call us back?" Sitra hollered over the wind. "We're doing just fine."

Lileth's eyes snapped wide, sending a spike of panic into their bond as she gazed towards the rear of the valley. They all prodded her with their minds, searching for the answer that she seemed momentarily incapable of. After several tense seconds, a single word escaped her mind.

Colossus.

CHAPTER 22

CORONATION

Cole turned to face the ocean. A mountain of a head rose with the unassuming speed of a distant cloud, followed by a pair of shoulders wide enough to fill the valley. Flickering dread wriggled in Cole's guts. It was impossible to tell how big the titan was, but it was certainly larger than the Alpha Colossus at Morthain.

Valen sent a surge of energy into the unit-bond, snapping them from their awe. They made for the Elders on the ledge, shooting up in a tight formation. Gale whipped across their path, giving them a trumpeting screech as he dashed out of the valley. Cole had a vague impression that Goran was nearby as they raced up the valley walls, though he could not see his friend anywhere. They came to a crunching halt atop the ledge. All eyes were upon the Elders.

"The lord of Hatred and Despair has arrived," Chiron said in a soft tone.

Alvani entwined her hands around Roth's arm, resting her head against his shoulder. "How do you know, Chiron?"

Roth's grating voice answered her, "Only Sorronis could have raised the Alpha Colossus from the floors of the White Sands. Looks like it took that rock wurm's plating for armor."

"And those are no storm clouds rolling in," Chiron added.

Billowing over the head of the Colossus was a black thunderhead. Veins of bloody lightning darted over its surface. The Colossus was entirely out of the water now, standing still at the valley entrance, a dark monolith nearly as tall as the Fangshards. The clouds continued to gather above it.

"Can we stop it?" Valen asked, unable to hide the trembling in his voice.

"You can't," Roth said. "You're going to plant yourselves right here. This one's a far shot out of your league."

The Unit let out a collective sigh of relief. There was no training to prepare them for an enemy of this scale. Cole's Rage wanted him to object, but what could he hope to accomplish? Even fully shrouded it would take him an hour just to dig his way to the bone nest. The Colossus swayed at the valley entrance, waiting for some unknown reason.

Chiron placed his hands on Alvani's and Roth's shoulders, rousing them with a gentle shake. "My dear friends, let us show Sorronis the might of the Unbound."

Alvani set a hand over Chiron's, giving him a warm smile. A look of dread washed over her as the valley took on a crimson glow.

"Hatefire!" Alvani screamed, throwing her arms out and pushing the group back with invisible force. Cole slammed into the others as if kicked by a horse.

The black thunderhead churned with bloody light, swirling to a fine point below. With a deafening roar, the bottom of the vortex opened, splitting the skies with a tornado of roaring fire. The whirlwind collided with the valley floor, filling it with unrelenting destruction. The tornado lurched forward through the valley, scorching the walls and obliterating everything in its path. Alvani threw her arms out, casting a glistening opalescent shield over the ledge.

Cole squinted, covering his ears as the roaring became unbearable. He wrapped his arms around his head as the Hatefire passed over them. When the light finally faded, he cracked his eyes open, checking his body to make sure the shroud had held up. He was not confident that his Rage would protect him from whatever that fire was made of.

Alvani's form blazed in a hazy silhouette as the torrent passed, her arms outstretched and breast pumping. Her eyes were locked in cold fury as she followed the column of fire. The tornado passed through the Domina, crisping them to charred heaps. Cole leapt to his feet, pressing his face against Alvani's shield. To his horror Oberon's forces had fared no better than the Domina. Megorien and her army were no more.

After annihilating all the length of the valley, the Hatefire swirled back up into the clouds above. The Colossus lumbered after the wreckage, running an island-sized hand along what was left of the paved trail. It scooped the charred bodies of the Domina into its maw. Somehow, the Domina were still alive, bleating and screaming all the while.

Chiron and Roth took up positions next to Alvani, bolstering her shield with their own Passion, which they projected from their palms.

Cole felt a smooth hand close on his munisica. Lileth looked up at him, Fear pooling in her eyes. Cole dismissed his Rage and embraced her, pulling her away from the view of the valley floor. He poured his Passion into her, but her mind was befuddled and resisted his touch.

He whispered into her ear, trying his best to make his words ring true, "We're gonna be okay. The elders will protect us."

"That complicates things a bit," Chiron said, watching the Colossus devour the last of the Domina.

"What is it?" Roth demanded.

"Sorronis may be mad, but he is as clever as the last time we met. Those Domina were *chosen* before the battle. The Hatefire acts as a substitute for the odium." Even as he said it, the Colossus bulged all over, swelling with new growth as the Domina's bodies were assimilated.

"Bet I can have that head off in ten minutes," Roth growled.

Chiron smirked, casting him a sideways glance. "Please Rothael, I'd be embarrassed to call you Unbound if it took you that long." A neat pair of jade wings curled out of Chiron's back.

Roth flexed his shoulders forward as his broad emerald wings erupted. "You coming, Alvi?"

She held her chin high as she maintained her shield with a single hand. "I will remain here to protect the young ones. You will both take my grace before you leave this ledge."

Roth shook his head, taking a step towards the edge. "No, keep it. We can look after ourselves."

She spoke with ironclad authority: "It wasn't an offer."

Faster than Cole could see, her free hand was suddenly on Roth's chest, fuchsia rays pouring in. A tingling sensation pricked over Cole's skin. He had no idea what Alvani had done, but he could feel an ocean of power in the transfer.

Roth's face slackened as his nostrils and eyes flared. His body took an aura similar to Oberon's chromatic surface. She repeated the process with Chiron, who did not object. When finished, she opened a hole in her shield. "Go now, last of the Unbound."

With a gust of wind, Chiron and Roth dove from the ledge. The air seemed to tear in protest to their speed. Alvani closed the gap in her shield and watched as the Colossus drew closer to their ledge. It was entirely unaware of two winged missiles blazing right for it. Inky droplets began to fall from the valley's clouded ceiling, staining the rock and rolling off Alvani's barrier.

Cole released Lileth, who trembled as she mumbled to herself. "Eliza, can you look her over? Something is wrong with her. Nothing I'm doing is helping."

"Of course," Eliza said, cradling Lileth against the valley wall.

Cole looked back to the Colossus. It was close enough now that he could make out individual bodies and smell their undying reek. The armor plating of the rock wurm lined its chest and arms in no discernable order, though it wore the beast's skull over its own in a crude battle-crown. Roth and Chiron were nowhere to be found. Cole rubbed his fingers to his eyes, sharpening his sight to the limits of his Wisdom. He saw a short curved pair of wings and a glinting body hanging in the air before the titan. Chiron was impossibly small, appearing no larger than the most diminutive insect.

An azure flash lit the space between Chiron and the Alpha Colossus, lifting its feet from the ground as if it had been struck by a battering ram. The titan collided with the opposite valley wall, causing numerous landslides. Seconds later, the noise from the spell reached the ledge, sucking all sound into an empty silence before a thunderous crack reverberated down the valley. The chaotic chatter of an avalanche came next.

Cole picked up a flicker of motion from above. Roth's wings were folded, his scintillating form stretched out into a living spear. Before the Colossus could gather itself, Roth buried himself in its neck, becoming a blur of wings and claws as pieces fell from the titan. To the Colossus he was hardly bigger than a grain of rice, but the damage already added up to a wide hole in its neck. Cole let out a nervous laugh. There was no way Roth would need ten minutes to decapitate the Colossus.

"Yes!" Sitra whooped, slashing the air. "Look at them go!"

"They had better end it quickly," Valen noted. "Sorronis's Harbinger has yet to show himself."

Cole's eyes scanned the bloody clouds. "Where would he be hiding?"

Alvani spoke in a steely tone. "The Harbinger is in the heart of the Colossus. They are attempting to draw him out into open combat."

Cole shivered. Even from this distance he could sense the power surging from Chiron and Roth. Thunderous magic reverberated down the valley, slamming into Cole's chest like a fist. The Colossus grabbed at the valley walls, pulling itself to its feet while explosions rippled from the hole in its neck. Cole found Chiron hovering chest-height to the titan. The elder gathered a ball of blue light in his hands.

The Colossus rose to its full height. Its chest swelled as smoke poured from its maw. Roth shot out of its neck, black soot dripping from his wings. With its gaze on the Bonebreaker, the Colossus wrenched open its jaw and spewed forth a geyser of rusty brown liquid. Roth dodged the attack, drawing it away, though its endless arms kept him from getting too far.

The azure orb in Chiron's grasp was now as large as he was. By unseen command, Roth changed direction, shooting for the stars as both of the titan's hands followed. Chiron thrust the magic towards the Colossus. The ball split in two, each half rocketing for the titan's shoulders. The resulting explosions were too bright to behold. Everyone on the ledge shut their eyes, and covered their ears before the sound could reach them, Alvani included. When the smoke and thunder had cleared, the Colossus stood readying another gout of vomit, except this time it had no arms. The limbs rolled down the valley wall, carried by rocky avalanches.

Before the Colossus could spray again, Chiron released a hail of the blue energy into its chest, smashing through its armor. The titan sputtered and fumbled, seeming to choke on its vomit. Seizing the hesitation, Roth dove in for a series of cleaving blows, cutting deeper into its neck.

The inky rain continued to shower the valley, growing thicker and obstructing visibility of the distant battle. The bloody clouds groaned overhead, looking as though they would release another tower of Hatefire at any moment.

Though Cole could hardly see Roth and Chiron, the Colossus was clearly losing energy. It took a knee, unable to stand under the bombardment of Chiron's destructive magic. Every blast of sapphire energy shattered its armor and sent hundreds of chosen raining to the ground. Roth's wings blazed with green light as they stretched to several times their size. With a final swoop, the head of the Colossus tilted and fell from its shoulders like a great tree. The rest of its body collapsed in a heap on top of its severed arms. Chiron gathered another orb, raising it over his head as it swelled larger than a house. He whipped his arms down, sending the magic screaming towards the Colossus.

Cole ducked, shutting his eyes and ears. The concussion knocked him off his feet. His back smacked the slate, driving the breath from his lungs. When he opened his eyes, there was a white mushroom-cloud rising up to the black cloud above. The others rose shakily to their feet. Alvani was still standing, however, her face locked in elegant wrath.

A moment later, a hole opened in the shield as Chiron and Roth flew in. They were both covered in the cloud's black water, though it hovered an inch off their skin. The taint dripped and fell from their barriers where it pooled on the slate at their feet.

"Do not touch the liquid," Chiron said quickly. "It is some wickedness of Sorronis."

They jumped back as Roth scraped dirt and stone onto the puddles. Cole gazed upon his Masters with newfound awe. They appeared no worse for wear, as if they had just returned from a stroll through the markets. Cole couldn't help but compare himself to the two Masters, feeling as if he could almost keep up with Roth. He was after all the only person to master Rage since before the banishing. If only he knew how to shoot those blasts of raw energy that Chiron used. Cole decided he would stand on Chiron's head until the elder showed him how to use such powerful destructive magic.

Sitra flexed her munisica. "That was carnage! There's no way that heap of shit is getting up from that!"

Valen peered over the ledge, inspecting the smoking remains of the Colossus. "I suppose he's not dead. Are those not Sorronis's clouds above us?"

Chiron swept over each of them, inspecting and filling them with Passion. "I'm afraid we only showed Sorronis that he will need more than an Alpha Colossus to best us." His voice dropped to a grim whisper. "Ready your hearts, children. The Harbinger approaches."

They all turned, slowly bringing their gaze upon the ruddy mountain of chosen. The Colossus undulated as it rose into the sky in an amorphous mass. The severed arms of the Colossus rose into the air carried by unseen forces, joining the throbbing city of broken corpses as it moved towards their ledge.

"Let him come!" Roth bellowed. His munisica snapped wide as the shroud crawled over almost all of his body. "I'll rip him in half and feast on his heart! Draw your blades, Warriors of The Sill! Let the Rage burn your bones!"

It was as if Roth's words were saturated with the red magic. White hot needles pricked their way up Cole's scalp as his Rage flared to life. His fingers lengthened and stretched, agonizingly yet gratifyingly. The shroud pooled over him from the inside out, bolstering every fiber of his body with Master's Rage. Every muscle in his body twitched, demanding violence. Cole filled his lungs and joined in the unit's battle cry, demanding Sorronis come face their fury.

The oily torrent surged in a thick deluge, casting the valley in dense shadow. Flashes of crimson lightning showed the progress of the floating remains of the Colossus.

After a tense minute, the writhing mass arrived directly in front of the ledge. The bodies were soaked with the greasy rain, though it wasn't enough to mask the stench from their charred flesh. Chiron slashed his palm over his head, bathing the whole area in brilliant white light.

"GET OUT HERE YOU SLIMY BASTARD!" Roth stamped his bladed feet, rattling the entire ledge. "YOU THINK YOU KNOW DESPAIR? BRING YOUR BEST OUT HERE AND BEHOLD THE MEANING OF SUFFERING!"

Thousands of bodies cried out in anguish as a fissure opened in the center of the heap. The gap stretched wider as the entire mass heaved, emitting a wrenching, wet lurch. The screams of the chosen rose as a nest of spiked bones the size of a city block hacked its way to the fore of the gap. A door hinged forward, slamming to the ledge like a drawbridge. From the shadows of the bone nest walked a man dressed in a neat charcoal suit. He was missing an eye and held a bundle of rags against his chest with one arm. He looked young and would have been handsome if not for the soot that stained his mouth and nose. Every feature of his face was etched with profound malice, as though he had been bred for the sole purpose of causing pain in others. The man stood upon his bony bridge, glaring at them with a bloodshot eye as he bared a mouth full of shattered, blackened teeth.

Cole shuddered as a horrible memory from the Devotion came to him. When Decreath had entered Kreed his face was stained in the same manner, broken teeth and all. This man was the Harbinger of Sorronis.

Alvani was first to speak. Her voice shook with horror. "Talin…my dear Talin…what have they done to you?"

The name clicked in Cole's memory. Talin was a unit-leader from The Sill. He'd seen him in between lessons and heard good things about the man. What misfortune could have brought Sorronis into his heart? Was he a traitor?

Talin's eye blazed as spit flew from the cracks in his teeth. He looked as if he would like nothing more than to murder Alvani on the spot.

Chiron reached out with a gentle hand. He spoke in a soft, timid tone, as if afraid Talin might explode any moment. "It's not too late, Talin. We can help you. There is still beauty and love in this world. Think of your family. Think of sweet Penelope."

Talin's head jerked as a fleeting, anguished expression twisted his features. He brought his glare to Chiron as he ground his broken teeth together. Blackened shards fell from his lips as he opened his mouth, his voice a smoky whisper. "*Liar.*"

Stung, Chiron turned his head and closed his eyes in a look of resigned disappointment.

"Save your sympathies," Roth grunted. "The boy's made his choice. I only wish I had the opportunity to kill him before he dishonored himself." He inclined his head, sneering at Talin. "What did you sell yourself for anyhow? How much did they give you? Wait, don't tell me. It was a release from the suffering, wasn't it? They tortured you a bit and you folded like wet paper."

Talin's lip curled in a wicked smile. "To live is to suffer, Bone-breaker."

Roth crossed his arms, sneering. "You don't say?"

Talin's head twitched again as he patted his free hand over the bundle that rested in his arm. "Your words are but empty lies. All of you. You sent children to fight for you. Filled them with promises of victory and glory. I see a few of your favorites managed to escape, but they'll join the others before long. They burn for me. They Hate for me, just as I Hate for you."

Alvani stepped off the ledge, joining Talin. Her shield bent and swelled with her, protecting her from the oily rain. Talin's face softened as her warm glow touched his skin. She reached for him, cupping his cheek with a hand saturated with strawberry light. Her voice was powerful and clear: "I release you from your Hatred."

There was a shuddering boom as Alvani's magic flooded into Talin, fixing his broken teeth and lifting the malice from his face. He inhaled, eyes searching as though he only just realized where he was. Alvani readied another spell, placing another hand on his breast.

"Alvi get back!" Roth roared, darting forward and snatching her back to the ledge.

Scarlett light bathed the valley walls as the clouds above opened once more. She wasn't ready. The Hatefire was upon them. Alvani cried out, throwing her hands up as she shoved more Passion into her shield.

Cole, however, was ready. With Varka's cape whispering hints, he dismissed his Rage and donned his Passion. Slapping his hands against the pearlescent shield, he infused it with his own Passion, strengthening it.

Screaming, the tower of Hatefire collided with the shield. The drain on Cole's Passion was immediate and rapid. He held on with everything he had, but it wasn't enough. Under the blinding fire he saw Chiron and Eliza raising their arms, bolstering the shield with their Passion. The load lifted from Cole, but after a few seconds he could feel their Passion faltering as well. As though it had only been toying with them, the tornado intensified, becoming a solid beam of fiery Hatred.

The shield vanished without warning, though so did the Hatefire. Great freezing drops of black rain smacked to Cole's naked skin, weighing him down with Despair. His heart broke when he saw the rest of his unit similarly affected. Even the elders had their backs bent by the weight of it. The significance of their failure was now painfully obvious to him. Every fat drop of the tainted oil battered his hope and showered him with regret.

Talin's head rolled back in laughter, only the sound that came was not meant for living ears. Helpless and soaked, Cole fell to his knees as the hellish noise filled him from the inside, overwhelming his senses. He felt himself sinking and slipping into every terrible memory he ever had. He scrambled desperately for the calming center of his mind, but the evil ramblings clouded and blocked his every thought. He was in the embrace of a god.

Weeping on all fours, Cole dared a glance at the others. Each of his unit was prone, possibly dead. The oily liquid flowed and bubbled up their bodies, covering them from head to toe. Flowing from the entire valley, the black tar converged on the ledge, as if drawn to its new victims. Seeing the others succumb to the evil magic ignited a modicum of Cole's Rage, just enough for him to rise drunkenly to his feet. Chiron and Roth were the only ones still standing. Alvani joined them after wobbling herself upright. Each of the elders maintained a barrier on their skin, keeping the oil from touching them.

Another bolt of crimson lightning flared. Needing no further encouragement, Roth dove for Sorronis.

"Rothael!" Chiron reached for him, but it was too late.

Before Roth's munisica met their target, thousands of ropey strands shot from the surrounding tar, wrapping him in place as surely as a fly in a spider's web. Roth thrashed, but the strands bent and stretched with him, halting his progress. His emerald wings erupted from his broad back, slicing through the black web as he spun on the spot. More strands joined the fray and broken fibers found new holds.

Chiron's hands became a blur as ribbons of flame shot from his fingertips, sailing and wrapping around Roth. When it became apparent the sticky substance wouldn't catch, the fiery ribbons became snakes of white ice, biting and freezing at the muck.

Roth bellowed through the web. "Don't waste your time on me! Put a blade to the bastard!"

Changing course, Chiron dismissed the snakes and floated from the ledge. His barrier stretched to a large orb as he levitated towards Sorronis. In each of his hands the sapphire energy gathered in thrumming lumps.

"Leave the boy, Sorronis," Chiron said, halting over the bony bridge. "You can't win against us. Despair and Hatred hold no sway over Rage and Wisdom."

With a roar, Roth threw off the black web, shoving it away with a blast of Wisdom. He stretched his own barrier in a wide orb like Chiron's, joining him on the bone bridge. Their defiance in the face of Despair sent a surge of Rage burning through Cole. It caught like wildfire, searing the rancid magic as the shroud enveloped him once more in a Master's Rage. The Despair would have no hold over him either. Rejuvenated, Cole joined Roth and Chiron. His munisica twitched, itching for an outlet.

Sorronis gazed through Talin's single smoking eye. Billowing smog poured from his mouth as the otherworldly sound keened louder, rising and falling in wailing laughter.

Cole gripped his Rage, wielding it like an ancient weapon. He could feel the haunting laughter echoing in the weaker parts of his mind, threatening to shake them loose and drag them into sickening Despair. His Rage bellowed in return, shattering Sorronis's taint from his mind as his Wisdom blew a cleansing breeze. Cole withdrew his Passion to his center, protecting it.

"You can't survive our wrath, hopeless one." Roth dismissed his shield. The black rain sizzled and evaporated before it ever touched his skin. Even the creeping tar fled from the heat of his Rage. "Give us the boy and maybe we'll kill you quicker."

Talin's head rolled from side to side as Sorronis's laughter warped into a banshee's wail. The shrieking vibrated the rain and shook boulders loose from the valley wall. Above them the sky cracked with bloody light as another tower of Hatefire descended. An electric green shaft of light rose to meet it.

Cole turned to see Alvani grunting with bladed hands over her head, a beam of jade Wisdom pouring up from her munisica.

The Hatefire bifurcated and rolled harmlessly around them, striking the mountain of chosen corpses before fizzling away.

Alvani whipped her clawed hands to her sides, screaming at the top of her lungs, "DO IT CHIRON. CAST HIM DOWN!"

Resignation fell over Chiron's face as he raised his energy-laden hands to Sorronis. The god keened horribly as the bundle on Talin's shoulder began to rustle and kick. The destructive sapphire magic swelled as Chiron readied the spells for release. The muscles in his arms tensed, but then Chiron paused, his head tilting slightly as his eyes sharpened. He lowered his glowing hands a fraction of an inch.

From behind the Harbinger, another figure strode out onto the bridge. He wore a suit of scarlet, the same cut as Talin's. The man strode out with a lazy grace, taking in the scene with a look of utter boredom. He was taller than Talin, and carried himself with lazy confidence, entirely underwhelmed by the chaos before him. Cole had a sickening suspicion that he already knew this man.

"There's nothing left of your Talin." The man's voice was derisive and clever, speaking through a smirk that accentuated the odd wrinkles on his face. "Hello, Dark Ones."

Confusion shook within the iron walls of Cole's Rage. "Habbad!"

"I told you I would never forgive you, Cole," Habbad said, hefting a black leather suitcase in his hands. With a lazy flick he summoned a green crystal table and set the suitcase upon it. "You promised me we would save Lexy. You failed of course, but it was necessary. Your failure was the catalyst that transformed both Lexy and me. To this day she serves Sorronis, just as I serve Grotton."

Sorronis raised Talin's free arm as the bone nest gave way to a thick appendage made from hundreds of arms and legs. The arm bent and curled, bringing forth the charred body of an impossibly small girl wearing a soiled dress. Lexy hung before Cole's face. Her unseeing eyes blazed with Hatred as her burnt voice hissed with Despair. Her crisped fingers reached for him, as her little voice fumed with murderous intent.

Cole threw himself into his Rage before the sight could shake him. The creature before him was no longer Lexy, just as the man in the red suit was no longer Habbad.

"Grotton's taking Underkin for Harbingers now?" Roth laughed. "The King of Hunger must be losing his touch."

Habbad licked his tongue over his teeth, scowling. "Grotton has yet to grace Aeneria with a Harbinger. Though after I give him the remaining two Unbound and their Passion-whore, I'm sure he'll crown me as his champion."

"You know not of what you speak, child." Alvani readied her own destructive magic in her munisica. "You sorely overestimate yourself if you think you will be more than a trifle to us. Not even Sorronis can hope to match us."

"I don't mean to match you. I don't need to." Habbad pulled a dusty grey feather from his sleeve, stroking it over the leather case. The case snapped open and three ebony needles floated from its depths. They were as long as Habbad's arm, and danced about his head as if they had a mind of their own. The needles kept darting for the elders, only to be yanked back by a waggle of Habbad's index finger. He grinned, seeing the revulsion on Chiron's face. "You know what these are, don't you?"

"You must be desperate indeed to parlay with the Cold Crows," Chiron said. Roth and Alvani perked up at the name, eyes widening in alarm. "To whom do the pithing shards belong?"

Habbad's grin darkened. "They belong to you of course. One for each of you."

There was a crack as each of the needles broke free from their bonds and shot across the bridge. Faster than thought, Chiron whipped his arms up as the Azure orbs in his hands widened into a broad slab, forming a thick shield. The shards passed through the magic unfazed. Each one found its home, piercing through Alvani's glowing hands, Roth's munisica, and Chiron's fading spell.

Cole watched helplessly as the needles buried themselves in each of the elder's chests. Their spells flickered and munisica faded as their bodies went limp, leaving the scene in quiet darkness as Chiron's white light vanished. As if waiting for the moment, the sticky black tar shot from the surrounding rocks, holding their bodies in midair. The elders didn't appear dead, but something was very wrong. Each of their faces drooped with hopelessness and their eyes scanned that which no one else could see. Roth's shroud receded entirely as his Rage failed him.

Cole's own Rage demanded that he dive for Habbad and rip him to pieces, though his Wisdom held him in place. There was no telling what Habbad was capable of.

"I'm sorry Cole, but I don't have one for you. I guess you aren't as important as we thought." Habbad strode forward and pushed Lexy aside. She lashed out with little fists as she disappeared back into the floating island of Chosen. "They're not dead, not yet anyway. Wouldn't want to spoil my gifts for Grotton." Habbad closed his eyes as snarling thunder echoed from the sky above. "Ah, yes. The Lord of Hunger arrives at last."

Cole leaped back onto the ledge, careful not to land on his unit, who all lay prone and still. The sticky rain had crept up over their bodies, covering them in black tar. Above him the bloody clouds split, revealing a speckled starscape and something immense descending to greet them.

A snarling swarm of rust fell into the valley, swirling into a thin spire as it quickened. Habbad raised his arms and threw his head back. "Come to me Grotton! Take your Harbinger and bring Hunger back to Aeneria!"

Cole backed away to the valley wall. If that thing really was Grotton then his Rage would spell certain death for everyone here. But he couldn't relinquish it, he needed the shroud to protect him from the oily rain. He had to think of something quick.

The ruddy essence of Grotton charged like a runaway locomotive. Cole felt naked and exposed, as if he were a field mouse at the mercy of a winged predator. The rusty mass halted above the ledge, bobbing back and forth as if it couldn't make up its mind. Cole dared not move, hoping it wouldn't sense his ripe Rage. He watched Grotton's churning mass with unblinking eyes, realizing the cloud was actually made of thousands, if not millions of tiny faceless mouths. Each one had a bundle of teeth the color of orange mold, which they used to tear and eat each other. A tendril broke free from the swarm, inching closer to Habbad.

"Grotton, I embrace your Hunger," Habbad cried, grinning from ear to ear.

The tendril shivered and recoiled, as if stung by something cold. It wormed its way away from Habbad, toward the elders.

Habbad's face twisted, desperate and confused. "No, no, no, I'm right here! Take me now!"

The rusty arm poked its way curiously over Roth. A few of the tiny mouths jumped free and set themselves on his bare skin, drawing blood and a breathless moan from the Bonebreaker. The orange cloud ceased its roiling as the tendril took greater interest in Roth. It tickled its way up his neck, reaching the corner of his lip. Without warning, the cloud shot for Roth as the tendril surged down his throat. The swarm howled as it took on the sole purpose of getting its entire mass within Roth's body.

"NO! IT WAS SUPPOSED TO BE ME!" Habbad wept, falling to his knees. "AFTER EVERYTHING I DID FOR YOU! YOU PROMISED ME!"

Roth's belly swelled to fantastic proportions as the last of Grotton forced its way into his mouth. Steam rose from his skin in a whining hiss as his stomach began to recede.

Habbad gathered himself, rising with a handful of fire bubbling between his fingers. The magic swelled as he aimed it for Roth.

A bolt of Hatefire screamed through the air and smote Habbad in the chest, sending him spinning like a toy over the bone bridge to the valley floor. Sorronis uttered a haunting moan, ignoring all else as he walked Talin's body over to Roth's, his free arm outstretched as if embracing a forgotten lover.

The Bonebreaker thrashed, becoming more coherent as the strands of tar fell from him. Roth's naked feet met the bridge as he stood swaying. Chiron stirred as well, eyes finally returning to the present.

Chiron's head flopped to face Roth, his voice feeble and hollow: "Rothael."

Roth gripped his hands over his stomach, which was now as large as the whole of his body. "Chiron, he has me. Get them out of here."

Chiron uttered a rasping groan. "I'm afraid I can't."

Roth strained, his munisica flaring and receding repeatedly. He grimaced as he found Alvani, bound and barely breathing. He looked back to Chiron, face heavy with defeat. "We were fools, weren't we?"

Chiron gave him a shaky smile. "Of course we were."

Roth let out a grating chuckle before doubling over. He landed on all fours upon the bone bridge, munisica snapping wide as he roared. Sorronis crouched, rubbing Roth's back encouragingly.

Chiron's head rolled towards Cole, peering at him with heavy lids. Maintaining his Rage, Cole took a step towards his Master, unsure of what to do.

Chiron's ancient song strummed into Cole. A weak smile stretched over the elder's face as he spoke a single word into Cole's mind: "*Varka.*"

"*I can't!*" Cole pleaded as Chiron's song began to fade. "*Master I can't do this alone! Fight it! Stay with me!*"

Chiron's lips parted, looking as if he were about to speak. His eyes snapped wide, suddenly clear and lucid. Bolstered, Cole took a step towards his Master, only to be halted by a blast of Wisdom. There was a loud crack and a puff of emerald smoke, and Chiron was gone. The strands of black tar searched the open air where his body had been.

Cole took another step. His Rage screamed louder, demanding action. His Wisdom scanned for an answer, anything that might present even a hint of help, but none came. His instincts took hold, melding with his Rage. Inaction would kill him more quickly than anything else. Roth was still fighting Grotton, but he wasn't gone just yet. That left only Sorronis. Grasping his Master's Rage, he threw a leg back and kicked off the valley wall as hard as he could, shooting off like a bullet.

The impact with which his munisica met Talin's body would have shattered any known material, though somehow Talin's body held fast. Cole and the Harbinger tore from the bridge out into open air. Cole dug his claws in, squeezing Talin with all his might, ignoring the muffled cries that came from the bundle of rags. When the force of his impact carried them as far as it would, Cole commanded his Wisdom to fly them farther still. Varka's cape snapped over his back, bending the magic to the perfect tune for Cole's mind. The air rippled and exploded around them as they accelerated beyond the speed of sound. Cole crushed Talin with enough force to cut through Morthainian glass, though somehow the Harbinger's flesh remained whole and hard. Cole urged his Wisdom on, aiming to take Sorronis as far from Grotton as possible. He might stand a chance against one god, but two was out of the question. Roth would make an unstoppable nightmare of a Harbinger.

Cole's Rage demanded more, so he gave it more. They were out of the valley and over the ocean, far enough from anyone he cared about. He also acknowledged a savage part of him wanted to see what he was really capable off. Giving Talin one more fruitless squeeze, he roared as he cast both him and Sorronis towards a small rocky island.

Cole stopped himself in midair as Talin struck the stone with the force of a small bomb. Cole let himself freefall to the island, scanning the hail of debris. His munisica crashed into a boulder, sending a shower of sparks and chips flying. He leaped from rock to rock towards Talin's crater. He wouldn't give Sorronis a second to recover.

Cole dropped into the crater, which was twice as deep as he was tall. Thick dust filled the briny air, obscuring his view. His ears pricked as a rustling came in the crater's center. Cole summoned a gust of wind, clearing the dust away. Black fist-sized rocks undulated at the bottom of the hole. Cole leaped once more, clearing the debris with raking swipes of his ebony blades.

A crimson hand shot from the loose rocks, snatching Cole by the wrist. The fingers elongated and sharpened into wicked claws as they crackled with sparks of Hatefire. The hand crushed and tugged. Cole yanked but the claws wouldn't break. They hurt.

A head covered in ruby bladed hair emerged from the rubble. Sorronis blazed with a world of Hatred through Talin's fiery eye. Cole balled his free hand into a massive spiked club, bringing it down on Talin's head with a hammer blow.

The air between them broke with a thunderous report, sending Cole flying away in a cascade of broken rocks. He steadied himself midflight, completing an awkward backflip before crashing onto solid rock.

Sorronis emerged from the crater, his short steps making much more noise than they ought to. The suit had been torn from most of Talin's body, exposing a blood-red shroud that covered every inch of his skin. His hands and feet were of the same color, only they were warped into munisica twice the size of Cole's. The bundle of rags he carried had somehow survived the trauma. It kicked and smoked as it squealed in agony. Cole was more worried about the bundle's contents than the approaching Harbinger.

Sorronis twisted and locked Talin's face into a menacing smile. He raised a twitching claw, pointing it at Cole as if in accusation. Before Cole could begin to wonder, a tight beam of Hatefire shot from the claw, striking Cole square in the chest.

Pain became him, threatening to shake the Rage from his bones. Cole shot behind a boulder. The relief was instant. He patted his chest, looking it over. His black shroud had been burned away, exposing raw muscle and bone beneath. Nothing was supposed to be able to pierce the shroud. Just then, Alvani's words from one of his first lessons echoed to the front of his mind.

"...As they gain mastery, the body becomes covered in an indestructible material, protecting them from any physical harm, though they are still vulnerable to the darker magics..."

This was the darker magic she was talking about. Hatefire could still harm him. Cole was so used to feeling indestructible, he hadn't bothered to defend himself while fully shrouded. How could he have been so careless against a god? He would have to mend the hole later, however. Sorronis's munisica chopped closer with every step.

Rage surging, Cole sank his munisica into the boulder. With surprising ease, Cole hefted the carriage-sized rock and hurled it towards the crunching footsteps. His Rage adored the challenge, demanding more. Quick as lightning, he charged after the boulder, waiting for it to find its target.

Time seemed to slow while his Rage burned hotter. After what felt like a minute, the boulder finally gave a shudder as it halted and split down the middle. Cole battered through the boulder, exploding through to the other side. His Rage growled with satisfaction as he saw the slightest twitch of surprise in Sorronis's eye. Roaring with bloodlust, Cole struck Sorronis in the gut as hard as he could. He felt a satisfying crunch as the crimson shroud yielded beneath his munisica. The god was not invincible.

Cole brought a bladed foot up next, intent on cleaving Sorronis in between the legs. A shrouded shin crossed his own, blocking the attack as the force carried Sorronis into the air. Cole crouched, preparing for another assault, but noticed something odd. There was a miniscule moment when Sorronis flailed before regaining his effortless grace. The motion was awkward, not at all befitting a god. The blunder, however small, showed that the Harbinger was not invincible, he was not perfect.

Emboldened, Cole launched after his enemy. Another beam of Hatefire screamed at him. He tried to alter his path with Wisdom, but there was no room left in his mind as the Rage filled every corner. The beam cut across his back, searing and stabbing a line down to his upper leg. He collided bodily with Sorronis, clinging to him with his munisica as they sailed high above the island. The red shroud sizzled and burned against his own. Cole ignored the pain and clenched all the harder while raining blows over every inch of Sorronis he could reach. Sorronis blocked most of his strikes, but not all. Cole's Rage rose to dangerous levels, blinding and consuming him while he grew faster and stronger. He no longer cared if he survived.

Soon Cole's attacks landed more often than they missed, though Sorronis seemed to be willingly handicapping himself by blocking with only one hand. His other was still occupied with the increasingly restless bundle he held on his shoulder. They flew higher still, now propelled by magic from Sorronis. Cole grasped with a pained grip while the Harbinger carried them over the water. His munisica felt as if they were shattering and breaking, but Cole could feel the red shroud crumpling and failing as well. Sorronis's movements became increasingly sloppy and labored, providing Cole with openings that he pounced upon without hesitation. Cole roared, allowing his Rage full control. A weary dread mixed with the waning Hatred in Sorronis's eye, but still he only fought with one hand, using the other to hold the bundle close to his chest.

With a final blow, Sorronis went limp, but Cole didn't relent. Sharp chunks of red shroud fell from the Harbinger's unprotected chest, exposing the flesh beneath. There was almost nothing left of Cole's munisica now. His claws had broken off, revealing angry wounds beneath. His body may have been failing, but his Rage was still on the rise. Cole pummeled the same spot over and over, feeling his own shroud breaking like cold wood and as he ignored the snapping from inside his arm. Sorronis closed his eye as his red shroud vanished, uncovering mortal wounds to his chest.

They were still somehow floating above the ocean. Cole held on with the remnants of his munisica, working out how best to tear the head off his enemy. Using his bladed feet, Cole shimmied up the limp body. In the quiet of the moment he realized the bundle of rags had been crying. There was a child beneath the folds.

The sound took his breath away. How in the world could a child be here? How could it have survived the trauma? How could it tolerate such proximity to an evil god? Frozen with curiosity, Cole took what was left of a claw and peeled back the rags, which were soaked and boiling hot. The child's wailing rose in desperation, grating on Cole's ears. He had to help it. As if his Rage knew the significance, the red magic gave his mind a few inches of clarity.

Cole threw back handfuls of the rags, careful not to harm the child. The wailing jolted to something morbid, creating a sound that could only be made by one experiencing ultimate suffering. Cole forced his munisica still, carefully peeling back the final wet layer.

The all-too-familiar smell of burnt flesh stung Cole's sharpened nose. The figure may very well have been a child at one time, but now it bore a closer resemblance to something scraped off a greasy skillet. Crisped skin melted seamlessly with Talin's naked chest, giving the appearance that he carried a rotting tumor with a little head and trembling arm. Cole couldn't fathom how this tortured creature managed to cling to life.

There wasn't the faintest whisper of a hope left for the child. Cole would have to kill it, no matter the cost to his own soul. This child had long earned a death. The embrace of the void would be the only escape from such prolific agony.

Just as Cole resigned himself to the act, the creature fell silent. Cole froze, hoping the child had suddenly died.

A shriveled arm uncurled from the charred lump, extending to a crude stick of a finger. Its head snapped free of the ash of Talin's chest, turning and revealing a pair of hazel eyes untouched by evil or flame. They were jewels, innocent and pure, embedded into a living nightmare. The eyes held Cole in place, flaying him as the finger pointed with the authority of Despair itself. The black finger caressed Cole's cheek and collided with his soul.

With no memory of letting go, Cole found himself falling through open air. Air rushed over his naked ears, chilling his skin. His Rage abandoned him, taking his shroud with it. The sky above him was devoid of even the faintest star. A canvas of evil clouds loomed, blocking even Oberon's warm glow. Odd concepts filled the gaps in Cole's reasoning, with one standing clear above the rest; he was quite sure that he was no longer on Aeneria.

He fell with his back to the unknown. There was a shadow just behind him, a burden he'd carried for far too long. It had been waiting, stalking every breath he took. It laughed at his empty promises, his attempts at wearing the mantle of 'hero.' Cole was nothing but the sum of his mistakes, piled on over years of ineptitude and callow yearning. His failures taxed the very lives and souls of those he loved. Cole could feel the shadow now, licking the back of his neck with fetid shame.

The significance of all his life's errors crashed over him as he dropped like a dead weight. Memories of everyone he cared for rushed to him, screaming and begging for his help. He saw his mother cowering in bed, eyes vacant and faded, her only moment of clarity coming when she offered him her Hatred. Nana Beth recoiled at the sight of him, abhorring the boy who had killed her adopted family. Habbad roared in hollow wrath, betrayed by the worthless liar who had promised him the life of his sister. Hopelessness pulled at Lexy's face, twisting it into unfamiliar agony as he watched the flames violate her. His unit closed in around him, Deekus and Eliza weeping, Sitra and Storn and Valen readying to attack. Lileth backed away, horrified at the man she had gifted her most fragile parts to. The Elders loomed over all, conjuring spells to obliterate the human who tore down Varka's barrier and brought endless suffering back to Aeneria. Each victim circled ever closer, demanding he give them back their trust and their lives.

Cole smacked into something solid. He didn't know how long he was unconscious for, but when he opened his eyes next, his sight was clouded and a searing cold stung at every inch of him. The impact had driven all the air from his lungs. He opened his mouth to breathe as icy water rushed down his throat. He was under water. He clamped his mouth shut and cut his way to where he hoped the surface was, lungs burning and demanding air.

He was surrounded by complete blackness with no way of knowing if he swam up or down. Red lightning cracked mercifully, flashing over the rolling waves too far above him. There was no way he could make the distance. His chest kept pumping for air, desperately attempting to suck in the freezing water. Cole adjusted course and made for the surface. Without warning his throat betrayed him like a greedy animal, sucking and dumping a mouthful of water into his lungs. Primal Fear fueling his every stroke, Cole charged through the water, determined to survive. With every stroke of his arms he expended more of his vital resources, but there was no alternative. He would live.

Bloody lightning flashed again. Only a few feet of cold water hung between him and the air he so desperately needed. Something crashed through the surface and sloshed down beside him. Even his screaming urge to breathe couldn't drown the sensation of an iron hand closing around his ankle, dragging him deeper. Despite the heavy weight, Cole managed to make progress with his waning strength. His hand broke through, heavy and chilled in the open air. His eyes and nose bobbed up next. He flailed against the dead weight, but his lips never met the life-giving air. The tides of struggle shifted against him. He sank back down into the darkness, utterly spent.

Cole dropped like a rock as his stiff fingers fumbled over his ankle. Lightning flashed again. Joshy dangled below him, his tiny white knuckles clenched firmly on his ankle. Despair tore Cole's heart wide open, dousing the final dregs of hope. They descended like a pair of falling stars, far away from the world to a place where hope and love had no home.

A calm acceptance fell over Cole. He would drown with his brother. He deserved it. His throat cracked open again, exchanging the last of his air with killing water. A faraway flicker revealed Joshy's dim figure once more. Wisps of ginger hair flowed over sad eyes. Upon seeing Cole, his face scrunched with profound sorrow, conveying remorse for what he was. His red jacket billowed as if on fire while his little Velcro shoes stuck out at odd angles behind him.

Cole pulled himself down with Joshy, wrapping his arms around his brother's body. Joshy embraced him, crying through the darkness. Holding each other close, they rushed to the void as the void rushed up to greet them.

I'm so sorry Joshy.

His brother's sobs shook into him, pulling him tighter as Despair embraced them both. They fell forever, beneath the world, beneath themselves.

After a lifetime, feeble curiosity joined their void. Were they dead now? Surely they were. Despair crushed the question. It didn't matter if they were dead; there was nothing worth living for. Cole pulled tighter, squishing Joshy's cold forehead into his cheek.

A defiant flower bloomed in the abyss, a realization of how things were. They had been falling forever, but it was no longer Joshy who pulled him down. Cole had been holding onto shame for his brother's death all this time. In life Joshy was a burden of fate's choosing. In Joshy's death Cole was finally freed of the charge, exchanging it for a burden of guilt which he neglected at every turn. He had to let go. A piece of Cole's heart that he never knew toppled into place, replacing the Despair with warm Passion.

Cole ran his hand up the back of Joshy's head, feeling his flowing hair between his fingers. He kissed Joshy on the brow, giving him one last hug. Joshy gazed into him with dreamy eyes, his lips pulled into a small, crooked smile.

I love you Joshy.

Joshy blinked and pushed his lips together. A sagely acceptance replaced his confusion as he gave Cole a single nod.

I know.

Cole's fingers slackened, releasing their grip on the red coat. Joshy sank beneath him, reaching up with pale hands as he entered the void alone.

Passion filled Cole from the inside out, wholesome and pure. He rose, quickly now. He would return to the world. There was still love up there, but there was also a shadow that threatened it. He would be the candle to stay the darkness.

At the thought of love, Cole felt several stars pop to life within him. They had been there all along, only he hadn't known how to see them. They were named Lileth, Sitra, Valen, Eliza, Alvani, and Goran. Cole embraced the stars, feeling their real-world counterparts miles away. Love became him, filling him with purpose. His friends were alive! Suffocating gloom pooled around their candles, but they still flickered. Cole gazed into the void below him once more, but his brother was gone.

Thank you, Joshy.

The surface of the water exploded as Cole erupted into open air. Varka's cape snapped to straight glass, tuning his Wisdom as Cole held himself in midair. He pressed a glowing jade hand to his chest and a gout of steam poured from his mouth, clearing his lungs of water. His hand then changed to lavender as the collection of wounds knitted themselves back together.

A kingdom of Passion welled up within him, swirling and dancing with other magics. The Passion blazed with potency equal to his Rage, enhancing it with righteous purpose without diminishing it. Newfound power rushed through him, sparking an introspective sense of wonder. Something had changed within his soul; however, now was not the time to acquaint himself with it. Six stars twinkled for him in the Fangshard valley.

Cole brought his Wisdom forth, commanding the assistance of Varka's cape. The cape obliged and Cole shot towards his candles with blurring speed, breaking the air as his Rage shrouded him.

As Cole soared into the valley, he realized one of his candles was unlike the others. Goran was not flickering, but beaming with a power that felt both ancient and wild as the Fangshards. Cole felt him keeping pace along the peaks of the valley. Goran nudged his mind with warm confidence. Cole would not face the enemy alone this time.

The churning island of burnt corpses floated before the ledge where the rest of his dimming candles clung to life. Cole zoomed his vision. Roth stood straight and still, eyes closed but no longer struggling against Grotton. Cole scanned him with a pulse of Passion, but the Bonebreaker's candle was nowhere to be found. Grotton now lived within the elder, just as Sorronis lived within Talin, who stood on the bridge as well. The Harbinger of Despair and Hatred waved a commanding arm at the tar consuming Cole's friends. The black muck churned and dragged their bodies to the bone nest.

Bracing himself, Cole put on one final burst of speed before colliding with the back of the floating mass of the Colossus, tearing through layers of cooked meat and bone. As he cut his way through, something oddly familiar struck a chord of his Passion. Altering his course, he found the anomaly and broke it from its fleshy prison, carrying it through the rest of the way. When he saw the light of the other side, he slowed himself and landed on the valley wall above the ledge. The writhing figure seethed under his arm, flailing and beating itself against his shroud. Its little fists spoke the Hatred that its mouth was no longer capable of.

Passion flared from Cole like a burning sun. The black tar fled from him as if blown by a strong wind, stripping the taint from the rock around him. Five lavender pulses shot from his chest, one for each of his candles. The Passion rushed into their prone bodies with rejuvenating magic. His unit stirred as Sorronis and the tumor-child emitted screeches that sounded like shearing metal.

It was then that Cole noticed two things. First, the mass of chosen began to flow back into the shape of a Colossus. Second, Roth's munisica and shroud had returned, but the elder grew larger by the second as his bulging stomach shrank. His expression was slack, though a burning Hunger sharpened his eyes. Roth was no longer Roth. He was the Harbinger of Grotton.

Cole silenced his own Rage, and his black armor shrank away before Grotton could take notice. Urgency fueling his Passion, Cole sent another rejuvenating pulse into each of his friends, rousing them from their stupor. Only Alvani remained on the cold ledge, hugging herself as she clung to life. Cole's Passion had no effect on her.

"Cole," Eliza called out, her voice cracking. "Cole what's happening? What's wrong with Roth?"

Lileth sprang to his side, munisica flashing like black daggers. "Sorronis!"

Valen took up a position on his other side, crouched and ready. Sitra and Eliza fell in behind him.

"Put your Rage away!" Cole blurted. "Grotton took Roth for Harbinger. We need to leave now."

"Master Roth? He *couldn't* have..." Sitra's voice rang with disbelief, but her eyes saw the truth.

"I'll explain later, grab Alvani quick." Cole eyed the Colossus taking shape before them. The screeching wails of Sorronis died away as the bone nest closed around him. Cole readied a spell, hoping it would be strong enough to carry them all.

Valen scooped Alvani into his arms. He inched away from Roth, who was now twice his normal height. His granite stomach had stretched into a rotund belly that shook with a thunderous chuckle. His eyes snapped to them, a grin of Hunger stretching his face wide.

"We're too late," Lileth whispered, her hands dropping to her sides.

"Roth you'd better put up a better fight than that!" Sitra roared as angry tears fell down her cheeks. "You can't let him have you! Fight it!"

The chuckling rose into an all-too-familiar sound that had no business in the world of the living. Grotton's beady eyes stared out from Roth's face, a horrible sight made worse by his nightmarish proportions. He glanced down at his ample stomach and gave it a pat. The shroud snapped over the rest of his skin, protecting him from the inside out. Cruel Hunger emanated from his hulking form. They were too late.

Now reformed, the Colossus stretched and flexed. It took one look at the unit and raised its island-sized fist, ready to smother them all in a meteor of corpses.

As the fist started its descent, a cracking rumble echoed from the peaks above. It sounded like thunder, but there was no lightning. Cole chanced a look above. A rolling landslide charged down to greet them, carrying boulders larger than houses. It was coming too fast. There was no time for a spell. His Rage was the only thing that could save him, but not the others.

Cole threw an arm up, pulling the tiny ashen body close with the other. It thrashed eagerly, greeting the death that bore down on them all. But death didn't come. The rocks cracked and roared past them, missing the unit entirely as if guided by unseen forces. Grotton smirked at the landslide, throwing a lazy munisica out to block the onslaught. A boulder the size of a Morthainian ship caught him dead on, sending him to the depths below. Every pebble of the falling mountain sailed harmlessly over the unit, seemingly hell-bent on striking Grotton's Harbinger.

Through the chaos, Cole felt the beaming star of Goran flying down the valley wall. The landslide thinned and Cole looked up, locking eyes with his friend for the first time in months. Cole's jaw dropped. Goran had gone through another transformation.

Flaming Ruby eyes larger than a man rushed towards them. They burned with intelligence, giving Cole a look of acknowledgement before setting their ferocity upon his next enemy. A mass of brindle fur sailed over them as Goran lunged for the Colossus. He was only half the size of the titan, but what he lacked in stature he made up for in violence. The two bodies collided with enough force to split a mountain. The valley shuddered, filling with the giant's thunder as Sorronis's clouds dissipated.

After triple-checking his bond, Cole rubbed his eyes, making sure that the massive beast really was his friend. Goran towered larger than the trees of The Sill, each of his brindle stripes wider than a city street. His white mohawk appeared to be made from snow, and his paws looked more like toothy peaks of the Fangshards.

Goran smote the Colossus, showering the valley floor with thousands of chosen, sending it careening onto its back. Though Goran seemed to be handling himself at the moment, Cole was eager to jump down and help. Perhaps their combined strength would be enough to fell the two gods.

A mournful keen pierced the battle-din as Lileth placed a hand on Cole's shoulder. "We must leave this place. Decreath could show at any moment. Three gods is too much."

As if in answer, a thudding of wings drew their attention as a massive creature descended from the sky. Gale landed roughly upon the ledge, chirping in desperate bleats. Cole let out a sigh of relief. He'd worried the winged feline had long abandoned them. Gale gave a soft chirp as he rubbed Alvani's body with his feathery head. Valen clambered up onto his back, nestling Alvani in the beast's plumage.

"Hurry, get on!" Valen cried.

Exhausted, Cole joined the rest of the unit on Gale's broad back, taking up a spot in the rear with Lileth sitting between his legs. He stuffed Lexy's charred body into a large saddle bag, ignoring her thumping racket as he buckled it shut.

Lileth leaned into him, pressing her body against his as she wove a hand up through his hair. She gave him a soft kiss on the cheek and whispered into his ear, "You are very important to me, Cole."

Cole blinked, squeezing tears free as he pulled her closer.

They stared into each other's eyes, indulging in the quiet of the moment as Gale sidled up the edge of the ledge.

"You sure you're up to this?" Sitra asked, giving Gale an encouraging pat on the flank. "Can you carry six of our fat asses out of this mess?"

Gale released a defiant bugle as he spread his wings and charged into open air. Cole turned, gazing down at the giants below him. Fortunately there was no sight of Roth, or as he was now known, Grotton.

Goran towered in a victorious posture over the prone Colossus, his arms, which looked to be made from blocks of granite, stretched out to his sides. Cole dove into their bond and attempted to convey their retreat. Goran heard him, but there was something greater, something far more important stirring within the gargantuan mirak.

Sensing Goran's intentions, Cole snapped his head forward and shouted with both his voice and mind, "Fly high! Get us out of the valley!" Cole readied himself to take flight with Wisdom, but Gale surged upwards. Hopefully the flying beast was fast enough. Cole looked back to Goran.

Great columns of rock shot from Goran's paws, embedding themselves in the valley walls. The mountains around them groaned as the Fangshards began to shudder. The valley walls moved. The pass was closing.

Cole grabbed hold of his Passion and brought all of its wild power to his hands, slapping his glowing palms into the feathers beneath him. Gale threw his head back and trumpeted his cry to the stars, snapping his wings with such force that it nearly unseated the lot of them. They rose higher as the valley walls drew closer. When he was sure they were clear, Cole glanced down once more, grim acceptance washing over him as the Fangshards snapped shut.

The saddle bag thrashed against Cole's leg as Lexy stormed her Hatred at the world. Cole gave the bag a sad smile, knowing that she would soon be freed of her torment. Lileth hugged him tightly as the others cheered in victory. They had escaped. They had survived two of The Three.

Sitra roared over the wind, raising her munisica to the stars, "Take us home Gale!"

End of Book 2

If you enjoyed your journey to Aeneria and want to help make it a real place, please take a moment and give this book an honest review.

For all Hate mail and love letters:
www.AeneriaIsComing.com/contact/

From the World of Aeneria

FROM THE AUTHOR

Greetings Traveler!

I've been writing sporadically for most of my life. However, it wasn't until January 2016 that I began to take it seriously thanks to one of my closest friends. While I'd like to be writing full-time, I (like most independent authors) have a day job, which is a logistician position in the National Guard. I joined in 2005, deployed twice, and have been active duty since 2012. The military lifestyle has had a tremendous impact on my life, filling it with more ups and downs than I can keep track of, as well as some lifelong friends.

My days are spent at a desk or bumbling around in a humongous truck. After work I get myself to a gym and do battle with my inner fat kid for a couple of hours, then rush home and hopefully start writing before 8 pm. I nurture a love for performance arts, especially plays and local stand-up. During summers I don't ride my motorcycle nearly enough, and the same goes for my snowboard during the winters. At least once a year I'll go abroad, usually your typical over-indulgent Caribbean cruise, though recently I spent a week in France, where I had the privilege of officiating at a wedding for two dear friends.

The stories I enjoy the most usually leave me shaken for a few days, not because I'm a glutton for masochism, but because they resonate with the wounded parts of me that I wouldn't ordinarily take notice of. With a somewhat busy lifestyle where stoicism has become my go-to survival tool, I need those stories that derail me from my daily grind, that kick me in the gut and make me feel something.

As of writing this I'm 30 years old and live in Manchester, New Hampshire.

-Joe

www.ingramcontent.com/pod-product-compliance
Lightning Source LLC
Chambersburg PA
CBHW070930100726
47908CB00001B/163